4/84

DED

HOT BUTTERED YUM

ALSO BY KIM LAW

HOT BUTTERED YUM

A TURTLE ISLAND NOVEL

Kim Law

Montlake Romance

Originally published as a Kindle Serial, October 2013

Published by Montlake Romance, Seattle

www.apub.com

ISBN-13: 9781477817568
ISBN-10: 1477817565

Cover design by Laura Klynstra

Library of Congress Control Number: 2013917818

Printed in the United States of America

To my Aunt Audra. You are the spirit inside of Mrs. Rylander. Sorry I couldn't fit her in the book without her panties. Maybe next time.

Chapter One

Strains of Rachmaninoff flowed from the Steinway grand piano, mixing with the ocean breeze that casually drifted in through the open dining room windows. Roni Templeman lifted slightly off the piano bench, one foot working the pedal, and picked up the tempo of the song. If there was anything she could get lost in, it was being at the keyboard. It had been that way her entire life.

Her hands flew in front of her. Up, down, pounding, caressing to the song's crescendo. She lifted her face to the cool breeze and sucked in a deep gulp of the morning dampness, knowing her cheeks had to be pink from her exertion. There was nothing like playing in the mornings when the rest of the world was still asleep.

Of course Turtle Island, just a ferry ride away from the southeasternmost corner of Georgia, had begun waking up well over two hours ago. Roni had welcomed the sunrise as she'd sat in her dining room—where most people would have a table instead of a black-lacquered, six-foot piano—as she did every morning. Tucked into the curve of the large bay window in her beach cottage, she had her routine, and she stuck to it. Occasionally, however, she did go beyond her allotted piano time and into her run-on-the-beach time. Because some mornings demanded she stay right where she was for just a bit longer. Today was one of those days.

As she neared the last stanzas, she watched through the plate-glass window as a distended bead of water clung to the leaf of a potted cabbage palm sitting on her deck. The sun had greeted the morning behind a hazy, slow rain, and though the sky was now a clear blue, promising a glorious early-December day, everything remained damp.

The droplet of water shook slightly, as if wanting to let go, but not quite certain it was ready to be free. Roni set her back teeth together and concentrated on the song, on the movement of her hands across the ivories, yet she couldn't take her eyes off that single leaf with the lone bead of water.

As she reached the final bars, her arms tensed with exertion, her breaths grew short. She was exhausted from the longer-than-normal session, yet at the same time, exhilarated. Playing had that power.

The tiny orb seemed to grow in size as she played, puffing up with bravery for a brief second before it vibrated with hesitation. Then, as if in desperation to move forward, it broke free, slipping silently along the leaf's vein and rolling down its length toward the tip. As it leaped from the greenery, Roni hit the last note and a crystal-clear, rich sound filled the room.

She let out a ragged breath.

Then her muscles went lax, and her body sagged against the bench as the bead of water splatted to the wood deck and the final note disappeared in the room.

Everything seemed overly quiet in the seconds that followed. But it wasn't, not really.

If she listened carefully, she could pick out the faint hiss from the gas fireplace burning in the connected living room. She heard the motorized hum of half a dozen ornaments hanging on her Christmas tree, slowly rotating while tiny people danced away inside.

She could hear the ocean a story below her deck; the swish and lap of the water was always there. Even more so after the wet greeting to the day.

Yet without chords coming from the piano, everything seemed so perfectly still.

She let out another slow breath and relaxed her shoulders before inhaling and filling her lungs once again. Then she blinked and looked around as if coming out of a fog.

She took in the cozy rooms with the cluster of unique furniture she'd handpicked from local stores. Her home wasn't tiny, having once housed a family of eight, but it wasn't too big, either. She liked having a bit of space. It was far nicer than the cramped apartment she'd rented in New York City. Or the hotel rooms where she'd spent the majority of her childhood.

The best thing about the house, though, was that it sat surrounded by almost an acre of land. This meant she could play in the mornings with her windows open to the sea and not worry that she'd wake her neighbors. The size of her yard was unheard of for a beachfront property in this day and age, but she'd lucked out when she'd moved here almost three years ago. The older lady who'd owned the property had refused to sell, even though she'd already moved into the smaller two-bedroom next door, until she'd found just the right owner.

Upon hearing that Roni intended to put a piano in the dining room instead of a fancy table for twelve, the eighty-year-old white-haired sweetheart had held out her gnarled hands, grasping Roni's in hers. "Welcome home," Mrs. Rylander had said. Roni had grown misty at the words.

Yes. It had felt like home. Turtle Island had always done that for her.

It was the place where she'd once met her two best friends. Where she'd spent every summer with them, from eight until eighteen. It was her home away from the hotels. She'd loved her summers here, not only because they were spent with her friends, but because it was uninterrupted time with her mother and brother. Her mother, a college professor at University of Alabama in Huntsville, had been able to take summers off, pack up her two kids, and spend the months at the beach.

Turtle Island was also the place Roni and her friends had all promised to return to someday. And they had. Only, Andie had married and moved to Boston earlier this year, and now Roni was . . .

What?

Unsettled? Bored?

She shook her head. No, she was happy. She loved the island. She loved her life.

She loved her house.

Though, granted, she hadn't been in any one place this long since she'd been six years old.

It was just this time of year. She always got a little melancholy in December.

The sound of "The Little Drummer Boy" sounded at her hip and she looked down to where she'd laid her cell before she'd sat down at the piano. It was her brother. She'd known Danny would call today. He always did.

Instead of answering, she pressed the button to send the call to voice mail and then headed across the room as she brought up the small text window. She keyed in a short message.

I'm fine. Really. It's been three years. I'm over it.

She ran a fingertip over the tiny Christmas village sitting on the mantel while she waited on Danny's reply. The glass pieces had been hand-blown by a local artist who rented space in the art gallery.

The phone sang out the words, "and a partridge in a pear tree." She had a text. At the same time, she caught sight of the usual spot of pale yellow bobbing across her yard and heading to the house next door. The tiny body below the scarf hustled faster than Roni thought an eighty-year-old probably should.

She looked down at her phone.

Then answer the phone when I call.

Roni smiled. She loved her brother.

I'll see you in three weeks. You'll see then that I'm fine.

Too long to wait. I'll call you later this week.

And she suspected he would. She would talk to him then. But right now, on this day, she didn't want to have a conversation with her brother about what she'd lost in the past.

It was over. She'd moved on.

Instead of dwelling, she wanted to head out to the beach and get in her morning run.

She wanted to wave good morning to the locals and tourists she passed. To enjoy her life—because it really was a good one. And she wanted to head over to the hotel and meet up with her friends for lunch while they giggled and fantasized over the idea of what they could all do with the twenty-four amazingly hot men that would soon be parading all over the island.

Because it wasn't every day a girl had that to look forward to.

Four hours later, a crisp breeze hit Roni in the face, lifting her dark bangs, as she sat at an outside table at the Turtle Island Hotel restaurant after downing a scrumptious meal. The morning rain had burned away and the temperature had risen to a pleasant seventy-two. Slightly higher than normal December temps, but perfect for lunch on the patio with the girls.

"I totally think you should go for it with one of them, Roni," Savannah Marconi said across from her. "When will you ever get that kind of chance again?"

Eight women, four on each side of shoved-together teakwood tables, all silently turned their heads to the eight men sitting two tables over from them. They. Were. Gorgeous.

Roni had met each of them briefly the evening before when they'd arrived at the hotel. Contestants one, three, eleven, twelve, fourteen, nineteen, twenty-one, and twenty-four. They had names, of course, but she couldn't remember them. She only knew their numbers now because each of them had a two-inch button attached to his shirt.

She'd met them with Kayla Morgan, head of Seaglass Celebrations, after the limos had brought the men from the ferry to the hotel. As master of ceremonies for the first-ever Mr. Yummy Santa competition, Roni had been asked to be there to greet all arrivals. Kayla had been with her, of course, to make sure everything ran smoothly and on time. And to hand out the welcome bags—which included the numbered buttons the men were asked to wear anytime they were in public over the course of the next thirteen days.

"Why don't *you* go for it?" Roni returned. She forced her gaze back to Savannah—because geez, they were pretty, pretty men. And because yes, she *would* like to go for it with one of them. It had been a while since she'd had that kind of fun. However, Kayla would have a conniption if she found out Roni even entertained the idea of having a fling with a contestant.

Not that it would really matter in the grand scheme of things. Roni got the same exact amount of input into the voting as everyone else did. But something told her Kayla would see it differently.

"Because she's married, you dolt." Samantha Greene chimed in. Samantha was Savannah's twin sister, and was sitting beside Savannah. Two long-haired, blue-eyed beauties, both with the Southern charm of Nashville that they'd brought with them—though Samantha was a bit more blunt and outspoken.

Samantha had moved to the island and opened a women's clothing boutique a year after her sister had arrived here with her husband. She eyed the men now as she took a long drag of her piña colada.

Roni shrugged at Samantha's words as if being married didn't matter, but the nonchalance was faked. She would never encourage a married person to have an affair.

"I'll do one." This came from the far end of the table, from shy and quiet Cookie Phillips. Everyone at the table knew there was no way Cookie would make the first move.

A couple of the men glanced over at them before turning back to their table.

"Me too," Ginger Atkinson spoke up at Roni's left. "I'm not married." Ginger's green eyes were glazed and dreamy as she eyed the tableful of ripped bodies. She was best friend number two, whom Roni had spent the summers with when she was young. The best friend who had been born on, and who remained on, the island. In fact, other than two years away at college, Ginger had never left.

Roni nudged her with her elbow. "Go for number nineteen. Did you see the size of his hands?"

"I saw." The words were said in sync, all with a tone of awe, by at least five of the ladies at the table.

One of the men leaned back in his seat at that moment, laughing heartily at something one of the other guys had said, and every single woman seemed to hold her breath. It truly was a crying shame Roni was out of the market for this impressive showing. These guys were taut, lean, chiseled, polite—if the brief greeting last night was anything to go by—and just downright doable.

A real crying shame.

"I really do think you should dip your toe into some of that," Savannah leaned forward and urged. "Maybe number one. His shoulders are broadest, and I know you like that."

His shoulders were broadest. And yes, she did like that. She'd also caught him checking her out a couple times during lunch.

"Imagine if you two fell in love," Ginger said in her dreamy, everything-is-romantic voice. "You'd have access to that body every single night."

"Only until he went back home," Roni clarified. Ginger turned everything into happily-ever-after. Roni kept it casual.

She picked up her own drink—a lemon drop that was far stronger than she should be having, considering she was about to meet Kayla to greet the remaining sixteen contestants—and gulped as she studied number one.

Dark hair, muscled chest and arms, pleasant face. It wasn't that she was so wildly attracted to him. Granted, he was good looking, and he had been super sweet the evening before. But it was mostly that she wanted something to take her mind off the next two weeks. December wasn't her best month. Plus, there was the master of ceremonies thing.

She might be the designated local celebrity—though she'd been out of that game for going on three years now—but that didn't mean she wasn't nervous about being the figurehead for this contest.

If she were to be entirely honest, though, the idea excited her more than she wanted to admit. She hadn't done much more than hang out on the beach with her friends or play hostess and entertainer at Gin's bar since moving to the island. So yeah, she was secretly thrilled at the idea of doing something new. Plus, it would help Turtle Island.

All of the women at the table, with the exception of Roni, were business owners on the island. They, along with several other merchants, had each contributed five thousand dollars, plus time and merchandise from their businesses, on the trust that this contest would up winter tourism on their tiny little island. They were literally betting their hard-earned money on twenty-four hot men drawing a crowd. Roni being the face that crowd would be seeing day after day.

It was a bit nerve-wracking.

Taking note of the number of tourists who had come and gone among the lunch customers, the majority of them women, Roni had felt a satisfied warmth spread inside her. Looked like the business owners had gotten it right. Mr. Yummy Santa was a good idea. It would be a success.

As long as Roni didn't screw it up.

Which meant no casual fling with one of the contestants. No matter how much fun it would be.

She sighed and turned back to the men, digging money out of her purse to cover her bill at the same time. "It's not going to happen, ladies. Kayla would—"

At that moment, eight handsome faces turned in their direction and a chorus of squeaks and giggles bounced around the table. The women straightened in their chairs, all looking dead ahead at the women sitting across the table. Not at the men.

But the guys were still watching them, Roni could tell.

It was as if a tanker of testosterone had been dumped in the middle of their table and none of the ladies could do anything but let out feminine giggles and wiggle in their seats.

Chairs scraped back as the men stood, and one by one, the women snuck glances in the direction of their table. The guys were leaving. But not without winks and smiles directed at them. Roni felt about fourteen, caught gawking at the senior football players.

Not that she'd ever attended a normal high school or had that experience.

But she had had her share of boy angst as a teenager. What girl didn't?

As the last of the guys cleared out, Roni was struck by another man now in her line of sight. In a small two-seater tucked just inside the furthermost corner of the patio, where the wrought-iron railing was at his back, sat a god.

A tall, broad, muscled, sculpted, testosterone-leaking-from-his-pores god.

Now *that* was someone she could get into for a little casual fun.

He had dark hair, short but with a bit of a wave to it, a nice tan on the tightly muscled arms coming out of his well-fit polo. And as far as she could tell, everything tapering down to his waist and hips in the exact way a man was supposed to taper.

Lunch didn't seem to be his priority as there was no plate in sight, only a half-full glass of tea. He had both hands on the keyboard of a laptop, his attention fully focused on whatever he was doing, and Roni couldn't help it . . . her fantasies flared to life.

"Roni?" Ginger jabbed her in the side.

Roni swatted away Ginger's elbow.

"Roni?" Another jab.

Again, another swat. Only this time, Ginger caught Roni's wrist and held it. Roni redirected her attention to her friend, only to discover what the problem was. Contestant number one was now standing directly behind Savannah, his deep green gaze plastered on Roni.

She looked up at him.

Whoa. That boy could smile.

"Nice to see you again, Roni," he said. He had a slight New England accent. New Hampshire or Connecticut, maybe. Not real strong, though. But there was a somewhat Southern charm to the way he stood there with his hands clasped in front of him and his head slightly dipped. And he was definitely a cutie.

But she still wasn't going to be tempted to sleep with him.

Roni put a polite smile on her face and ignored the snickers around the table. "Uh . . ." she started. Oh crap, why hadn't she bothered with their names?

"Gus," he supplied. He gave a little nod. "I was wondering if we might find a few minutes to talk at the reception tonight."

The reception?

"I'd love to have the chance to get to know you better," he continued.

Roni blinked. Several times.

Ginger leaned in and whispered, "We have the reception with all the contestants tonight. To welcome them to town. And to meet the—"

"Right," Roni cut in, her chin lifting slightly as she spoke. "To meet the members of the community who pulled the contest together."

Of course. Why had she gone stupid at the sight of one gorgeous man standing three feet away from her? She'd seen plenty of gorgeous men in her life. Case in point . . . she snuck another glance at the god in the far corner.

Exhibit one, your honor. Gorgeous specimen of a man.

She turned back to Gus. How did she politely discourage his attention? "I'll be chatting with everyone tonight, Gus. I'm sure our paths will cross."

Kayla chose that moment to appear at their table, standing immediately to Gus's left. That helped. But again, Roni felt like the fourteen-year-old caught gawking at someone she had no business gawking at.

"Hello, Mr. Thompson," Kayla said. She was only two years older than Roni, yet when she wore her stern face, there seemed to be at least a decade between them. "How are you this afternoon?"

"Wonderful," Gus mumbled. Even he wore a look of guilt himself, as if he knew he shouldn't be fraternizing with the forbidden.

Roni gave him a little shrug as if to say, What can I do? while Kayla frowned at him.

Kayla was a good person, and Roni knew Andie wouldn't have moved to Boston so quickly if she hadn't had Kayla here to run Seaglass for her. Yet it bugged Roni that Kayla rarely seemed to relax enough to enjoy herself. Life wasn't all about work. Roni knew that better than anyone.

"I'll . . . uh . . ." Gus fumbled for words, then his neck turned red as all eight of the women at the table, *and* Kayla, gazed silently at him as if to ask, "Were you really here to flirt with our Roni?"

Roni smiled politely. Possibly she batted her eyelashes innocently.

"I'll see you at the reception, then," he mumbled and then fled before Roni could form a reply.

She couldn't help it. She laughed.

"Kayla," she admonished. "You're heartless. You just scared that poor boy to death."

Because yes, the more she'd looked at Gus, she'd determined he was closer to boy than her twenty-eight. He couldn't be more than twenty-three, and probably not even that. And though a twenty-three-year-old hottie could be fun, and likely he'd show up with loads of stamina, he was still a contestant.

And she was just too old for twenty-three these days.

Or at least she felt like it.

Which was just sad.

She peeked at the man in the corner.

"He was hitting on you," Kayla informed them, as if all eight of the women weren't aware what Gus had been up to.

"And I was encouraging her," Savannah added drily.

Kayla's mouth tightened. "Roni—"

"I know," Roni said. She held up her hands as if in surrender. "It would be inappropriate to sleep with the contestants. Not to mention, who has time for twenty-four drop-dead gorgeous hunks, anyway?"

Kayla blushed at Roni's implication. Roni may have her fun on occasion, but she was most definitely selective.

Yet she couldn't help picking on Kayla.

"I want to do a good job for Andie," Kayla said in a pleading tone. "For Seaglass."

"I understand." Roni nodded. This was the first non-wedding event that Seaglass had been hired to do. It was important. They were branching out. She'd heard this a number of times in the weeks leading up to the event. Kayla was nervous. And Roni wasn't a bad person; she wanted to help. Plus, it was her friend's business, after all.

Not to mention, she was the face of the contest.

"Spoilsport," Savannah tacked on. Several at the table laughed under their breaths.

"I promise to behave." Roni said contritely. She once again peeked at the dark-haired Adonis in the corner, his attention still buried in the laptop in front of him.

She turned back to Kayla and gave her a wide, guileless smile.

"Twenty minutes, then I need you out front," the other woman said. "The ferry will be docking soon."

Sixteen more gorgeous hunks, heading her way. Oh, what fun.

Suddenly, the six long months since she'd been naked with a guy seemed like six years.

Kayla left the table and Roni stood before she talked herself out of it, quickly gulping the remainder of her drink. Her attention was focused on the man at the corner table.

"Where are you going?" Ginger whispered. Her hand reached out as if to stop her, but she let it drop when Samantha and Savannah both spoke at the same time. "Oh," they practically moaned the word. "Even better."

They'd followed Roni's gaze. Roni nodded. Even better.

"Go get him, girl," one of the others whispered as she passed.

Oh yes. She intended to.

CHAPTER TWO

Roni was most of the way across the bricked patio before it occurred to her that she had no idea what she would do—or say—when she got there. With that thought finally entering her mind, she stopped, barely ten feet from the man, and simply watched. He still hadn't looked up from that computer.

He was in the seat that she chose anytime she came over to the historic hotel alone for lunch, though he wasn't making the same use of it at all.

She liked to sit there not because she was shying away from the crowd, but because she enjoyed watching them. Some would show up in the middle of the day in their Sunday best, and others came in tourist-casual attire. Occasionally women would arrive looking as if they'd stepped off a Paris runway. Those were her favorites. She liked to dream up stories of where they would head to next.

Computer guy had no idea anyone else was in the vicinity.

He was staring so intently at the laptop, his fingers tapping rhythmically on the keys, that he still hadn't noticed Roni. Which meant she could continue taking her time noticing him.

Her eyes dipped as far down the red polo as she could see, and then she tilted her head, wanting to see below the table to determine if the goodness continued all the way down. But before she could assess, a soft sound to her left caught her attention. Glancing over, she found a red-haired server with a high ponytail on the back of her head smiling at her from ear to ear.

"Oh yeah," the younger woman murmured. "He's as good as you think. Only, not the talkative type. He's been sitting there for going on two hours, doing nothing but working on that laptop." The waitress gave her a sideways look as if sharing a government secret and added, "And downing a mammoth sandwich. Our grilled chicken. Only, he added an extra piece of chicken."

Roni looked back at the man. He was big in the small seat. Wide shoulders, long legs. Probably over six feet. And he certainly filled out the space. But he didn't strike her as the type to overeat.

Maybe it was to provide energy to all those muscles.

"Talking *is* overrated," Roni found herself replying.

The waitress giggled so loud that everyone in the vicinity lifted their gazes to them.

Everyone except the hunk sitting in her seat.

Roni narrowed her eyes. Desperate measures suddenly seemed in order. She wanted that man's attention.

She looked at the waitress, glancing at her name tag.

"Cindy," she said. Roni nodded toward the occupied table in front of them, sweeping her hair out of her eyes when another gust of wind caught it. "Would you mind bringing me a glass of tea, please?"

Cindy's eyes widened in question.

Roni gave her a devilish smile. "I'll be joining the gentleman."

The waitress nodded in a quick head bob that made her ponytail bounce and headed off, and Roni asked herself what she thought she was doing. It was rude to intrude upon someone who was obviously looking for some time to himself. She could understand that need. For the most part, she liked being around people, but she also knew how to appreciate a quiet corner all to herself.

Yet she couldn't make herself walk away.

Maybe simply because he was so oblivious to everything going on around him.

And maybe because she suddenly found herself unable to think of anything but getting naked with him. Nothing wrong with that. She was a normal, healthy girl. And Mr. Oblivious looked to be a normal healthy guy.

Even if a bit too into his computer.

Without questioning herself further, she finished the final few steps, stopping only when she reached the chair opposite him. He still didn't look up at her. Annoyance flitted through her and she dragged the chair back from the table—intentionally *not* lifting the legs.

The man's long fingers stilled on the keys at the sound of metal legs scraping over the brick. His shoulders stiffened for a millisecond, so fast she almost missed it. And then those muscles relaxed, and Roni had the thought that he was forcing a calmness he didn't quite feel. If he was anything like her when she was into one of her daily practice sessions, he'd been deeply entrenched in whatever he was working on.

She almost felt bad for interrupting him.

But then he slowly curled his fingers under his palms and she found herself forgetting her rudeness and holding her breath as she waited for him to look at her. He didn't lift his head so much as shift his gaze. It landed somewhere around her middle before his lids lowered and he trailed down over the A-line blue chambray skirt of her dress.

The dress was a favorite. The skirt ended just above the knees and had tiny blue- and sienna-colored flowers, the reddish-brown color matching the wide braided belt at her waist, and the bodice and three-quarter-length sleeves were white and covered in eyelet lace. She'd paired the outfit with her favorite cowboy boots. The ones that had turquoise stones on the pull tabs on either side of her calves.

After a slow perusal—all the way to her boots and back—the man finally removed his hands from the keyboard and his body went from straight back, good posture to what she would call casual-sexy-slump. Her blood pumped harder in anticipation.

Then he lifted those eyes to hers.

A deep blue the exact color of the first car she'd owned stared back at her. Along with a slow curve of full lips that made a spot a few inches below her belt wake up and say hello.

Oh. My. Lord.

He might just be more man than she could handle.

She wet her lips and forced the smile she'd thought she'd already been wearing. She'd apparently been gaping instead. But good grief, he was hot.

It wasn't just the muscles and the eyes and that mouth . . . *swoon, that mouth!* . . . it was the twinkle and the charm that somehow seemed to emanate from him while he did nothing more than shoot her a lazy look and an if-you're-not-already-thinking-dirty-thoughts-I-can-make-you-think-them naughty grin. And there was just something about him that shouted that he should be wearing a cowboy hat and saying, "Howdy, ma'am."

A man shouldn't be able to exude charm like that without trying.

"Well, hello," he said. His voice was as delicious as everything else about him. "What can I do for you?" One eyebrow lifted the slightest amount with his question and she would swear his deep, slow timbre made her womb quiver.

You can invite me up to your room and have me for dessert.

She blinked at the thought, then lowered herself quickly to the seat. She wasn't so hard up that she'd invite herself to the man's room without at first getting to know him.

But then again . . .

Reaching a hand across the table, she upped the wattage of her smile, determined to take control of the conversation. "Hi," she said, drawing out the word and using the Alabama drawl she'd outgrown the first year her father had taken her on tour with him. "My name is Roni."

His gaze quickly crawled over her face.

"Lucas," he drawled out, showing a Southern accent of his own. His sounded more Texas, though. It only added to the cowboy-hat fantasy.

She forced herself not to audibly sigh at the warm feel of his skin as he closed his fingers around hers, then chastised herself for her silliness. He was merely a nice-looking man. She'd met hundreds of nice-looking men during the years she'd traveled from one side of the world to the other as a concert pianist. Had met a decent share of them since she'd lived here.

Nice-looking men came to the beach all the time.

So this one had tightly bound muscles just waiting to explode everywhere, so what? And a jaw with the absolute perfect amount of scratchy stubble. Not to mention the easy charisma that she suspected was currently pulling at every woman within a twenty-five-foot radius. She swallowed against her dry throat.

He was *still* just a man.

She let go of his hand and put hers in her lap. She could handle "just a man" any day of the year.

With that thought, she relaxed back into her chair, crossing one leg over the other, and took pleasure when his gaze flicked down to follow her move. She didn't have long legs, but she made good use of what she had. She never missed her morning run on the beach. Good health and good legs, all in one fell swoop. It worked.

Especially when she wanted to use those legs to capture a man's attention.

She stared at Lucas now, having no idea what she should say now that she was here. But she trusted her instincts. So she opened her mouth. And then almost laughed at what came out. "You're in my chair," she told him.

His blue eyes widened. "I . . . uh," he stammered. A look of innocent confusion swept over his face and she quickly saw that he was even more disarming when he didn't purposely turn on the charm. "I'm sorry?" he asked.

With a small motion, she nodded in his direction, forcing herself to not let her smile out. "My chair, Lucas. This is where I sit. You're in it."

"Oh." His mouth rounded with the word, and then humor passed over his strong jawline. He ducked his head, looking around as if checking out the sides and back of the chair. When he finished, he gave her a crooked grin and lifted his hands, palms up. "I don't see a label anywhere, Roni. Are you *sure* this is where you sit?"

She liked that he was mimicking her by using her name as she'd done his. He was fun.

Cindy appeared at that moment with her tea, and Roni simply grinned across the table at him. After Cindy set it down, Roni pointed one finger at the glass. "That's my tea," she said. "Guess it is my seat."

Lucas laughed, the sound ringing out long and warm, and Roni caught herself leaning into the table to soak it in. She even inhaled deeply, as if she could somehow smell that yummy sound. She didn't have to look around to know that every female head on the patio had turned in their direction. His laughter was the kind of sound any woman would want to get closer to.

A strange kind of honor passed through her that she was the one he was directing it at.

It made her enjoy the moment even more. Even if it went no further than this conversation, she was glad she'd come over.

"You here on business?" She motioned to the laptop. "Did I interrupt something important?"

Lucas's face went still for a brief second as he glanced back at the computer. Then he closed the lid and turned all his focus on her. "Nothing I can't take care of later."

"Good," Roni said. She turned up her glass of tea and took a deep gulp, suddenly nervous with all of that maleness directed at her. He was far more potent than any of the men who'd just left the restaurant. Too bad he wasn't in the contest. He would win hands down.

As Lucas watched her, seeming to wait for her to make the next move, heat fluttered across her cheeks. She should have thought this through before coming over. It wasn't like she could just say, "Hey, it's been a while for me and I'm feeling a bit of an itch. Want to scratch it?"

Not that she would do it quite so casually, anyway. Even if it was the only thing she was currently thinking about. She had some standards, after all.

Get to know a guy a bit. Require a dinner or something.

Not simply *Hi, nice to meet you, let's get to it.*

"There seems to be a tableful of women watching you, Roni," Lucas informed her. His voice was halfway to laughing as his gaze drifted over her head in the direction from which she'd come. "And now they're all smiling at me." He shifted back to Roni. "Clearly I'm missing something."

Her cheeks had to be deep red by now. She could even feel her ears burning. "I suspect that's the group of women I just had lunch with." She cringed as she uttered the words. "They're waiting to see what happens over here."

Where had her spine gone? Why was she suddenly a fragile flower wilting under the intensity of this man's charm? Not good. She had to turn this around.

"Ah," he murmured before taking a drink of his own tea. "So this *isn't* your seat?"

"Yes, it is." She nodded quickly, but then paused and gave him an apologetic grimace. "When I come to the restaurant alone."

"And I'm guessing from the looks of that table, you didn't show up alone today." The gleam that shone from his eyes was laughter. At her expense. Obviously, her not-so-subtle flirting would be more effective without her many backseat drivers.

"Actually . . ." she started. She glanced back at the girls and shot them a hard look, hoping it would make them quit staring. Instead, they all waved. Even shy Cookie tossed up her hand. Perfect.

Lucas chuckled and Roni's body parts reacted to the low, scrumptious sound.

Maybe she shouldn't have had such a strong drink before coming over to talk to this walking, talking every-woman's-fantasy.

She gave up on her friends and returned to Lucas, pulling out her bravado once again. It was just flirting, after all. She'd done flirting for years. "You shouldn't laugh like that so freely, you know? It's not nice."

"What's not nice about it?" He looked honestly confused.

She waved a hand at her body, moving it in a circular pattern, palm toward her, up and down in front of her chest and abdomen. "It does things to a woman. Messes with her."

He grinned suddenly. Not the slow, sexy smile he'd given when he'd first noticed her. This one was fast and real. It said, "I'm a fun guy."

It said, "Baby, you're in trouble now."

"Seriously," she groaned out. "Stop it. You're killing me."

He laughed loudly again, lines creasing on either side of his mouth and out from his eyes, and she was just about to lean in to soak it up once more when the sound abruptly cut off. His dark-blue gaze flicked to a spot above her shoulder a second before she felt heat there. Someone had stepped up behind her.

She glanced up. It was Kayla.

Roni gulped.

The frown on Kayla's face looked as if it had been etched there all her life. When she glanced at Lucas, it grew even harsher. Without a word, Kayla tapped the face of her watch, eyeing Roni. Reprimanded again.

"Uh-oh," Roni murmured. She dropped her gaze to the table and stood, reaching into her purse to pay for her tea. "I've got to go."

"I've got it." Lucas had his wallet out and had a five tossed on the table before Roni could protest.

"Thank you," she said earnestly. She caught his gaze. "Maybe we'll . . ."

Suddenly, the thought of not seeing him again was more than the loss of a potential fling. He'd been fun to talk to. Fun to just sit here and share the space with. She wanted more of that.

"I'll be around for a couple weeks," he told her. "Maybe we will."

Roni flushed again, strangely flattered.

She nodded and turned to follow Kayla out of the restaurant, but peeked back over her shoulder before she'd taken more than a few steps.

Lucas sat watching her. He wore the same look in his eyes that she was feeling in her gut.

Maybe, just maybe, he wanted to spend more time with her too.

CHAPTER THREE

As Lucas Alexander stepped inside the room, shards of light from crystal chandeliers reflected off the high ceiling and walls of the meeting space on the second floor of the hotel. He stood by the door, taking it all in. Classical Christmas music played from the high speakers, though not too loud to disrupt conversation, and a light mix of reds and greens was interspersed throughout the room. Mostly, though, the decorations were white, silver, and gold. Someone had done a nice job. It looked like Christmas in here.

Along with the classiness of the setup, Lucas could see a stage at the front of the room with twenty-four chairs, twelve on either side of the podium, each with a large number in a circle on the wall behind it.

Welcome to the Mr. Yummy Santa contest, it shouted to him. Where men leave their dignity by the door, but just might go home with fifty grand to the charity of their choice.

He forced himself not to roll his eyes at the name of the contest. He supposed it was a fair trade. It wasn't that he minded twelve days of prancing in front of oohing and aahing women. He'd put himself through college doing just that. It was that he felt too old for it these days.

Not to mention, the guys he worked with would have his balls if they found out what he was doing. But then, they'd also die laughing if they realized he graced the covers of quite a few romance novels too. Probably novels their own wives read.

But a man had to pay the bills. Or these days, contribute to a good cause. Because he had plenty of reasons to want to give back.

Spotting a handful of guys he'd worked with in the past, he made his feet move and headed across the room. After his very pleasant conversation with Roni—he'd not gotten her last name—in the restaurant that afternoon, he'd returned to the software program he'd been fighting with all morning and had lost track of time. He'd worked right through meeting the event coordinator in the lobby for his welcome packet. However, asking at the front desk had led him here for the reception. Looked like he'd come to the right place.

No one stopped him as he made his way to the side of his buddy, Kelly Griffin.

Lucas was closer to him than anyone here. They were the same age, and while Lucas had been putting himself through college with his modeling income, Kelly had been making waves in the clothing world full-time. He'd scored more than one high-name contract over the years. Underwear, T-shirts. Even a commercial or two.

He was also the only one here who really knew Lucas. Who knew about his home life. He'd been around when Lucas had been with Des.

"Hey, man." Kelly slapped him on the back and pulled him into the group he was chatting with. There were three other men he'd met before—one who was a douche—who would be in the contest, and then there were four women and two men he didn't recognize.

That wasn't actually true. He did recognize two of the women. They were twins. They'd been at the table of women today who had been staring at Roni and him as they'd been talking.

Flirting.

Heat pooled low in his abdomen at the memory. Yes, it had been flirting. He may not get out much these days, but that didn't mean he didn't recognize the casual banter for what it had been.

Seeing the two dark-haired women now made him wonder if Roni would be there tonight as well. This was a meet-and-greet with the business owners and local townspeople who'd put the contest together. Could Roni be a part of that?

He hoped so.

He wanted to find out her last name.

He wanted to spend more time with her.

And if spending time with her led to more . . . as the flirting had implied it might . . . all the better. Especially since the only times he let himself have that kind of fun these days was when he left Dallas.

And he'd only left Dallas a very small number of times over the last few years.

"How've you been?" Lucas gripped Kelly's hand and gave it a pump. "How's Becky?"

A quick strike of pain crossed his friend's face at the mention of his wife.

Ah, hell. They'd broken up?

"Really?" Lucas asked. "But you two were so—"

"Things change." Kelly cut him off, clearly not wanting to talk about his wife or whatever had gone on there. "About time you got down here. Where've you been?"

"I caught an early flight out. Had work to get done before the festivities could begin."

"Still work-before-play-Alexander," Kelly teased. "You haven't changed."

Nope. He didn't change. Much to his ex's disgust.

He glanced around the group, letting Kelly introduce him.

"Kristi Bagley," a curvy, pretty woman said. "I own Turtle Tracks and Lobster Claws, an ice cream and doughnut shop here on the island."

"Cute name."

Kristi's face lit up with the compliment. "Thanks. Come by and I'll give you one of our signature pastries, the Lobster Claw."

"Sounds like a plan." He turned to the next person.

"Mac Spiner." A thin, graying man gave him a crushing grip. "The dairy-goat farm down on the south end of the island. Hope you make it to Eight Maids-a-Milking. The challenge that day is at my place."

Each of the twelve days of the contest went along with the theme from the well-known song, though the participants had no idea what those specific daily competitions would be. They would learn them along with the crowd the morning of the event. Apparently, if he stuck around long enough, he'd have his hands on some teats before the week was out.

When Lucas turned to the first twin for an introduction, instead of giving him her name, she said, "Oh. You're a contestant." The two sisters exchanged a look.

She sounded disappointed.

"Yeah." Why else would he be here? And then he saw the numbered buttons the other guys were wearing that signified them as part of the competition. Ah. He didn't have his button. He looked around as if he had any idea where to get one. "I guess I need a button."

"Kayla's here somewhere," the first twin said, flipping her hand in the air. "I'm sure she'll find you, probably sooner rather than later." She held out her hand to him now. "I'm Savannah Marconi. I own the Two-Step Bar and Grill, and my husband is manager here at the Turtle Island Hotel. Come on out any evening for some dancing. We do classes if you aren't familiar with line dancing. But even better, come for the Italian special of the night. My husband's recipes. And welcome to Turtle Island, Lucas. I hope you enjoy your stay."

Lucas kept his expression polite with the bombardment of words. She was a chatty one.

After Savannah, he shook her sister Samantha's hand, and watched them exchange another look before Samantha informed him, "You know, Roni is here too."

Nice. He didn't even have to ask. He forced his smile to remain polite when what he wanted to do was grin like a child who'd been let out for summer break two weeks early.

"Good to know."

"Who's Roni?" Kelly asked.

"A woman I met at lunch today."

Kelly shook his head as if impressed with the speed with which Lucas had moved. He didn't bother telling Kelly that he hadn't even managed to get her last name. He was losing his touch.

Lucas tried not to look too anxious to find her, but couldn't keep his gaze from scanning the room once more, now looking for a petite, black-haired woman who had large brown eyes, one of which had a dot of green on the outside of the pupil.

Samantha smiled behind her glass of champagne before sliding her eyes off to his right. He followed her gaze.

Bingo.

Probably no more than five feet tall, the woman he'd barely gotten the pleasure of meeting stood with her back to him, a slim black dress hugging her curves, and he knew he'd recognize her anywhere. Her short, sleek hair swept to one side, she stood with her back straight, polite but not stiff, as she charmed several other contestants. He couldn't blame their slack jaws and goofy smiles. He'd been charmed in the few minutes he'd had her attention too.

He was suddenly in a hurry to finish the introductions and move across the room.

Fifteen minutes later, after too many polite conversations and not nearly enough glances at Roni, he had a glass of champagne of his own, and was crossing the plush carpet on the hunt. She'd shifted around the room several times since he'd come in, talking with people who stood alone, pulling them into larger groups. At the moment, she had the attention of three more contestants, all wearing the same wowed look the earlier men had worn.

Lucas's blood kicked into a higher gear well before he got anywhere near her.

On the way over, he caught sight of the short-haired brunette who'd taken Roni away from him earlier that day. She seemed just as stressed as she had that afternoon, only tonight she held a clipboard in her hand and was watching the crowd more than being a part of it. She tucked her hair behind her ear in a nervous gesture and he had the thought that she might be the Kayla that Savannah had mentioned. If so, she'd have the button indicating he was a contestant.

That would just have to wait.

Right now he was five feet from Roni, and nothing was changing his course.

By the time he stopped at her side, the only person still talking with her wore a button declaring him contestant number one. Roni didn't stop speaking, but she did glance Lucas's way to politely include him in the conversation. Only, when she caught sight of him, she did go silent.

Her gaze flicked to his chest before returning to his face. Then she visibly shook herself and returned, uninterrupted, to the sentence she'd been in the middle of before he'd walked up. Contestant number one appeared somewhat smug that he'd recaptured her attention.

Good luck to him. Lucas knew he was about to take it away.

In the first break of words, he took a half step closer. "Good evening, Roni."

Her eyelashes dipped. They were so long they seemed to touch her cheeks. And then they lifted and those brown eyes turned up to him. He was lost.

"You've met Ms. Templeman?" This came from number one.

Confusion attached itself as Lucas, forcing his attention away from Roni, searched the area immediately surrounding them. He was aware that concert pianist Veronica Templeman was to be master of ceremonies. He'd been looking forward to meeting her, especially given that he'd been a fan since he'd first heard her play five years ago. In fact, he had a bit of a celebrity crush.

Only, he hadn't seen her yet. He didn't see her now, either.

"Is she here?" he asked. He wasn't anxious to leave Roni's side, but he *did* want to say hello to Ms. Templeman.

The next instant, Roni stuck out her hand, smiled wryly at him, and said, "Roni Templeman."

The floor could have opened him up and swallowed him whole.

Roni. Veronica.

Of course.

How had he missed that?

He closed his hand around hers for the second time that day, not unaware of the heat that traveled up his arm as he did.

He'd only seen Veronica—*Roni*—from a distance or on CD covers before, so he'd never realized she was so tiny. But also, he'd never seen her with anything but wavy, jet black hair down to the curve of her rear.

The hair was still jet black, but it was completely straight and barely hit her chin.

Roni's lips curved before him as he stood there gaping like an idiot.

"I take it you didn't recognize me?" she murmured softly. She'd turned fully to face him, and out of the corner of his eye, he saw contestant number one move hesitantly on to find someone else to talk to. The two of them were alone.

In the middle of a roomful of people.

But still, he had her alone.

And he still had her hand in his.

"I had no idea," he said. The thought that internationally renowned concert pianist Veronica Templeman had been flirting with him earlier that day was almost enough to make him giggle like a schoolgirl. "You look different than when you were performing."

She'd always been stunning in her promotional photos. Not so much model-perfect—her chin was a little too round and her eyes a bit too wide set. But rather, as if there were a unique, magical aura about her. It made her appear almost ethereal. In person, however . . .

He glanced from her black hair to the lips that bore the faintest hint of a coral color and then on down to the creamy skin peeking out above the modest neckline of her dress.

In person, she short-circuited his brain.

She laughed, the sound light. Sexy. It made him want to stand even closer, touch her even more.

"I've changed a bit," she admitted. "Without the hair, very few people recognize me at first sight." Her voice dropped lower and he had the idea that this was what she'd sound like after a rousing night in bed. "So you've heard my music?"

"A time or two." The first had been with the Dallas Symphony. He'd been dating Des then, and at twenty-two, had tried to impress her with a fancy night out. He'd been the one to come away impressed, though. By the guest appearance of Veronica Templeman.

He'd been a fan of classical music since a required class his freshman year had introduced him to it, but he'd never been to a live performance. And he'd never heard of Veronica Templeman. Watching her on the stage that night had touched him. Not merely because she was so good. And "good" was a mild word for it. She'd been brilliant. Phenomenal.

But she'd also seemed as swept away by her own music as the rest of the crowd had been. When she'd finished, she'd appeared . . . moved. Exactly like everyone else in the room.

With her having played professionally for seventeen years, it had shocked him to see her pure enjoyment. It hadn't felt like it was just a job for her. And he hadn't been able to get enough.

He'd bought all of her CDs after that night and then attended a solo concert two years later when he'd been living in Houston. He hadn't realized at the time that it would be one of her last.

Which made him wonder what had caused her to walk away from it all.

She probably didn't need the money, but still . . . a person does something their whole life, gets accolades and recognition—it was hard to imagine they'd just up and walk away without a look back.

Though he shouldn't be surprised. He'd witnessed firsthand how a woman could up and walk away. He pushed the irritating thought from his mind and returned to the present. To Roni.

To the fact that she was looking at him as she had that day at lunch. As if she could be his for the taking.

If he wanted.

And he was no idiot. He wanted.

He studied the gentle features of her face before admitting, "I'm definitely a fan."

Her lips curved. The color on them made him want to lean in and taste her. "Maybe I'll play for you while you're here, then."

"So you still play?" The idea of a private show just for him made standing in the middle of a crowd difficult. He wanted to drag her off and be alone with her right then.

She gave a small shrug. "You can take the girl out of the per-forming . . ."

But she was still a pianist. That was very good to know. He closed his other hand over where their two remained joined. He wanted to close the distance between them completely.

"You're accent isn't as heavy tonight," he remarked. The very attractive pink color that had touched her cheeks at lunch was back. He liked that she blushed so easily around him.

"I was laying it on a little thick earlier," she admitted. "Some men like the accent."

"Ah," he murmured. "And some men like the whole package."
Lord knows he did.

She blushed a deeper pink.

He couldn't quite put his finger on what it was yet, but she drew
him to her. Instantly and hard. This would be a couple of fun weeks
if he had anything to say about it.

Someone bumped into them and they both shuffled a couple
steps over but didn't look around, neither wanting to let anyone else
into their private conversation just yet.

"Please tell me you don't have anyone waiting for you back
home," she whispered.

Hot damn. And no. Not in the way she meant. "Not a soul."

"Good."

That's all. Just "good" and then a soft smile.

It was a done deal. He was going to see this woman naked.

His mother's voice chose that minute to pop into his head. *If it seems
too good to be true, Lucas Eugene, then likely it's going to come with trouble.*

But he couldn't see where trouble would show up with Roni. Two
weeks of casual, easy fun and then he'd head home. The thought of
having only two weeks poked at a spot behind his rib cage, but he
didn't let himself explore it. That's the way it would be. No need to
play the what-if game.

"Maybe we could talk more later?" she suggested. She cast her
gaze around quickly, seeming reluctant to pull away, but they both
knew they couldn't stand there alone in the middle of the room for
the remainder of the night. "After I'm finished here."

"Absolutely."

A small horizontal line formed across her brow. "I'm confused,
though," she said. "Other than 'Lucas,' I'm not sure who you are. I
don't recognize you."

"Alexander," he said. He squeezed her hand between his. "Lucas
Alexander."

She nodded but the line didn't disappear. "And why are you . . ." She lifted her shoulders slightly before finishing with, "here?"

Ah, she didn't know he was a contestant. He really needed to find that button.

"I'm—"

"Not at all good at following directions." Clipboard lady was now standing at his elbow, eyeing his and Roni's hands clasped together. He let go, feeling like he'd been caught touching a body part other than her hand.

The newcomer stuck out a slim, white plastic bag with a logo for a local bakery on it. "Kayla Morgan," she said. "You were supposed to be on the one-thirty ferry this afternoon, and then subsequently, in the lobby to be greeted appropriately at two o'clock."

Lucas took the bag. "Sorry about that," he mumbled. He glanced at Roni as if she might offer him some help, but instead, she stood there with a look of shock on her face. Mixed with the shock seemed to be disappointment.

"We're putting on a highly organized event here, Mr. Alexander. I'd like to welcome you to the island, and let you know that if you should need anything at all throughout the next two weeks—" she nodded at the bag in his hand "—my number can be found on my card. But I do ask you to please, follow directions from here on out. I need that cooperation from each of you to ensure that everything runs smoothly and as planned."

Silence filled the space when she quit talking.

Lucas didn't know whether to go sit in the corner as punishment or to laugh at the woman, who seemed strung way too tight.

"Your button is in your bag," Kayla tacked on when he said nothing.

He looked at Roni again. She'd lost the look of shock, to have it now replaced by a bland, polite expression. Her loss of animation made the area between his shoulder blades itch.

When he continued not speaking, and Kayla continued standing there staring at him, Roni finally nudged her chin in his direction. "She's waiting for you to agree to follow the schedule."

Oh. He nodded quickly. "Yes. I'm sorry. I'll absolutely follow the schedule. I apologize again. I ended up catching an earlier flight out and got busy working and simply forgot the time."

The pinch on Kayla's face implied she didn't care. "Just let me know if anything else needs to change. In advance, please."

And then she was gone and Lucas was left standing alone once more with Roni.

"Wow," he said. "She's intense." He had the thought that her idea of fun was probably sitting at home at night in flannel pj's, dreaming up ways to scare people into order.

"She's stressed, is all. She's a good person. She wants to do a good job." The flirty lift to Roni's tone was gone and a heaviness crept inside Lucas's chest at the loss.

"Think it would help if I sent her flowers or something?" he teased. He wanted to see Roni smile again.

Instead, she locked her brown eyes on his, nothing but cool politeness remaining, and said, "I apologize, Lucas. I didn't realize you were a contestant. I shouldn't have come over at lunch today."

"Wait." He reached out to stop her though she hadn't yet turned away. Her words seemed to impact his ability to pull in a deep breath. "What do you mean?"

She cocked her head at him and gave him a dry look. "There's no need to beat around the bush. We're attracted to each other, we're doing the dance, trying to decide if we want a fling or not."

She shook her head and opened her mouth to say more, but he jumped in and stopped her.

"I've already decided," he said.

"We can't."

"I do," he insisted. "We can." He grabbed her hand. "We *should*."

She raised an eyebrow, then disentangled her hand. "We *can't*."

"Well, why not?" Nothing about the last few minutes had indicated this was the way their conversation would end. He would have sworn she was just as receptive to the idea as he.

A sigh slipped past her lips, her shoulders sinking at the same time. "I'm the face of this contest, Lucas. That's why not. I can't be . . ." She glanced around, then leaned slightly in and whispered, "Sleeping with a contestant."

"Then how about I promise to keep you up all night?" He couldn't help but try. He gave her his best smile. She was right, there was attraction there. A lot. The chemistry between them sizzled. He put one hand over his heart. "I solemnly swear *not* to let you sleep for one single minute while we're together."

A hint of a smile played around her lips. It even made it to her eyes. But she still shook her head. "Sorry. Not gonna happen."

Damn.

It wasn't merely the loss of the chance of exercising a few muscles that had been dormant for too long. It was her. He liked her. She was straightforward, she was gorgeous, she was fun to be around. And from what he'd seen here tonight, she was nice. She'd been going from person to person, drawing them into conversations. Making sure no one stood alone.

She'd wowed and charmed. She'd been real.

He liked real.

And now he had to walk away from that.

Or so *she* said.

But that didn't mean he had to play by her rules.

CHAPTER FOUR

adies and . . ." Roni began. She stood in front of the packed convention center Monday morning, her shaking hands hiding behind the lectern, and wasn't sure how to end the sentence. "Gentlemen?" she finally said, making the word a question.

Laughter swept through the crowd like a wave in an arena.

"Welcome to Turtle Island and the Turtle Island Convention Center." Cheers erupted. "We're thrilled to see so many out-of-towners joining us here today and we hope your stay is a very pleasant one."

More clapping, and now screams were added in. These women were ready to see some men.

Roni said a few more words in greeting, but soon gave up. They hadn't come to hear her talk. She glanced at Kayla standing in the wings. Kayla nodded, then gave the sign to someone Roni couldn't see. The curtains swung open behind her, and Coyote Creek, the country band hired for opening-day activities, began playing.

They played a brief version of "Here Comes Santa Claus," then backed off the volume and settled into background music. The crowd got louder, and Roni smiled broadly. It was nothing but a loud buzz of energy in the room. With any luck, the excitement running through the auditorium would help tamp down her ongoing nerves.

Though why she was so nervous, she had no idea. It wasn't like this was the first time she'd been in front of a large crowd before.

It would be the first time she'd sat at the piano in front of one in a long while, though.

Her stomach did a flip-flop, and with an exaggerated motion, she turned to the side and swept an arm across the festively decorated stage. She shouted to be heard. "I give you this year's contenders for Mr. Yummy Santa."

The place went crazy.

A line of men appeared on either side of the stage, and on cue, one by one, they headed to the center mark, where they waved, preened, and jokingly flexed their muscles before heading off the other side of the stage. They were dressed in alternating red and green low-slung swim trunks, no shirts, no shoes, and all wore a Santa hat with the white ball on the end flopped to the side of their heads.

The whole thing looked like a badly done Miss America contest, but it was a blast.

The women in the crowd were having fun, as were the men onstage. The men were yukking it up for attention. And the women were giving it to them. It bode well for the money to be raised for local charities throughout the upcoming days.

Roni even caught herself smiling in pure pleasure instead of the polite charm she'd been going for. She had to admit, she was impressed with the quality. She supposed that's what fifty grand would get you. It brought out the big guns.

Her smile vanished the instant contestant number seven made his appearance. As Lucas crossed the stage, she caught herself holding her breath. The man had about driven her crazy the night before. Even after she'd said no to the unspoken question they'd both been toying with, he'd constantly shown up in her line of sight throughout the remainder of the evening, directing a charm so compelling it should be bottled and sold. If it were, she'd certainly buy some.

The guy could flat out make a girl forget her name. Probably make her shed her panties if he got her alone long enough.

As she watched now, she confirmed what she'd only before suspected. Lucas sans shirt was a sight to behold.

A fine brushing of hair across the middle of his chest. Abs that really needed to be explored in detail by her fingers. And a sexy, thin trail leading from his navel down until it disappeared under his swim trunks. Kind of like an arrow, pointing the way to the pot of gold.

She swallowed against her dry throat.

Darn the man for being a contestant.

She'd been knocked for a loop when Kayla had shown up and thrust the welcome bag at him. He hadn't been wearing the oversize contestant button either time she'd seen him, and it had honestly never crossed her mind that he might be in town for any reason other than work.

Possibly because she so desperately wanted him not to be part of the competition.

Since leaving her career and moving to Turtle Island, she'd made the decision to live her life by going with her impulses. If it felt right, she did it.

And flirting with Lucas Alexander had felt right.

Too bad her impulsiveness had burned her this time.

She continued to watch the remaining men stride across the stage as part of the opening to the upcoming two weeks of activities, and while the crowd clapped with wild abandon, she agreed with her prior assessment. This event would be a success.

The committee, who had worked tirelessly over the last six months, was to be commended. As well as the business owners who'd contributed the prize and Kayla for the highly professional job she'd done. Roni only wished that Andie was here to see it. She would not only be proud of Kayla and Seaglass Celebrations, but she would enjoy the display of hot, hunky men as much as every other woman in the room.

When contestant twenty-four disappeared off the stage, a whoosh went out of the crowd. They still tittered in their seats with smiles on their faces—because they knew more was heading their way—but it felt almost as if the air had been let out of all of them simultaneously.

The air disappeared from Roni's lungs too, but for an altogether different reason.

Within minutes, she would be sitting at the piano onstage with the band. Playing with them.

It was silly that this bothered her so much, but there it was. She was a ball of nerves. But she had to focus and move on through the next few minutes before she could worry about what came next.

Clapping along with the crowd, she turned back to the podium and leaned forward to speak directly into the microphone.

"Now wasn't that a nice way to start off the week?" she said. Laughter once again bounced through the room. "Rarely have I had a more entertaining Monday morning."

Each day of the competition would start off like today. At eleven in the morning they would gather to greet the remaining contestants and learn of the day's challenge, then she would draw the names of the lucky audience members who would be assigned their very own contestant for the day. The selected women would then spend the afternoon helping with the day's challenge, and they'd all return to the convention center in the evening for the wrap-up and reveal of the day's winner. At the same time, two contenders would be kicked out of the competition.

Day twelve would crown the winner, and on day thirteen there would be a parade showcasing every contestant and all the businesses who'd sponsored any part of the competition, and highlighting this year's Mr. Yummy Santa. Roni would lead the parade as part of her master of ceremonies duties.

"Now for the really juicy part," she said into the microphone again, waggling her eyebrows as she spoke. "Let's bring these guys back and take a closer look. Maybe learn a thing or two about them."

The cheers started again as the men returned to the stage one by one.

Roni announced each man's name, reading their information off the provided index cards as they made their way to the middle of the stage. This time, they barely had to do anything for the encouraging cheers, but that didn't stop them. Muscles bunched, six-packs rolled. It was every girl's fantasy come to life.

When she got to Lucas, her body began a slow burn from the toes up as she watched him move across the space. She didn't understand how he got her so turned on with nothing more than a smile and a glance when any number of these men should be able to do the same. But facts were facts. He lit her fuse.

He stopped at the designated spot in the middle of the stage, and when he shot her a look, she shot him one back. "Look at the crowd, not me," she silently told him. But when she caught sight of Kayla scowling at her from the shadows, she realized that the looks heading her way were because she'd quit talking.

Her eyes went wide. She was gawking instead of reading off his stats.

Good grief.

She turned a too-wide smile to the crowd and flipped to his card.

"Lucas Alexander comes to us from Dallas." A roar filled the room. Yep, he was going to be a fan favorite. "He's twenty-seven, a mild-mannered computer programmer by day"—which explained the single-mindedness with the laptop the morning before—"and a cover model by night. He loves to take women to the symphony . . ." She paused, caught off guard at the thought of him watching her play. He'd admitted he was a fan, but she'd assumed he'd heard her recorded music only. Had he actually seen her perform in person?

Kayla shot her another glare and Roni glanced back at the card in her hand. "And he says his weakness is avocados," she continued.

Funny.

"His charity is the Dallas Leukemia Foundation," she continued. "He's six-two, one hundred and ninety pounds, and eight percent body fat."

Sheesh, didn't she feel all dumpy.

She waved the card in front of her face to cool herself as the women squealed and Lucas did a little turn and pose. He flexed the muscles in his back and the noise level hitched up.

When he'd finished taunting the females, Lucas headed in her direction and her heart seized. Oh geez, she was going to have a really hard time ignoring him for the next two weeks.

He winked as if he'd read her mind, then swung around to land in the spot he'd been assigned. She needed to get her head on straight and quit thinking about him like that or playing the piano would be the last thing she'd be nervous about. She would instead need to worry about not making a fool of herself fawning all over Lucas Alexander in front of the whole darned island.

With determination, she finished introducing the remainder of the men, then moved to the large ball cage that had been positioned at the edge of the stage. The ball held the names of every woman who'd donated ten dollars to be put into the drawing. All the money collected today would go to the local sea turtle rescue.

"As you know," she began, "we're counting down the twelve days of Christmas to find our Yummy Santa." More screaming. "We're kicking things off today with a tree-decorating contest. There are twenty-four Douglas firs positioned around town, each currently bare. Every contestant will have the same selection of ornaments and lights."

She held up a small hand-painted figure that went with the theme for the day. "In his box he'll find twelve drummers drumming, along with an assortment of other decorations. It'll be your job to help him turn the tree into something to marvel at. The goal, of course, is to make it look better than anyone else's."

They would have from noon until four to decorate the trees. At that point, judging would begin. Each person could buy as many votes as they wanted. Each vote cost one dollar. This was made to be fun, but it was also about charity.

"The two men who come in last will be eliminated tonight."

With a wide grin, she grabbed the handle of the enclosed cage of names of donating women and began cranking the arm. The crowd once again went wild. She drew out twenty-four cards, one at a time, announcing the name on each. The winners jumped up and down and threw their hands in the air as if they'd won a new car, then they were directed to a waiting area.

"The contestant with the most number of votes will be pronounced the day's winner at this evening's ceremony," she continued. "At that time, you will all be treated to a concert by Coyote Creek."

At which, she would *not* have to participate. Thank goodness.

Cheers went up and the band once again broke into song. The men were directed offstage, and Roni slipped from the front and headed to her makeshift dressing room. The band would play alone for several minutes while Kayla got the women into T-shirts with their contestant's number on it, and then prepared everyone for one last parade across the stage. Then Roni would be up.

At that point, she'd have to face the crowd whether she was ready to or not.

~

Roni paced the twelve feet of her dressing room, pivoted, then headed back. She focused on pulling in breaths deep enough that they expanded her chest, held them for a count of five, and then let them out again. She was trying to get into the routine she'd spent years doing before concerts. The pacing was new, but the deep breathing had always helped her focus.

She wiggled her fingers at her sides, loosening up her hands.

The band continued to play out front as she turned and took equal-distance steps back across the room. Someone would be rolling the piano out toward the stage soon, getting ready to push it to the center. Then it would be time for her.

Her fingers clenched into her palms and her deep breaths stopped.

She'd like to believe the nerves were something other than what they were, but she couldn't hide from the truth. She was experiencing pure terror at the idea of playing for an audience. A large audience. A real one on a real stage, not casually like at Gin's. She played at Gin's all the time without any problem.

The bar could be overflowing with customers and it didn't faze her.

But the crowd here at the convention center?

She pulled in another lung-filling breath. Today reminded her of her years of being front and center. Was it the size of the audience? The lights and stage? She wasn't sure. But either way, this felt more important. It felt real.

If felt like she'd gone back three years and was once again facing her demons.

She closed her eyes as she moved, concentrating as she placed one foot in front of the other, and tried to think of something other than stepping back out on that stage.

Lucas Alexander's evil smile popped to mind. She moaned in torturous ecstasy as she silently counted the steps she took across the room. That man registered a twenty on her Richter scale.

She'd dreamed about him last night. In the dream, he'd smiled at her, flirted with her, and then he'd taken her in his arms.

And she'd taken him for a spin.

Only he was more like a shiny sports car sitting on the showroom floor. One that she wasn't allowed to touch.

She made a face at the thought.

Stupid hormones. They had to go and get all worked up over someone she couldn't have.

She turned and headed back the other way. She needed more than twelve feet to get a good pace going. Next time she'd head out the back door to the beach.

It was silly, really, when she thought about it. Why couldn't she have a little fun with Lucas? It wasn't as if she had any real say in the voting. She could pay to vote just like anyone else. Other than that, she had no sway over matters whatsoever. She was merely there to help with the show. She would entertain with witty banter, announce the day's competition, then spin the lottery wheel and draw out the names.

Easy. Simple. Not a conflict of interest.

Ugh.

Only, she knew she was making excuses. It wouldn't look good. Kayla would worry it would hurt Seaglass. And Roni didn't want to hurt anyone, least of all her friend's business.

So yeah, she supposed sleeping with Lucas wouldn't be a good idea. Unfortunately.

She just had to keep telling herself that every time she caught a peek of him.

Right now, though, she should focus on something else. Something other than what she wanted to do with Lucas.

Like the fact that she was about to take to the piano on a stage for the first time in three years.

She thunked the palm of her hand against her forehead and squinted her eyes closed tighter. She still couldn't believe she'd agreed to that.

Step, step, step. Pivot.

Somehow Kayla had talked her into it. A guilt trip. She'd explained what a thrill it would be to both the contestants and the crowd to have Roni give a special "mini-performance" with the band. They'd be brokenhearted if she didn't. And Roni had fallen for it.

She supposed it would be a bit of a thrill for her too. She loved performing. Or she had. So how could it not be exciting? If she were to be honest, she'd also admit that she missed the rush of it sometimes. A little.

Not enough to go back, though.

Yet playing just one song . . . well, one song with the band and then a small solo number . . . was fine. She could do that. It would be fun. But she had not allowed herself to be talked into a full concert at the end of the two weeks. That would be going too far.

Pivot.

She was retired from all that. She played for fun now. Only.

That's why she refused to take any money for her performances. And hey, what wouldn't be fun about playing "The Twelve Days of Christmas" with an up-and-coming country band, along with twenty-four gorgeous, half-naked men gracing the stage?

So yeah, okay. She could do this. Do her master of ceremonies duties . . . and stay focused only on that.

And do *not* do Lucas Alexander.

She slammed into something hard, only then realizing she was still walking with her eyes closed. When she opened them, she wished she'd kept them shut.

Lucas stood in front of her.

Big, wide, bare chest. And of course, he was wearing the requisite smile. The man had to know what that smile did to her.

Her heart tried its best to pound its way out of her chest.

"Morning, gorgeous," he said.

She gave him the evil eye. He sounded gravelly and satisfied, as if they'd just crawled from beneath warm sheets together.

He chuckled, apparently unimpressed with her mean look.

"Shouldn't you be out front getting ready to go back onstage?" she grumbled.

"Probably. In fact, Kayla will likely hunt me down any second now. She caught me heading this way."

Roni shot a look at the now closed door. She'd left it open when she'd come in.

"You closed my door," she pointed out.

"I did."

"Why?"

He leaned in and put his mouth to her ear. She could smell mint on his breath. "Because I wanted to be alone with you," he whispered.

Her treacherous hand reached out and pressed, palm flat against his heated chest, and the muscles behind her panties did a little spasm.

Damn the man.

"There's no good reason to be back here alone together," she spoke into his neck, since he was still leaning into her. His hands had crept to either side of her waist and his cheek was so close to hers that it would take only a tiny shift to press her skin against his. If she hadn't been concentrating so hard on not letting her fingers burrow into the soft hair on his very, *very* hard pecs, she might have been embarrassed by the shaky squeak of her voice.

"Any chance I could change your mind today?" Heat dampened her ear as he spoke.

Her shoulder inched up, closing the gap to her ear, as if he'd touched his lips to her instead of merely whispering a hair's breadth away. The hair on her upper body stood on end, and her lower body melted. He didn't have to say what he wanted to change her mind about. Her. Him. And a little something that would end with a screaming orgasm or two.

Her eyes popped open. She'd closed them again. *Sigh.* And her hand was still planted firmly in the middle of his chest.

And no, unfortunately, she was not going to have any screaming orgasms anytime soon.

Drat.

She pushed against him, putting a few inches between them, and then forced her hand from the firm, tanned flesh. She closed her fingers in her palm and lowered her arm to hang at her side. Kayla made an announcement over the back speakers. Time to line up.

"No," she muttered. "I'm not changing my mind." She knew she sounded pouty. But dang, he would have been a good diversion for the next couple of weeks.

Lucas wrapped his fingers around her clenched fist and leaned in again, putting his mouth back to her ear. "It would be fun," he cajoled. "Hot," he whispered. She shivered. "And not a single person other than us would have to know."

Right. Because it was so easy to keep a secret on this small island.

His thumb stroked along the outside of hers, each movement licking heat along the underside of her wrist before zipping up her forearm. His touch frustrated her even more. But she didn't pull her hand out of his.

Because she liked it.

She tilted her head back, lamenting the fact that she was only five feet tall. Even in heels, he still had almost a foot on her.

It was a shame, really. That they couldn't have a good time. Because she liked him. Not only did he have that fun vibe going, not only was he sexy as sin, but she'd bet big money that he knew how to handle a girl. And yesterday at lunch he'd pushed his work aside and returned her attention when she'd sat down with him.

Charles had never put work aside for her.

"I'm the face of the competition, Lucas," she whispered. "I'm the one everyone will see. Every day." Geez, how she wanted not to care about that. "I can't . . ." She trailed off as she realized his fingers were now entwined with hers.

She looked down at their hands and gave a halfhearted tug, but he kept hold of her. When he didn't turn her loose, she made a face at him. He smiled in return. The corners of his eyes crinkled with the action.

"Someone could come in here and see us holding hands," she pointed out, her tone droll. Not at all accusingly as she'd intended. "Do you want to get me in trouble?"

"I want to get you to smile." His words were simple and honest.

She let out a soft breath. "Lucas." Her voice was pleading. He seemed like a good guy. Really, he did. She'd paid far more attention to him the night before than she should have. He'd been polite and pleasant. He'd chatted up everyone, making people laugh and seemingly having a good time. And other than teasing Roni mercilessly, he'd been adorable. "I'm sorry I flirted—"

"No, you're not," he said. "You're sorry it's more complicated than you thought. But it doesn't have to be."

The band quit playing and the crowd went silent. Her mouth turned dry.

The curtains would be closing and the piano rolled to the stage.

"I see no reason—" Lucas's words stopped and his features hardened. That's when she realized that the edges of his blue irises were trimmed in a thin strip of gray. They were intriguing, beautiful.

"What's wrong?" he asked.

"What do you mean?"

His hand squeezed hers. "You're shaking. What's wrong?"

The man had gone from teasing and playful to take-charge and intense in an instant. She looked down at their hands twisted together. Yes, her hand was shaking. Her whole body was, actually.

Then she heard her cue and knew that the curtains would be opening again soon and she would be up. "You've got to go." She shoved at him. "I have to take my spot."

Instead of leaving, he gripped her hand tighter. He peered down at her. "You're nervous?"

She shrugged, embarrassed. "Apparently."

He stared at her for two long seconds and then brought her hand to his mouth. He pressed his lips to the spot above her knuckles. "You're going to wow them, you know."

"What?"

"You will be amazing. You're brilliant onstage. All you have to do is put your fingers on the keys, close your eyes, and nothing else in the world will matter."

He was trying to calm her nerves. What a sweetheart. And the fact he'd keyed in on exactly what her issue was didn't miss her.

She swallowed around a lump in her throat. She was going to be okay. She could do this. She was exemplary at this.

And anyway, they were talking one song. One and a half. His hand tightened around hers again and he whispered, "Knock 'em dead."

Then he was gone, and she got to her spot just as the curtains began to open.

It was go time.

CHAPTER FIVE

The curtains parted, revealing Roni at the piano surrounded by the band. Her wrap dress with its vibrant mix of colors crisscrossing her body pulled all eyes to her.

Instead of greeting the crowd, the group launched immediately into an intro to "The Twelve Days of Christmas." No singing, merely playing. Letting the crowd absorb and appreciate Roni.

Lucas wanted to stand in the shadows and watch her. That's all. Just watch. Wait for her to finish so he could go to her and make sure she was okay. The audience seemed transfixed. It was an honor to see her play. Everyone in the room seemed to understand that fact.

She wasn't looking at anyone now. She hadn't so much as lifted her head.

She was watching only her own fingers. Yet he could tell that the tension was already disappearing from her shoulders.

Lucas had been shocked to feel her shaking in her dressing room. The quieter the crowd had become, the more her body had quivered.

At first he'd been egotistical and thought it was his touch.

But he'd quickly realized that though they may have off-the-charts chemistry, even he wasn't that good. The woman had radiated fear.

He'd read through the schedule the night before and had seen that she would be playing today. He'd been exuberant at the thought.

Yet as she'd stood there, vibrating in his hands, it had clicked. Something had made her walk away from playing. Something that had turned the brown of her eyes to a bottomless pool of worry.

This woman had played for packed houses with large symphonies. She'd played solo concerts all over the world. She'd even once played a special event for the president and first lady of the United States.

Yet she'd looked today as if she'd rather run from the building than head out to the stage.

He had to hand it to her, though. She didn't shirk her responsibilities. When the time had come, she'd done what she had to do. She'd tossed her head back and walked right to the middle of the stage.

And she was shining out there.

He glanced down at his partner for the day, Melody Harper, an older lady who stood at his side. Both of them, along with eleven other contestants and their helpers, were ready to head out when given their cue. Melody was alternately smiling at him and then at the band. Or maybe she was smiling at Roni. It was hard to tell. Especially when he could barely pull his own gaze from Roni long enough to pay much attention to anything else.

Kayla Morgan marched back and forth in front of the line of them, a pencil tapping against her clipboard as she counted out a silent beat. She was wearing a headset with a small microphone positioned in front of her mouth. He saw her speak into it, presumably to the person she had on the other side of the stage lining up the remaining contestants over there.

But at the center of it all was Roni, her fingers gliding over the keys and her face settling into a comfortable glow.

His eyes drifted to her hair. The interesting thing about her today—along with her being almost too scared to walk out on stage—was that her hair seemed to better fit what he knew about her. It had lost yesterday's smooth, contained style, and today it was literally exploding around her head. Black curls were everywhere. They were glorious. It felt more like the pianist who played with wild abandon.

~

The instant Roni's fingers had touched the keys, she'd been transported back in time. She'd been doing this since the age of three, trained by her father, who'd also been a child prodigy. He'd begun taking her on the road with him at the tender age of six. She'd loved it.

She'd missed her mom, of course, but overall, she'd loved every single second of it.

With each "day" the band sang now—first day of Christmas, second day of Christmas—the men reentered the stage with their designated helpers, stepped to the center to wave, then edged back, leaving a gap for the crowd to see the band.

Roni watched until she saw Lucas and his partner come onstage, and then she closed her eyes.

She got lost in the music. The sound of the guitars and drums pumped through her, but it was the touch of the ivories under her fingertips that she felt the most. And the crowd. She knew the excitement wasn't for her. Not yet. But she fed off the energy.

Her fingers glided over the keys as she thought about all she'd walked away from. She'd had to walk. She'd been too broken.

And she'd never regretted it.

But she did miss it. She missed this.

This excitement. This feeling of doing what she was born to do.

"Ladies and gentlemen," the lead singer spoke softly into the microphone several minutes later. The band faded out and the singer announced reverently, "Ms. Veronica Templeman."

A spotlight shown down on her as she transitioned into her solo and everything else seemed to fade away. She played a medley of Christmas songs, with her own classical spin thrown on top. She'd recorded the piece on her last CD and had been practicing it in a new key for weeks.

The crowd quieted as her hands flew in front of her.

There were no nerves now, only contentment. And coursing adrenaline. She played as if she were the only one the audience was there to see.

As her fingers reached for each note with exact precision, Roni let her mind drift to the first time she'd played at Carnegie Hall. She'd been ten. The specialness of that performance had been that her mother and brother had gotten to come up.

Then she thought about the children's hospital in New York City. Her first time there, hundreds of kids had sat in the audience. Kids there for nothing more than getting tubes put in their ears, or possibly just visiting their less healthy siblings. Kids who'd called the hospital home for months.

Some who'd had no idea that they would never get the chance to go home again.

Unwanted emotions threatened to creep into the edges of the music and Roni stubbornly pushed them aside. She was playing here now. On Turtle Island. Not in New York City. And not for anyone but a rowdy crowd of women looking to have a good time and spend a little money.

She was not playing for a child who had no mother.

Or a child who had no home.

She shoved everything from her mind but the song pouring from her fingertips and the fact that this was her one and only shot. Then she would go back to playing at Gin's.

She raced toward the end, and felt tears slip from her eyes.

When she hit the final note, she stood.

Shoulders back, chin up, she felt twice her size. The place exploded.

Her hands tingled with the flow of blood, and her body shook from excitement. That had been euphoric.

That had been living.

That had scared her to death.

She didn't mean to, but her gaze sought out Lucas's. He was standing with his partner, but he seemed to have forgotten she existed. He stared at Roni with an understanding that made her breath catch. Somehow, he knew what she'd just felt. She had no doubt about that.

He knew he'd just witnessed her coming alive.

And she had. She loved playing. She loved performing. She missed it.

But she couldn't go back.

She couldn't live without the pieces of her heart it took from her every time.

CHAPTER SIX

At five o'clock that evening, Roni stood twenty feet from the shoreline behind her house, her hands tucked deep into the pockets of her faded blue-gray capris, her feet bare. She stared out at the water, barely seeing more than the mix of the late-afternoon colors and the gray of the ocean. Soon she'd have to return to her house and dress for that night's event. She didn't want to be late.

But not yet.

First she needed a few more minutes to herself.

So many things had been on her mind that day. Playing the piano at the convention center. *Enjoying* playing the piano at the convention center. Enjoying the hushed awareness of the crowd before the eruption of applause.

She pinched her lips together.

Watching Lucas after she'd played.

She pulled cool air in through her nose and closed her eyes as her mind raced through the other memory that had been eating at her that day. Going to the children's hospital for the last time. She didn't like knowing she was still so raw from that.

Her hair whipped in the wind and she lifted both arms, digging her fingers into the curls on either side. She held there like that. Arms up, elbows out, hair back off her forehead. And turned her face up to the deepening blues and purples of the sky. She often thought of letting her hair grow back out, but it was too much here on the beach. At the length it was, it was manageable. Her life was manageable. Best to keep it short.

"That was quite the performance this morning."

Roni dropped her arms to her sides and looked back and to her right. Mrs. Rylander was making her way across the beach, wearing a chunky turtleneck, wool pants, and green rubber boots up to her knees. Her curly white hair was held in place by a sheer yellow scarf, tied securely at the loose skin of her neck. Clearly her neighbor didn't appreciate the crispness of the December breeze like Roni did.

"Did you stand below my deck listening to me play again this morning?" Roni asked. About six months ago, she'd realized that the former owner of her house often snuck over in the mornings and listened to her play. Now Roni watched for her to head back across the yard when she finished each day.

Rarely did Mrs. Rylander acknowledge she was there. Nor did Roni let her know when she saw her. It was kind of their "thing."

"I'm not talking about at your house," the older lady harrumphed, as if the mere suggestion that she listened in on Roni's practice sessions was ludicrous. "I mean at the Hunky Santa thing. It was different than what you do at the house. A different feel to it."

Yep. It had been.

"I didn't realize you were in the crowd." Best to avoid topics one didn't want to discuss.

Being so short left Roni at about the same height as her neighbor, so she got the full impact of a sharp, are-you-kidding-me look as the woman made it to her side. "There's twenty-four men walking around this island, reminding me of when my Henry was young. Henry could have competed right along with those boys, you know?" She shook her head. "No chance I'm missing any part of that."

Roni laughed softly at the thought of Mrs. Rylander in line, buy-ing up tickets to every event. Also, she'd seen pictures of Mrs. Rylander's late husband in his older years. The man's nose and ears had dominated the photographs. She'd just have to take her word on whether or not he could have stood a chance beside the likes of Lucas and the other twenty-three in his early days.

"And don't be changing the subject on me," Mrs. Rylander added.

A wave broke and landed within feet of Roni, the foam reaching out in slow motion until it almost touched her toes. She turned toward the dunes. She should get ready for the upcoming evening anyway. Mrs. Rylander trudged along beside her, not picking up her feet as she shuffled, scooping handfuls of sand up with each forward movement. Most of the sand bounced off the back of Roni's calves.

"I'm not changing subjects," Roni began. She studied her house instead of looking at her neighbor. "I just don't know what to say. I agree. There was something different."

This wasn't the first conversation they'd had on the beach. It had become another of their "things." When Roni had something on her mind, she often found herself standing on the beach. More often than not, her neighbor joined her.

Roni hadn't thought she'd done it intentionally, but thinking about it now, she wondered if maybe she did. The woman had seen eight decades of living. Surely she had some knowledge to impart. Maybe Roni had subconsciously been hoping to pick up a tidbit here or there.

"You know what it was, don't you?" Mrs. Rylander asked. Her breathing had grown short and rapid so Roni slowed her pace. She took in her neighbor from the corner of her eye but didn't say any-thing. Just kept walking.

"It was desire."

Roni jolted to a stop.

"Desire?" She echoed. She eyed her neighbor. Had Mrs. Rylander somehow picked up on her attraction to Lucas?

"Oh, good grief." The elderly woman waved a hand in the air. Her mouth puckered, and the corners of her light-blue eyes wrinkled as if disgusted. "You young people today, that's all you think about. Though I could tell you a story or two about desire. Why, in my time—"

"Mrs. Rylander," Roni warned. She did not want to hear about Henry or his conquests.

"I'm not talking about *that* kind of desire," Mrs. Rylander grumbled. "But I suspect there's some of that going on too."

Only every time she got a glimpse of a certain contestant. "Then what are you talking—"

"I mean the desire to be there. In front of the crowd. You weren't just playing this morning. You were somewhere else. You wanted to *be* somewhere else."

Roni remained immobile in the sand. She was only a few feet from the walk that would take her up under her deck and away from this conversation, but she felt like she'd been dropped out in the middle of the ocean. Her chest burned as if she were being held under the water, unable to breathe. She didn't have the desire to be in front of that kind of crowd again. Not really. She'd given that up. It had been her choice.

And she hadn't been anywhere else but the convention center that morning.

But she had been thinking of someone else.

A different pair of light-blue eyes appeared in her mind, ones that weren't eighty years old, and she squeezed her eyes shut. She shook her head. "No," she whispered. "I don't. I love living here. I love what I do."

"Playing at that bar?"

"I teach piano too." She opened her eyes and shoved the past back where it belonged. "And I volunteer. I even help Ginger out on the boats on occasion." Ginger had inherited her Daddy's ferry business when he'd died suddenly, and since coming back home from college, she'd added fishing and tour boats, as well as dinner cruises.

"You piddle to keep busy," Mrs. Rylander accused. "Because you're afraid to look at what you gave up."

She glared at her neighbor now. They'd never had a discussion of this kind before. In fact, they'd never talked about her piano career at all. "You have no idea what you're talking about."

"I know what it's like to lose something you love," the elder woman said. She stuck her nose proudly in the air. "Sometimes you have control over it, and sometimes you don't."

Most times you don't.

"Don't you think you've been hiding long enough?" Mrs. Rylander said in a rush, her words ending in a near whisper.

Roni stared at her. She tried to force herself to look away, but she couldn't. The blue eyes, faded with her years, were watery now, and her chin trembled just the slightest amount. The sadness looking back at her suddenly reminded Roni of the stories she'd heard about why the woman had sold her house and moved next door to the smaller one.

Her kids wouldn't visit her here.

She'd had six kids with her Henry—but if Roni remembered correctly, had lost one when he'd been a teen. And not a single one of the remaining five visited her.

It was sad.

"Mrs. Rylander," Roni started. She reached out and put a hand on the other woman's frail shoulder. "Are you okay?"

That chin inched up higher. "I'm perfectly fine, dear. I'm always fine."

Why did it sound like she'd said those words before?

"Can I do something?" Roni asked.

The glassiness from her neighbor's eyes cleared and the shrewdness returned. "You mean other than admit you made a mistake?"

Roni clenched her teeth together. "I did not make a mistake."

"Decisions like yours don't lead to daily three-hour sessions at the piano."

"I still like playing the piano."

"Obviously."

A sigh slipped out, though Roni had been trying hard to hold it in. This had been a rough day already. She didn't need her neighbor being difficult on top of it.

"I'm going in now, Mrs. Rylander. I assume you can get yourself back to your place?"

As in, go away. Leave me alone. Don't say another word.

But Mrs. Rylander either didn't read the underlying message, or she didn't care.

Instead of heading back to her place, she plopped her hands on her hips and scrunched up her face. "And just for the record, I saw the way that boy looked at you. As well as the way you looked at him."

"Again. I have no idea—"

"Desire," she bit out. "That other kind. Contestant number seven."

Roni started to shake her head in denial, but Mrs. Rylander held up a single bony finger. Roni ceased movement.

"You can lie to yourself all you want. You can lie to me. But your face doesn't lie." Mrs. Rylander softened her voice. "And your heart doesn't lie. Listen to it."

~

Lucas lined up with Melody Monday night as they waited to be given the go-ahead to head onstage. Melody was a sweetheart. In her late fifties, and so excited to have been selected to help with the first challenge of the competition. She'd ridden down with a group of friends from Savannah.

She'd also been a shameless flirt. But an innocent one.

They'd had a really good time throughout the afternoon. First they'd checked out their tree and box of decorations, and then they'd grabbed a meal and used the time to formulate a plan. He stunk at putting lights up. He'd certainly heard that enough over the last few years. But Melody had sworn she knew what she was doing. She'd done the job each year during her thirty-five-year marriage.

Since her husband had passed away two years earlier, she'd let the grandkids handle the decorating, so she'd taken today's opportunity to heart. She'd wanted the chance to see what she could do again.

Lucas had lucked out. This woman could have whipped a Charlie Brown tree into shape. They'd both ended up proud of the job they'd done. He'd seen plenty of admirers, too, as he and Melody had stood by their decked-out tree during the judging process.

Many people had oohed and aahed over their creation.

Who he hadn't seen, oohing and aahing or otherwise, was Roni. She'd been suspiciously absent since the curtain had closed on her solo that morning.

He pictured her as she'd been at the piano and felt the power of what he'd witnessed. If he hadn't seen it himself only a short time beforehand, he would have never believed she'd been racked with fear. Her talent hadn't slipped one bit in her absence.

He'd gotten lost in the sound as she'd played her solo, and had forgotten there were more than the two of them in the room together. He'd watched her. And he'd wanted to go to her.

"There she is," Melody whispered beside him. She slipped her arm through his and squeezed.

He followed her gaze, but knew who she was talking about without asking.

Roni was coming from the back and heading to the stage. She very carefully was not looking around as she walked.

She wore another dress tonight, this one silver and more formal. It hit her at the ankle on one side and was pulled up to mid-shin on the other. There was a thin line of sequins running in a path down to the bunched material at her shin, then edging the bottom of the dress all the way around. It wasn't overly flashy, but spoke of class and style. It was perfect for her.

As was her hair. The short black tresses had once again taken on a life of their own.

"She's beautiful," Melody said in slight awe. At least he wasn't the only one being blown away.

Melody had explained earlier that she'd been a private piano teacher in Savannah until she'd retired. She'd followed Roni's career for years. When Melody hadn't been talking about her deceased husband throughout the day—or flirting with Lucas as if she were thirty years younger—she'd been talking about Roni. The woman was definitely a fan.

Roni was the reason Melody's friends had been able to convince her to come down with them. Until they'd brought Roni up, Melody hadn't realized she lived so close by.

"We came in Saturday," she told him now. "And went to the bar where she plays."

"She plays at a bar?" he hadn't realized that. At least she hadn't completely walked away from it.

Melody nodded. "A cute little place called Gin's. It's about a quarter mile up the beach. She's apparently been there since she moved here, both as hostess and playing the piano. But it's not the same as what we saw this morning. At the bar, she eggs on the crowd to get them going. She's more just having a good time. This morning . . ." Melody paused and closed her eyes as if reliving the moment. "This morning she breathed the music into her lungs," she whispered.

Yes. That's exactly what she'd done. She'd lived it. Breathed it.

"I heard a rumor that she's giving a concert after the parade next weekend," Melody said.

Lucas went still. "Really?"

He hadn't seen that mentioned anywhere. And he'd been looking.

Melody nodded, her short blonde bob moving up and down at his shoulder. "Could you imagine? If they want to draw a crowd, that's the way to do it."

He would have to agree. Roni would attract way more people to the island than he and his colleagues had.

The crowd hushed and Roni took the mic. He liked the slightly Southern, slightly husky sound of her voice. Just a hint to show her roots.

She welcomed the audience back, and then Kayla gave the signal and the men and their partners began filing onto the stage to welcoming cheers. As he entered, he kept his gaze on Roni. Just looking at her soothed him.

Which was silly. No woman soothed him. Women were good times. He enjoyed the occasional hookup when he was out of town. But they weren't *soothing* in any manner.

What they were was fun. Plain and simple.

They weren't steadying, they weren't calming, and they certainly didn't soothe.

When the clapping died down, he watched as Roni was handed a sealed envelope. She turned to the men, but didn't make eye contact with him. That irritated him.

She seemed to look at every other man onstage.

"I have in my hand the names of the two contestants with the lowest scores." She waved the envelope in the air and boos filled the auditorium. She gave a shrug and the sequins that were also running down the sleeves of her dress glittered under the lights. "Sorry, ladies, but we have to let two go. Otherwise we never get to our winner."

Nerves tightened Lucas's gut before he remembered a couple of the other trees he'd seen. Those men had clearly *not* had the help of someone with thirty-five years' experience putting up lights.

When Roni called out the first name, he recognized it as one of the men who'd lacked in Melody's talent. The second name followed suit. The guys and their partners in crime took to the front of the stage and accepted their demotion bravely before being hustled off to the right.

Next, Roni was handed another envelope and she swept one more glance over them. This time, her eyes tripped over his.

She looked at him with reluctance in her eyes. As if not wanting to see him. Or have him see her.

It was because of that morning. Because he *had* seen her. As she'd been playing. She knew he'd witnessed her feeling far more than fun and good times as she'd played.

She'd felt exposed.

And he was the one who'd witnessed it.

Melody squeezed his arm again and when he looked down at her, she smiled brightly. He knew she'd enjoyed herself today. Which made him wonder if this was the first time she'd had such fun since her husband had passed. He hoped they won for her.

Roni pulled the card from the envelope and once again waved it in the air. The crowd started shouting numbers of the contestants. He heard several sevens for them and gave Melody a wink. She blew him a kiss in return.

"And today's winner is . . ."

"Seven!" someone shouted from the audience.

Melody laughed and leaned into him to whisper, "That's my friend, Rebecca."

"Lucas Alexander," Roni announced, "and his partner, Melody Harper, from Savannah."

The crowd whooped, Melody pumped an arm in the air, and Roni headed their way with a gift basket.

"Congratulations," she said, handing the basket to Melody. She turned brown eyes to his and he knew they had to talk. That night.

~

The day had ended pleasantly enough, and now all Roni wanted to do was head home and crawl into bed. It had been a long day.

First was everything she'd felt when she'd stood from the piano that morning.

Mrs. Rylander had been right. She wanted it. She wanted to be back in front of the crowd night after night, doing what she loved.

Then she'd thought about the two-month sabbatical she'd taken after her last tour. Before realizing she couldn't go back to performing at all. She'd never been that low in her life. Or alone. And she'd never wanted to feel either again.

She'd come close to it today.

Everything from her past had hit her at once and she'd headed to her house to take refuge. She hadn't participated in the tree decorations, nor had she so much as cast a single vote. That had not made Kayla happy, but Roni had discovered she was still capable of having a day where it was not only hard to raise her head off her pillow, but almost impossible to step outside and be around other people. Kayla would just have to deal.

Roni changed out of her heels and slipped on the flip-flops she'd brought to the convention center with her. She hadn't driven over, so she would walk home. It was only half a mile.

As she stepped out onto the back deck, closing the door to the sounds of the band, she heard the surf pounding below and drew in a deep breath of salty air. It was nearing eight and close to high tide. She headed for the stairs. She'd prefer to walk home by way of the beach and dig her toes in the sand. The dampness would give her a jolt and help keep her from returning to where she'd spent most of the day's hours. But she didn't want to risk ruining her dress, so she'd stick to the sidewalks tonight.

At the very moment her foot touched the ground at the base of the steps, she heard the door above her open and close. The stairs wound down in a way that ended up slightly underneath the overwide deck. A heavy footfall landed on the top step a couple of seconds later.

She didn't wonder how she knew, but she had no doubt that it was Lucas who'd come out after her. He'd been watching her all evening, though not with the same flirtatious look he'd chased her with the night before.

Tonight had been different.

He'd seen her earlier when she'd ripped herself open with emotions, and he was apparently not going to let it go without attempting to get her to talk about it. But she didn't want to talk.

She also didn't want to hide tonight.

She could use someone holding her up for just a moment.

Lucas appeared at the bend in the stairs in worn jeans, cowboy boots, and a white button-down under a sports jacket. He stared down at her. Roni stood there waiting; she hadn't made another move toward home. Pressure built in the back of her eyes, alerting her that if she wasn't careful, she would cry.

She could remember crying at some point in her life. As a child.

But not when her father died.

Not when she'd walked away from Charles.

And not—

"Are you okay?" Lucas asked.

Roni shook her head from side to side.

Then she dropped her shoes to the ground and reached out for him.

Chapter Seven

Roni stood for several minutes wrapped in Lucas's embrace, both of them quiet. The only sounds were the muted music from indoors and the much louder rush of the ocean from behind.

And Lucas's breathing.

It was a steady in and out. Similar to the strong heartbeat she felt beneath her cheek. She was thankful he didn't ask questions. Also thankful he'd somehow known that she'd needed a shoulder to lean on.

Since moving to the island, she'd worked hard to be carefree and untroubled. Not sharing her past issues with anyone, not even her closest friends. Because she'd moved on from her previous life. She was making a new life at a place she loved.

She'd never told them the truth about what had brought about the end of her career.

She had also never let herself break down on them.

Yet here she was, holding tight to Lucas as if he'd been in her life forever and knew just what she needed.

Thankfully, the feeling of crying had passed so she didn't have to worry about that at least, but now that the initial swell of emotion was over, she feared Lucas would want to know more.

She couldn't tell him. She didn't talk about it.

Her loss was in the past. Reliving it would do no good. She simply needed to move on. As she'd always thought she had. Until she'd spent the afternoon curled in the fetal position in her bed.

Her grip loosened around Lucas's waist, but she didn't step back. He pulled slightly away, though, and looked down into her face. It was a dark night, but lights from upstairs shone out through the glass doors and leaked between the slats of the deck, providing enough filtered light so they could see each other.

"Want to talk about it?" he asked.

She shook her head.

"Okay," he said gently. He didn't push. She appreciated that. He simply tucked her back against his chest and rested his chin on the top of her head. Then he ran his hands up and down her back.

They stood there with the ocean breeze blowing over them for several more minutes until Roni recognized that she'd moved into holding him simply for the pleasure of it. It wasn't right, but he felt so very good pressed against her. He was strong and hard. Solid.

And his body was warm against hers. She'd forgotten to bring a coat with her when she'd walked over earlier, and now that the sun had dropped, it was chilly.

They separated at the same time, as if a thought had been mutually spoken aloud, and Lucas tucked his fingers into the front pockets of his jeans. He rocked back on his heels. "So you were just going to sneak out?" he asked.

She forced a smile. "I did just sneak out."

"Only not quite unseen."

She lifted a shoulder. "Quit watching me like a hawk and maybe I would have been unseen."

He reached a hand up and brushed a finger along the underside of her jaw. It made her toes curl into her flip-flops. "I can't seem to stop watching you." He said the words softly.

His finger was still on her so she reached up to brush it away, but instead she ended up holding it in her hand.

"I'm still not going to sleep with you," she informed him. Her tone didn't sound too convincing, but she ignored that. His being in the contest was bad enough, but him knowing when she needed someone? That scared her.

She would just have to put her hormones back into hibernation.

"I think you're making a mistake," he told her.

Possibly. But she didn't think so. "I should go home," she whispered.

He nodded. "Then you need to turn loose of my finger."

She jerked her attention to their hands in between them, where she wasn't so much "holding" his finger as fondling it.

"Oh, good grief," she muttered. She released him and smirked when he chuckled.

Then he pulled his sports coat off and wrapped it around her shoulders. "You're shivering again, but this time I think it's from the cold."

It was from the cold. And from him. It was harder than she'd have thought not to lean back into him.

"Will you answer me one question before you go?" he asked.

She eyed him carefully. Something told her to be very wary around him. "Possibly."

"Wait," he said, holding up a hand. "Two questions. But the first is an easy one." He continued before she could butt in, "Will you let me take you home?"

"I told you I'm not—"

"Just take you home. Not go in, though you know I want to." He motioned to the path leading toward the sidewalk. "It's cold. Let me drive you instead of you walking."

"How do you know I walked?"

He bent over and picked up her silver heels, dangling them in one hand by the heel straps. "Because you changed out of these."

Hmmm. Good observational skills.

"No," she said. She wasn't letting him get anywhere near her house. "Second question?"

Eyes that she knew were almost as dark as the night sky shone back at her. "Will you kiss me?"

Her mouth fell open.

"A kiss doesn't have to lead to sex," he pointed out.

"But you're hoping it will."

"Sweetheart, right now I just want to have a single taste of you. You wouldn't believe how many times I've dreamed about it."

Which reminded her of what he'd said before she'd gone onstage that morning. "You've seen me play before, haven't you? This morning you said I was brilliant onstage. Like you'd seen me." Her words slowed and she asked more hesitantly, "Or was that just to calm me down?"

He studied her silently in the dark. Finally, apparently pleased with what he saw, he gave a small nod. "Twice. I would have attended more if you hadn't quit."

She glanced quickly away, willing him not to ask her why she'd quit. A gust of cool air caught her in the face and neck as she turned toward the ocean. She burrowed deeper into his jacket.

"So . . ." he said from behind her.

She steeled herself for his next question. They were having such a nice moment. She wasn't ready for it to end.

But she also wasn't talking about her past.

"About that kiss," he finished.

She glanced back. Stupid as it may be, she wanted to kiss him too. Though it would only make her want more.

"Then you'll leave me alone?" she asked.

He didn't answer.

She huffed out a sigh and faced him. "It's not going to change anything, you know?"

"Meaning, I'll still be in the contest and you'll still think it's unprofessional?"

Pretty much. Or that she knew Kayla would think it unprofessional.

"Kiss me," he urged.

And he finally won. Yes. Her breath grew shallow. Yes, she was going to kiss him.

Then she would march herself home, pull out her favorite adult toy, and imagine it was Lucas.

Still, she stalled. "Just once?" She watched a muscle in his jaw twitch.

"If that's all you want."

Looking at the man in front of her, she thought it might be all she could handle.

Two small steps and she was back in front of him. She had her arms crossed over her chest, each hand grasping a lapel, and she tilted her face up to look at him. They were a foot apart, and he had about a foot of height on her. *Hmmm.*

"Just a minute," she murmured.

She stepped around him and moved up two steps before facing him again. Then she nodded. This would work. She was now much closer to his eye level.

"You about ready?" He was laughing at her.

She gave him an evil eye. "If we're just going to get one kiss, it should be done right, don't you think?"

A dangerous gleam of white came from his mouth with his quick smile. "Oh, darlin'." He took a step closer, butting his chest against her crossed arms. "It's going to be done right."

She suspected it would be.

KIM LAW

Goose bumps lit over her body. Her breath caught in her throat and she didn't know what to do next. She just wanted his mouth on hers.

"You going to start it?" he asked softly.

Nerves had her clenching her fingers tighter against the lapels. She nodded.

But she didn't close the distance.

A thump came from above as if someone had bumped into the door, and she froze. The breath she'd been holding slid out.

Lucas didn't let the noise bother him. He leaned forward, bent slightly at the neck, and brushed his lips against one of her cheeks. It was a small, velvety touch. So soft she wouldn't have been sure what it was if she hadn't been watching. It made her ears ring.

He didn't pull back. "I'm waiting," he whispered against her skin. His heady, masculine scent surrounded her.

"Someone might see us," she whispered back. Her entire body hummed.

"Kiss me, Roni."

Crap. The man was going to make her lose her mind.

But she was going to lose it in a very good way.

In a quick move, she turned loose of the coat and lifted her arms. They went around his neck, and he turned his lips to hers. She stared at him for one second. Looking straight into his eyes even though it was too dark to see.

And then she closed her eyes and closed the distance between their mouths.

CHAPTER EIGHT

A groan slipped from the back of Lucas's throat as Roni's lips settled onto his.

Her arms were bent at the elbows and locked around his neck, and her chest—her small, firm breasts—pressed into him.

He didn't move at first, simply let her touch settle on him. He didn't want to miss a moment. If this was going to be his first and last kiss, he was going to savor it.

Only, she parted her lips and the tip of her tongue touched him.

And hell, he was a goner.

He still held her silver heels. He dropped them and closed his arms around her waist with a moan. He crushed her, hips to shoulders, against him, and then he opened his mouth in return.

She slipped in before he could.

Then they both went into a frenzy.

They couldn't get close enough to each other, couldn't get a good enough taste. Hands and tongues stroked. He slid his palms to her rear. She went up on her toes and reached for more.

He kissed her as if his life depended on it.

He kissed her until neither of them could draw in air.

They parted, gasping for breath, foreheads together. His hands remained on her rear and he squeezed, closing his eyes and savoring the feel of her taut curves. The door above them creaked opened and they both froze. Female laughter bubbled out, at least two women. He did not want to stop.

Apparently Roni didn't either, since she didn't move away. Instead, she cupped his jaw and brought his mouth back to hers.

This time it was slower.

He teased his tongue inside her mouth, capturing her soft moan, and she roamed her hands down over his chest. He could feel her fingers smoothing over him, missing nothing. As if painting him in her mind. A heady power surged through his body to know that this woman wanted to examine him so thoroughly.

One hand cupped the back of her head and he drank from her, tilting her head up to his and holding her steady so he could get his fill.

He feared he would never get his fill.

Her hands slid lower and he sucked in a sharp breath. They trailed beneath his navel, but then circled around to his back. He released the breath and buried his mouth against her neck. She smelled like berries.

The door above them slammed closed and feet moved across the deck.

Roni didn't stop. She reached her arms up to his neck again, arching her body into his and he understood her needs. He had the same. She wanted his hands on her.

He was nothing if not obliging.

With one hand now at the base of her spine, he trailed the fingers of the other softly over the smooth skin of her neck. As his thumb slid from the underside of her chin to the base of her throat, her lips separated from his and she angled her head back. She was like a cat stretching in the sun.

Only, she was stretching in his *very* capable hands.

His coat lay on the stairs behind her, and the bare skin of her upper chest glowed in the night light. She was creamy and white and soft. And he was so hard it was painful.

He dipped his fingers lower, trailing down her front. He brushed over the top curve of one breast before following with his mouth.

He put his lips to the spot above her breast, right above the neckline of her dress, and gently sucked. She shivered.

Then he dropped his hand to her waist, almost afraid to touch what he wanted.

They were in public, with at least two women not fifteen feet above them, and he wasn't sure he could stop if he ran his hands over her curves. She didn't seem to have the same concerns. She reached for him and slid his hand with hers up her body.

He grew harder.

And there was no way in the world he wasn't going to do exactly as she wanted.

With a silent plea for help, he crossed over her rib cage and circled his hand around her breast.

"Oh, God," she whispered. The words floated upward and Lucas thought the movement above them stilled.

He reached his mouth for hers to capture any more noises she might make.

Then he gently squeezed his fingers, pressing into her soft curve. He cursed the fact that some women could feel so good. She fit his palm perfectly.

When she moaned again and pressed more insistently into him, he slid his thumb over her nipple.

At the touch, his eyes crossed, she ripped her mouth from his and groaned, and one of the women above whispered, "I think someone is down there."

That finally got Roni's attention.

Her eyes went wide as she looked at him, but he didn't remove his hand. He'd noticed something very interesting, and those women could come down the steps if they wanted, but he was going to find this out before he turned Roni loose.

He moved his thumb again, slowly over the crest of her breast.

Her eyes closed as if in pleasurable agony.

His balls tightened the same.

"Is that a nipple ring?" he asked. He'd put his mouth to her ear and whispered as softly as he could. His voice demanded an answer.

He felt her throat move up and down in a swallow before she hesitantly nodded.

Oh, sweet Jesus. His fingers clenched around her again and he knew that he would give any amount of money in the world to see her naked.

"I need to go," she whispered. She pointed above them to the deck.

Right. She needed to go. They were about to get caught.

Only, his thumb was resting on her nipple ring and he wasn't sure he could let go.

"Let's go down there," a voice came from above.

Shit.

Lucas uncrossed his eyes and somehow forced his hand from Roni's breast.

He looked at her but she was diverting her gaze and straightening her clothes.

What in the hell had just happened out here? He had never been knocked for such a loop.

And the woman had a nipple ring!

"Roni," he whispered. It came out like a plea.

She put a finger to his lips and reached up to press one more—*very tiny*—kiss to his mouth. "I've got to go," she breathed the words. And then she was gone.

He was left standing there, an erection the size of Texas, his coat and her shoes spread out around him, and two nosy women heading his way.

Without a thought, he scooped up the clothing and headed to the opposite side of the building toward the parking lot. Presumably, he should stay longer and mingle with the guests. The contest wasn't just about winning challenges, but becoming a fan favorite. He'd seen enough reality TV to know that the favorites got the votes whether they deserved them or not. But there was no way in hell he was going back into a roomful of strangers when he had the idea of Roni's pierced nipple running through his mind.

Probably no way he was getting any sleep that night either.

But he gave himself kudos for not following her down the street.

Because no way did he think that either of them was going to be happy with just one kiss.

~

The clink of glasses sounded from behind the bar at Gin's as Roni led two women barely in their twenties to a table by the all-glass patio doors. They'd requested the seat so they could see the beach while they had a drink. Roni smiled politely. She knew exactly what was out on the beach that they wanted to see.

The same thing she'd been sneaking peeks at since she'd gotten here.

She placed menus on the ladies' table, forced herself not to look out the patio doors, and headed back to the hostess stand. She glanced across the room to the bartender, Kevin Morris, as she went. It was two in the afternoon and Gin's was mostly vacant. Kevin seemed to be playing a game with the bottles of liquor, moving them in and out on the display shelf. He was clearly bored.

The outside door opened again and sunshine came in with Ginger. She stopped just inside the door and stared at Roni, mouth agape, her blonde hair glowing like a halo around her. Her personality was perfectly on display with the ruffled, feminine blouse she wore, along with the faded jeans and work boots to her knees. She pointed toward the back of the bar in the direction of where the two women were seated. Roni waggled her eyebrows at her friend.

"I take it you know what's going on out there?" Ginger asked.

Oh yeah. "Every woman on the island knows what's going on out there," Roni told her.

It was day two of the competition and the men had been assigned their "attire," along with their partners, earlier in the day. Currently, they were busy preparing for the Eleven Pipers Piping challenge.

Twenty-two buff, hot men were spaced out along the coastline wearing kilts and learning to play the bagpipe. Tonight they would stand in front of the audience and their partner would blindly pull a Christmas song for them. Then the men would have to play it.

Votes would be cast for best performance, and if the partner guessed the actual song that was played, they earned bonus points.

Roni had not spoken to Lucas at that morning's drawing. She hadn't spoken to him since she'd run away the night before. But she was keeping her fingers crossed that he was musically inclined. She'd hate for him to get kicked out so soon.

"Why aren't you out there with them?" Ginger asked.

"Why aren't you?"

Ginger rolled her eyes and headed toward the patio doors. "I just got in from a nature tour."

Ginger had started the tours for school groups last year. She picked up a pair of binoculars from the storage box tucked behind the piano.

"There are binoculars?" the too-perky, blonde guest asked.

Roni smiled and grabbed two more pairs. "Enjoy, ladies," she said as she handed them over. "Your server should be out any minute."

"No hurry," the blonde murmured as she and the brunette stood from their seats and put the binoculars to their eyes.

Roni watched the three women standing shoulder to shoulder at the doors, their backs to her, taking in the action on the beach. She heard a harrumph and caught Kevin shaking his head at the small crowd. Yet if there had been a gaggle of supermodel-caliber bikini-clad women out there, Kevin would be the first to stare.

"Oh my," one of the younger women said softly. "He is *hot*."

The brunette briefly pulled back from the glasses. "Which one?"

"The one straight ahead." The blonde pointed. "I heard he was caught making out during the party last night. Underneath the deck."

Roni stilled. Crap. They were talking about Lucas. And her.

They had to be. How many people could have been making out under the deck last night?

Casually, she grabbed her own set of binoculars . . . not that any of them needed the glasses to see the men. The bar was nearly on the beach. She stepped between Ginger and the brunette, scooting her friend over, and zoomed in on the sight the other three women were glued to.

Lucas and his young, cute partner for the day had moved down the beach and were now right there. Right outside her window. Roni had never seen a kilt look so good.

She chewed on her lower lip as she tried to nonchalantly eavesdrop.

"He was seen carrying a woman's shoes to his car," one of them said.

Roni's shoulders tightened. She'd forgotten her shoes! She supposed that meant she'd eventually have to speak to Lucas again. She only hoped she could do it without sticking her tongue down his throat.

Or tugging that bottom lip between hers.

Oh my geez, that man had the best mouth. And he knew how to use it.

"The woman wasn't with him?" the other asked.

"No. She probably met him at the hotel."

"Barefoot?"

"Who knows? Jamie and Rhonda caught them and she ran off. Must have taken her shoes off at some point and didn't have time to put them back on."

"Well, who was it?"

"No idea. But Rhonda heard her moaning. *Loudly*." This last was followed by a moan of her own.

"I'd let him make me moan any day," the brunette pronounced.

The two women grew silent, probably lost in their own fantasies about just what Lucas could do to make them moan. The waitress arrived and the women returned to their table to order drinks and appetizers. Ginger scooted in closer to Roni.

"Who is he?" she whispered.

Roni eyed her from behind her binoculars. Ginger hadn't been able to make the reception to meet the contestants the other night, nor had she been at the convention center yet. Work kept pulling her away. And apparently she didn't recognize Lucas from lunch at the hotel.

"Lucas Alexander," Roni said. "Contestant number seven."

"Have you met him?"

What was she supposed to say? She'd come darn close to offering herself on a platter? She nodded and licked her lips. "Briefly." Her voice came out pinched. "I've met them all."

Ginger gave her a wry stare as if trying to figure out why Roni suddenly sounded as if she were incapable of pushing oxygen through her windpipe. Roni *would* tell Ginger about Lucas. She had to. She had to tell someone about that mind-melting kiss. But she wasn't about to do it where the other women could hear.

They both returned to perusing the beach, and while Roni kept her glasses trained directly on Lucas, she wished Ginger would focus farther down the sand where contestant number twelve was practicing. He even had a dog with him. Weren't men with dogs supposed to be a lure? Instead, Ginger lowered her glasses and turned to Roni.

Roni saw the movement out of the corner of her eye but didn't return the look.

"Did you drive over last night?" Ginger asked.

She was very astute. And she knew her friend well.

"I walked, actually." Roni's voice sounded a bit too prim and proper to her own ears.

Ginger nodded, then looked through the patio door once again, this time without the binoculars. A few seconds later, she turned back. "What did you wear?"

Dang it. "That silver dress I wore to the plated-dinner fund-raiser at the hotel earlier this year."

"Hmmm. And the shoes? If I come to your house, will I find the shoes in your closet?"

Roni lowered the binoculars and pressed her lips together. When she met Ginger's eyes, she had no doubt that she'd been found out. Ginger knew which were her favorite shoes to wear with that particular dress. Roni had gone on and on about it when she wore the combination last spring.

Ginger would also know that Roni wouldn't walk half a mile in four-inch heels.

She shot Ginger a hard look and then motioned with her eyes to the two women who'd once again joined them at the doors. Ginger swung her light-green gaze in the direction of the women. Finally, she slumped her shoulders and overplayed a mopey look. She knew she wouldn't be getting details today.

"Then I've got to go," she grumbled. "Grocery shopping to do since the store should be empty of other women right now. They were all clumped along the boardwalks as I drove past." She returned the binoculars to the case behind the piano and stopped and stared at the instrument.

Roni followed her over. She'd had the piano delivered when she'd first moved to town.

"There was talk on the ferry this morning about your performance yesterday," Ginger told her. "Some of the regulars from in here."

Roni sat on the bench and put her hands on the keys, softly starting to play Bach. There were plenty of people that lived on the island who went over to the mainland for work every day. "Never thought they'd see me with a country band, huh?"

"Actually, it was about the solo. They knew you were good—or used to be—but they'd never seen you in concert. Seems you impressed."

She gave a shrug. Apparently she had. She'd heard it from a number of people herself.

"You given any more thought to a full concert after the parade next week?"

Roni didn't hesitate. "I told Kayla no."

She had agreed this morning, though, to play a couple songs with the band when they returned for the final night. Their songs only.

Ginger sat on the bench as Roni continued playing. Roni caught sight of the two women still at the doors, now holding their drinks. Suddenly their faces turned in her direction and their eyes grew round.

"You're...?" the brunette mouthed, one finger pointing helplessly toward Roni.

Roni smiled and nodded. Yes, she was the pianist from the Mr. Yummy Santa contest. The one who used to be famous. This wasn't the first time she'd been asked that question today.

The women returned to their seats, moving almost reverently. Apparently Roni was now more exciting than Lucas in a kilt. At least for the moment.

"But why won't you?" Ginger asked quietly, pushing the idea of the concert. The spot between her brows pinched into a vertical line. "What happened, Roni? Why won't you perform anymore?"

Roni looked at the person she'd known longer than anyone but family. She should have told her friends years ago. When it had first happened. Just possibly, they could have helped her through it.

That burning sensation of impending tears appeared again.

"Not today, Ginger. I don't want to talk about it today." She didn't want to talk about it at all, but lately she'd been feeling the need to.

Bach continued coming from her fingertips. She didn't even have to think to play. She stared out the back doors and let the music flow, while she felt Ginger continue to watch her.

Fifteen seconds later, Ginger leaned in, one arm going around her waist. She squeezed. "When you're ready, sweetheart," she said. "We're here when you need us."

The three friends may not all be in close physical proximity anymore, but they were still tied by the heart. Plus, Andie was only a call away.

Roni tilted her head and rested it on Ginger's shoulder. "I know," she whispered.

Ginger touched her own head briefly to Roni's, and then she patted Roni's leg and stood. "Call if you need anything."

Ginger left the building and Roni once again disappeared into the music. She let her hands feel the notes. Striking out sharp, hard beats, and then caressing. Whatever the music called for. And she let her mind drift back three years.

It was a rare thing that she let herself go there. She'd learned early on that you dealt with your problems quickly, and then you moved on. Her father had taught her that.

Parents get divorced? Give Mom a hug and head back out on the road. No time to fret.

Lose your father? You've got a concert to get back to.

Have your heart ripped from your body and thrown off a cliff? Don't loiter feeling sorry for yourself. Suck it up, move on. Put on your brave face.

It had always worked.

Until she'd found herself unable to step back onstage.

She snapped her eyes open and returned from the past. It did no good to hash through what couldn't be changed.

Letting her fingers fly, she finished out the piece, realizing when the last note ended that she was out of breath. She lifted her hands and looked around. She'd forgotten she was at Gin's.

Kevin was still behind the bar, but he was no longer playing with the bottles. The two women in the dining room seemed to have no interest left in the men. And the waitress and chef had come out from the back.

All of them silently stared.

And then one of the women started to clap. She began slowly until the others joined in. Then there were five pairs of hands showing their admiration. There was little expression on their faces other than shock. She supposed she had just impressed again.

She sighed. She couldn't seem to stop doing that lately.

But the interesting thing was, she kind of liked it.

CHAPTER NINE

Music blared from inside the bar as Lucas made his way across the parking lot. It was Wednesday night. They'd been through three challenges and he was still alive in the contest. The fifty thousand remained within his reach. But he was tired of Roni ignoring him. So tonight he was seeking her out.

As was, apparently, everyone else.

The door of Gin's opened below the huge caricature of a happy, red-headed smiling face, and raucous laughter billowed out. Along with very loud music. He shook his head at the contradiction. The bar looked . . . not upscale so much . . . but not honky-tonk, either. More like it catered to both mild-mannered sports fans and well-dressed women looking for an afternoon glass of wine.

Yet he could see several of the guys inside partying it up, and heard more than one good-natured catcall. And he would swear the parking lot was shaking with the noise level.

He'd heard plenty of talk about Roni over the last couple of days. He wasn't the only one smitten with her. She spent mornings cutting up with the guys. Teasing and flirting. Then again in the evenings. She'd even come out to the obstacle course today. He'd seen her on the sidelines, a big floppy hat and a breezy skirt swirling around her ankles, cheering people on.

But she hadn't uttered one single word to him since Monday night.

He looked back at his rental car, where her heels were still tucked safely inside the trunk. He'd been carrying them around like some Prince Charming, looking for a time to get her alone. Only, he didn't just want to get her alone to give back her shoes. Most notably, he wanted to know if that kiss had kept her awake all night or if it had been just him.

The good thing was, being unable to sleep for thinking about the way her body had so easily molded to his—along with that piercing he'd felt!—had allowed him to get plenty of work done for the day job. And since that was what kept the lights on, he had to get that in.

He'd been a telecommuter for years now, working for a large insurance company out of Houston, and they were used to him putting in odd hours. It had started three years ago when he'd had to move back to Dallas. He'd spent so many daytime hours at doctor's appointments, the evenings had been the only time to get the work done.

As he was their top systems architect, they'd gone along with it.

His cell buzzed and he pulled it from his pocket. He had a text from home. He moved to the shadows, standing on the boardwalk instead of heading directly into the bar. The ocean was licking up on the dunes at his back and the bright, friendly atmosphere of the bar was at his front.

He punched out a quick reply. It had been a long time since he'd been away from the house for more than a couple nights, and he was discovering that it was harder to do than he'd thought. He kept the occasional modeling job because it allowed him to get away. A little distance and he stayed sharp. Thankful. He didn't take anything for granted.

Plus, these days he put everything he made through modeling into charities. He wasn't sure where he would be without them.

A couple more texts back and forth and he tucked his phone back in his pocket and stared at the bar. It was just casual fun he was looking for, he reminded himself.

So why did he suddenly think he should get back in his car and forget that he'd ever had his hand on Roni's breast?

"Alexander, is that you?" A voice called from the patio. The doors had opened and it looked as if the crowd inside was expanding to take up the space on the outside. Kelly was waving him over. "Come on in, man. This chick is fantastic."

Roni being the chick, he supposed? "Heading that way." As if he had a choice.

He could no more get in his car and drive away than he could ignore her for the next ten days.

~

Roni looked up from the piano as someone shouted a song title. "I don't know that one," she yelled back.

The men—and quite a few women—were enjoying piano karaoke tonight. And they were bad. But the bar manager was happy. Singing, dancing, drinking. It was the right combination for this kind of establishment.

Plus, Roni was having a great time. Even if her ears were bleeding from the tone-deaf singing. Good thing these guys didn't have a talent show coming up in the contest.

Another song was shouted out and she nodded. She had to think about it, but she could do that one. Closing her eyes in concentration, she went into the song as someone in the middle of the bar began bellowing out the lyrics.

A cool breeze swept in from the opened patio doors and she lifted her head to let it wash over her face. It had become stuffy inside the building over the last hour. The group of men had all followed her there immediately after the ritual kicking off of two of the guys. Those two didn't seem so down, though. They'd so far talked adoring fans into buying all of their drinks for the night, and they looked to merely have to choose which ones they wanted to take back to their hotel room for the evening. What players.

But hey, at least a good time was being had by all.

Mostly all. She hadn't seen Lucas come in. Which was good. Since she was still avoiding him.

She opened her eyes when someone sat down beside her. Contestant number nineteen—a way-too-young-for-her cutie from Des Moines—gave her an ear-to-ear grin.

"Sure would like to dance with you tonight," he said in his Iowa dialect.

She gave him a smile. "Hard to dance when I'm playing, Jason."

"I could put some money in the jukebox," he suggested. "Find a good slow song."

Oh, she bet he could. But she was not going to be seduced by a twenty-one-year-old, no matter how cute. Or how worked up Lucas had gotten her the other night. She gave Jason a letdown wink. "Sorry, sweetie, not gonna happen."

He lifted his hands in an I-had-to-try kind of way. "Can't blame a guy. Let me know if you change your mind," he said as he stood.

Yeah. She'd do that.

She suddenly felt old. Last year she might have even considered taking him up on his offer. But tonight she felt . . .

Her shoulders slumped as she played. She didn't know what she felt. Out of sorts.

She turned her face back to the breeze, and her gaze landed on the man in her mind. He was standing, arms crossed over his chest and a shoulder leaned against the doorframe.

And *he. Looked. Good.*

He stared at her, unwavering, and she suspected her time in hiding had come to an end. He motioned with his head, asking her to come outside. His steady gaze never broke from hers.

No! she silently screamed.

She gave him a nod.

She didn't want to avoid him any longer.

What was life if you didn't live a little?

Lucas disappeared back into the dark of the night and Roni finished the song. Immediately more titles were shouted out.

She stood and held up her hands. "I need a break, guys."

Number nineteen looked up quickly from where he leaned on the bar, a hopeful expression on his face. She shook her head. Still not going to happen. He shot her another grin, dimples flashing. Got to give the guy credit for trying.

Downing a drink of water from the bottle sitting on top of the piano, she closed the cover over the keys and headed for the main door, all the while wondering what she was doing. She'd been perfectly fine keeping her distance, and now with one crook of his head, she was following Lucas out into the dark?

The door swung closed behind her and the noise level dimmed. A cool breeze kissed her heated face.

Yeah, one crook of his head and she was following him out into the night.

And she was fine with that.

Chapter Ten

Roni stood in the dark, wondering where Lucas had disappeared to. She couldn't imagine he'd remained on the patio, but she didn't immediately see him anywhere else, either. Once her vision adjusted to the night, she stepped to the parking lot and began walking slowly toward the cars, letting her gaze roam as she tried not to appear as if she was looking for someone so much as just going outside for a break.

The night was dark, but not so much she shouldn't be able to see Lucas. There was no moon, yet the stars were out in full force.

Two trucks pulled into the lot at the far end, one after the other, and their headlights flashed across one of the trees that had been decorated Monday, before hitting the ocean beyond. As the lights swung on around, a faint glow touched the walkway heading out to the beach. She could see a lone figure standing at the end.

The breadth of the man's shoulders suggested it was Lucas.

Joining him in the dark with the ocean as a backdrop was not the smartest move she could make. The best thing to do would be to go home. Forget the feelings that teased her every time she looked at him. Forget that when he'd kissed her he'd touched something she'd wanted to remain buried.

A deep, soul-wrenching need for more.

She didn't have a place for that in her life. She couldn't do "more."

She shook her head as her feet turned toward the beach and she headed out to Lucas.

As she approached, she could better make out his form. He'd worn jeans again tonight, along with a different pair of cowboy boots. And he had on a crisp, long-sleeved white shirt, tucked into his belted jeans. Nothing overly special.

Yet he definitely had something special.

When she was within feet of him and he didn't turn her way, she paused. Unsure. He had to have heard her. She suspected he wanted to talk about the other night. The kiss. But what could she say? *In one move you put all the guys I've known before to shame?*

She couldn't tell him that. A man couldn't handle that kind of ego stroke.

Yet she also couldn't turn away and *not* have whatever conversation he wanted to have. She found herself anxious to hear what he thought about that kiss too. Masochist.

She joined him at the top of the steps without saying a word. They stood there, arm to arm, both staring out at the water. The tide was heading back out, and she had a moment of feeling the same way. As if she should be running away instead of walking to him. She inhaled the damp night air into her lungs and held it there.

"You about finished avoiding me?" he finally spoke.

The air leaked slowly from her chest. *Keep it simple.* She nodded. "If I have to be."

He turned his head and peered down at her. The reflection from the stars lit his face. He looked too serious. "We could go on playing this game," he told her. "Or we could play a different one."

Games. Yes. That was the way to do it. Keep it fun. Light.

She lifted one shoulder. "What did you have in mind?"

His eyebrow rose suggestively.

"Sex?" she asked. So he didn't want to talk about the kiss? He just wanted to take her to bed? That should be a good thing given it was what she really wanted anyway. No complications. Just easy, casual fun.

Except she wasn't going to sleep with him. *Right*. Because it was unprofessional.

She held in her sigh.

He didn't immediately reply, just kept watching her. But the mood in his face did seem to lighten a fraction. "I like your bluntness, Roni. It's enjoyable. A man doesn't have to worry where he stands with you."

She gave an unconcerned shrug. She was what she was. A gust of wind blew into their faces and she crossed her arms over her chest.

"But sex wasn't what I had in mind," he confessed.

"Good, because I'm still not sleeping with you." Again, she did not sound convincing.

He chuckled. "I like your humor, as well."

"It's true." She smirked. She sounded like a petulant child.

"Okay."

She shut her mouth. Who was she kidding? Get her alone and she'd probably be naked in under a minute, conflict of interest be damned.

She glanced at the bar, seeing even more people hanging out on the patio, framed by the twinkling white lights that had been strung up around the doors and along the wooden railing of the perimeter. It was a happy, relaxed scene. She could hear light laughter and the jovial voices of the customers. They were having a good time. She probably should have stayed up there with them.

"They're talking about you," she informed him. She returned her gaze to Lucas. "At least the women are. Trying to figure out who you were with under the deck the other night."

"I heard."

If someone happened to look in their direction at that very moment, it wouldn't take much to put two and two together. "Did you tell anyone?"

That eyebrow thing again. "You think I'm the kind to kiss and tell?"

"I have no idea what kind you are. All I know about you is that you're an amazing-looking guy, you're from Dallas, and you're a computer programmer." She paused, then shot him a grin. "And that you're a weak man around an avocado."

His grin met hers. "Had to give them something, right?"

The local grocery store owners probably loved the shared tidbit as much as the women did. Given that she'd bought a bagful herself, with Lucas in mind, she'd put money on her not being the only female who had more of the green fruit lying around right now than they needed.

"And thank you for the compliment," he added. "You happen to be an amazing-looking woman yourself."

Flattery seemed to work on her, if the squishy place in her heart was anything to go by. She barely kept from leaning into him. "Thank you," she mumbled politely, instead.

She was in so much trouble with this guy.

As if in unspoken agreement, they both headed down the steps together. They got to the third board from the bottom and stopped. She was wearing jeans tonight, and didn't mind getting sand on her rear. They lowered to the riser, putting Gin's and its cheery lights out of sight. They could no longer see the bar. Therefore, the people at the bar could no longer see them.

Lucas leaned back, resting his elbows on the step three above where he sat. She kept her focus trained forward. The ocean felt less threatening than the man at her side. The wind swirled curls in her face and she tucked them behind her ear.

"You know something else about me, as well," he told her.

She shot him a quick glance. "What's that?"

"That you like kissing me."

There it was. She knew it would have to come up.

There was no sense hiding from the fact. She nodded. "I do like kissing you. It was quite enjoyable, in fact."

"Good."

He said nothing more, as if he'd merely needed the confirmation and now he was free to move on. Only, he didn't take the conversation anywhere else, either. He just sat there. Mute.

She studied the ocean a bit longer before peeking at him once again. "I also know you're a cover model." She hesitated, feeling intrusive, but she'd been wondering about something all week. And if he wasn't going to keep the conversation going himself . . .

"I don't understand the model *and* the programmer thing," she blurted. "How did that happen?"

One side of his mouth hitched up and he slowly sat upright. He took her hand in his and flipped it palm up, then brought it to his thigh and began absently tracing her fingers with his.

"I modeled to put myself through college," he told her. "A woman from a romance publisher's art department noticed me at a Starbucks my first year. I looked like I was already in my twenties, and I'd been working out hard for the previous couple of years so I was fit. Apparently, that was what it took."

If he described himself simply as "fit" today, he was sorely missing the boat.

"Sounds easy," she said. She liked the way he touched her hand.

He flattened all five of his fingers on top of hers, putting them palm to palm, and sat there, head tilted, looking at the two of them together. Her fingers were long for her size, but his dwarfed hers.

"Sometimes a guy gets a break." His voice was easy when he finally spoke, yet she detected a tenseness to it.

"Did you ever regret doing it?"

He looked at her and she wished it wasn't so dark that she couldn't read his eyes. "My parents would rather I had made money some other way. But they also knew they were in no position to help with tuition.

Blue-collar workers. They did their best. Still do, in fact. They're pretty terrific."

"So you still have them both?"

His finger paused while tracing a circle in the middle of her palm. "That's right. Your father died when you were young, didn't he?"

"I was eighteen," she pointed out. "Not exactly young. And how did you know about that?"

A grin popped on his face. "Because I was a beginning stalker before you disappeared on me. There was plenty of info to be found about you and your father playing together up until he passed." He grew quiet as if respecting the loss of her parent, before adding, "I also happen to know that we have the same birthday. One year apart."

Having the same birthday was kind of cool.

"You're . . ." she racked her brain to remember what had been on his index card. "What? Twenty-seven?"

"Yep. And you're twenty-eight. Will be twenty-nine on February twenty-third. I always did like an older woman." He winked.

She rolled her eyes. "Don't try so hard. I like you better when you don't."

His grin inched a few degrees more wicked, and her nether regions turned to blaze. Dang, but she liked this guy.

"So your parents?" she asked, pulling her mind back from thinking about how much more she could *like* him if she let herself. "You're close to them?"

He nodded and returned to exploring her hand. "Very. We live in the same neighborhood, actually. I bought a house down the street from them a couple years ago."

That piece of info set Roni back. Okay . . . he held down a good job. He had a house. In a *neighborhood.*

Suddenly he was coming across as a bit more settled and "serious" than she'd imagined.

"But you don't have a wife, right? Living in that house with you?"

He gripped her hand and pulled her to her feet. "I already told you I don't."

She glanced over at Gin's. She wasn't ready to go back in. Looked like the place had quieted down, though. The patio doors were still wide open, but everyone had gone back inside.

She and Lucas stood facing each other. Tonight's three-inch stacked heels barely made an impact in matching up to him.

"What are we doing here?" she asked. She held up their joined hands and used her other to motion back and forth between them. "Why'd you want me to come outside with you?"

"To talk."

"But why?" she asked. "And if you didn't want to talk about that kiss from the other night, if you're not going to try to get into my pants tonight, then what *are* you doing? What game are you playing? I like to know the rules before I participate."

Lucas let go of her hand, but only to slide his fingers to her wrist. He circled the bone and did the same with the other arm. Then he moved one step down and turned her to face him. She now looked out toward the ocean while he faced the boardwalk. The difference in their height was much more manageable.

"I brought you out here," he began, "because I *did* want to talk about that kiss." He put his hands at the base of her spine, keeping her wrists bound and pulling her arms behind her back. "And of course I'd like to get into your pants. What man wouldn't?" He gave her a teasing wink when she made a face at him. "And the game tonight is exactly what we've been doing." He leaned in to whisper. "We're getting to know each other."

His chest wasn't quite touching hers, but with a deep breath it would be.

And she was quite fond of the feel of being shackled by his hands.

"Then why didn't we talk about the kiss?" she whispered.

He nuzzled her ear. "We did. You said you liked it."

"That's it?" She tilted her head, giving him better access to her neck. "That's all the talking you wanted to do?"

His mouth brushed the underside of her jaw, just below her ear. She sizzled to her toes.

"I found out what I needed to know. Did you want me to tell you that I liked it too?" he asked, his voice going husky as he continued nibbling at her neck. "Because I did. I thought about it all night long. And I thought about your breast." He inhaled and his chest almost brushed hers. "And the piercing on your nipple." His lips were back to her earlobes. "I got myself so hard thinking about it that I had to take matters into my own hands." He nipped at her lobe. "Twice."

Her breathing had turned to pants.

"And yet I still couldn't sleep," he told her. "I put in hours of some of the best work I've ever done for my company, all because I was so juiced by the thought of getting my hands back on your breasts. Only next time, I want to touch flesh."

"Well," she breathed out. "*Oh-kay.* I think we've sufficiently talked about that."

Lucas chuckled. The sound hit the side of her neck and crept over her shoulders and down her spine. "I could tell you what I imagined you doing while I jacked off," he offered.

"No, no. I'm . . ." She panted, trying to get her breath. She squinted her eyes shut tight as if that would help her concentration. Her tongue touched her top lip while she imagined him lying in his hotel bed with his hands on himself. Thinking about her. "I'm perfectly fine not knowing what you imagined."

He chuckled again. This time her nipples lit up. That piercing he was so interested in—which was actually a small barbell instead of a ring—rubbed against her bra and she went a little weak at the knees.

"What was the next issue you had?" he asked.

He lifted his face from her neck and she whimpered at the loss. "Oh, yeah," he murmured. His white smile flashed again. She would drop her panties for that smile if he asked. Then he put both her wrists in one of his hands, still behind her back.

"You wanted to know . . . in *your* words . . . if I wanted in your pants."

He used her own hands to press her forward, into his erection. His size made quite the statement.

She whimpered again.

His free hand cupped her jaw and held her face up to his. He rubbed his thumb over her top lip, tracing the upward curve before dipping in the middle. "I do," he whispered. "And I intend to. I really like those pants."

They were designer jeans. And they were made to get noticed.

"Then why all the other talking?" she asked. Her voice barely made any noise at this point. "Why not just seduce me?"

"I am seducing you." The hand that held her jaw lowered to trail down the middle of her throat. The backs of four fingers whispered along her heated skin. When he hit the pulse at the base, he changed to using only one finger.

Roni's heart raced as the pad of that finger kept going and neared her chest. She shivered.

"You know," he said conversationally. "It's December. If you'd learn to wear winter-appropriate clothing outside, you might not shiver so much."

She had on a soft cotton blouse with flutter sleeves that came to her elbows. She'd picked up the shirt in Paris the summer before she quit touring. "It's a perfectly fine shirt," she told him.

"It's short sleeves."

"I'm not cold."

His finger hit the lowest part of the vee in her neckline. Right between her breasts. "You're shivering for another reason then?"

He was such a tease.

"Why all the talking, Lucas?"

His finger slipped over her shirt and circled down below her curves and she couldn't help the way she pushed her chest out. She wanted his hand on her.

"You owed me," he muttered. He seemed fascinated with the path his finger was taking. "You've been ignoring me for two days."

"So you're . . . what? *Punishing* me by making us chat about our pasts?" She forced her mind away from his roaming finger long enough to think about their conversation, and then she accused, "You didn't even bring up the past yourself. That was me. How did you do that?"

He trailed back and forth, right at the base of the breast that wore the piercing. Her hands were still trapped behind her back, thrusting her toward him, and she would swear she could have an orgasm right then and there if only he'd land on her nipple. She pushed closer, nudging at his finger.

"I've watched you for the last three days," he told her. "I knew that all I had to do was remain silent and you'd fill the void. Plus, we didn't talk about your past. You just asked about mine." His gaze lifted to cling to hers. "We can talk about yours later."

She strained her back in a tight arch and let out a low growl when his finger made a slow, deliberate swipe up and over the lower heaviness of her breast, coming within millimeters of the most sensitive spot.

"That wasn't very nice," she whispered, her voice as shaky as she was. She could either be talking about him remaining silent to get her talking earlier, or about him *almost* touching her nipple now. She wasn't even sure which she was referring to.

"I had to do something," he whispered. He'd moved in without her realizing it and his mouth now hovered against hers. "You said you weren't going to sleep with me."

He sucked her lower lip into his mouth before letting it go with a pop and she tugged against the hand holding her wrists. She wanted to touch him.

He didn't release her.

"Let me go," she begged.

He shook his head. "I like this game."

"What is this one you're playing now? You were supposed to tell me the rules."

"The rules are simple. I do whatever I want."

"And me?" She was panting again. "What do I do?"

He eyed her in the dark. The stillness on his features had her shaking in his hands once again. "You also do whatever I want," he murmured.

She grew still. She could feel dampness between her legs, her blood coursing through her veins. He had her on the edge. Which was bad. Bad, bad, bad. She'd never been one to have a lot of control when it came to not going after what she wanted.

"And what is it that you want?" she finally whispered.

Inside, she silently begged that he didn't say he wanted her in his bed. She couldn't do that to Kayla. But she had no idea how she would be able to say no.

He gripped her wrists with both hands again and leaned in. He let his chest brush over hers this time as he touched his lips, first to one corner of her mouth, then the other. Then he grazed along her closed eyelids as she stood there, mouth hanging slightly open, legs shaking beneath her. Every place he touched, she sparked. Setting her on fire.

She burned. Everywhere.

She wanted. *Everything.*

He pulled back and slowly released her wrists. But instead of allowing her to touch him, he clasped her hands together in between their bodies. She wasn't sure she had the strength to lift her fingers and touch him at that moment anyway. The man was serious about seduction.

Then he leaned in one last time and planted the tiniest, most innocent, yet wildly sexual kiss against her lips. It was barely more than the flap of a butterfly's wings but she groaned as if he'd just slid inside her.

"I want you thinking about *me* tonight," he told her. "While you lay in bed. Naked. I want you to picture me." One more tiny touch of his lips and he whispered, "And I want you touching yourself while you do it."

With his words, he stepped around her and was gone. Up the steps, long strides heading toward the parking lot, while she stood there watching him go and shaking like a leaf.

The man wanted her thinking about him?

Done.

In bed while she touched herself?

She almost laughed, but didn't have the strength for it.

No doubt that would happen too.

CHAPTER ELEVEN

Feminine squeals erupted inside the convention center Thursday night as the next two contestants appeared on stage. Roni had done the introductions to the night's event, and then she'd joined the audience members. This was one contest she most certainly wanted to participate in. They were into the Nine Ladies Dancing theme, and had the largest turnout yet.

Only, those weren't ladies up on that stage. And they weren't merely "dancing."

They were stripping.

Six contestants had already shaken their groove thang, and now it was the next duo's turn.

Lucas and contestant number twelve, Kelly Griffin, gyrated across the stage. Both of them wore Santa hats and what looked to Roni to be more of jesters' costumes than anything that could remotely be misconstrued as sexy; however, that didn't seem to slow the women down.

Nor did it her, to be fair. Though maybe that was because, thanks to Lucas, she'd done nothing for the past twenty-four hours but think about what might be inside those striped pants. The man was evil.

And no, she hadn't immediately run home the night before and pleasured herself to Lucas-induced fantasies.

She'd waited at least a full thirty minutes before doing that.

"So," Ginger whispered at her side. "Spill."

Roni squeezed her eyes shut. Ginger had been trying to get the goods from her since she'd sat down, as Roni still hadn't explained how Lucas had managed to run away with her shoes the other night. Roni looked at the other women around their table. None of them seemed to be paying the least bit of attention to anything but the men. That didn't mean that couldn't change in an instant, though.

"Shhh," Roni shushed her. "We'll talk later. Not here."

"I don't have time later," Ginger insisted. "I have to get to bed as soon as this is over. I have an early charter scheduled for tomorrow."

"Then we'll talk tomorrow afternoon. Or this weekend."

"But I want details now."

Roni looked at her friend, her style almost identical to Roni's tonight. Dark-washed designer jeans, a feminine, ruffled top. But where Roni's hair was its normal wild and unkempt style, Ginger's blonde locks fell smoothly around the curve of her shoulders. Her fine hair was accented by the kelly green of her blouse, and dipping toward her cleavage was a lovely woven-knot necklace in sterling.

If not for the whining coming from her friend, Roni would be highly impressed with the sophisticated look. Ginger had put in more effort than normal tonight.

"There aren't really any details to share," Roni insisted. "Nothing has happened."

Except a mouthwatering kiss and some dirty talking on the beach.

The men jerked the tails of their shirts out of their pants, and Roni and Ginger took a moment to pause and watch. If abs were about to make an appearance, they didn't want to miss it. But apparently the guys were only teasing. The way the two men worked in unison led Roni to believe this wasn't the first time they'd danced together.

Ginger tugged on the sleeve of Roni's shirt and leaned in close. "I heard he was at Gin's last night."

Roni didn't let herself be goaded. "Everyone was at Gin's last night."

"I heard you disappeared shortly after he arrived."

Roni swiveled her head around to her friend. "Who told you that?" Oh geez, had someone seen them out on the beach? Not that they'd done anything.

But still.

"What are we talking about, ladies?" Mrs. Rylander's tight curls popped in between Roni and Ginger. She twisted a bony shoulder sideways and pushed forward, and the next thing Roni knew, her miniature neighbor had somehow parked a chair between them and had herself plopped down on it. She lifted her face and smiled from one woman to the other, her pale-blue eyes shining with mischief. "Roni's boy crush?"

"Mrs. Rylander," Roni whispered. "I don't have a boy crush."

"Well, honey, that boy certainly has a crush on you."

Ginger met Roni's gaze over the top of Mrs. Rylander's head, a smug look giving her a tight smile. "Told you," Ginger mouthed.

Roni twisted up her face in a return smirk and then refocused her sights on their topic of conversation. Lucas had been working it at the front of the room thus far, shaking what his mama gave him, but as if he had some kind of sixth-sense, he shifted his gaze at that very moment.

It landed on her.

She exploded with heat.

"Look at that." Out of the corner of her eye she watched her neighbor nudge her friend. "She blushes every time he looks at her."

"I do not," Roni growled out.

"I see it," Ginger said. "And she does that every time, you say?"

"Every time he turns those big blues in her direction." Mrs. Rylander nodded her head in overdefined up-and-down movements.

Roni lifted her hand to her heated cheek. "It's the glass of wine I drank," she muttered.

Two of the ladies at their table glanced in their direction, their gazes flickering over Roni's burning cheeks, and Roni wanted to duck her head. But Lucas was still staring at her.

He gripped the corner of his bright-red bow tie and tugged. Hard. The material slipped free from his neck and slid through his fingers. He never glanced away from her. Holy, mother of . . .

Roni's chest burned from lack of oxygen. She wanted to help that man right out of his clothes.

"I think they should get a room," the eighty-year-old trouble-maker whispered in a loud, non-whispering sort of way. "That boy watches her like he knows what she tastes like."

"Mrs. Rylander!" Roni gasped. She broke connection with Lucas long enough to gape in shock at her neighbor. Ginger's eyes widened and then she laughed so hard she doubled over at the waist. Roni watched as she wiped tears with the back of her hands.

"Shhhhh," came from several of the other women at the table.

"Is she sleeping with him?" This from somewhere behind her.

"If not, she needs to. I certainly would if he looked at me like that."

Roni had no idea where that last comment had come from, but was dying of mortification. If she decided to sleep with Lucas, she really didn't need the entire room to know about it. She opened her mouth to explain to those around her that he was only working it, just like all the other guys that night. Their goal was to get the most singles from the crowd.

But before she could speak, everyone at the surrounding tables went wild, and Roni jerked her attention back around to the men. Their shirts had come off, and two six-packs had made an appearance.

"Oh, mama," Ginger whispered. "He looks as hard as a freaking rock."

Roni couldn't help it. Evilness and the desire to get back at her friend's enjoyment of Roni's current torture had her leaning into Mrs.

Rylander and pressing closer to Ginger. "He is," she murmured. "At least his pecs."

She lowered her gaze to his abs and remembered trying to outline them through his shirt.

"And his abs," she admitted. She shot Ginger a naughty look, and Ginger fanned herself with a napkin.

"I think you should most definitely go for that," Ginger said. Mrs. Rylander bobbed her head up and down again. "And marry it as soon as possible," Ginger finished.

"What?" Once again, Roni stared at her friend, her mouth hanging open. Ginger was the "sweet" one of the group. The romantic. She saw moons and stars with every potential relationship.

She turned those romantic green eyes on Roni. "Imagine how good he would take care of you if he takes care of himself like that."

Interesting point. But no.

The volume of their tablemates grew to a shriek, and instead of replying to the nonsense Ginger was preaching, Roni returned her attention to the men. Kelly had moved across the room, walking on the tables that had been butted up together for just that purpose.

Lucas was doing the same, only heading her way.

The women were salivating, fake dollar bills waving in the air, and a prick of irritation hit Roni. Couldn't they have a bit more class?

Lucas stepped in the middle of their table and swung his butt around in a hypnotic move, impressing her with what the man could do with his hips. She gulped.

The sudden appearance of a very tiny pair of red Speedos in her face made each woman at the table gasp, and the mistletoe design cupping the front bulge made Roni go stupid.

"Oh my geez," she whispered to no one.

She wanted her hands on that.

"He sure looks big," Mrs. Rylander said from the other side of Roni. She had her head craned around to the front of Lucas and was peeking up, her eyes wide.

Lucas looked down at the woman and gave her a wink.

Then he looked at Roni and smoldered.

"Don't worry about a thing," Mrs. Rylander said. She patted Roni's forearm as she continued watching Lucas's one particular body part. "My Henry was a big boy too. But it never hurt me none."

"Oh, good grief." Roni buried her face in her hands as everyone at the table laughed.

Then they all grew quiet. Pinpricks tickled the back of Roni's neck. Terrified to see what had caused the silence, but unable not to look, she finally forced her face out of her hands and lifted her gaze. All eyes were on her. Including Lucas's.

He was dancing solely for her now. His eyes had hooded and she would swear there was smoke coming from him. She gave him a hard look.

Go away. Don't be so obvious.

Only he didn't move on. He kept dancing. Then he nodded to the dollar bills she had clutched in her hand.

Oh! He wanted her dollars.

The rules were that everyone who wanted to play could buy in with the nightly fee, and in return they got twenty-five fake dollar bills to give to whichever contestant—or contestants—they wanted to move on to the next round.

Women weren't allowed to stick the bills in the dancer's trunks themselves for fear of . . . uh . . . inappropriately touching the man's "junk." And once a person's bills were gone, they could continue to watch and enjoy, but they were out of the game.

The two contestants who collected the least money would be done.

Lucas's hips swirled in front of Roni's face, trying hard to make sure he wasn't one of the two sent home.

His waistband was stuffed full of the fake bills he'd already collected from the other women and Roni handed up one of her own. The crowd cheered. Lucas shoved it in his Speedo and kept dancing, right where he was.

The gleam in his eyes matched the wicked in his smile, and she couldn't help it. She flushed again. It seemed the entire room was watching them now. And they had to know what the both of them were thinking.

Going along with the show, she counted out five more bills and passed them up.

A couple whistles sounded as Lucas also tucked those into his trunks. He still didn't go away. Nudges and whispers worked through the crowd, along with wide smiles. These women were enjoying watching Lucas flirt.

Then the lady to her right leaned over and said—loudly enough that everyone at their table and all the surrounding tables could hear, "I think he wants all of it, honey."

Lucas's smile turned wolfish. Oh yeah, there was no doubt that he wanted all of it.

Covering her eyes with one hand, she lifted the other and shoved the remainder of her bills at Lucas. Rowdy whooping and cheering made her shake her head.

He owed her.

He owed her big.

She just had to figure out how she was going to make him pay.

~

"You've slept with him, haven't you?"

Roni sat immobile in her seat, glancing to the floor beside her to stare at the toe of a classic black pump, the tip end shiny patent, tapping repeatedly on the wood floor. She followed the line of the leg up and over a pinstriped pantsuit paired with a starched white blouse buttoned all the way to the neck, until she landed on the heated face of an agitated event coordinator.

"Hello, Kayla." Roni tried a smile, but didn't expect it to do much good. She lifted her glass of ice water and took a long sip.

She was in the convention center's green room, sitting calmly in a plush, square-backed chair and staring out at the darkness of the beach. There was one light glowing in the corner of the room by the door. She'd been there since finishing her duties after the night's striptease show.

The follow-up entertainment had ended about thirty minutes earlier, and given the lack of noise coming from the remainder of the building, the audience had all left for the night, as well. The place was essentially deserted.

Only, Roni could still feel Lucas in the building. She hadn't seen him since the contest had wrapped up, but he was around.

"You slept with him?" Kayla repeated.

Roni shook her head, but a guilty shame crossed her features. She touched the side of the glass to her cheek. "I have not slept with him."

But she wanted to.

And she suspected she would.

Especially after tonight.

Lucas hadn't won the competition—probably because he'd spent way too much time at her table and not getting more money from others—but he'd not been in the bottom two, either. Roni had been unable to think of anything but the way he'd looked at her as he'd danced, his blue eyes telling all the things he wanted to do to her when he got her alone.

So she'd escaped to this room in the back corner of the building. Alone. As she'd tried to sort through her feelings and figure out whether she would let him do those things or not.

Kayla's hands flapped at her sides, reminding Roni of a baby bird trying to figure out how to fly for the first time. "Roni," Kayla groaned. "You're a part of this competition. You can't just go around sleeping with the contestants."

"I'm not going to sleep with all of them." Roni tried the smile again. No impact. "It's only the one I want," she finished lamely.

She felt bad about it. Truly. She didn't mean to upset Kayla. But how was she supposed to ignore the chemistry between her and Lucas? She'd never been a part of anything with quite that kind of pull.

A thin, high-pitched noise squeezed out of Kayla and Roni cringed. It sounded like air being let out of a balloon by pinching the neck. Thankfully, it only lasted a couple seconds.

"I'm sorry," Roni began. She uncrossed her legs and stood, reaching for Kayla's hand. "Really. I'm sorry this worries you. But it won't be a problem."

She'd made up her mind already. She was going to sleep with him.

"Of course it'll be a problem. I've been hired to put on a professional event."

"And you're doing an amazing job of it."

Kayla snorted. "Not if my master of ceremonies goes to bed with one of the contestants. That is not an amazing job, Roni. *That* is a conflict of interest."

"No, it's not." And Kayla would realize it once she calmed down.

It may not be the most professional behavior Roni could exhibit, but obviously this connection between her and Lucas couldn't be hidden. Everyone in the auditorium had witnessed it, and in fact, no one would be shocked to discover that she and Lucas had decided to spend time together outside of the competition.

Though Roni would do her best to keep it on the down-low. She didn't want it to be talked about any more than Kayla did.

A frantic whimper came from Kayla. She turned her back and paced to the middle of the room, her arms crossed tight over her chest.

The darkness outside the floor-to-ceiling windows seemed to close in on her as she turned to face Roni. She appeared tiny in the middle of the black night. "How will I explain this?" she asked.

Her toe started tapping again.

Roni really did feel bad for upsetting her. She liked Kayla a lot, even if the woman was strung so tight Roni suspected she'd hum like a guitar string if plucked. Roni hadn't set out to add to the stress.

"Think about it," she said now. She headed toward Kayla and spoke calmly, hoping to soothe frayed nerves. "I'm only the person reading off the script. I don't really have any importance in the grand scheme of things. I don't get a say in who stays or goes unless I buy in to vote. Just like everyone else. I couldn't impact the winner of the money if I tried.

"So if I spend a few nights with one of them . . ." she finished, holding her hands in the air, palms up, "it doesn't really matter."

"*Ohmygod*," Kayla muttered. "A few nights? How many nights do you plan to spend?"

If the other woman weren't so stressed, Roni would laugh. Her freak-out was pretty funny.

Before she could tell Kayla that she would likely spend as many of Lucas's remaining nights on the island with him as she was invited to, a door slammed somewhere down the hall.

"Kayla," Roni spoke quietly. She had the sense that Lucas was moving closer. "It won't impact anything, I swear."

"Andie will have my hide if I screw this up."

"Andie won't have your hide," Roni assured her, "because nothing is going to get screwed up."

"I promised her when she moved to Boston that I would do nothing to harm the company's reputation." Kayla hands flapped again, but least she'd stopped tapping. "How am I supposed to explain this to her if the committee fires me?"

The door opened to the room and Roni looked over to find Lucas standing in the doorway. His face was expressionless as his gaze took in her and Kayla. Without a word, he stepped out of the room and closed the door.

"Roni," Kayla's harsh whisper caught her attention. "What am I going to do?"

Roni forced herself to look away from the door and concentrated on breathing steadily and thinking rationally. Facts were facts. She was about to sleep with Lucas Alexander.

He'd come for her. He wanted her.

And she was going to have him.

She took Kayla's hands in hers and shoved Lucas and his abs from her mind.

"You're going to keep doing exactly what you've been doing," she told Kayla. "Pulling off the best darned event Turtle Island has ever seen."

That high-pitched noise leaked from Kayla. This time her shoulders deflated with the sound.

"It'll be fine," Roni assured her. "I wouldn't do anything if I thought it would hurt you or Andie. You know that. And I'll talk to the committee myself if anything was to come of this. I'll talk to Andie too. I'll explain everything to her. She can be mad at me if she wants, but you haven't done anything wrong, Kayla. No one will be upset with you. And no one is going to fire you."

Kayla shoved her hands into her hair on either side of her head and pulled. "I just want to do a good job."

Kayla's words came through gritted teeth, and Roni couldn't help it. She finally let out the laugh. "You *are* doing a good job. A wonderful job. I've heard nothing but compliments since we started."

The other woman's eyes narrowed as if she didn't believe her. Her hands lowered to her sides. "Really?"

"Really." Roni nodded. "Lots and lot of compliments."

A tremulous smile tried to form on Kayla's mouth before falling off. She grunted. "I still don't agree with this," she said. She lifted her

112

chin and her gaze drifted to the darkened night. A forlorn look painted across her face. "But if I had a man looking at me the way he looks at you . . ." She shook her head. "I can't say I wouldn't do the same thing."

With that, Kayla turned and headed across the room. She swung the door open and at the sight of Lucas waiting there, she ducked her head and hurried down the hall.

Roni laughed again, a small sound barely making it out of her body, and had the thought that Kayla *needed* a man to look at her that way. Maybe then she'd unwind just a bit. There was more to life than being stressed. She caught Lucas's eye from across the room and he shot her a wink. Her clothes suddenly felt too tight.

"Want to go for a ride with me?" he asked. The steadiness with which he watched her let her know that he wasn't just talking about a ride. Well, not only in his car.

Her grin was wide and fast. *Oh, yeah.*

"Only if it ends at your hotel."

CHAPTER TWELVE

The ride to the hotel was short and silent. Lucas had hustled Roni out of the convention center and into his rented sedan before she came to her senses and told him to take a hike. If her hand on his thigh was anything to go by, though, she had no intention of changing her mind.

He turned into the hotel parking lot, heading toward the valet area, and gripped her creeping fingers in his. His hold was too tight to be polite. She had him on the cusp by doing nothing more than tracing tiny circles on his upper thigh for the five-minute drive over.

"Is your intention to draw unwanted attention to me as we walk through the hotel?" He tugged her hand closer to his crotch to make his point, but stopped just short.

She didn't seem to have the same hesitancy. Her fingers stretched forward until they slid over his straining length. He groaned, and when she squeezed him through his jeans, he almost drove through the valet stand.

"Christ, Roni."

She giggled. She already had the look of a woman who'd been thoroughly loved, and he hadn't put a hand on her. Her cheeks were flushed, her brown eyes hooded. She was blazing hot.

He braked in front of the hotel, but held her hand where it was, letting her feel his blood pulsing through him. "Did you think of me the other night?" he asked her. His voice was tight as he pictured her in bed alone. Thinking of him. "Did you touch yourself?"

The way her gaze dipped to their joined hands and the rushed rise and fall of her chest gave him his answer. Christ almighty. He may not be physically able to step out of the car.

When an attendant headed their way Lucas turned loose of Roni's hand and practically shoved it back to her side of the car. He grabbed a jacket from the back seat and shoved it in his lap. Roni giggled once more and he shot her a look. He wasn't upset. But damn, it would be nice if he could actually *walk* through the hotel instead of hobbling.

"I owe you," he threatened.

"I think we might be even after the dancing you did on my table tonight."

He shook his head. "Not even close."

The deep brown of her eyes went hot, and she ran her gaze quickly down to his lap once more before coming back up. "Then show me what you've got, big guy," she taunted.

Sweet Jesus, that didn't help his predicament any.

Doors opened and they both stepped out. The shaggy-headed kid who approached took a longing look at Roni before eyeing the jacket Lucas dangled at his waist. He gave Lucas a conspiratorial look. Lucas handed over his keys and a couple of twenties.

Keep your mouth shut, kid. No one needs to know about this.

The attendant gave him a too-wide grin. *Hell.* Word would be spread within minutes that one of the contestants had arrived back at the hotel with a hot woman and a raging hard-on. Just what they needed.

He narrowed his eyes on the valet, considered ripping the twenties back out of his hand, then slammed the car door and rounded the hood to Roni. If he took the bills back now, it would only make the story worse.

"You just lost money," Roni told him as they entered the hotel lobby through the middle set of double doors. The amber lighting cast a seductive glow down on her. "He's going to tell everyone he knows."

The nonchalant way she stated the obvious surprised him. "And you're okay with that?"

"Well, I'd prefer he didn't." Her tone was sarcastic. "But what can we do?"

"We could have gone to your house," he grumbled.

Roni just shot him a roll of her eyes and jabbed the elevator button. He'd suggested her place when they'd left the convention center, but she'd shot him down. Hotels kept things simpler.

The excuse had irritated him.

"The damage is done," she said. "Plus, it's not like it'll be the first time I've shared an evening with a man."

Of course not. She was a beautiful woman. She'd traveled the world. He knew she wasn't celibate.

However, jealousy flared at the thought of her with other men.

The elevator doors slid open and he took her hand. After the unloading passengers exited, the two of them moved inside and stood quietly facing the front. The doors closed and he considered jumping her right there. He wanted to kiss her. He wanted her to forget—for just a minute—that she'd ever been with another man.

He wanted not to be jealous. It wasn't like *he* had been a monk.

The doors slid open and he started to step forward, his hand still clasped around Roni's, but stopped when he once again saw the lobby. Three people boarded. A man and woman a few years older than them, and a boy who looked to be around ten. The doors slid silently closed.

Lucas remained where he was, dumbfounded until Roni leaned into his side and whispered, "We forgot to push the button."

The woman peeked at them over her shoulder and smiled around a laugh.

Embarrassment heated Lucas's neck. He reached out and jabbed at the buttons, catching both the three and four. They should have just taken the stairs.

The family got off on the second floor, the woman once again shooting them a smile.

"Which floor are you on?" Roni asked gently.

"Four," he growled. At least his erection had gone away. Mostly.

Roni laughed softly, then gave his hand a squeeze. "You're acting nervous, but I don't believe for a second that this is the first time you've taken a woman to your hotel room."

He stared at her, wondering how many times she'd gone to some man's hotel room. Then he wondered why he cared.

"No," his voice deepened and he backed her into a corner, "not the first time. And don't worry; I'm not nervous." Just more excited than usual. He lifted her chin and focused on her lips. They had a slight natural curve at the corners that had the ability to draw the eye whether he wanted to be looking at her mouth or not. "I know exactly what I'm doing."

He covered her lips with his, inhaling the sweet fragrance of her when she clasped both hands on his shirtfront and held on as if afraid he might get away. He wrapped an arm around her and brought her against him. He groaned at the feel of her softer body pressing into his reappearing erection.

The elevator dinged softly at the third floor, but they ignored it. If anyone saw them, it was just too damned bad. He wasn't ready to turn her loose yet.

The doors swished closed again, and when the bell sounded once more, he forced himself to take a step back, noting that he wasn't the only one struggling for breath. When he turned to the open doors, they came face-to-face with another contestant.

The other man's eyebrows shot up toward his forehead.

"Great," Lucas murmured, wondering what else could happen before they got to his room.

The guy's expression quickly changed to envy, and he eyed Roni as if wondering if it might be his turn next.

"Not on your life," Lucas ground out as he dragged Roni from the elevator, growling in frustration when she tossed out a flirty hello to the other contestant.

She laughed with a teasing, light note when Lucas tugged her behind him harder. "You're acting like a caveman," she pointed out.

He swiped his keycard over the entry panel and opened the door, letting a shaft of light into the room. "I feel like a caveman. Do you have to flirt with every man you meet?"

"Are you jealous?"

He practically shoved her into the room and she turned to him with a taunting smile. He followed her in. "I don't get jealous."

Liar!

The door closed and the room went dark. He had her against him before she could accuse him of anything else. He didn't need her to point out that his actions were a direct contradiction to his words. He was well aware of that. What he didn't understand was why he felt jealous at all; he was going to be with this woman for, at most, ten days.

Roni's hands slid up over his chest and landed at the base of his neck, and he scooped her up, dangling her in the air. "You're too short," he muttered.

"My mother's fault," she whispered. "I look just like her."

Her legs wrapped around his hips and he grunted in appreciation. She felt good pressed against him. He fought the urge to shove her against the wall and continue what he'd wanted to finish in the elevator. He wanted to explore her first.

And he wanted to see that damned piercing that had about driven him out of his mind.

He lowered his head and kissed her, his mouth taking it far slower than his pounding blood insisted. She was a combination of sweet with just a hint of lusty. He didn't think he'd ever tasted anything so tantalizing.

Her tongue brushed his and he gripped her tighter. He saw stars behind his closed eyes.

Needing to put distance between himself and the wall before he changed his mind and took her there, he headed across the room. He moved easily in the dark while her hands burrowed into his hair. Their mouths never parted. When he reached the bed, instead of setting her down, he reached behind his back with one hand and went to work on her shoes.

"How do you get these things off?" He pulled his lips from hers to speak, already missing her eager mouth.

"There's a zipper." Her voice was raw. "Hold me and I'll do it."

He kept one hand on the curve of her butt and braced the other against the middle of her back. She reached down while lifting her leg higher. The movement rubbed her more intimately against him and he buried his face in her neck. "Hurry," he encouraged.

A zip and then a thump sounded behind him.

"That's one," she whispered. "They're cropped boots so they're easy to—"

"I don't care," he interrupted impatiently. "Just get them off before your wiggling causes the wrong kind of ending to this."

She giggled and switched arms and legs, still squirming dangerously against his dick.

"Roni," he warned. "You're doing that on purpose."

Zip. "Maybe." Thump.

With rapid speed, he unwrapped her legs from around his waist, but instead of laying her on the mattress, he stood her on it.

"What are you doing?" her voice was a surprised whisper coming from above him in the dark.

"You'll see."

He gripped her at the hips and tugged her a couple inches closer, bringing her almost to his chest, her breasts practically touching his face. He let out an anguished groan.

"Don't let me fall." Fingertips clung to his shoulder.

"I would never let you fall."

He would eventually turn on a light because he was dying to see her spread out on his bed. But for the moment, he enjoyed the heightened sense of touch and taste the darkness provided.

He could smell her—she always carried the scent of berries, along with a hint of soap and the salty breeze of the ocean.

"Lucas?"

He spread his hands wide on either side of her tight jeans. "Yes?"

"This feels . . ."

He slid upward, slipping his hands under her untucked shirt and over the heated skin of her waist. Her stomach dipped in with a harsh breath.

"Yes?" he asked when she said nothing else. "It *feels* . . . what?"

His thumbs met in the middle of her bare stomach and smoothed back down. She let out a breath, ruffling the top of his hair. When he reached her jeans, his thumbs inched underneath.

"Roni?" he said. The breathing, a few inches above his head, was getting louder.

"What?" she bit out.

He lowered his thumbs further inside her jeans, searching for the top of her panties, and focused hard to keep his own breathing steady. "Does it feel okay?"

"Yes." The word was short and hurried.

"Should I stop?"

Both hands now held his shoulders, her fingers digging in. "Only if you want to die."

He chuckled. "Not today."

He removed his hands from inside her jeans and palmed her ass, hugging her against him, while he buried his face between her breasts. The feel of her made him break out in a sweat.

A soft moan slid down from above and he gritted his teeth to keep from letting his mouth seek out the nipple that he was so desperate to touch. He wondered if it was just the one that was pierced, or if she'd done both.

With forced effort, he moved her back from him and brought his hand around to her waist. "I'm going to take off your jeans now. Is that okay?"

The sound she made couldn't be considered a word, but it was answer enough.

He undid the button and lowered her zipper, his eyes rolling back in his head at the brush of heat across his knuckles. He didn't have to touch her to know she was already wet. Then he peeled the denim down her hips, gliding his palms over her smooth skin as he went.

The rustling sounds of the fabric were overly loud in the quiet room. Seconds later, the material was at Roni's feet. He drew a deep breath in through his nose, wanting to drown in what he knew was in front of him.

"Lift your leg," he instructed, his voice rough.

She did and he pulled the material over her foot. Silently, they worked together to do the same to the other.

Once they'd finished, he closed his eyes and pictured what she must look like. Wild hair at the top, eyes glazed and half-closed. Probably biting her lip. He could see her standing there only in her panties and shirt, those silky smooth legs gloriously bare. And behind that shirt . . .

He wet his lips and swallowed.

He would bet his house that her nipples were rock hard. Same as his.

With concentrated effort, he somehow managed to continue going slow. He began at her calves, trailing his fingers over the lines of her muscles. Next were her thighs. They were shapely and lean under his palms. He could tell that she worked out. He didn't stop to linger, though. He had another destination in mind.

When he reached the back curve at the top of her thighs, he paused.

Roni swayed toward him and the softness of her breast brushed against his cheek. The muscles in his neck tensed.

"I've never had someone undress me in complete darkness before."

Good. He wanted to know that the next time she took her clothes off in a dark room, she would be thinking of him. He didn't speak. Wasn't sure he could at the moment. With great effort, he ignored the piercing that taunted him only a few inches from his mouth and focused all his attention on his hands.

Her behind was curvy and he palmed it in his hands. It was almost completely bare.

"Your underwear doesn't seem to cover much," he informed her. His fingers slid over her flesh and she swayed again.

"They get the job done," she murmured.

He trailed slowly along the lace on either side of where her cheeks came together. She dug harder into his shoulders.

"What color are they?" he asked.

"White."

He followed the line of the fabric over the outside of her hips and trailed around to the front. "And your bra?"

There was a tiny pause before she whispered, breathless, "They match."

He smiled in the dark. He could easily imagine her in white lace.

The panties rode low, and he knew he was brushing just above her pubic line by the way she shook in his hands.

The next instant, he hooked the lace with his fingers and tugged down.

"Oh." The sound was a sigh.

His dick throbbed behind his zipper but he ignored its plea. He wanted to feel her first. He wanted to taste her.

The underwear passed her hips, then her thighs, and before he could ask, she was lifting each foot for him to remove the scrap of cloth. When it was free from her, he tossed it over his shoulder in the direction of her jeans.

"Spread your legs." He touched the backs of his hands to her inner thighs and she jerked. Not away from him, but more like a small spasm. "You okay?" he asked.

"You betcha." The sound was tight and he couldn't help but laugh.

"I'm going to taste you now," he told her.

He felt her body move slightly in a small rhythmic pattern and suspected she was nodding.

"You knew that, didn't you?"

"I was counting on it."

He grinned again. He loved her spunk.

With his fingers, he continued his exploration, this time up her inner thighs. She vibrated slightly with each stroke.

"I'm afraid I might fall." She sounded more matter-of-fact than concerned.

"Hold my head when I bend down."

"That—"

"I told you. I won't let you fall."

"My knees, Lucas," she said urgently. "I'm not sure I can stand on the bed while you—"

Her words cut off when he touched one finger to her.

"*Oh, crap,*" she whispered.

"Don't fall," he commanded. "I want to taste you like this."

"I don't—" She went silent when he spread her and put his mouth to her. When he flicked his tongue back and forth, she gripped his hair. "*Ahhhh.*"

He buried his nose, almost too turned on to continue. She was slippery and hot, and if he wasn't careful, he would be the one too weak at the knees to stand.

She tilted her hips, seeking more, bumping against him, so he refocused and gave her what she was after. He stroked with his tongue, his fingers. He nudged her with his nose. He used every trick he'd ever learned to drive her right up to the edge, ready to jump.

His thumbs parted her wide once again and he closed his lips over her, sucking gently. She shook in his hands. He gripped her around the thighs so she wouldn't fall.

"Lucas?" Her hands pressed his head into her.

"What?" he mumbled the word deep in her folds. She tasted tangy and luscious, and he wanted to stay right where he was for days.

"If you don't stop . . ." Her words trailed off as her fingers clenched reflexively in his hair.

Like he was going to stop.

He redoubled his efforts, focusing on her engorged flesh, and within seconds he felt her legs stiffen. Her hips clenched and the weight of her shifted as her body arched backward. He put one hand to the small of her back to keep her from falling over, but did not take his mouth off her.

"Oh," she moaned. "I'm. Oh. God." She ground out the last word as her orgasm took control of her body.

Lucas held her against him, his thigh muscles and biceps shaking along with her, but he didn't let up until he felt her weaken. She released one final breathless sound and slumped. Not falling, but he could tell it was only because he held her up.

He straightened, keeping his arms around her and sliding up her body. When he got fully upright, she grunted and dropped her forehead to his shoulder.

His ego ratcheted up a few notches.

"I knew you would be dangerous to my well-being," she whispered. She turned her face into his neck and hot breaths bathed his skin. "Will you let me down now?"

He shook his head. "Not yet."

"What?" She lifted her head from his shoulder. He could picture her shooting him a dirty look.

"There's one more thing I need to do first."

"Well, I'm not sure there's one more thing you're getting out of me right at this moment."

"Oh yes, there is."

He turned loose of her and stepped back.

"Lucas?" Her voice jumped an octave. He held his hands up in the space in front of him in case she tumbled forward until he was certain she'd righted herself.

"Don't fall," he repeated as he took a small step away. "I'm going to turn the lamp on."

"Okay."

"But I need you to do something before I do." He stepped to the bedside table and put his fingers on the switch.

"What's that?" she asked.

"Take off your shirt."

CHAPTER THIRTEEN

Renewed desire coursed through Roni at Lucas's command. She nodded, though there was no way he could see her in the pitch-black room, then quickly grabbed the hem of her shirt and yanked it over her head.

She tossed it across the room and heard it land with a near-silent *whoosh*.

"Now your bra."

Her nipples beaded at the thought of stripping for him. She couldn't believe he'd made her come while she stood on the bed in the dark, but after that, she'd do anything he asked.

"You don't want to do it?" she asked, just to be sure.

"Not this time." His voice was low and rough. Controlled. He'd done nothing over the last few minutes to take pleasure of his own, only handing it out. She could only imagine how tightly he was wound.

With anxious fingers, she reached behind her and released the hook. She let the straps slide down over her shoulders and crossed her arms beneath her breasts, cupping herself to keep it from falling all the way off. She closed her eyes at the feel of the lace pulling gently on the little barbell she had through her left nipple.

She must have made a sound because Lucas asked, "What are you doing?"

"I'm . . ." she paused and licked her lips. "I'm taking off my bra."

"Why is it taking so long?"

She ran her thumb across the jewelry. "Because it feels good."

A soft groan sounded from about three feet away from her an instant before he turned on the light.

Lucas, fully dressed, stared at her as she stood on top of the bed, her legs still parted and her hands cupping her bra to her. His nostrils flared, reminding her of a bull before it charged a cape-waving matador, and she couldn't help it, she ran her thumb once more across her nipple.

"Roni?" he spoke very slowly, very deliberately.

She nibbled on her lower lip. "Yes?"

"Don't move."

Lucas came back to her and stood where he'd been before. His face was directly in front of her breasts. And that was where he was looking.

Her nipples ached for him to touch them.

"I was wrong," he said. He lifted his heated gaze. "I want to take it off."

And darn if she didn't grow even wetter.

The desire emanating from him was tantalizing. "Should I fasten it back—"

"No." He shook his head. "You should stay exactly as you are."

Then he lifted one hand and ran a finger from her left shoulder, down to where the strap lay loosely against her arm.

"You're beautiful," he murmured.

All she could do in reply was watch. He seemed transfixed. It was empowering.

Next was his thumb. He stroked it across the top curve of her breast. The barbell twitched against the lace and she groaned in the back of her throat. His eyes turned so dark she was certain they were now black.

"So it's only one that you have pierced?" he asked.

She nodded.

"Why?" That thumb took another swipe, this time in a downward path, but remained above the lace. He pressed slightly into her skin, causing her nipple to lift behind the cup of her bra. Her knees wobbled and he shot her a quick look. "Don't fall."

She shook her head obediently. "I won't."

His look was intoxicating. Weakening. But she would make absolutely certain to do nothing to change it. If that meant standing there naked before him all night, then that's what she would do.

Because the man wasn't only a good kisser.

He was just good. At everything.

"Why?" he repeated.

"Huh?"

His thumb began sliding slowly over the lace, from her cleavage heading horizontally across the fullest part of her breast. There was only light pressure, making her fight to keep from pushing into him. When he got to the center, he touched her. Right on the tip.

Then held his thumb there, unmoving.

She couldn't look away. The contrast of his tanned hand against her lighter skin and white bra would have turned her on if she wasn't already well beyond it. The fact that he touched her directly on her piercing just about did her in.

"Why do you have only the one pierced?" he asked again.

"Oh." She inhaled deeply and her breast pressed into Lucas's thumb. His eyes narrowed at the movement. A muscle ticked in his jaw. "Because the first one hurt too much."

Dark eyes flicked up to hers. "Does it hurt now?"

She gave him a slow smile. "Oh, no."

His thumb moved on and she let out the breath.

"Will you do something for me?" she asked. It occurred to her that they were missing one important piece in their game.

His hand stilled where it had shifted, now tracing over her other breast. "Maybe. Depends on if I *want* to do what you ask or not."

Before she could voice her request, he tugged down the lace, baring her unpierced nipple. The muscle in his jaw twitched again. Then he leaned forward and lapped his tongue over her and she almost turned loose of herself and her bra and reached for him. She caught herself at the last minute.

Panting breaths had her chest rising and falling when he pulled his head away and looked up at her. "I've decided to continue the game from the other night," he told her. "I do whatever I want. *You* do whatever I want." He gave her a lazy look and a naughty lift of his lips.

Her nipple remained uncovered, wet from his touch, and she decided that she liked his games. But she wanted to be disobedient for just a minute. She wanted to give her own order. "Take off your clothes," she demanded.

She needed to get her hands on all those muscles. If he wouldn't let her touch, she should at least be able to look. He eyed her. She could see him thinking, trying to figure out if that fit into his plans. Finally, he gave a small nod, and a happy whimper slipped from her throat.

He stepped back a few feet and brought his hands to the buttons of his shirt. "Make sure you don't move."

"Wouldn't dream of it."

As his shirt parted, she almost begged him to let her down. She wanted to touch him as he'd done her.

When the cotton dropped to the floor, she touched herself instead.

Her thumb brushed her left nipple.

"You're moving," he growled.

"Is that really bad?"

He popped open the top button of his jeans and the sound of the zipper filled her ears. "I suppose I can let that one pass," he said.

She touched herself again, and couldn't help a smile when his gaze narrowed in on the movement. Then she moved her other thumb and scraped the side of her nail across that nipple. Lucas yanked off his boots and threw them in the corner.

The next instant he was back in front of her and his mouth was covering her bared breast, capturing her thumb between him and her. She continued moving over herself, mixing in with Lucas's tongue, groaning when he closed an arm around her hips and crushed her to his hard chest.

Her arms were crossed over her, holding her bra on, and were now trapped between them. His mouth was still busy at her breast.

Just when she thought she would scream from wanting him to touch her piercing, his hand came up and settled over her. She jolted. His teeth and lips nipped and plucked at her softly on the one side while his thumb and finger mimicked the action on the other, pulling gently against the barbell through the lace.

She went white-hot. She wanted his hands everywhere on her, and she wanted her hands doing the same. With an uncontrolled wriggle, she pressed harder against him, wishing she was lower so she could feel his erection against her.

As if to stop her fidgeting—or maybe to encourage more of it—Lucas spread his hand wide on her rear and feathered a finger down her crevice. He reached around until he made contact with her front. When his finger slipped inside her, she cried out and bucked.

"Please," she whimpered. "I want to touch you. I want my turn."

Out-of-control eyes turned to her, seeming unfocused. She remained there in front of him, hands cupping herself, not daring to move until he said to. She had never been so turned on in her life, and if he wanted to go a little longer down this path, she would follow along nicely.

But she might continue begging.

Suddenly he gave a quick nod and pulled her bra from her body. He scooped her off the bed and stepped back. When she'd cleared the mattress, she slid down the front of his body.

A guttural sound ripped from both of them as she edged over the denim he hadn't yet removed and felt him straining against her.

"Hurry," she whispered.

He set her on her feet and she went to work on his jeans. Shoving them down, she forced herself not to touch him just yet, but couldn't take her eyes off his size. It may not be the most professional thing for her to go to bed with one of the contestants, but she'd given up professionalism years ago.

She was a breezy beach girl these days. And that meant that if she wanted to spend the next ten days naked with this man every spare second she could find, then that was what she was going to do.

He kicked his jeans from his feet then tugged her with him to the bed.

As she tumbled, she reached out and closed her fingers around him. It was time for him to be tortured.

CHAPTER FOURTEEN

Lucas opened his eyes in the darkened room. He knew it would be five o'clock. That would make it four at home, and he always rose like clockwork at four. He had to or else he couldn't get his workout in before the day started.

He glanced at Roni beside him in the king-size bed, outlined by the glow of the bathroom light. He'd left the light on earlier when he'd gotten rid of the third condom of the night.

She slept on her stomach with one arm thrown out across the mattress, her fingertips just barely brushing his chest, and the other arm bent at the elbow and pointing toward the headboard. There was no pillow under her, and her face was turned toward him. His chest tightened at the sight of her bare back, the way it sloped down and dipped so erotically as if making a grand entrance to the swell of her rear. The side of her breast just barely peeked out under her arm. He wanted her again.

Which blew his mind. Not that he'd expected one night to be enough, but at this point, he was beginning to wonder if he could get enough. Never before had this been a problem.

Rather than selfishly wake her, he rolled to his side where he could simply watch.

And think.

If their first kiss had knocked his socks off, last night had left him naked in the middle of a snowstorm.

She was glorious and fun. And she made him want things.

He pictured her as she'd been standing on the bed the night before, her breasts and that scrap of a bra cupped in her hands. Her thumbs sneaking touches. He grew hard again just thinking about it. He liked her boldness. Both in and out of bed. She did what she wanted, and she made no apologies for it. He could go for that.

A soft noise slipped from her and he held his breath. He wasn't sure if he wanted her to wake and find him watching her, or if he wanted a few more uninterrupted minutes alone.

Her lips moved and she made a soft mewling sound, and then she settled back down.

It reminded him of the years he'd spent with Des.

Roni was nothing at all like his ex—which was a good thing. Terrific, actually. But he had enjoyed waking up with a woman during those days. Just like he enjoyed waking up and seeing Roni there now.

Her fingers moved against the mattress as if searching. They'd lost contact when he'd rolled to his side, but now they wiggled and shifted, not stopping until they once again touched his chest. She grew still, with the tips of those fingers planted firmly against his skin.

A band constricted around him at the intimacy of the moment.

Suddenly her arm stiffened and her eyelashes fluttered. Her eyes opened. She didn't speak, merely stared across the bed at him. Then a sexy smile slowly curved her mouth.

"Morning," she murmured. Her eyes were droopy with sleep, and he knew that she was the best thing he'd ever seen at five o'clock in the morning.

"Sleep well?" he asked.

"*Mmmm.* Not nearly enough." She yawned, covering her mouth with the hand that had been touching him, and rolled to her side.

Sadly, she tugged the sheet with her as she shifted so that both breasts were covered. It was a shame. "I'm not complaining, though."

He laughed lightly. "I hope not."

She grabbed a pillow and shoved it under her head so they both lay comfortably on their sides facing each other. Neither seemed to be in a hurry to change the moment, so he took the opportunity to ask a question he'd wondered about all week.

"Do you ever miss playing professionally?"

Her dark eyes popped wide in the darkened room. "Starting serious this morning, huh?"

He hadn't meant to, but he found himself wanting to know more about her. He'd enjoyed the few minutes they'd spent talking at the beach a couple nights ago. How he got into modeling had never been a secret, but rarely did someone look beyond the surface enough to ask.

He wanted to scratch her surface too.

"Avoiding the question?" he accused.

One shoulder gave a half shrug and she yawned again. "Maybe."

"Why?"

She didn't answer, but he could see her thinking about it. Her entire body grew tense.

"Okay"—he interrupted her thought process, suddenly worried the question would send her right out of his bed—"then how about this one? Tell me what it was like growing up the way you did. Traveling. Playing all over the world with your dad."

She blinked as if readjusting her thoughts, and melted back into the sheets. An easy look touched her features. "It was the best time of my life," she finally admitted.

He took her hand and held it between them on the bed. "Tell me," he urged.

So she did.

"I was six the first time he took me with him." Her mouth fell into that natural curve and her dark eyes warmed. "He came home from a month of being away and I ran immediately to the piano and played for him. I'd been practicing a new piece the whole time he'd been gone. Hours every day. I was so serious, I remember. And I tried my absolute best for him that day. I wanted him to be proud of me." Her lashes dipped and when she looked back at Lucas her eyes burned with pride. "He was. When I finished, he nodded and told Mom to pack me a bag. I jumped up on the bench and threw my arms around his neck. I was deliriously happy. Dad didn't hug a lot. But that day he did. His arms were like a vise around me," she said. She laughed lightly. "And then he told me to practice it again."

Lucas studied her in the dark. She still wore pride on her face, but there was something else mixed in too. A look that came with age, he supposed. Memories weren't always exactly the same when you looked back.

"Six is young," he pointed out. "Did that bother your mom?"

"A little, but she'd known this was coming. It was who Dad was." She paused for just a second and her top teeth sank into her lower lip. Then she dropped her gaze to their hands. "It was who I was too," she said softly. "I'd known I would be there beside him since the first day I sat at the piano."

He pulled their hands closer to his chest. "And that's what you wanted?"

She peeked at him from beneath her lashes and nodded. "That's what I wanted."

"I wish I could have known you then."

She twisted up her mouth. "You wouldn't have liked me. If you didn't play piano, I had zero time for you."

He laughed and pressed a kiss to her hand. "Tell me about the first night you performed. Do you remember it?"

"Duh," she said. "It was only the most important night of my life."

She shook her head and scrunched her shoulders up, and he saw that she went to a different place in her mind. A good place.

"I'd been bouncing with energy all day, getting on everyone's nerves. I couldn't believe I was finally going to be onstage with my dad." Her fingers moved under his hand. "Thrilled doesn't begin to describe it," she said. "I had on a gorgeous dress. It was black and sophisticated, but had the most beautiful lace covering it. It felt so girly. And my dad was really going to let me play with him. Then right before the concert started—I wasn't going on with Dad until later—I peeked out from behind the stage."

Her gaze locked on his. He could feel his heart pounding in his chest as he waited.

"I saw this huge crowd of people. More than I'd ever seen in my life. I almost started crying I was so petrified. All those people were going to see me play. And what if I messed up? Dad would be so upset." She swallowed. "Then the curtains opened and my dad stood there in front of them." Her gaze drifted away, and her voice lowered. "A gush of energy swept through that room," she murmured. "The noise level rose. People were clapping so hard I kept thinking that they had to be hurting their hands. And the smiles." She closed her eyes and let out a soft moan. "Oh my goodness, they were so glad to be there. Just to see my dad."

She stopped talking long enough to pull in a deep breath. She opened her eyes and rolled her lips together. A small line creased her forehead. "And then he sat down and put his hands on the keys, and I'd never seen a room go so quiet so fast."

Lucas didn't say a word. He was mesmerized by the look of amazement on her face.

"I'd never seen anything like it," she repeated. She returned her gaze to his. "They sat there, all their attention focused on him while he played. I would have sworn that not a single one of them moved."

"That's pretty hefty to witness as a kid."

"That was what I wanted." She didn't look away. "With every tiny fiber in my six-year-old body. I wanted those people looking at me the way they looked at Dad." She blinked. "The way they clapped for him again when he finished. I suddenly had a mission in my life, and it was to get that reaction."

Her passion echoed out of her as she lay there.

"Did you get it?" he asked.

She nodded. "I did. Maybe not quite as much that first night, but it was close. All my fear of playing in front of everyone vanished. I just wanted them to love me. And *ohmygod* they did." Her head shook back and forth. "It was powerful stuff, Lucas. I could suddenly understand why the piano was the most important thing in my dad's life."

He couldn't help but wonder if that meant the piano came before her too.

"I love that energy," she whispered. "It gets me going."

He nodded. He'd seen that Monday morning, but he didn't admit it to her. "You also just love playing."

She grinned. "Oh God, yes, I just love playing. I started when I was three. It came naturally."

"Bet you put the other preschoolers to shame," he teased.

The soft sound of her laughter reeled him in deeper. He wanted to be inside her, both physically and mentally.

"I'll admit I wasn't the other kids' favorite person," she said. She rolled to her back and picked up his hand, holding it above her stomach while tracing the edges of his fingers with hers. "When it was free time, I always wanted to play the piano. Fortunately for me, the teachers loved it. But unfortunately for the others, I think it got old fast."

He weaved his fingers between hers. "I can picture you at that age. Thinking they must all be crazy, and continuing to play despite them."

She chuckled. One side of her mouth twitched up sarcastically. "Pretty much."

"Your parents divorced at some point, right?" He changed the subject to something else he'd wondered about, and ignored the little voice pecking away inside that asked him what he was doing. Sex. Fun. Easy. Not *what makes you* you? "Did that interrupt your travels?"

"No." Roni shook her head, a faraway look sweeping across her face. With her free hand, she continued drawing small patterns on the back of his. "I remember we came home so Mom and Dad could go before the judge to finalize it. There were a couple arguments while we were home, of course. They were arguing a lot by that time. But then the next day we were back out on the road. We didn't miss a concert."

"How old were you?"

"Eight."

"And you continued as you had been at that point? Traveling with him?" He couldn't imagine doing that as a child. It seemed like all the travel would force a kid to grow up way too fast. Plus, children needed mothers. Especially girls. They needed a woman around.

"I traveled with Dad and my tutor," Roni said, pulling his head back from places it didn't need to go. "I didn't go to regular schools because I was on the road so much, so my tutor went with us. And I didn't see Mom and Danny as often, anymore, either. I was pretty much raised by my dad."

She didn't sound sad by the fact, but he could see it in her eyes nonetheless. She'd missed them.

"Danny is your brother?"

She nodded.

"How often did you see them?" His tone was barely a whisper in the room.

She shifted her gaze to his and studied him for a minute before answering. "I went home several long weekends during the year, but

I got summers off. Mom, my brother, and I would spend those weeks here."

"On the island?"

She nodded again. "I actually met my best friends here. Mom always liked the beach so it became our tradition. Danny liked it too, but not as much as the two of us. We would hit the road almost the minute I arrived in Huntsville each summer. I think it was her way of trying to give me something special. Like she thought she needed to compete with Dad."

"But she didn't?"

Dark eyes studied his. Sad. Lonely. "Never," she whispered.

He inched a foot over until his big toe touched the arch of her foot. "Your friends?" he asked. "Are you still close to them?"

"Very." She scooted her hip closer. Absently, as if she didn't realize she was doing it. Then she slid her leg over the top of his, tucking her toes in under his calf. Heat coiled around him where she touched him, then oozed up and over his body, spreading to cover him like a sheet, warm from the dryer.

"And your brother?" he asked. His voice had tightened a fraction.

Her eyelashes swooped lazily down over her eyes, and her face softened, her smile became wistful. "He's as annoying as ever."

Ah, she loved her brother. He'd like to meet the man who gave her that tender look.

"How about your mom?" he asked. They were lying there, smiling and holding hands, their legs now intertwined, but the atmosphere had shifted. It was thicker. More serious. More intimate. He wanted to pull her close and hug her tight. He wanted to scrub away the memories of all the hurts. "Are you still close to her?"

Roni nodded, but it was a slow, deliberate movement, and her expression flattened a bit.

"Not as much as I'd like," she finally admitted.

Lucas's chest squeezed as he watched the emotions flicker across her face.

"But I will be seeing her soon," Roni offered. She shot him another smile, this one a bit forced, but it was real enough. "My brother and I always go home for Christmas. I look forward to it every year."

"I'm glad," he said. He was close with his family, and the holidays were special for them too. It pleased him to know Roni had that in her life, even if it wasn't perfect.

Roni suddenly went still. She didn't say anything, merely lay there, staring up at him. Watching him. Her thick lashes framing almost-black eyes and her mouth with that slight tilt to the corners. And he felt like he'd been cut open and was being dissected.

It took all the control he had not to look away.

"We are keeping this casual?" Her words came out quick. "Right?"

He swallowed. "Of course." Though he still had that urge to pull her close and offer nothing more than a hug.

"Because you had a look about you," she said.

"No look." He shook his head. He hadn't had a look.

Nor a thought of wanting to take care of her.

He had enough to take care of.

She watched him a few seconds longer and then her eyes narrowed the slightest amount as if she considered questioning his statement. But then the moment passed and she inched closer. He couldn't help but notice that the sheet slipped as she moved. The tiny silver barbell now winked out at him.

He gulped and lost his train of thought completely.

"It's my turn," she said.

He nodded. Whatever she wanted.

She shifted back to her side and pulled her hand from his. She pressed it to his chest and immediately started exploring. "Tell me about modeling," she said. "It put you through school, I know, but why do you continue to do it?"

The tips of her fingers scorched him. She circled a nipple with her nail, then dragged a fingertip through the hair and down the middle of his chest. He sucked in a breath and watched her actions, trying valiantly not to let all the blood leave his brain.

He failed.

"You're making it hard to concentrate," he told her.

"I can't help it. I like touching you."

He crushed her hand in his before it dipped under the sheet. "Ditto," he growled out. "But did you want an answer to your question or did you want me back inside you?"

Her eyes darkened, and he almost lost the fight when her tongue peeked out to touch her lips. "Can't I have both?" she asked.

He nodded slowly. The truth was, she could have anything she wanted. Which was not a good thing at all. And was not exactly in line with keeping this light.

"I do it for the charities," he blurted. He gripped her hand tighter when she tried to touch him again. "And because I enjoy it. I get to see new places, meet new people. It's never boring."

She grinned. "You probably enjoy the women throwing themselves at you like I did."

He'd had his share of hookups over the years, it was true. But they were few and far between these days. Plus, he'd discovered that that way of living was losing its luster. He wanted something deeper.

And he wanted someone who saw that need in him. Not just someone who saw his body.

But he wouldn't admit that out loud.

"The hookups get me through," he said casually. He released her hand and reached for her. His fingers circled the weight of her breast, squeezing gently, and he smiled at the hitch in her breath. He rolled his thumb over her piercing. "Some better than others," he murmured.

She glazed over as he tugged at her. He'd had plenty of time to test things out the night before, and he'd learned how sensitive she was and how she best liked to be touched. He tried to do that for her now.

"What other questions?" he asked hoarsely.

Brown eyes studied him through lowered lids before she said, "Why the Leukemia Foundation?"

His fingers stilled. He hadn't been expecting that question.

"I've had experience with it in my family," he answered. He wanted to tell her about it, about the fear that had lived inside him. That sometimes still flared back alive. But that wasn't what this was about. Casual hookups didn't discuss cancer.

"I'm sorry," Roni said solemnly. "I hope things turned out okay."

Things could have been a lot worse. "It left a lasting impact, is all."

Enough talking. He grabbed a condom and rolled under the covers until he was on top of her. She was warm and soft and she immediately opened her legs so he could slip between them.

"Anything else you want to know that can't wait?" He propped himself on his elbows to look down at her. He adored the wild curls framing her face.

She shook her head.

"Good." Ripping open the packet, he lowered his hand to put the condom on. Then he dipped his mouth and pulled against her nipple. "Because I'm about to show you how much I've missed being inside you since I was last there."

A low giggle sounded deep in her throat, easing the heaviness that had settled in the room. "Since three hours ago?"

He curled a lock of hair around his finger, taking in her disheveled look and her parted lips. And reminded himself to keep it light.

"Three hours was far too long to wait," he murmured.

He plucked at her nipple again, and then without another word, slipped deep inside her.

CHAPTER FIFTEEN

Two hours later, steam from her shower filled the hotel bathroom as Roni brushed her teeth with the packaged toothbrush she'd found in the amenities basket. She stood naked in front of the fogged mirror, and wondered briefly if she could entice Lucas into the room for one more go. They could see how that big shower worked with two people in it.

But no, he was busy, and she needed to get home. She had her routine to keep. And she was already behind schedule.

She hadn't meant to fall back asleep after they'd finished earlier, and when she'd awoken for the second time, she'd discovered that Lucas had not had that problem. He was showered and shaved, and had been sitting at the desk, working at his laptop.

Not ready to open the door yet and leave her private cocoon, she grabbed a hand towel and wiped a circle of fog from the mirror. Then she made a face at her reflection. Her hair was going to be a mess without her defrizzer. Even better would be if she had her flat iron. But she detested the thing. She preferred the curls, yet felt that for special occasions she should at least try to look more polished.

She dug her fingers into the curls and plumped, knowing that no matter what she did, she would still look less than flattering.

What better way to do the walk of shame through a hotel lobby than with wild hair and last night's clothes?

She pinched her cheeks to try to add some color and then remembered that she had lipstick in her purse. And maybe a mascara. At least she might not scare people as she slunk down to catch a cab.

Grabbing the hotel robe from the back of the door, she slid her arms through the sleeves, but didn't bother belting it. No reason to be modest at this point. She cracked open the door and peeked out. No Lucas, but she did hear the sound of computer keys clicking from the small living room. He was still at work.

As she searched for her purse, she realized that last night's clothes were now draped over the back of a chair. Her clothes. His were nowhere to be found. Apparently the man didn't like sex-discarded clothing loitering up the place.

She tiptoed to the chair and dug into her purse, pulling out a lipstick, mascara, and a wide-toothed comb she'd forgotten she had in there. Then she saw the blinking green light on her phone. She pressed the button to see that she'd missed a text.

It was from Andie. And it had come in only ten minutes earlier.

I hear you're sleeping with a contestant.

Ah, geez.

Roni gathered her items, tucked her purse back where she found it, then snuck a quick glance around the open doorway. Lucas was still at the desk, head tilted slightly down, and appeared to be hard at work. He'd explained that though he was here for the contest, he wasn't actually on vacation. He had a deadline to get a project turned in so he got up early each morning to work.

She liked that kind of dedication. It reminded her of her years on the road. Just because you'd had a full day of travel didn't mean you slept in if there was work to be done.

And it had seemed like there was always work to be done. Let yourself slide, and suddenly you're number two in the world instead of number one. She didn't like number two.

With one last look at Lucas and a longing look at the bed, she snuck back to the bathroom and closed the door soundlessly behind her. Once inside, she let everything but her phone tumble from her hands to the counter. She wasn't going to text Andie back. If her friend was up, Roni wanted to talk.

Yes, she'd just had sex with a contestant.

And yes, she intended to do it again.

Thirty seconds later the phone was answered in Boston and Roni sat on the edge of the tub and grinned as if she knew the secret to instantaneous orgasms. "He's six-two," she started, "a body begging to be explored, and he understands the word *foreplay*."

Though this morning had been more talk than foreplay, but it wasn't as if she hadn't been ready for him.

"Oh. My. Stars!" Andie's voice burst through the phone. "Ginger called me and got me out of bed this morning to tell me you didn't go home last night."

"Ginger called?" Roni pulled the phone away to look at it. "Not Kayla? Wait . . ." She shoved the phone back to her ear. "How did Ginger know I wasn't at home?"

Not that it was that wild of a guess after the way the man had danced for her last night.

"She went by there on her way to the dock and knocked on your door."

"And what if she'd woken me up?"

Roni could picture Andie shrugging in unconcern. "Apparently she was going to give you a hard time if you had gone home last night instead of going with that tall drink of water. *Ohmygod* Roni, is he really as good as she says?"

"So much so, you'd consider dumping Mark for him yourself," Roni assured her.

"I doubt—"

"You would." Roni interrupted. "You may not do it, but you'd consider it. And he's not just hot, he has a personality. He's nice." She glanced up in the mirror that was no longer fogged and looked at the stupid smile she couldn't seem to remove from her face. "He's fun."

"Most men you hook up with are fun," Andie pointed out. Not that Roni was always hooking up with people, but yeah, she tried to find the ones who weren't dull.

"Okay," Roni agreed, "but I can't stop . . ." What? Wanting more? Wanting to sidle up next to him and hang on until he pried her loose? "I don't know. He just makes me feel good to be around him. I can tell he enjoys life. I like that."

"I can tell," Andie muttered. She went quiet, then her next words were spoken carefully. "So . . . is this . . . something?"

"No." Roni answered quickly, shaking her head as she did. She looked in the mirror again. She was still smiling. "Of course not. It's just fun."

"It's just a lot of fun," Andie said.

Roni snickered. "Exactly. *A. Lot.*"

Andie guffawed and Roni could tell she'd gotten her meaning.

"Oh my God." Andie was laughing so hard Roni had a hard time understanding her. "Do tell. No wait. Don't. Mark is out of town right now and I don't want to have to—"

"You are so out of control." Roni grinned even wider as she remembered lying in her bed a couple nights ago, thinking about Lucas. Time to change the subject! "How are you?" she asked. "How is everything? Life still good as Mrs. Kavanaugh?" They usually talked at least once a week and often e-mailed in between. But that didn't mean Roni didn't miss her friend like crazy.

"Terrific. How's the contest going? Kayla says it's good, but she sounds like she's about to snap in two."

"She is," Roni agreed. She stood and took three steps to the other side of the room before turning back. "She's also ready to beat me for coming back to the hotel with Lucas last night. I had to promise her you wouldn't fire her."

"Of course I won't fire her."

"I know. She thinks either you or the committee will. Thinks my sleeping with a contestant . . ." Roni let her words fall off. She found herself cringing, nervous that Andie *would* have a problem with it, even though they'd just been talking about the man as if he were a top-grade side of beef.

"I know that Kayla is professional," Andie said. "And I know you are too. You wouldn't do anything to hurt us."

Roni plopped back down on the side of the tub. "Thank goodness," she breathed out.

"You thought it would bother me?"

"No." She shook her head. She'd just been *afraid* it would, she supposed. She didn't want to have to stop. "Never mind. Tell me what's going on with you. We miss you."

"I miss you guys too. And Mom and Aunt Ginny." Andie paused and seemed to hold her breath for a long second. "So I'm coming down next weekend," she finished quickly.

"What?" Roni stood from her perch on the tub once again. "Really?"

"For the parade. I can't wait."

"Ah." Roni nodded. Her eye caught on something she hadn't noticed before and she tilted her head as she studied it. "So you'll get here in time to see the men before they leave," she murmured, her mind already somewhere else. "I think your true colors are coming out, my dear."

Happy laughter rang through the phone and made Roni smile once more. She was so glad Andie and Mark had worked out their differences. She'd never seen two people so perfect for each other.

"I'm definitely coming before those men get out of town. I may be married, but I'm not dead." Andie talked a couple more minutes, filling her in on what was going on in Boston, and about her latest philanthropic efforts with her mother-in-law, while Roni studied Lucas's toiletries to the left of the sink.

She had no idea how she'd missed that before.

There wasn't a lot there. Shaving cream, a razor, cologne, toothpaste. And a handful of other essentials that could come in handy on a long trip. Nothing out of the ordinary.

Except how they were all lined up across the vanity.

Like little army men, they stood one by one in single file. Tallest to shortest.

What person was this organized? Then she remembered the papers she'd caught sight of on Lucas's desk as she'd been talking to him before she'd come in to take a shower. There had been no less than three lists at his work area. All handwritten with precise penmanship. And then there were the clothes laid carefully over the back of the chair.

The man was a neat freak.

This tidbit made her smile turn wide. And then into a laugh.

"What is it?" Andie asked.

Roni laughed even more. Lucas Alexander, the sexiest guy she'd ever met. The man who'd worked muscles in her last night that she'd forgotten existed, was a neat freak.

He lined up his toiletries!

She picked up his cologne and smelled it, and heat stroked through her at the rich scent of spices and warmth. It made her want to grab Lucas and drag him back to bed.

"Roni?" Andie got her attention. "What's so funny?"

"I found his quirk," Roni said.

She set the cologne back on the counter exactly as it had been. It wasn't like she was a slob, but now she almost wished she'd agreed to go back to her place the night before. As a rule, she didn't take men to her house. However, being that she hadn't really cleaned in the last couple of weeks, she would've liked to have seen Lucas's response to her sink full of dirty dishes. He probably would have either run from her house or started doing them himself.

The idea of it was cute, actually.

Lucas being too anal to just let loose.

Though the man did know how to let loose in the bedroom.

"I've got to go," she told Andie. "I've got to tease him about this. I'll send you a picture."

They said their good-byes and she snapped a photo of the army-men toiletries and sent it to Andie. Then she went in search of Lucas.

Before she made it to the living room, though, she heard him talking. She paused, wondering if another person had come into the room, but then registered from the lower, more intimate tone that he was most likely on the phone.

"I drew you a picture."

Roni paused at the clearly audible sound of a child's voice.

"Will you save it for me?" Lucas asked. "I have the perfect spot just waiting for it on the fridge."

Childlike giggles erupted through the room. "Daddy. You're so silly. The fridge is already covered with my pictures."

Roni felt as if all the blood had drained from her body. She froze to the floor. *Daddy?*

She swallowed against a dry mouth and looked around as if in a panic. Daddy?

"Guess what?" the kid asked from the other room.

"What?"

Oh . . . my . . .

Roni's insides roiled. She pressed a hand to her stomach and then looked down. She was still wearing the robe, but it wasn't tied around her. Her hand was on her bare skin.

She snatched at the sash, missed, and had to force herself to slow down and do it again. Then she tied the ends together and jerked them tight around her.

Lucas had a kid?

Lucas had a kid!

"We found the dog, Daddy," said the voice in both a pleading and awestruck kind of tone. "The one I love and want forever."

Roni stepped carefully to the door and leaned forward slowly.

"Gracie," Lucas used what Roni recognized as a "Dad voice." "We've talked about this. Remember? We aren't sure you're ready for a dog yet."

Roni peeked.

Lucas was still at his desk, his back to her, but he wasn't on a speakerphone as she'd assumed. He was on his laptop. On a video chat. And on the other end of that connection was one of the cutest little girls Roni had ever seen.

Young, maybe four or five. Brown hair, huge blue eyes.

The hair was shorter than Roni's, but the curls were about as wild. And she looked just like Lucas.

"I am." Those curls bobbed up and down now. "I promise. Grandma got me a movie about it and ever'thing. I learneded how to take them for walks and make them poop. And how to pick up the poop in the purple poopie bags."

Roni almost laughed as a vivid picture of her two nephews popped to mind. Apparently saying *poop* over and over wasn't solely a male thing.

"Can we discuss this later? After I get back home?" Lucas asked. Roni could see the frustration in the stiffness of his shoulders, but he was careful to keep it out of his voice. She suddenly knew without hearing anything further that he was a good father. She pressed the heel of her hand to her chest.

"Okay," the little girl said. "But I'm gonna watch the movie again while I wait."

"That sounds like a good plan. Make sure you're good for Grandma today," he told her.

The pressure in Roni's chest increased. She'd once wanted a kid so badly.

She'd come so close.

"Okay, Daddy." The little girl's voice penetrated through the cloud of pain. "I'll be good. I promise. I already have been. You can ask her."

"I believe you, sweetheart. You're always good, aren't you?"

Curls bobbed again.

Fire burned in the back of Roni's throat. Life wasn't fair sometimes.

"Daddy, who's that in your room?"

Roni's gaze flew to Lucas's as he jerked his head around and looked over his shoulder. A scowl covered his features before he quickly wiped it from his face. "It's . . . a friend of mine, baby. She's . . ."

Roni watched the indecision flash through his eyes. Why had she stepped around that corner?

"She's playing the piano for the contest I'm doing." He turned back to his daughter. "You remember I said I was here for a contest? And she's really good."

Innocent blue eyes grew wide and round and the girl sucked in a dramatic breath. "I love the piano, Daddy."

Lucas nodded. "I know. Maybe I can get her to show me how to play something and I'll come home and show you."

The small face grew larger on screen until it took up the whole thing. "Could she come here and show me how to play?"

Roni's heart thumped hard. She should just leave. She didn't need to see Lucas's kid.

"I don't think—"

"I have my own piano." The words were spoken a bit too loud, as if the child were no longer speaking to Lucas, but trying to talk around him.

Roni peeked back up. She'd dropped her gaze to the ground. Lucas was watching her again, this time with an odd expression on his face.

"Did my Daddy tell you? I haf my own piano, but I haven't got the lessons yet. What's your name?"

Fear kept Roni's feet from moving. She wanted to run, but Lucas was watching her. He nodded his head just the slightest amount toward the laptop. As if suggesting to Roni that she should speak to his daughter.

She opened her mouth and moved her lips but nothing came out.

"Her name is Roni." Lucas scooted back so that he wasn't between the computer and Roni and motioned in introduction. "Roni, this is Gracie."

Roni's throat squeezed shut as if someone were choking her. She shifted her gaze back to Lucas and he nodded once again toward the computer.

The smile she forced to her face felt brittle. "Hello, Gracie," she eked out. She cleared her throat and tried to wipe the panic from her voice. "It's nice to meet you."

The child's face bounced up and down. "I love meeting Daddy's friends. The boys at his work think I'm cute. He doesn't work with much girls though."

Did that mean he just didn't introduce his daughter to girls? Yet he hadn't turned the computer away when Gracie had seen her. Heck, he could have said she was a maid. End of discussion.

But he hadn't.

Roni took a step toward the desk.

Gracie's head bobbed again. "Could you teach me to play the piano? Daddy gots me one for my birthday, but I don't know how to play."

Roni looked at Lucas then. He wore a chagrined expression, as if he'd been caught lacking as a father. "How about I talk to your Dad? Maybe I can help him find someone to teach you to play."

"Will you?" Her words were breathless again. "Then I'll show my new puppy how to play too."

"Gracie," Lucas butted in. "We're going to talk about the dog situation after I get home."

"Okay, Daddy." Gracie turned her blue eyes back to Roni. "I love *Lady and the Tramp*," she said. "It's my favoritist movie. I'm going to name my dog Lady."

A chuckle escaped Roni at the miserable look on Lucas's face. If she had to guess, the man was soon going to own a dog.

"Do you have a dog?" the girl asked. The child certainly wasn't shy.

"I don't. Because they're a whole bunch of responsibility. And I'm not sure I'm ready yet." There. Maybe that would help.

The small face in front of her—Roni glanced around and realized that she was now standing within feet of the computer—scrunched up in concentration. "Does your Daddy not let you have one either?"

Oh geez, this child was too precious.

"Gracie," Lucas cut in again. He swung back around so Gracie could see him more clearly, which put his shoulder resting flush against Roni's hip. "How about you say good-bye to Miss Roni, now? Okay? It's time for Grandma to get you your breakfast."

An older lady suddenly appeared behind Gracie. She had the same blue eyes.

Roni's pulse fluttered in her throat. Lucas's mom was staring at her. In his hotel room. While she talked to his daughter.

How had this happened?

The next couple of minutes passed in a haze. Roni thought she said good-bye to Gracie, but she couldn't be sure, and then Lucas swiveled around in his chair and looked up at her.

She turned and fled to the other room.

"Roni, come on." Lucas said behind her.

By the time he caught her in the bedroom, she was working furiously, trying desperately to shimmy into her jeans. The sides of the robe kept getting in her way and she shoved at them so she could see to fasten her pants.

Lucas held out his hand. "Come sit with me. Let's talk."

She took a step back. "You have a kid," she said, stating the obvious.

He nodded slowly as if to a child. "I do."

Roni bit down on the inside of her jaw. Now that the call had been disconnected, the confusion had flooded back in. She didn't get involved with men who had kids. "I don't understand," she whispered.

They were supposed to just be having fun. An easy, casual thing. A fling.

But he had a kid.

How did someone with a kid do casual? Or did they?

"Her mother isn't in her life. She and I never married," Lucas explained patiently. He held out his hand again. "Let's talk."

He was not only a dad, but a single father, raising his kid alone. *Sonofagun*. He was going to make her want more without doing anything but being a good guy.

Roni shook her head when he took another step toward her. She could feel her hair swishing back and forth, her damp curls brushing against her cheeks. "I need to go."

"We need to talk."

"No. I need . . ." Crap, she didn't know what she needed. She shot her gaze around the room, not seeing anything that made sense. Could she reverse the last twelve hours? No, thirty-six. She should never have gone outside with him at Gin's the other night. Wait. The kiss. She shouldn't have kissed him under the deck.

Oh, geez.

"Roni," Lucas's tone was a mix of stern and pleading. "It's just a daughter. It doesn't change anything here."

"I know." But that wasn't true. She lifted a hand toward her face but didn't know what to do with it so it just hung there. She saw him differently now. He wasn't just a good time. He was a dad. "I've got to go."

"We'll talk tonight," he told her.

She stared at him, at the solemn look on his face, and wondered why she'd ever thought he was the carefree type. When she'd met him, he'd been working so hard he'd tuned out anything and everything around him. When she'd ignored him after they kissed, instead of moving on to the next girl, he'd patiently sought her out.

And he lived in a subdivision, for crying out loud.

All the signs had been there.

Her chest ached as if it was being crushed. These were not the habits of a carefree guy.

"Tonight," he reiterated. "After we finish at the convention center. We'll talk then."

She nodded. She supposed they should talk. But she needed some time to think first. Time to grieve the ending of a really hot fling. "Okay. We'll talk tonight."

No way were they going to talk tonight. Every time she got alone with him she found herself with diarrhea of the mouth. She didn't trust herself not to open up and tell him even more about herself. Or ask even more about him.

But neither of those things needed to happen because they were done. He had a kid.

And she didn't.

"Nothing here has to change," he repeated.

"I got that."

She grabbed the remainder of her clothes from where they were draped over the chair and hurried to the bathroom. It was probably ridiculous to cut a wide berth around him, but that didn't stop her from doing it.

She closed herself up in the room and leaned back against the door, her clothes held tight to her chest. She stared at the toiletries, glanced at the shower, where she'd already made plans to have her way with him next, then closed her eyes and pictured the fair skin and fine brown curls of his daughter.

He was wrong.

Everything here had changed.

Because seeing Gracie had cracked open a hole she'd superglued shut three years ago.

CHAPTER SIXTEEN

C an you believe they have us milking goats?"

Lucas ignored Kelly's words. He wasn't in the mood to talk. Hadn't been all day.

They were standing slightly apart from the rest of the group while two other contestants made their way through the gladiator-type course, heading for the goats at the end.

Kelly stood next to him, leaned back against the barn with his arms crossed over his chest, leg bent at the knee, and his foot propped on the weathered wood beside his other knee. Stick a cowboy hat on him and a piece of straw between his teeth and he'd be the picture of a romance book hero.

Lucas stood, arms locked over his chest, scowling at the ground. The brooding hero, he supposed.

More like the pissed-off reject.

Roni was avoiding him again.

He knew this though they hadn't made it to the end of the day yet, at which time they were supposed to have a talk. Not for a single second had she looked his way throughout the morning . . . and now, not throughout the afternoon. Furthermore, he suspected that, come the end of the evening, she would be nowhere to be found.

He wanted to go to her and demand she talk to him. Now.

He couldn't get the picture out of his mind of her practically running from his bedroom, as if the sight of his daughter was the most nauseating thing she'd ever seen.

"They'd better not ask us to drink it, is all I'm saying." Kelly muttered.

Again, Lucas ignored him.

And really. The look on Roni's face had been more disgust than anything.

It was a daughter, for heaven's sake. Not a two-headed cow he was keeping in his bedroom as a pet.

And then that escape attempt she'd tried to maneuver after she'd come back out of the bathroom. A low growl came from the back of his throat. She'd intended to run out of his hotel room and not even let him take her home. He didn't do things that way.

"Now if *that* was at the end of the course . . ." Kelly spoke under his breath. "I would have no problem doing *whatever* she asked."

Lucas lifted his head from staring at his boots. "What are you rattling about now?"

But Kelly didn't have to answer. Lucas saw what he was talking about. Roni stood about fifty feet away, her back to them.

Her arms were propped across the top rung of a fence, one foot hooked on a lower slat, and the position pulled her shirt snug across her back so that the slope of her body and dip at the base of her spine was molded perfectly under the material. Below the shirt was another amazing pair of jeans. Almost as good as the ones he'd peeled off of her the night before.

"I'm just saying," Kelly added, "that if she needed milking . . ."

Lucas slowly turned his head to his friend. He lowered his arms to his sides and clenched his fists. He'd known Kelly a long time, and didn't want to kill a friendship by breaking the other man's pretty nose.

If the man didn't rely on his nose to get him jobs, however . . .

"You might want to lay off," Lucas spoke slow and careful, his tone menacing.

Kelly merely smiled. "That's what I thought," he said.

"*What* is what you thought?" Irritation seeped in with the anger that had been steadily building all day.

"You and the piano player."

Lucas eyed his friend.

"After the dancing last night, I can't say I'm surprised. But I am impressed."

Three breaths in and out didn't help matters much. "So what? You think it's your turn next?"

Kelly laughed loud enough that Roni peeked at them over her shoulder. When Lucas met her gaze, she quickly turned back around.

"No, you idiot," Kelly stated. He pushed off the side of the barn and stood straight, feet shoulder-width apart. "And even if I wanted to head down that road, I don't want to take you on. That would get ugly for both of us." He jabbed Lucas in the arm. "But I do want to hear about it. I mean, other than from some loser at the bar."

Lucas came away from the barn himself. "What are you talking about?"

"The idiot valet. He came into the hotel bar last night after he was off the clock. He was too young to buy a drink, but that didn't stop him from standing around, running his mouth about how one of the "older" contestants and a cute, short sexy thing had been all over each other. I suspected Roni, given how short she is, and your ugly mug came to mind when he mentioned an old man. Plus, I knew it wouldn't be long before you'd at least *try* to get some of that."

Lucas stared at his friend, his mood not improving. Might have known the jerk valet would embellish things to make it even worse. "We were *not* all over each other," Lucas muttered. "What else did he say?"

Kelly smirked. "That you couldn't stand straight when you got out of the car."

The first smile Lucas had produced since that morning cracked over his lips. "That part was true."

"Heard a couple murmurs this morning, too, that she'd been seen heading through the lobby on the way out the door. Said you were barely keeping up with her, she was moving so fast. What happened? She wake up and realize what she'd done?"

Lucas smirked. "No, you jackass. She woke up and wanted more."

Before she'd run.

He went silent as he thought about the conversation they'd had in the quiet of the morning. He'd enjoyed the moments of talking, had enjoyed hearing about her years with her dad. He still didn't get how she'd just walked away from that.

Then she'd asked if they were being casual. As if to make sure he remembered the rules.

Of course they were being casual.

He didn't bring women into Gracie's life. If her own mother wouldn't stay, why would anyone else?

"What is it?" Kelly asked.

It may have been a couple years since the two of them had spent a lot of time together, but that didn't mean he and Kelly weren't still good enough friends to know when the other was working through a situation.

Lucas lifted his shoulders and rolled them toward his back, stretching out his joints until they popped. He twisted his neck in a similar fashion, then faced his longtime friend.

"She saw Gracie," he admitted.

Kelly's easy manner disappeared in an instant. "Gracie is here? Is she okay?"

"No. I mean, Roni *found out* about her. Well, no, she saw her. Talked to her. Through Skype."

"She talked to her?"

Lucas nodded. He felt sick to his stomach. He looked across the field to where Roni remained, her back and cute ass still facing their direction. He'd never let a woman he'd slept with talk to his daughter. "Gracie called this morning and I was talking to her . . ." He paused, silently chiding himself for not getting off the call sooner. Even worse was his encouraging conversation between the two. "I didn't hear Roni come out of the shower."

Kelly's gaze scrutinized Lucas. "And what? The two just struck up a conversation?"

"Not at first. But then Gracie saw her standing on the other side of the room." Lucas shrugged as if it had been out of his hands at that point. He could have lied about who Roni was. He should have turned the computer away. "You know how Gracie can be."

Kelly nodded. From the minute Gracie had learned to talk, she hadn't figured out how to stop. She could ask nonstop questions for hours on end. And if she wasn't asking questions, she was sharing things. Like, "I want a dog," "I have a piano," or "My dad hasn't gotten me piano lessons yet."

Which was simply because she was too young. He probably shouldn't have bought her the piano.

Only, she'd been through so much. He'd wanted to give her whatever she'd asked for. And of the two things she'd requested for her birthday—a piano and a mother—the piano was the one he could manage.

"What did they say to each other?" Kelly asked.

Lucas closed his eyes as he replayed the few minutes his daughter had been talking to Roni. Roni had been hesitant to speak with her at first. In fact, she'd looked terrified at the thought of it. But then she'd moved across the room and come closer. And then she'd smiled.

His stomach turned into a hard knot.

As Gracie had been going on and on about wanting a dog, Roni had eased into the moment. She'd appeared to be enjoying herself.

And she'd looked at his daughter as if Gracie had mattered. As if she was just a normal kid.

A kid anyone could love.

Then she'd run from the room and accused him of being a father in such a way as to imply the fact could start a chain reaction that would lead to the end of the world as they knew it.

"Lucas?" Kelly nudged his elbow into Lucas's, bringing him back from the recesses of his mind. "What happened? Did you tell her about the leukemia?"

Lucas jerked back. "Of course I didn't tell her about the leukemia. That isn't who Gracie is. It doesn't define her."

"I didn't mean it did. I was just . . ." Kelly stopped talking and held up his hands.

Kelly and his wife, Becky, had been the ones who'd been there for him during the worst of it. As well as Lucas's parents. Chemo was not an easy thing for anyone. It was brutal.

Kelly scrubbed a hand across his jaw and wore an apologetic grimace. "You looked like something had happened," he finally said. "Leukemia was just a guess."

Lucas shook his head. "I don't tell people about that."

Hell, as a rule, he didn't tell people about Gracie. Period. Not the people in his modeling world.

And certainly not out-of-town hookups.

He shook his head again, aware that the time he'd spent with Roni had felt suspiciously like more than an out-of-town hookup. He wanted to simply be in the same room with her—whether she was ignoring him or not. He wanted to make her smile, to wipe away the faint sadness he occasionally caught in her eyes.

He wanted to kiss her.

He wanted to know why his daughter scared her to death.

Focusing on her now, his eyes traced over the outline she made against the fence. She appeared casual and relaxed, as if she were enjoying herself. But he noted how her elbows were tucked in front of her on the fence and her arms crossed tight over each other, each hand grasping the opposite elbow. Also, she stood by herself, away from everyone else.

She was tiny to begin with, but he realized that she often made herself even more so.

As if she felt alone.

Was she lonely?

A spot burned inside him and began to spread.

He ran a hand through his hair. *He* was lonely.

"Of course I didn't tell her," he grumbled. He forced himself to take his eyes off Roni. "She'll never meet Gracie, anyway. So it doesn't matter."

"Are you sure?"

Lucas stared at his friend, unblinking, as a question flashed through his mind as clear as if it were painted in bright neon red. Could he let Roni meet Gracie in person?

No.

But his blood surged through him so quickly, so fiercely, that he felt as if his insides trembled with the gush.

He shook his head. No. He couldn't introduce his . . . whatever Roni was . . . to his daughter. It wasn't right. He didn't do that. But at the same time, more questions spun through his head.

What if he did?

Would Gracie become too attached if a "friend" happened to stop by?

Would his mother look at him like she knew what he was up to? Would she be disappointed in him if she did?

He glanced once more at Roni.

Could he even talk her into a trip to Dallas?

Before he could figure out the answer to any of the questions, a goat screamed, the noise sounding disturbingly human, and both men cringed. They looked at the pen where one of the guys was sitting on a stool beside the animal. His partner was trying to explain how to milk the goat, and apparently the process was not going well. Nor were the goat's rear legs shy about kicking.

Lucas shifted his gaze to the woman chosen for him today. She was twenty-five, looked about fifteen, and stood with the other women in a clump on the other side of the pen. The women had been shown how to milk the animals earlier in the day, while the guys hadn't been allowed in the barn. When it came time to do the deed, the women had to talk the men through it. They couldn't show them, and they couldn't help them. Only explain with words.

The goat kicked out once again and the metal bucket underneath the frustrated animal rolled to its side. The thin dribble of milk that had managed to be retrieved trailed in a narrow path over the rim and dropped to the dirt below.

Kelly wore a grin. "Twenty bucks says he's done tonight."

"I am *not* taking that bet," Lucas said.

The goat kicked once more, then got away from the contestant. They'd apparently forgotten to secure her collar to the platform.

The owner stepped in to retrieve the animal and the moment passed. Lucas found himself standing shoulder to shoulder with Kelly, neither man talking. He wanted to explain how he'd watched Roni and Gracie that morning, and how he'd found himself wanting more. How he'd worried every day for the last three years that Gracie didn't have a mom to grow up with.

She had a grandmother. That's the reason Lucas had moved back to Dallas. He wanted his daughter to grow up close to her grandparents, but more importantly, to at least have one female influence in her life.

But as he'd watched Roni standing in a bathrobe, her hair wet and cheeks flushed, talking to his daughter . . . for the first time he'd admitted to himself that he wanted more. More for himself. And more for Gracie.

It didn't mean he could get it.

But he wanted it.

"She's pretty special," Kelly said.

Lucas had no idea if he meant Gracie or Roni. Didn't matter. The answer was the same.

He nodded as he watched Roni raise her hands and clap for the poor guy who'd finally gotten a decent stream of milk coming from the goat. "Yeah," he said. Something tightened behind his ribs. "She is."

CHAPTER SEVENTEEN

Roni clutched at the catch in her side as she ran. She focused her gaze on the back of her house in the distance, and refused to slow though the pain was growing unbearable. Her breathing came in gasps. She dug her feet in and pushed harder.

The ocean glistened to her right, its calm waters shining under the cloudless blue sky and bright sun. The wind weaved softly through the tufts of weeds in the dunes on her left. It was Saturday morning. It was a beautiful day.

Lady Antebellum blasted through her earbuds.

Life was good.

Yet Roni ran as if her past were a mere two steps behind her.

Her fingers intermittently worked the area at her waist that threatened to bend her in two. She counted her steps as she ran to concentrate on anything other than the pain.

She pumped her arms. She dropped her shoulders. She lifted her face to the sky.

Nothing worked.

She couldn't run fast enough.

It was just a normal day, she kept telling herself. A normal run.

Only she was lying. It was anything but normal.

And she was anything but okay.

Her feet stumbled and she cried out as she threw her arms out to catch herself. She didn't fall, but she came close. The shout hadn't been from the pain. Not the physical one. The jabbing in her side was nothing compared to the hurt in her soul.

It was December ninth.

She'd gone to the children's hospital for the last time on this day three years ago.

She stumbled again and this time went down. Three seconds later she was back on her feet, moving forward, but with a limp. Every time her right foot landed, she listed to her side. She kept this up as moisture appeared in her eyes.

Life was not fair.

She'd walked away from Charles for Zoe.

Roni stumbled again, and this time went down. She stayed there.

On all fours, she dropped her head so it hung limply between her shoulders and sagged. Her breaths heaved in and out. She'd been too late.

A buzz began at her waist and she sat back on her haunches to pull her phone from the hidden pocket behind the waistband of her pants. She was early for her run today. She hadn't been able to sleep and had gotten out as the sun was coming up.

Her brother wouldn't know that, though. He'd think he was catching her right as she finished with the piano.

Still breathing raggedly, she wiped sweat from her brow and yanked the earbuds from her ears. She brought the phone up, staying where she was in the sand. She wasn't inclined to move just yet, though her house was now only fifty yards away.

"Good morning, Danny," she answered. Her brother could always be counted on to check in on her during her rough days.

"Hey, sis. How are you?"

She shook her head from side to side. A tear seeped from the outer corners of both eyes and she let them roll down her cheeks. Her brother was the only one who knew about Zoe. "I'm just finishing up a run."

"You're early."

"I couldn't sleep."

Her brother might check in with her on this day every year, but he didn't always know how to start the conversations.

"You exercise too much." This was an ongoing theme between them.

"I exercise just enough," she clarified. "Dad died of a heart attack at forty-eight. I won't be next."

Their father had been a type A personality. He'd focused on his career with single-minded determination. Roni had once been just like him.

There was a brief silence from the other end of the phone, and then her brother said, "You can't bring her back, you know? No matter how hard you push yourself."

Pain sliced through Roni.

"Ah, shit," Danny muttered. "I'm sorry. That came out wrong. It was insensitive. Kathy tells me I'm a jerk all the time." He waited three seconds while Roni said nothing. "Roni?" he said, almost pleading.

She remained silent.

"Don't hang up. Please. I'm sorry. That came out wrong."

"You said that," she whispered. "I'm not deaf."

Just broken.

"Oh, sis. Are you okay? I should have called earlier in the week. I should have—"

"I'm fine," she muttered. "It's just a shitty day. Too many—"

She stopped midsentence. Too many memories, but also too many wants. Too much loneliness.

And talking to a cute, brown-haired, blue-eyed little girl yesterday hadn't helped matters any. Her heart squeezed at the cuteness of Gracie. Lucas was so lucky.

Some days, Roni admitted to herself now, she *didn't* love her life. Some days it just sucked.

"I should have come down there this week," Danny said.

"I told you. I'm fine." And surprisingly, she realized, that wasn't a complete lie.

Though she had seen better days.

"Then why do you continue to push yourself so hard? Why do you kill yourself with these runs?"

"You're a doctor. You should understand the value of an exercise regime."

There was silence on the other end of the phone before Danny sighed. "I understand exercise. I get up every morning and do my own. But no matter how healthy you are, you can't change the fact that Zoe was sick. You've got to give yourself a break."

"I run because I don't want to die like Dad."

Because it was easier to run than face her world.

She'd needed Zoe.

And Zoe had needed her.

"Want me to come down?" her brother asked. He was a pediatric surgeon in Cincinnati. "I'm off for the next four days. There's a flight leaving out of here in three hours."

When she hadn't come home for Christmas three years ago, Danny had flown to New York to find out what the problem was.

"You can't leave Kathy and the kids," Roni pointed out. His wife was a doll, but two young boys were a handful for anyone.

"They'll be fine for a few days. Plus, I could use something other than the drizzly cold we've been having here."

Roni unfolded her legs from beneath her and stretched them out, propping her elbows on her knees as she did. The dampness from the sand seeped into the back of her compression pants. She would be frozen if she didn't get up off the ground soon.

"I'm fine, Danny. Really. I told you, it's been three—"

"I know how long it's been, Roni. I was there, remember? I saw you at your worst."

No he hadn't. He'd seen her only at the beginning of her worst.

"I can tell today is bad," he said. "I hear it in your voice. Let someone help."

She shifted her eyes to her house and studied it. She did need to let someone help. She should have let them years ago. She had friends who loved her as much as she loved them. "You're right," she said at last. "How about if I promise to tell Ginger and Andie? Will that keep you in Cincinnati?"

"Today?"

The ache behind her breastbone burned. "Tomorrow," she said. She didn't want to talk about it today.

A movement caught her attention on her deck but then it stopped. Probably a shadow from one of the trees in her backyard.

"Promise me you aren't lying," Danny's stern big-brother voice said in her ear.

Her brother was only two years older than her, and though they'd spent the majority of their childhoods apart, they were close.

She smiled. "I'm not lying. As soon as I hang up with you I'll text them to set up a time."

He went quiet and she could picture him with a smug look on his face, thinking he'd just accomplished something she wouldn't have done alone. The truth was, she'd been thinking about talking to her friends since she'd left Lucas's hotel the morning before.

"You'll be home for Christmas, right?" Danny asked, changing the subject. "The boys are looking forward to seeing you."

She'd only ever missed the one year.

"Of course I'll be there." She inched her smile up, hoping the sentiment would make it through the phone. She was looking forward to seeing his boys too. Her nephews were nine and six, and though she sometimes felt a little envious of the life that Danny had built for himself, she would never let that come between her and seeing her family. "Have you met Tom yet?"

Their mother had a new boyfriend.

Danny laughed lightly. "I have. He's a good guy. He moved to Huntsville last year and is teaching at the college with Mom. He worships the ground she walks on."

"That's good to hear." Their mother was a strong woman, but she'd had a hard time getting over their dad. She'd dated two other men fairly seriously over the years, but so far, nothing had stuck. Danny and Roni were hoping this was the guy.

They said their good-byes, then she held her phone up in front of her as she typed out a message. The run had done her good. As had the chat with her brother. But Roni was ready to talk to her friends.

The message went to Ginger:

Can we talk? My house tomorrow morning? I'll skip my run.

She'd talk about Lucas too.

Not that it mattered at this point. It was over. Certainly he'd gotten that message when she'd given him the cold shoulder the day before.

That didn't keep her from wanting to talk about him, though.

She glanced back at her house, didn't see anything out of the ordinary on her deck, and crossed her arms over her knees as she waited for a reply. She lifted her chin and enjoyed the sunshine warming her skin. It was a gorgeous morning.

Everything okay? The message came back.

Really good. And it was. It was way better than when she'd started out that morning. **We'll call Andie. I need you both. Things I should have told you a long time ago.**

171

I'll be there. The reply was immediate. **And I'll let Andie know.**

Roni could always count on her friends.

Rising, she began moving toward her house. She had extra time before she had to be at the convention center, but her rear was frozen from sitting in the sand. She needed to get out of her wet pants.

"Yoo-hoo." A voice came from somewhere above her.

Roni squinted as she looked around, trying to make out where the sound had come from. Finally, she saw a small head sticking up above the railing of her deck. A bony arm waved back and forth, wildly enough that it could be trying to flag down a ship.

"Yoo-hoo."

The head had what Roni knew to be white curls covered in a sheer yellow scarf. Mrs. Rylander.

"What are you doing up there, Mrs. Rylander?" Roni shouted back. She picked up her speed, worried that the older lady would head down the steep steps before Roni could make it up to her. Mrs. Rylander may think she was only fifty, but the facts were, she had three more decades on her. Roni didn't want the woman to lose her balance and break her lunatic neck.

"You have company, dear," the woman's thinner voice yelled back. "I brought over tea."

Roni's feet quit pushing through the sand. She lifted one hand above her brows to block the sun. She could only see her neighbor on her deck.

She began moving again, dusting the sand off her rear as she went. When she made it to the base of her stairs, a much larger figure appeared beside Mrs. Rylander. Lucas, looking scruffy and rumpled like he'd just crawled from bed, stood there, his hand huge around the delicate teacup he held, his white T-shirt emblazoned with "Turtle Island rocks!" stretched tight across his chest and shoulders. Roni's breath lodged in her throat.

Geez, he made her weak at the knees every time she looked at him.

He made her want to march up the stairs and muss up his hair even more than it already was.

She should have known he wouldn't get the hint from yesterday.

"Morning, Roni," he said. His voice touched her like a summer rain shower, sprinkling down over her from above. Warmth covered her, and she shivered.

She pulled her gaze from his and shifted it back to her neighbor. Mrs. Rylander smiled brightly in her fleece jacket that hung to her knees, its collar turned up at the neck, fluttering her lashes in innocence as old as time itself. The woman was in so much trouble. Lucas wouldn't be on the deck right now if not for her.

With a silent groan, Roni moved forward. Might as well get this over with. The man wasn't likely to leave until they did.

Fifteen steps up and Roni stood before Lucas. As with every time, he dwarfed her. He seemed twice as wide as her, as well as the substantial inches he had on her in height. He was also eyeing her as if he knew a secret she didn't want to share.

Sitting on the small glass-topped table behind him were the silver stilettos she'd left at the convention center the first night he'd kissed her.

"Well," Mrs. Rylander said, pressing her hands together in front of her. She turned toward the massive beast of a man and patted him on his chest. Roni noted that even at eighty, the woman let her hand linger longer than necessary. "Now that the lady of the house is home, I'll leave you two to talk."

"Thank you, Mrs. Rylander," Lucas began. He reached out and gripped her hands in his and met her wide, blinking gaze. "I appreciate the hospitality from such a gorgeous lady. I hope Roni knows what a lovely neighbor she has in you."

What a suck-up.

The older lady laughed, the sound high-pitched and girlish. The paper-thin skin of her cheeks even blushed.

Roni stared at her, aghast. What a flirt.

"Oh, you charmer, you," Mrs. Rylander cooed. "I'm sure Roni would have done the same for me if I'd had an unexpected guest." She patted his chest one more time—tossing in a bit of a stroke at the end—before turning her back to him and facing Roni. Then she winked. The sky-blue eyes laughed as if she thought she'd pulled something off. What did she think? That she'd done Roni some sort of favor by capturing and keeping him here until she'd returned?

Roni shook her head at her neighbor, letting her know that she wasn't getting away with anything. And Roni *would* find a way to get her back.

"You keep the tea set for now, dear." Mrs. Rylander said. "I brought over a cup for you too." She headed for the stairs, her head bobbing with her steps as she seemed to have a bit of a limp. Had she hurt herself?

"Wait."

"Let me help you."

Roni and Lucas spoke at the same time, both taking a step toward her. Roni glanced at him. He ignored her and continued on to Mrs. Rylander. "Please allow me to help you down the stairs."

"Well," Mrs. Rylander said. She peered down the steep steps before looking back at the two of them. The woman might be spry for her age, but honestly, she had no business on those stairs. One finger lifted to toy with a tight curl just below her ear. "I'm sure I could do it."

Roni's jaw dropped. Mrs. Rylander was doing the oh-innocent-me hair twirl? At her age? The woman had no shame.

"Please," Lucas said, "I'd be honored."

Assuming he would hold her arm, Roni watched as Mrs. Rylander stuck out her elbow, but Lucas surprised both of them by scooping her up, one arm behind her knees, the other at her back.

"Oof." The sound came from Mrs. Rylander a second before both hands clutched tight around Lucas's neck. She peeked over his shoulder and smiled wickedly at Roni.

The sneaky little thing.

Lucas swung around, Mrs. Rylander in his arms, and pinned Roni with his gaze. "Do not go anywhere," he said. "We have a conversation you ran away from yesterday."

"Really?" Mrs. Rylander swiveled her head between them. "Did something happen?"

Roni glared at her but didn't answer.

"Oh," Mrs. Rylander said, drawing the word out as if she'd just seen what seemed to hang between them every time the two of them got within twenty feet of each other. Mrs. Rylander then smiled brightly at Lucas. "I'm sure she'll be right here waiting for you. Who wouldn't want to have a conversation with a handsome young man like yourself?"

Eyes more stormy than clear shifted from Roni to her neighbor. "You'd think so, wouldn't you?" His voice made Roni fidget where she stood. It had a way of twining around her, while simultaneously reaching out and stroking her. "Yet amazingly," he continued, "she seems to enjoy avoiding me whenever she thinks she can get away with it." He took a step down the stairs. "If she's smart, she'll realize this is not one of those times."

Mrs. Rylander giggled again and the two of them headed down the steps. Roni's gaze caught on the muscles bunching under the back of Lucas's T-shirt. There was a lovely grace about the rigid planes as they tightened and lengthened with his moves. A sexy grace.

She'd touched and seen each and every one of those muscles up close the other night.

And she found herself wanting to do it again.

Regardless of the fact that the instant she'd caught sight of him on her deck, she'd realized that she hadn't only run away from his daughter the morning before. She'd run away from him too.

But he was a good guy.

He was carrying an old woman down the stairs, for crying out loud. Who wouldn't be swept away by those kind of manners?

Right before they disappeared from sight, Mrs. Rylander looked back one last time. She waggled her eyebrows at Roni and Roni flushed in embarrassment when she realized she'd been caught ogling.

But dang. If an eighty-year-old could act feeble just so the man would carry her down the stairs, how was Roni supposed to stand a chance around his charms?

Because she didn't.

She was already thinking that she'd overreacted. So he had a daughter. So what? He also had a few moves in the bedroom she wouldn't mind trying out another time or two.

Surely she could keep things compartmentalized.

He was a fling. She wasn't going to fall for him.

Easy peasy.

His dark head reappeared at the bottom of her stairs a couple minutes later, and his gaze lasered on hers. Hot desire shot through her body.

Oh geez. She was in trouble.

This was not going to end well.

Chapter Eighteen

By the time Lucas got to the top of the stairs, all he saw of Roni was her retreating behind in her tight black-and-blue running pants. She did leave the sliding door standing open, though. Inviting him in? Or possibly, conceding defeat.

Either way, he was entering her house and she was allowing it. Score one for him.

He stepped cautiously inside and found himself standing alone in her living room, which was actually only one part of a much larger space. The entire room comprised her living room, kitchen, and dining area. It had high ceilings and elaborate crown molding, with the detail of the molding mimicked in the woodwork of the kitchen. The cream cabinetry and light-stone tile floor gave it a wide-open feel. The room was huge.

Not that he was surprised. Her whole house was huge. He'd seen that from the outside.

What did surprise him was the piano in place of where he would expect to find a table and chairs. A large piano. One that took up enough space that Roni could easily fit a table for twelve there instead.

There were papers scattered on top, along with a couple pencils. A few more papers were crumpled and pushed to the side, and a couple had tumbled to the floor. A squat, seemingly forgotten plant sat brown and dry in front of the floor-to-ceiling bay windows that were directly behind the piano.

Next was the kitchen.

The stainless-steel range was industrial-size, and the counter space would be a culinary student's dream come true. If there wasn't such a mess scattered about.

A coffeepot sat next to the sink, its lid removed, and two brown trails of stains dribbling from the spout. Several mugs littered the area around the pot. The cabinet door above the area hung open, with more mugs and a stack of bowls perched on the shelves.

Running parallel, an oversize island spanned the room, with a small sink on one end. The opposite end held the tea set Mrs. Rylander had brought over, along with an unorganized cluster of plates. It looked as if Roni had sat at one of the padded barstools to eat, but then pushed the dishes aside instead of taking them to the dishwasher.

Or even the sink.

Several times.

Not that the place was a disaster. Just . . . untidy. There was a clump of bananas shoved haphazardly to one side of the stove, and two oranges that looked to have rolled away from the rest of the fruit lay butted up to a plastic mesh bag of avocados. There were also two empty baskets sitting alongside the fruit as if only waiting to hold everything.

Appliances of all types and sizes dotted the granite countertops, and a short hallway led to the open door of what he could only guess was a room-size pantry.

He scanned his way back to the living room, bypassing the foyer and the attached room with the French doors, and his gaze landed on the table bumped up behind the sofa. It was covered in pictures. His feet moved forward, but he caught himself before picking up any of the photos.

There were several of Roni from different ages. Each was of her standing proudly beside a piano, not smiling, but looking like she wanted to. In the most recent one, she had on a midnight-blue gown and her black hair swung loose to her waist, draped softly over her narrow shoulders. This was the Veronica he remembered from when he'd seen her play before. The picture couldn't be more than a few years old.

Next to it was one of her and her father. She stood by one piano, and on the opposite side of it was her father standing with an identical one. Lucas had seen this photo online before. If he remembered correctly, Roni had been eighteen and it had been taken only a short time before her father had passed away.

Mixed in among the pictures of her were what he assumed to be family photos. A man with Roni's black hair and features stood with a woman and two dark-haired boys. This same grouping was in at least four other pictures, as well. There was an early shot of Roni with what he assumed was her brother, her father, and her mother. And then another of her, her brother, and her mother. That one looked to have been taken here on the island when she'd been in her early teens.

The enormous leather sofa was a burnt-red color. And tossed over the far corner were two blouses. In front of the couch was a coffee table, where the silver shoes he'd brought back to her were now perched.

He glanced toward the hallway, following the trail of sand, and wondered what she was doing. And why she hadn't taken the shoes with her.

In the living room stood a dark Christmas tree in front of the glass window overlooking the ocean. The tree was filled with an assortment of ornaments of every size, shape, and color. If there was a theme, he was missing it. Gracie would approve. Gracie hated her grandmother's snowflake-themed tree and her Christmas village–themed tree. She wanted everything mixed together.

Roni padded into the room then, no longer wearing the snug bottoms and top she'd had on for her run. Instead she had on a pair of gray cotton, loose-fitting pants with a drawstring at the waist and a cropped T-shirt that ended right where her waistline began. Her hair was still damp from the run, but her cheeks weren't quite as flushed. Her eyes implied she was irritated with his mere existence.

"I brought in the tea," she said by way of greeting. "I assumed you were finished with it."

Lucas cracked a smile. She was already trying to get rid of him.

It was going to take more than that.

"Gracie is four and a half," he started, his words blunt and to the point. They had a conversation that needed to be finished and he intended to do it. Before she *did* kick him out.

Roni didn't say anything, just crossed the tile floor in her bare feet and plugged in the tree. It came to life, including several of the ornaments tinkling and revolving on their hooks.

"Her mother and I got together when I was twenty-two," Lucas continued. "I took time off from school during my fourth and fifth years to earn the money to finish up. Des was a makeup artist on several of the shoots I did."

"I didn't ask," Roni pointed out.

"But you need to hear."

She eyed him, unimpressed. It didn't stop him. What he felt for her scared him.

And he hadn't cared enough to be scared in years.

"So it took you five years to graduate college?" Roni asked. She tossed him a superior look down her nose before stooping at the fireplace and popping the igniter. Flames burst to life, casting a faint glow around her hair.

That's what she'd gotten from his statement? That he'd attended college for five years. "Four and a half, actually. I got a double major," he pointed out. "Computer Science and Math."

"Ah." She rose and faced him, her hands clasped in front of her. "You're a brainiac?"

She was trying to derail him. Why?

He narrowed his eyes on her. Because she didn't want to know about Gracie?

Or because hearing about his past made her nervous?

Option B, he thought. And it was too damned bad. Because he was nervous too.

"Exactly," he acknowledged, ignoring the bored look on her face. "Des was twenty, and going on about sixteen." She'd had stars in her eyes about what she wanted from life.

It had been even worse when it'd come to what she'd expected from him.

Unfortunately, he'd been too wrapped up in his own plans to notice.

"We were stupid." He felt stupid thinking about it now. "And we weren't always as careful as we should have been. I was getting ready to go back to school when we found out she was pregnant. It was October."

He was rattling, but he couldn't seem to stop.

"I graduated in May, got a job in Houston, and Gracie was born in June. I was ecstatic. I've loved Gracie from the minute Des told me she was pregnant." He swallowed and then stalled by walking to the tree and watching the tiny scene of ice dancers skating around a frozen pond. "Des was . . . *less* than ecstatic. Motherhood wasn't what she wanted."

Neither had been living in a Houston suburb with a corporate suit for a husband.

His bad for not noticing.

"She wanted to be in Hollywood," he blurted. He turned back to Roni and crossed his arms over his chest. Des had wanted *him* to be in Hollywood with her. Since he'd been a model, she'd had visions of him being the next Brad Pitt while she would do makeup for the likes of Angelina Jolie.

When she'd told him she was leaving, he'd gone so far as to suggest he move there and give it a try. Not because he couldn't stand the thought of losing her, but because he couldn't stand the thought of Gracie growing up without her mom.

He wasn't sure how to continue his story without sharing all that Gracie had been through, and he wasn't ready to do that. He hadn't been kidding with Kelly. Leukemia didn't define his daughter. He never wanted anyone thinking of that first when they thought about Gracie.

"What happened?" Roni asked.

He looked at her. He'd gotten her attention. "When Gracie was eighteen months," he began, "Des walked. She'd had enough." He glanced over her shoulder to land on the pictures sitting behind the sofa. He liked seeing her family all clustered around her. "She left us and a week later I got papers from a lawyer, along with a bill. Since we weren't married, we didn't have that to deal with, but she'd signed away her parental rights. She didn't even want updates on her own kid."

Roni moved her head from one side to the other, as if she intended to shake her head "no" but was unable to make more than that one small motion. "She legally declared she didn't want to be Gracie's mother?" she asked, the swoop of her lips turning down. "What is wrong with people? How could she do that?"

She spoke the question so quietly he felt she was almost talking to herself. Then she moved to the other side of the Christmas tree and stared out the window at the beach. The day outside was bright and beautiful.

Roni glanced over at him, her brow furrowed into a scowl. "Gracie didn't deserve that."

"I know," he said. He nodded and repeated, "I know. I've never understood it."

Of course, there was more to it. Des had walked out the morning after Gracie's diagnosis. She hadn't signed on for cancer, she'd said. She would never get a Hollywood career if she was stuck in a three-bedroom ranch in Houston, taking care of a sick kid.

She'd packed and been gone before he'd gotten out of bed the next morning.

It still made no sense. She was Gracie's mother.

"That's when I moved back to Dallas," he added. "I'm from there originally."

"Your parents live there."

"Right." He nodded. He'd told her that the other night on the beach. "I wanted Gracie to be close to them since she didn't have her mom."

"Was it that or did you move back so you could get your mother to take care of your kid?"

Anger flared.

"Clearly you still travel." Her words were blunt. They were facing each other now, with the edge of the gaily decorated tree sparkling brightly between them. "I mean, you're here. Someone must be watching Gracie. I assume that was your mother I saw on your computer yesterday morning."

He forced his jaw to loosen. He didn't care for the implication that he would ditch his child off on someone else.

"I do travel," he began slowly. Calmly. "But it's rare. Having the occasional time away allows me to concentrate more fully on Gracie when I am at home. It helps me be a better father. More grateful. And yes, it gives me a bit of a break. I think every parent needs that, but especially the ones doing it on their own. Plus, I rarely leave. It's been eight months since my last trip, and that one was for only three days."

He hoped she was getting that it had been at least that long since he'd been with a woman, as well. He didn't do flings lightly anymore, even though he did keep them casual.

Until now.

Letting Roni talk to Gracie had blown casual right out of the water.

And she was just going to have to deal with it.

"What else?" she asked.

"What else what?"

She lifted a shoulder in a shrug and shifted her gaze to the ornaments hanging from the branches. "You wanted me to hear this story, so what else do you have to tell me?"

Meaning, get it over with and get out of my house.

He studied her tight jaw and the way she was careful to avoid eye contact.

She was trying to act like this conversation was no big deal. That his being in her house was nothing. But being here was showing him *her*. And what he saw told him that she was far deeper than she pretended.

She had a piano as a focal point in her house, for heaven's sake. Not to mention enough rooms to sleep a small army.

The space was adorned with pictures showcasing her talent and her career. Her family. There was a Christmas tree and a cozy fire.

This wasn't the setting for someone only looking for casual hookups and a good time. This was a home. This was also where she was hiding from the world.

It was time to turn the tables on her. "Why don't you play professionally anymore?" he asked. A woman who had a piano for a dining table missed her career.

Her head snapped up at the question. Her eyes grew cold. "That has nothing to do with your story."

"Yet it's a valid question." He took a step in her direction but stopped when her entire body stiffened.

He wouldn't force himself on anyone.

"We're talking about you." Her words were hard.

He had to push. "Yet I'm standing in your house, and I suspect I'm actually seeing *you*." He took one small step around the edge of the tree. "Why don't you play, Roni?" he cajoled. "Mrs. Rylander says you spend hours practicing every morning. Yet no one hears you but customers at Gin's."

"I played somewhere else just this week." The words coming from her seemed strangled. As if she couldn't get enough air from her lungs to push the words fully up and out.

"You played one song," he pointed out. "And that one song ripped you apart." He curled his fingers into his palm to keep from reaching for her. "What happened?"

She closed her eyes and as Lucas watched, he saw her pulse pumping in the side of her neck. Ornaments beside them buzzed as they circled happily in place. A clock from somewhere in the house steadily ticked off the seconds.

He wanted to hold her. There were demons she was fighting, and even if she didn't want to share them with him, he wanted to pull her close and offer comfort.

But he did nothing but wait, knowing that he'd probably already pushed too hard.

He glanced to the front of the house where the door stood at the other end of the foyer. He suspected he would be walking through it very soon.

Finally, Roni moved. She shook her head in denial, and he watched as her throat rose and fell. She opened her eyes and looked at him. "Why did you come to my house?" she asked.

"Because I knew you wouldn't come to me."

Because he hadn't been able to keep away.

"You have a kid. It's best to—"

"You like kids." It was a guess, but there were gifts stacked under the tree, most of them wrapped in boy-themed Christmas packaging. SpongeBob and Teenage Mutant Ninja Turtles, along with several covered in cowboys. He suspected those would be going to the two boys in the pictures on her table.

Brown eyes drilled him. "Of course I *like* kids. Most people like kids. But that doesn't mean—"

"My kid is in Dallas," he stated. "You and I are here. The two don't have to merge."

He held his breath as he waited for her reaction. That would be the smart way to play it. But he hadn't been able to stop asking himself all kinds of questions for the last two days. He wanted to delve into this thing with Roni. He wanted to see if something was there.

"You aren't exactly carefree," she accused. "Not with a kid at home. That's more than I signed up for."

"And you aren't exactly leading a simple beach-girl lifestyle."

"Sure I am."

He scanned his gaze purposely around the rooms. "You have a house large enough for a family here. Or two."

"That doesn't mean anything."

"Do you regularly entertain overnight guests, then? Does someone use the spare bedrooms I know you must have in this place?"

She looked away from him again. "I like my space, is all. I spent years living out of hotels."

That could be all there was to it, but he didn't think so. His intuition told him there was way more to the story. And quite possibly, whatever it was had to do with why she'd walked away from her career.

"Listen, Roni," he began. He moved away from her, needing to put some space between them. Stopping on the other side of the fireplace, he rested his hand on the mantel and turned back. "I'm not saying we have to take this anywhere more than the few days of fun we originally intended. But I am saying . . ." Fear almost choked off his air. He didn't have faith in anyone sticking around for the hard times. He shouldn't be *saying* anything.

"I'm saying," he started again. "That I like you. I think you like me. I want to spend some time hanging out together. Getting to know each other. And if that were to turn into wanting even more . . . well . . ." He swallowed against the knot wedged painfully in his throat. "Then I might just want to see where that goes too."

Chapter Nineteen

Roni blinked at Lucas. First he'd shown up at her house unannounced. Disrupted her day. Then he just put that out there like that?

He likes her. He wants to get to know her. And oh, by the way, he might just want more.

And she noticed that she wasn't immediately screaming *no* herself.

"I don't know, Lucas." She wet her lips. She wanted to shove him out of her house. "I don't do serious."

"I don't either."

She nodded hesitantly, even more bewildered. Then they *were* on the same page?

"I also don't introduce women to my daughter," he stated.

Yet he'd introduced her. As a friend. But still. They'd met. They'd talked. He'd encouraged the conversation with the head nod toward the computer.

Was he implying she was already more than casual?

The funny thing was, she suspected she could say the same thing about him. Maybe it had been only when he'd scooped up Mrs. Rylander that morning that had done it. Or maybe it had been when he'd had the look in his eye that he knew he would soon be buying his daughter a dog.

He was a sweet guy. He cared about people.

She hadn't had the chance to get to know a lot of sweet guys in her life.

She ached from the inside out and found herself wanting to step into his arms as she'd done that first night under the deck. He'd held her and asked no questions. She should have known then that he was different. She should have run right at that very moment.

But if they went back to that night, she would step into his arms again. Sometimes, a girl just needed to be held.

Clearly he wasn't just casual. But she wasn't quite sure what he was.

She lifted her gaze to his face and studied the hard planes. Six days ago she'd seen a good-looking man. A really hot, crazy-sexy man. Today she saw a good guy.

A dad. A caring person. A man who didn't let little old ladies break their fool busybody necks. A man who smiled and laughed and enjoyed life.

A man just like she'd once imagined falling for her and Zoe.

Damn.

The back of her throat and nose burned with unshed tears as she met his azure gaze. "You can't push me about the piano thing," she demanded.

He gave a brief nod. "I won't push about the piano thing."

"And as far as I'm concerned, this is still just having fun. I don't believe for a minute it'll go anywhere else." She glanced away from Lucas and her gaze fastened on the locked wooden box sitting on the bookshelf at the back of the room.

"We each have our own beliefs about that, I suppose." His voice was deep and calm.

She swung back to him. "Do you really believe this could be more?" She paused, then whispered when her throat closed, "Do you want it to be more?"

His mouth moved as if intending to form words, but then his shoulders sagged and he blew out a harsh breath. He scraped a hand down over his face. "Honestly? No. Gracie and I are good. We don't need anyone else. But I look at you, Roni, and . . ."

His deep gaze seemed to penetrate her skin and see into her soul. And her stupid soul was reaching out its greedy little hands, begging him to say he wanted more.

Goose bumps raised on her arms as she stood in front of him. She had no idea what to say. Or what she wanted to hear.

"I like that even though you would've rather kicked my butt back to the other side of the island when you saw me here," he started, "you faced reality and knew we needed to talk. I like that you clearly have your ghosts to bear—and no, I'm not asking about them. Yet. But ghosts or not, they haven't stopped you from living. You enjoy life, even while you hide from it at the same time. And you look at me like you want me to hold you, and it takes everything I have not to move mountains to do just that."

She lowered her gaze to the ground. She did look at him that way. Because she *did* want him to hold her.

"Roni," he whispered. He was in front of her now and he reached out and lifted her face to his. "I like that you smiled and talked to my kid. I like that me having a kid scares you."

"You like to scare me?" she asked. She really needed the moment to be lightened.

"You understand that being a father is a part of who I am."

He saw parts of her that she didn't show to the world too. And she kind of liked that herself. Even if she didn't want to talk about it.

"This could be fun, Roni. Or this could be more." His hand slipped over her jaw and his thumb caressed her cheek. His skin was rough against hers. It made her remember how his big hands had caressed her body in his bed.

"Say yes," he urged. He cupped her cheek in his hand. "Let's see what it is."

Her heart thudded so hard she could feel it pounding in her ears. She searched over his hard jaw, trailing over the stubble. Her gaze edged over his thick lips and she thought about having them on her. It had been fun and good times she'd felt in his kiss, but even before she'd gotten out of bed yesterday morning, she'd understood that it had been more too. They'd connected when they'd talked.

Their lips had clung together as if they could hold on to something neither of them had seen yet.

Then she thought about the look on his face when he'd encouraged her to talk to Gracie.

He was as lonely as she was.

She lifted her eyes back to his. And nodded.

They would see where this would go whether either of them wanted to or not.

"I'll come over tonight," she suggested. "I'll drive my car, though." She didn't want him getting in the habit of thinking he had to bring her home every morning.

"How about I come here?"

Oh geez. Her heart contracted. The man didn't know when to stop.

"I get up and practice before dawn," she said, hoping to discourage him.

"I'll head back to the hotel to work." The man didn't discourage easily.

They stood there, both of them unmoving. Facing each other. Both wanting more, but terrified to believe they could get it.

And then she gave a final nod.

The hardness of his face eased and broke into a gentle smile.

She couldn't believe she'd just agreed to . . . what? A relationship? A trial relationship?

Whatever it was, she found she actually wanted to do it.

She glanced down and looked at her hands. They were shaking again.

And then Lucas leaned in and brought his mouth ever so gently to hers.

Her hands quit shaking and she lifted them to capture his face.

His lips were soft. Almost hesitant. As if he were trying them out for the first time. He slid his hands into her hair and tilted her face up higher. Then he stepped closer and the heat of his body seared her from head to toe.

The kiss wasn't like what they'd had before. This one said that it knew what it was doing. And what it was doing was starting something new and fresh. Something that could be special.

A knot twisted in her stomach at the idea of falling for Lucas and Gracie. What if she fell in love with them?

What if they got within her grasp but she couldn't keep them?

She didn't want her heart to be broken again. And she also knew that if she fell for one, she would fall for the other.

It was a really big risk.

Lucas's lips released her and he pulled back. She opened her eyes and stared up at him. He hadn't turned her loose, and she still had his face in her hands. They looked at each other in the middle of her living room, with her Christmas tree glowing on one side of them and her fireplace burning on the other. It was a warm, cozy scene. All she needed were three stockings hanging from her mantel.

She bit her lip at the thought.

Then she thought of Zoe.

She'd planned to give Zoe the best Christmas of her life.

Tears rolled from the corners of Roni's eyes and dripped down to her ears.

"What is it?" Lucas asked. His tone was gentle. Letting her know she could talk to him, but he wouldn't push.

She shook her head. She was terrified, but at the same time, a light burned inside her that she hadn't felt in years. "Kiss me again," she whispered. "We have time before we have to be at the convention center."

His pupils dilated.

This time when his mouth met hers, it was harder. His tongue parted her lips without hesitation and heat swirled low inside her body.

She wanted him. And she wanted him right there in the middle of her house.

He roamed his hands down her back and then up and under her shirt. His skin burned where he touched her.

"Make love to me," she whispered. She stepped into him and shivered at the feel of his hard erection pressing against her stomach.

He lifted her up and she wrapped her legs around him.

"The kitchen counter," she muttered. She buried her face into the side of his neck and took a naughty little bite. He tasted of sweat and man. She wanted to taste him all over.

She lifted her head when he didn't move toward the kitchen.

"What's wrong?" she asked.

"You have stuff everywhere."

She twisted around in his arms and took in the counter space. "Over there." She motioned to the corner on the other side of the stove. "There's plenty of space."

When she looked back at him she laughed at the look on his face. She'd never seen a mix of heated desire and barely contained disgust together before.

"I promise it's just a few dirty dishes." She stroked a finger from his ear down over his strong, corded neck. She smoothed over the red spot where she'd nipped him. "I wipe down the counters and everything."

He shook his head as if he couldn't believe what he was about to do, but his feet headed toward her kitchen. "You're a mess."

She laughed. "Just wait until you see my bedroom."

His feet paused and he groaned. She laughed again.

Then she put her lips back to his neck and sucked on his heated skin. "I was coming out of the bathroom yesterday morning to tease you about your toiletries," she murmured against him.

He plopped her down on the countertop and gripped the bottom of her shirt. In one motion, it was over her head and tossed to the floor.

"You're really good at that," she said. She peered around him to where her shirt had landed on the tile. "And it's funny how you don't seem to be the least bit fazed by a lack of tidiness when stripping me of my clothes."

He unhooked the front clasp of her bra and peeled it from her shoulders. Her nipples said hello while her bra went flying.

"What about my toiletries?" he growled. A muscle ticked in his jaw as his gaze raked her over.

He put his hands around her waist, and she looked down at them. His thumbs touched just above her belly button. He tugged and her bottom scooted out farther on the counter. She spread her legs and he stepped closer.

She looked up at him then and the air around them thickened. His eyes were hooded, and instead of staring at her breasts, he was looking at her face.

"You line them up like little army men," she whispered.

She wanted this, she realized. Not just the sex. But the man. The dream. She wanted to believe this could be something.

She wanted to believe in them.

"I'm efficient," he told her. He caught her chin and lowered his head to hers.

The kiss was similar to the one from a few minutes before. He barely brushed his lips to hers before lifting away. Then he dipped and brushed again. This time he slipped inside and searched out her secrets. He explored her. Caressed.

He let her know that she wasn't just sex.

So she showed him the same thing.

She lifted her hands and held his face in her palms, and she poured all of her hopes and fears into the kiss.

When they parted, both of them stared at each other.

She nodded. He nodded back.

Then he scooped her up and headed down the hall.

"Which way to your bedroom?" he asked. He wasn't asking permission, and she liked that about him.

As she lifted her arm to point out the right room, his phone rang from his pocket. He went still.

"*Shit*," he ground out.

"What?"

"That's the ringtone for Skype."

Ah. Her ardor cooled. "Your daughter is calling."

He nodded, his apologetic gaze steady on hers. "We talk every morning," he explained.

"Then let me down," she said. "You talk to your daughter, and I'm going to go shower."

She slid down his body until she landed on her feet.

"I'll make it short," he said.

"No." She shook her head. "You take your time. Your daughter needs her time with you. I'm going to shower." She wrinkled her nose. "I'm kind of grungy anyway."

He studied her, his phone now in his hand. "Can I join you when I'm finished?"

She glanced at his phone and then at the man. She had no idea what she was getting into, but she was plunging full-body into it. She nodded. "I was hoping you would."

195

CHAPTER TWENTY

R oni scribbled on the piece of paper lying on top of the piano
before putting her hands back to the keys. She played the stanza
again, shook her head, then tried it a different way.

That one brought a smile to her mouth.

She hurried and corrected the notes on the sheet before playing it
once more to make certain it was what she wanted. She nodded. Perfect.

It was almost eight-thirty on Sunday morning and she'd been at
the piano for going on three hours. Ginger would be there any minute. Roni had let her know that breakfast would be waiting. It was
the least Roni could do after asking her friend to stop by so early on
a weekend morning.

She moved to another section of the piece she'd been struggling
with and ran her fingers along the keys as she worked through the
notes in her mind. She'd written a few concertos in the past, most of
them while working with other people. She'd also taken more popu-
lar songs and changed them up, adding a classical spin. But lately she'd
been experimenting with her own stuff.

And she had to admit, she wasn't bad.

The front door opened across the room behind her but she didn't
look around. She'd left it unlocked when Lucas had headed back to
the hotel that morning.

"I have a quiche warming in the oven," Roni said, still concentrating on the music. She closed her eyes and played the last six bars again. Yeah, that was it. "Make yourself at home. I'll be done in just a sec."

She quickly scribbled the notes and played it again, then moved to the next section.

Ginger didn't say anything. She merely sat down next to Roni on the bench.

"Mmmm," Roni murmured as she erased a whole line of notes. She was close to what she wanted, but wasn't quite there yet. "You smell terrific."

Then she caught the scent of another perfume right behind her.

She looked up and swung her head to the person beside her. And her eyes went wide.

"Andie!" Roni shouted.

Her friend laughed out loud and then Roni, Andie, and Ginger were all hugging and jumping and squealing like little girls. Roni felt like she was a teenager again and she'd just arrived on Turtle Island for the summer and met up with her friends. She pulled back a bit and looked Andie up and down. Her hair was longer, and her curves were just as awesome as ever.

"You look terrific," Roni gushed. "What are you doing here? When did you get in?" The words poured out. They hadn't seen Andie since October when she'd made a quick trip down to spend the weekend for her mom's birthday. "I thought you weren't coming in until the parade next weekend."

Andie lifted a thin shoulder covered in pale-green cashmere. Earrings with several long dangles tinkled together with her movements. God, she was gorgeous. She was practically glowing. "I'm staying *through* the parade now," Andie said. "I took an early flight down this morning. I heard you needed us."

Roni went still. She looked from one friend to the other. Then she felt tears speeding to the surface and she pulled the two of them in for another hug.

"You came down from Boston because I wanted to talk?" Roni spoke through a suddenly stuffy nose.

"I came down from Boston because you wanted to talk," Andie confirmed.

One more tight hug and Roni felt like she could speak without emotion clogging her throat. She swiped at her eyes. "You are the greatest." She looked at Ginger. "And I assume you had something to do with this?"

Ginger gave a quick nod. "I had a feeling this was going to be a biggie."

Roni swallowed. She wiped at her face again and then pulled her hands away and stared at the wetness on her skin. She was crying. Good lord, she hadn't cried in years. She'd come close recently. A tear here or there. But right now, she had tears streaming down her face.

She lowered her hands and smiled at her two best friends in the world. Talking about Zoe would be hard enough, but as if they'd completely understood what she needed, they'd just made it loads easier. "I love you guys."

They hugged once more and then Ginger stepped away. "I'll get the quiche," she said. "I'm starving."

"I'll get the glasses." Andie held up her hand and displayed a bottle of champagne. "We're having mimosas with breakfast."

"Perfect," Roni murmured. She glanced over at the piano. "Just let me scribble out one last thing before I forget?"

"Sure." Ginger and Andie both headed to the kitchen and Roni returned to the piano.

"I have the table set up on the deck," Roni muttered, motioning with one hand in the air. "Just grab another place setting and we'll eat out there."

Roni replayed the last few bars she'd been working on and then worked furiously to get the correct notes on the page. When she finished, she sat up straight and looked around. She was alone in the room, and another fifteen minutes had passed.

Ginger and Andie were both on the deck, as was all the food.

"You found the avocado and strawberries I'd cut up," Roni said as she stepped through the sliding glass door. She squinted against the brilliance of the sunlight.

"You had the bowls stacked beside the juice in the fridge. They seemed to be there for a reason." Andie fussed with the linens and silverware Roni had set out.

Roni had cleaned the kitchen after Lucas had left that morning, so while she'd been at it, she'd pulled out her grandmother's china and the napkins she had picked up in India to celebrate her twenty-fifth birthday. They'd been used only a handful of times.

"Is that your neighbor?" Ginger stood at the railing, looking out across the yard.

Roni jerked her head around. Sure enough, Mrs. Rylander was beating a path from under Roni's deck, back across the yard to her house. "Hang on," Roni murmured. "I need to talk to her."

She ran in to grab the tea set Mrs. Rylander had brought over the previous morning, then took off down the back steps. She caught the woman about fifty feet away.

"You're fast for an old lady," Roni said.

"Oh!" Mrs. Rylander squawked and whirled around, bringing her hands to her chest. "You're not supposed to see me," she accused.

Roni laughed with the pure pleasure of the moment. She'd put a small table and two chairs under her deck months ago so the woman wouldn't have to stand when she came over to hear Roni play, and Mrs. Rylander still wanted to pretend that she didn't sneak across the yard most mornings.

"I'm sorry." Roni tried to sound apologetic. "Let's pretend it's not morning and I didn't just finish playing the piano." She wrapped her arm through the woman's elbow and turned her toward her smaller house. "I wanted to bring you your tea set back. I also wanted to ask if you enjoyed your little ride yesterday."

"What ride?"

"Uh . . . the one down my stairs?"

Pale eyes turned to hers and Roni noticed for the first time that her neighbor looked closer to her age today than she normally did. The creases around her eyes seemed deeper, and her mouth was turned down. Also, her skin had a sallow color to it.

"Are you okay, Mrs. Rylander?" Roni reached out, intending to make sure she wasn't running a fever, but Mrs. Rylander jerked her head back.

"Of course I'm fine. I was just out for a walk."

"I know." Roni patted the arm in hers. "Your walks must be interesting, given the fact you take the same path every morning," she murmured wryly.

Mrs. Rylander twisted up her face. "If you want to insist on pointing out that I like to listen to you play on occasion, then I'll point out that you had company overnight. *Thankyouverymuch.*"

Roni chuckled again, enjoying her neighbor, and smiled even wider when she heard the happy sound of her laughter echoing back to her. "It was a good night," she conceded.

"Should have been. That man may not be my Henry, but he's close. He's a very good-looking man. And whew," Mrs. Rylander waved her free hand in front of her face. "The muscles on that one. They sure are nice."

Roni thought about how those muscles had pinned her up against the shower wall yesterday morning. "That they are, Mrs. Rylander. That. They. Are."

The older lady cut her eyes over at Roni then, before glancing behind her at the way they'd come. When she turned back, Roni thought she saw a bit of loneliness clinging to her features.

"You seem to have more company this morning too," Mrs. Rylander murmured. "You're quite the social butterfly lately."

"My girlfriends are here." Roni glanced at her deck herself. "We're going to have a long-overdue talk." She had the urge to invite Mrs. Rylander over, but she needed this time with her friends.

She needed to tell them about Zoe.

And she wanted their take on this situation she'd found herself in with Lucas.

"Would you like to come over for breakfast someday, Mrs. Rylander?" Roni asked as they stepped through the gate separating the two yards. "I could fix pancakes or waffles, or—oh!" Her eyes rounded. "How about eggs Benedict? I haven't fixed that in years."

Charles had always wanted eggs Benedict when he'd stayed over at her apartment. That hadn't happened too often since one or both of them was usually traveling. They'd rarely been in the same city together. But Roni loved to cook. She'd become quite the expert on hollandaise sauce over the years, and she thought she might still be able to whip up a batch.

"After your run someday?" Mrs. Rylander asked. She untied her customary scarf from under her chin as they reached her back door. "I usually eat earlier than that."

Roni was giving up her run today—the first time she'd done that voluntarily since she'd moved to the island, and she certainly didn't want to get in the habit of it—but she suddenly wanted to skip it again. For her neighbor this time. She also wanted to use that time to try to wheedle some information out of the woman about her kids. Was it true none of them ever visited her?

Mrs. Rylander was clearly lonely. Roni wanted to help. Maybe she wouldn't solve anything, but if she could be an ear on occasion . . . she wanted to do that for her neighbor. Just like Mrs. Rylander was there for her for their beach talks.

"After I finish on the piano, then," Roni suggested. "How about Wednesday?"

"This week?" Those pale-blue eyes had a bit more life in them now.

Roni squeezed her neighbor's hand and then passed over the tea set. "This week."

Thin lips slipped into a hesitant smile and Mrs. Rylander gave a small nod. "I would like that, I suppose."

Before she could change her mind, Roni leaned in and gave her a quick peck on her cool cheek. Mrs. Rylander stiffened, but she didn't pull away. They'd never had these kinds of moments before.

"Don't come up the stairs by yourself," Roni admonished, as she turned to go. "After you get through eavesdropping on my playing, I mean. I'll come down and help you up."

Mrs. Rylander blew out a huff. "You could invite that hunk to stay for breakfast and he could come down and help me. I'm a feeble old woman, you know?"

"You're full of crap," Roni tossed over her shoulder. She threw up a wave. "It'll just be me and you. He leaves before I get to the piano."

"You might want to think about keeping him."

Roni stopped at the quickly spoken words. She turned back. "What?"

"Keep him," Mrs. Rylander said with a sure nod. "He's a good one."

A breeze picked up and skated across them, and Mrs. Rylander brought a hand to her hair as if afraid her curls would get mussed in the wind. The hair on the back of Roni's neck stood on end.

"You think so?" she asked. She'd already decided that Lucas was a good one. She didn't know if that would be enough to "keep him," or if she even wanted to, but she had to agree with her neighbor's assessment.

"Have you watched him this week?" Mrs. Rylander asked. "He holds doors open for women." The smile on the other woman's face hinted that she was drifting away to another place and another time. "And he talks *to* people. Not at them. He pays attention when others speak." Her gaze emptied a little and her smile flattened. "He sometimes reminds me of my Henry. The good parts."

A look of loneliness passed over the thinner, wrinkled skin of the other woman again and Roni fought the urge to step back over and wrap her arms around her. Maybe someday. But for now, an invite to breakfast seemed like far enough to push.

"I'll see you Wednesday morning," Roni said.

The white head bobbed, and Mrs. Rylander gave one more slight smile. "Thank you."

Roni turned and fled. She didn't want to think about the sadness that had been reaching out to her as she'd stood on the woman's patio. Mrs. Rylander clearly had hurts in her past. So much so that she was now here all alone.

A chill raced up Roni's spine, and she couldn't help but wonder if Henry had somehow played into that. Mrs. Rylander had clearly loved him, but there had been something else in her eyes just now when she'd mentioned her husband. Something that had looked a bit like regret.

Roni skidded to a stop as she approached her deck and looked up. Both of her friends stood at the railing, mimosas in hand, and sent up a silent toast with their champagne flutes.

"When did that start?" Ginger asked.

Roni hurried up the steps. "Mrs. Rylander? She's been sneaking over for months. I thought I told you that."

"You did. I didn't think you two acknowledged the fact, though."

Roni grabbed her own drink and took a sip. Delicious. Then she looked at her friends and stated, "There are a lot of things I haven't been acknowledging. I'm trying to change that."

Her words set the tone and the three women settled down to breakfast. They passed the quiche and fruit around the table, and then Andie lifted her glass in a toast.

"To the best kind of friends," she said. "The ones I want to celebrate everything with. And the ones I'm fortunate enough to always have on my side." Her gaze landed on Roni. "Just like I know you two know I'm there for you. No matter when, and no matter where I am."

Affection swelled inside Roni. She missed their times together.

They clinked glasses and took a sip, and Roni noticed both of them eyeing her over their rims.

"So . . ." Ginger began when it became clear that Roni was stalling. Ginger popped a slice of strawberry in her mouth, chewed, and then said, "Should we talk men first?"

The tension eased from Roni's shoulders and her face split into a wide grin. "Yes," she breathed. "Men first." She thought of the conversation she and Lucas had had in her kitchen yesterday morning and blurted, "*Ohmygod*, I think I'm in a relationship."

Ginger choked on her mimosa, and Andie rolled her eyes and took another drink.

"Honey." Andie reached over and patted Roni's hand. "I could have told you that when we talked the other day."

"You knew she was in a relationship?" Ginger yelped. "And you didn't tell me? I thought she was just having sex!"

Andie swallowed a bite of her quiche. "She thought she was just having sex too."

Roni placed her fork carefully beside her gold-trimmed plate and clasped her hands in front of her. Her breakfast would just have to get cold. "What . . . *exactly*," she started, her attention turned to Andie, "made you think it was more?"

Because Roni was fairly certain she'd only said that they were having sex.

Andie's eyebrows rose above her blue-gray eyes. The color of her eyes had always reminded Roni of the calm surf glistening in the bright morning sun. "I believe your exact words were," she began, "'He just makes me feel good to be around him.'"

Ginger sucked in a breath. "She said that?"

Roni shot both of them a scowl. They ignored her. "Enjoying being around someone does not mean it's more than sex," she pointed out.

"I'm so happy for her," Ginger said in a hushed tone.

Great. Roni could see her friend's romantic streak coming to life—while both her friends seemed to have forgotten that Roni was right there with them.

"Mark makes you feel good to be around him," Ginger asked Andie. "Right?"

Andie nodded. "And when I'm not around him. Just knowing I get to be around him again works too."

Roni wanted to make a face at the sickeningly sweet sentiment, but she'd seen Andie and Mark together. It was true. They each made the other feel good. Just being around one another.

"And she's like that with Lucas?" Ginger pressed.

"That's what she said."

"Hello?" Roni clanged her fork on her glass. "I'm right here."

And *she* should be the one to determine when it had turned from sex into a relationship.

She looked at Andie, prepared to argue the point, but then slumped in her chair. "Damn it," she muttered. She should have known it the instant she'd seen Gracie on that computer. "How did you know that? *I* didn't even know at that point."

"Of course you didn't," Andie said. "You can't see it when you're right in the middle of it. Especially when you think it's just sex."

"And you couldn't have bothered to tell me?" Roni grumbled. Not that she would have believed her. Heck, she still didn't know what to make of it.

Ginger scooped up a bite of eggs and watched the other two women. Andie swallowed a bite of berry before wiping her hands on the napkin in her lap and pointing an accusing finger at Roni.

"How long did you date Charles?"

"Two years." They'd met the season they'd both played with the Chicago orchestra, and had stayed together after that. She'd later flown Andie and Ginger to New York to meet him. "Why?"

"Did he ever make you feel better to be around him?"

She opened her mouth to say that of course he had. She'd thought she wanted to marry the man, for heaven's sake.

"I enjoyed my time with him," she hedged, thinking back over the years spent with Charles. They'd shared a lot of the same likes and dislikes, and had both understood the pressures of the business. They'd respected one another, as well as their talents. They'd also rarely been in the same city together. And she had been fine with that. But no, she realized, he hadn't made her simply feel good to be around him. Not the same way she got with Lucas.

"We were both worried, waiting for you to tell us you were going to marry him." Andie motioned between her and Ginger. "But we could see he didn't do that for you. He was just . . ." Andie shrugged. "I don't know. Comfortable."

Roni nodded. "He was comfortable. We both understood each other well." Charles was as driven as Roni had been.

"And then you moved here," Ginger jumped into the conversation. "And we didn't push because we didn't want you to go back to him."

"You didn't like him?" Roni asked. Someone could definitely have told her that.

"We liked him fine," Ginger said. "But he wasn't the one. He didn't make you get all swoony."

Roni shook her head. There was more to making a relationship work than getting all swoony. Her dad had made her mom all swoony for years, and even with that, they hadn't been able to make it work. He hadn't paid enough attention to her.

Just as Charles hadn't paid attention to Roni.

"We had a lot in common," Roni argued, knowing the point was moot. "He understood my passion for playing, and I understood his." Charles had played the violin. He still did.

And then it dawned on her that her friends had assumed she'd moved here because she'd been running from a bad relationship. They thought she'd given up her career over Charles?

"I didn't move here because of him," she said with a healthy amount of incredulity.

"Okay," Andie accepted the statement.

Ginger looked uncertain for a few seconds and then scratched at a spot on her neck. "Okay," she parroted. "Then why did you? And what happened with Charles?"

Do or die, Roni thought. It was time to tell them.

She took a deep breath, pulling in the scents of their mostly uneaten breakfast and the honeysuckle bushes surrounding her deck from below, then let it back out. "I moved here because he made me choose," she stated flatly. "And then my choice eventually broke me in two."

Two confused gazes stared back at her.

"I'll start at the beginning," she said. "Three years ago I played a charity event at the children's hospital in New York. I'd done plenty of similar events before, so when my manager suggested the hospital, I loved the idea. What better way to give back than to put a smile on a kid's face? It was June, and I was doing one concert. When I got there, I was overwhelmed. There were so many kids in the crowd."

Ginger leaned her elbows on the table, and Roni watched her eyes mist over. Ginger would make a great mother someday.

"I looked out over this crowd of miniature people and was over-whelmed with the spirits pouring back at me. Some looked at me as if I was the most magical thing they'd ever seen. Some as if I were the *only* magical thing they'd ever seen.

"And there was this one little girl," Roni continued. She could picture Zoe so easily in her mind. "She watched me with no expression whatsoever. She just sat there and took it all in. It wasn't that she was incapable of expression or feelings, but it was as if she wanted to make absolutely certain about something before sharing with me even the barest hint of herself."

"She was protective," Andie said.

Roni nodded. She'd recognized it the instant she'd laid eyes on Zoe. "I could see that from where I sat at the front of the room. This little girl, so tiny she could get lost in the crowd, was sitting there, afraid to so much as spare me a smile."

Roni sat back in her seat and placed her hands in her lap. She had to concentrate to tell the story without letting grief take hold. "She was seven, and her name was Zoe," she stated. "When I finished and asked if there were any questions, Zoe raised her hand." Roni closed her eyes and pictured the slight girl with the thin blonde hair and slightly too-large head.

"What did she ask?" Ginger whispered.

Roni took a long drink and finished off her mimosa. When she set her glass down, she dug her teeth into her top lip before answering, "She asked if I had a mother." Roni swallowed. It had been said with the most wishful voice she'd ever heard. "And then if my mother had been the person who'd taught me to play the piano."

She closed her eyes again as her chest burned.

"I got to know her over the next six months." Roni thought about her visits to the hospital. About the terror that would squeeze the breath out of her each time she approached the front doors. "Every time I walked into that hospital, I feared it would be the last. So I'd stop by to see her whenever I was in town. I sent her postcards from the places I traveled. She loved to see the cities I visited. I even gave her lessons on the piano a few times. She'd developed Alexander disease before she was two. Her mother hadn't been overly responsible up to that point, and had left Zoe with her grandmother much of her first two years of life. Then when Zoe went into the hospital for the first time, no one ever came to pick her up."

"Oh my." Ginger put her hand to her mouth. "She was just . . . deserted?"

Roni nodded. "Her mother never showed up for court dates after the abandonment, and eventually lost parental rights. Not that she wanted them, apparently. Zoe lived in and out of foster care and hospitals at that point. Alexander disease is fatal, so no one wanted her long-term."

"How awful." Andie looked a little green at the thought. "What happened to her?" She reached over and held Roni's hand. Ginger did the same.

Tension squeezed from the base of Roni's stomach, up to the back of her throat. Tears once again leaked from her eyes. "I fell in love with her," Roni whispered brokenly. The back of her nose burned as she tried unsuccessfully to keep in the tears. "I'd taken one look into her pale-blue eyes that first day, at the fear radiating back at me, and I had the strongest urge to run to her. To scoop her up in my arms and hold her so tight. I wanted to help. And I wanted to make her smile." She sucked in an unsteady breath. "I wanted to be there for someone.

"I went home that day a changed woman. It took a while, but I reevaluated my life. I took a long, hard look. And I didn't like what I saw. I was heading down the same path my father had chosen. Profession over all else. I loved my career. Very much. But I didn't want to be alone the remainder of my life. And I didn't want to die knowing that all I had for anyone to remember me by was the piano."

Those months of self-evaluation had led to a major decision.

She'd scale back. Teach at Juilliard instead of performing. She'd give everything she had to Zoe.

She would change her life for the child.

"I wanted to be Zoe's mom," she told her friends. Her voice shook when she spoke. "I had it all figured out. Charles and I would get married, and I'd cut back. I'd stop playing completely if I had to. So that I could be there for Zoe. I knew she had limited time to live."

"That's a huge thing to do," Andie spoke softly. Her fingers stayed wrapped tightly around Roni's. "I take it Charles didn't like the idea?"

A dry chuckle came from Roni. "Charles didn't waver for a second. He said he would marry me—*he supposed*—but he wanted no part of having a kid." Roni glanced down at the food on her plate as she continued in a whisper, "And certainly not a reject who would take time away from his music. Only to end up dying in the end." Her voice was monotone by the time she finished relaying Charles's words. Shame filled her for ever having loved the man.

"Zoe or him, he'd said." She lifted her face and smiled weakly at her friends. "And he was arrogant enough, he thought I'd choose him."

"He was an ass," Ginger's tone was harsh. Harder than anything Roni had ever heard come from her. "And he didn't know you at all." She used her free hand to wipe the tears from Roni's cheeks. "You've always wanted a family."

Roni blinked at that, pulled out of the past. "What?"

She'd never even thought about a family until she'd met Zoe. And then the thought had only crossed her mind because the girl had so desperately needed someone. Roni had realized that she'd needed someone too, of course. Not just someone. She'd needed Zoe. She'd wanted to give the girl everything she'd never had before.

And she'd wanted to make sure that Zoe never felt alone again.

"When we were little, you were the one who always wanted to play 'house.'" Andie added to Ginger's statement. "You were the mother, I was the kid, and Ginger was your husband."

Roni let her eyes lose focus as she went back in time. She remembered playing house with her friends. And yes, she had wanted to do that. All the time. Funny, she'd never thought about that being so telling. But maybe she had wanted a family, even then. Or maybe it had simply been because her own family had splintered.

"Sometimes that boy would play with us," she muttered. "What was his name?"

"Carter," Ginger answered. "He would be your pain-in-the-butt son."

Carter had lived on the island year-round. He'd been Ginger's friend. Roni had another memory and she grinned suddenly at Ginger. "When he was around, you always wanted to play 'wedding.'"

Ginger blushed. They'd teased her endlessly as a teenager about her crush on the boy next door. Carter had been their age, but he'd looked older. He'd filled out and was muscular by the time he was thirteen. And he'd moved on from playing house with silly girls. Ginger had been chunky and shy, and easy to ignore at that point.

"We're not talking about me." Ginger smirked at the two of them.

"Have you seen him recently?" This came from Andie. She leaned forward in her chair, though neither woman had turned loose of Roni's hands. "Is he still hot?"

The blush deepened, turning Ginger's cheeks a deep crimson. "He hasn't been home in years. I have no idea what he looks like."

"Ah," Andie thunked back in her chair. "Too bad. I'll bet he's still a catch."

"I'll bet he's bald and fat," Ginger grumbled. "And has a nagging wife. Maybe an ex-wife or two, as well. Probably a houseful of unruly kids."

Not that she was bitter, apparently. Throughout their teens, Carter had remained Ginger's friend, but he'd never looked at her the way she'd looked at him.

Andie turned her shrewd gaze back to Roni. "I hope you told Charles he could rot at the bottom of the ocean while the crabs picked his eyeballs out of his head."

Roni nodded. "Pretty much. And you two were right. We'd worked together as a couple, but he wasn't it for me. Even before he turned into a first-class jerk. We were simply comfortable together."

That didn't mean Lucas was it, either. But he was definitely farther ahead in line than Charles had been.

"So what happened to Zoe?" Andie returned them to the story.

The muscles along Roni's neck and shoulders tensed. She knew the smile she tried to wear came across as heartbroken instead of happy, but it was the best she could do. She was hollow inside. "I was out on tour when I decided I wanted to adopt her. I called and talked to my lawyer, and we had a plan in place. The minute I had a day to run back to town . . ." She choked on a sob. "It was three years ago yesterday," she whispered. "I headed straight to the hospital to tell Zoe that I wanted her. That she would never be alone again."

Tears dripped off her face and landed on their clasped hands. "She'd died six days earlier." Pain crushed in her chest. Her voice grew so quiet that Andie and Ginger practically leaned into her chair to hear. "I should have been there," Roni finished.

"Oh, honey." Ginger was the first to move. She had Roni wrapped up in her arms, and then Andie closed hers around both of them. Ginger stroked Roni's hair. "I'm so sorry."

Andie pressed her cheek to Roni's and Roni realized that Andie was crying too.

Something else occurred to her as well.

This was the first time she'd really cried over losing Zoe.

She'd shut down. Quit functioning. But she hadn't cried.

"Why didn't you call us?" Ginger asked in a desperate plea.

Roni shook her head in the circle of her friends' arms. "I couldn't." She squeezed them tight. "I had two weeks of my tour to finish. Had to be back onstage the next night. So I hopped a plane, and I tried to put it out of my mind."

"Oh baby," Ginger soothed.

"I know," Roni whispered. "I'm so sorry I didn't tell you two. You're my best friends. You deserved to know what was going on in my life."

"You deserved to have us hold your hand through it, but that's not you, hon," Andie added. "And that's okay. You've always held yourself in a little tighter than us. We knew you'd come to us when you were ready."

Roni nodded. "I just wish it hadn't taken me so long. I went back to New York after my tour, and Danny showed up a few days later. I hadn't gone home for Christmas, so he'd known something was wrong." Roni sniffed. "I told him everything. At that moment, I needed someone to know that I was broken. That I wasn't okay. He stayed for a few days, and then after he left . . ." Her neck lost the ability to hold her head up and she laid there, her head lying against Ginger's. "I didn't leave my apartment for the next two months. I didn't answer the phone, or even open my blinds. I just sat there. Until I couldn't even stay there any longer."

"And then you came here," Andie stated.

Roni nodded. "And then I came here. I needed my girls. I couldn't bring myself to talk about it. I didn't want to feel the pain again. But I needed to be with you. And I needed to be away from there. The mere thought of playing on a stage again made me see Zoe's face. It reminded me that I hadn't been there for her. I'd let her die alone."

"Oh, sweetheart," Ginger cooed. "Of course Zoe knew you loved her. I'm sure she looked at those postcards every day. You gave her something in those six months that she'd never had."

"Maybe." Roni wiped at her eyes. "But I'd failed her when it mattered the most."

She'd failed Zoe even worse than she'd just admitted to her friends. But some things she had to keep to herself.

The three of them sat there, huddled together for several more minutes as each of them shared Roni's grief, until Roni finally made herself confess as to what had brought this on.

"Lucas has a daughter." She spoke into Ginger's hair. Ginger pulled back.

"What?" she asked.

"Lucas," Roni repeated. "He has a daughter. Her name is Sophia Grace. She goes by Gracie, and she's four and a half. I accidentally met her over a video chat the other day."

Andie's eyes went wide and round as she slowly sat back into her chair.

"I talked to her," Roni admitted. Her chest ached. "She wants a dog. And to learn to play the piano."

Discovering Gracie had knocked her out of her locked-down life. It had made it impossible to keep Zoe contained in the back of her mind.

"And you didn't run away?" Andie asked.

"I did." Roni nodded. "But Lucas came after me."

"Ooooh," Ginger's romantic tone was back. "That is so sweet."

Roni chuckled. Mental exhaustion made the sound come out sad. "He showed up here. I tried to kick him out, but instead I ended up doing him in the shower. *After* he convinced me that there might be something more to this than just sex. He likes that I enjoy life even though I seem to have my fair share of hang-ups. He accused me of having this big house because I wanted to fill it with kids. And he claims that I look at him like I want him to hold me. Oh," she paused, but knew she had to put the last thing out there too. "And he thinks that I miss playing the piano professionally."

"Do you?" Both of them asked.

Roni nodded.

"I have *got* to meet this guy," Andie murmured.

Roni rolled her eyes sarcastically. "He's just like any other guy."

But he wasn't. He wasn't at all like any other guy.

"He's dreamy." Ginger picked up her drink. "And he has these abs," she said. She turned up the glass and drained it. "I had naughty dreams about those abs the other night."

"Oh my God," Roni groaned.

Ginger shrugged. "Sorry. It's been a while."

The two of them laughed while Andie just stared at Roni.

"He pushed you for more." She pointed out. "He didn't take your crap and walk away, even when you told him it was over. No one has ever done that to you."

Ginger nodded in agreement, her eyes growing sober. "She's right."

"*Ever*," Andie reinforced.

Roni reached for her glass, but it was empty. Before she could get up for a refill, Ginger ran to get the champagne and orange juice from the fridge. While she was gone, Roni thought about what Andie had said. No one had ever done that to her.

She'd dated a few guys after her dad had died, but none of the relationships had felt right. When she'd suggested they see other people, not a one of them had protested. Then there had been Charles. He'd made her choose.

And no one since she'd moved to the island had ever come close to meaning more. They'd been good times. They'd been fun guys. But if they hadn't figured out on their own that it was just a fling, Roni had soon made that clear.

Until Lucas.

She looked at her friends now. "Why is he different?" she asked. It still scared her to death.

Ginger smiled in the dreamy way they were all used to. "Because he's special."

Andie shot her a look and shook her head, and then turned to Roni. "Because he has abs that you might want to keep around for a while?"

She winked before growing serious and topping off her own drink with the juice. "And because it sounds like he sees who you really are."

Roni tapped the pad of her finger against the tines of her fork. "I'm not sure I know who I really am anymore."

"You'll figure it out." Ginger patted her hand. "And when you take wrong turns, we'll be here to shove you back on the right path. Assuming he doesn't do it first."

Roni knew that they would.

She reached out and wrapped an arm around both of them, pulling them all in close so they practically huddled around the table. "Thank you for being here for me," she said sincerely. "I suspect I'm going to need you again before this is over."

Andie nodded her head. "Me too," she mumbled.

Roni laughed. "You have great faith in me, huh?" she teased.

"I mean . . . *I'm* going to need you both too. But . . . I'm not sure I should talk about it."

Ginger and Roni whipped their heads around. "What's wrong?" they asked.

Andie looked pained. "I'm nervous to tell you. Not after what you just told us."

Roni turned loose of her friend and studied the serious expression on her face. "Whatever it is, there's never a better time than when we're together, right? Tell us."

Ginger nodded and reached over to clasp Andie's hand. "Tell us."

Andie eyed Roni another few seconds and then picked up her glass and grimaced. She held it over the table between the three of them. "There's no champagne in my mimosa."

Neither of them got it for a moment, and then they simultaneously squealed. A lingering bout of sadness washed over Roni for what she didn't have in her life, but she was so happy for her friend. They pulled Andie to her feet, and the hugs began again.

"When are you due?" Roni asked. She peered down at Andie's smooth stomach, wanting to reach out and touch it. "And I'm so glad that you told us."

Andie flattened a hand over herself. "Seven months," she said. "I just found out yesterday. I haven't even told Mark yet."

Tears came from all three of them, and Ginger once again smiled in her gooey, romantic way. "We're going to be aunties!"

CHAPTER TWENTY-ONE

Tuesday morning in Lucas's hotel room held the soft click of computer keys. No television, no sound of water from the shower, no slight breathing noises from his bed. Roni had risen when he had. She'd tugged on a pair of jeans and a T-shirt. And then she'd headed out the door, almost before he could sit down at his laptop.

Lucas logged onto his company's server, checked in all the files he'd been working on, then typed up an e-mail to his boss. He'd met the deadline. He was finished.

Now he was officially on vacation.

He hit Send.

Then he dropped his head to the seat back and stared out the window to the blue sky.

He was careening down the hill toward love and he wasn't sure if Roni was following along in his tracks or not. They'd spent a lot of time together the last few days, and both of them seemed to enjoy it. In fact, other than the hours between five a.m. and when they saw each other at the convention center, they spent all their free time together.

The morning hours were their own, though. She played the piano and went for a run, while he put in a few hours of work and got in a workout. But after they finished with the competition for the evening, they came together and either made their way back to the hotel or to her house. Last night they'd ended up here.

And he'd almost begged her not to get out of his bed and leave so early.

Time was running out. He needed longer than five more days.

No. He shook his head. What he needed was to figure out how to bring up the idea of Roni going home with him to Dallas. He wanted her to meet Gracie.

A knock sounded on his door and he shot a look at the digital clock sitting on the end table. It was barely seven. His pulse spiked as he thought about Roni coming back. Maybe she'd been reluctant to leave that morning, after all.

He swung the door open and his excitement deflated.

"Well, don't look so damned sad that it's only me," Kelly said. He was dressed in a tight Under Armour shirt, shorts, and tennis shoes, and shoved his way into the room. Following along behind him was a thirty-pound, solid-black mound of fur. The dog's tongue lolled out and she immediately came over to Lucas for a rub.

"I still can't believe they let you keep her in the hotel." Lucas studied the animal, which would eventually grow into the size of a human and wondered if Gracie needed a large dog or a small one.

Kelly had brought Mako with him, since she was only three months old. He hadn't wanted to leave her alone for two weeks, and had found a dog sitter on the island to watch her while he was out during the day.

"I offered to stay at a different hotel," Kelly said, "but they wouldn't hear of it." Kelly stood in the middle of the room now, hands on his hips and an irritated look smearing his pretty-boy face. His dog moved to a corner, plopped down, and promptly forgot the both of them existed. "I need your help," he announced. "Can you put work aside this morning? Let's go to the gym in town today."

They had been meeting in the hotel's fitness center every morning before going over to the convention center, but the equipment in there left a little to be desired. Lucas glanced at the laptop still sitting open on the desk. "I just finished, actually. Let me talk to Gracie first and I'm all yours." Gracie should be calling any minute. Lucas headed into the bedroom to the dresser. "What's up?" he asked as he rummaged through a drawer.

He replaced the T-shirt he'd pulled on when he'd gotten out of bed with his own Under Armour.

"Today's a year since we split." The words were growled out and Lucas poked his head back around the wall to study his friend. Kelly had very carefully *not* mentioned anything about Becky the whole time they'd been here. He ran a hand through his hair and a sigh sounded in the room.

"I'm sorry, man."

Lucas had been at Kelly and Becky's wedding five years ago, and he still couldn't believe they'd broken up. It had been love at first sight when they'd both been sixteen.

"Yeah." Kelly mumbled.

What else was there to say? Yeah. Breaking up sucked. Even when you didn't love her with your life. Lucas couldn't imagine what Kelly had gone through.

But then, he wondered if he could now. He glanced at the rumpled bed and thought about not seeing Roni again. The mere idea didn't sit well.

It didn't sit at all.

"Want to talk about it?" Lucas dragged his eyes from the bed and plucked his shoes from the lined-up row of footwear at the bottom of the closet. He thought about Roni making fun of his toiletries and figured she'd have about the same thing to say about his shoes. "Or are we just going to pound out our frustrations and pretend nothing else is bothering us?"

Kelly's jaw tightened. "What good would talking about it do?" He shrugged. "We fucked it up." He shook his head and Lucas was at a loss as to how to help. Finally, Kelly said, "I swear I keep seeing her on the island the last couple of days. Everywhere I look. It's making me insane. I should be over her by now."

And Lucas shouldn't be falling for a woman that he wasn't sure could fit into his and Gracie's life. But sometimes the heart was in charge, apparently. Not that it made it any easier to accept.

"We'll just pound out our frustrations, then." Lucas suggested.

A sound came from the computer speaker and he moved back to the desk. He tapped his mouse and his daughter's face appeared on his screen.

"Good morning, sweet Gracie," he said.

She giggled and rocked back and forth, her legs crossed Indian-style, only with both feet on top of her thighs. She was sitting on the floor with the camera pointed down at her.

"Good morning, sweet Daddy!" she shouted. "Grandma says it's only five more days 'til I see you again."

He smiled broadly. He missed his kid. "That's right. Can you count to five?"

She went immediately into counting, holding up a finger for each number until she had four held up on one hand and one on the other. While she counted, Lucas glanced at Kelly and motioned to the screen, silently asking if he wanted to say hi to Gracie. It had been a couple of years since they'd seen each other.

Kelly's eyes shifted to the computer and his jaw hardened even more. He shook his head.

"Then we can get the dog, right?" Gracie asked. At the word "dog," Mako lifted her head from the floor as if knowing that her type was being talked about.

Lucas flailed in his mind. He didn't want to talk about getting a dog right then. And he certainly didn't want Mako wandering over into Gracie's line of sight. He motioned to Kelly and then to the dog, trying to tell him to keep her out of sight. "How about we wait and see if Santa brings you one?"

Crap. He cringed as the words left his mouth. That was worse than letting Gracie see Mako.

"Oh." Gracie's eyes brightened. "I didn't think of that. I bets he'll have the most beautiful dog in the world for me."

Yep. He was about to be the proud owner of a dog.

"What's your Grandma doing this morning, Gracie?" he asked. He wanted to talk to his daughter about Roni, but he wanted to do it alone. If things progressed and it looked like he might be able to talk Roni into coming to Dallas, then he'd bring his mother into it. No need to hear her opinion until he made up his own mind.

"She's fixing me pancakes," Gracie said. "And sausages. She said I could dip the sausages in the syrup. But not in my orange juice."

Lucas watched the screen as his daughter talked. When she finished telling him about the pancakes and sausages, she began a rundown of her evening from the night before. She'd made her grandparents watch *Lady and the Tramp*, yet again.

She was Lucas's joy. His life.

She was his everything.

Was he really ready to risk interrupting that by bringing a third party into the mix?

The picture of Roni lying in his bed that morning, the way she'd been when he'd awoken, popped to mind. Her legs had been tangled with his, her warm body curled against his side. Her head had rested on his shoulder, and her palm had been planted dead center on his chest.

He'd lifted his head from his pillow and peered down at the two of them, and he'd known that he needed to tell her about Gracie's cancer.

Which mean that, yes, he was ready to bring her into Gracie's life.

The leukemia may not define his daughter, but it was a part of who she was. It was a part of who *they* were. And he wanted to share that with Roni.

He could trust her. She was the type who would be there for the hard parts.

And she was the type who could love Gracie as much as he did.

Which he would insist on if this was going to go anywhere.

"Hey, Gracie," he interrupted his daughter, who was now showing him her pink toenails and explaining how Grandma had let her do them herself. He wanted his daughter's thoughts on the matter before he did or insisted on anything, but he also worried about getting her hopes up.

"What, Daddy?"

Bright eyes blinked at him in complete and utter trust and his heart seized. He would do anything in the world to keep from hurting her.

"Do you remember my friend from the other day?" he began slowly. He couldn't believe he was asking this, but he couldn't just spring Roni on her, either. "The piano player that was here when we were talking?"

She nodded, her green barrette slipping to hang precariously on the end of her fine hair. "She had pretty curls like me," Gracie said. Gracie's hair had grown back curlier after the chemo. "Is she there? Did you learn to play the piano?"

The child never quit talking. "I haven't learned to play yet," he said. Nor had Roni played for him—which he was hoping to change. He wanted a private showing. "I was thinking . . . how would you like to talk to her again sometime?" He rushed his words now. "What if she stopped by the house someday? Just to say hi."

He caught the raised eyebrow on Kelly.

"Would she teach me to play the piano?"

He could imagine Roni sitting on the bench in his great room with his daughter, showing her where to put her fingers on the keys. She would be a patient teacher, he suspected. But taking her home with him wasn't about the piano.

"I don't know, Gracie. Maybe. But how about if she just came for a visit sometime?"

"Why?"

He smiled at her curiosity.

"Because she's a special friend and I thought she might like to meet you," he explained. "And I thought you might like to meet her too."

Gracie pursed her lips as she thought it through, her eyebrows lowered. Her thinking took all of two seconds. "I think I might like to," she declared. "Would she play dolls with me?"

Lucas chuckled as the weight low in his stomach began to ease slightly. "She might," he said.

"When will she be here? Are you bringing her in five days when you come home? Hey, Grandma." Gracie suddenly shot up from the floor and ran out of sight of the camera.

"Gracie . . ." he started, but stopped. She was gone. Nerves tingled up his arms and around to the back of his neck.

"You're taking Roni home with you?" Kelly asked quietly.

Lucas shrugged. "I'm thinking about it. If she'll come."

The line of his friend's mouth shifted from the flat, hard mark it had been in since he'd arrived, to a smile. It wasn't huge, but Lucas could see it was heartfelt. "Congrats," he said. "She seems like a great gal."

"Daddy's bringing home a friend." Gracie's voice could be heard offscreen.

Christ. Lucas wasn't ready to explain to his mother that he might be risking bringing home another woman who wouldn't stay.

"What's that?" He heard his mother ask.

"A special friend," Gracie said. "Daddy's bringing her home."

Kelly snapped for Mako and the dog stood. They both headed to the door. Kelly was giving him some privacy. "Meet me in the lobby in ten?" he said.

Lucas nodded. He needed the extra-hard workout himself.

Gracie was suddenly in front of the monitor again, staring straight into the screen. "Can she stay with us?" she asked. "I can share my room with her." She bit her bottom lip for a second before adding hesitantly, "I'll sleep in the top bunk if she's scared to. I'm a big girl now."

A flutter tickled just behind Lucas's ribs. Up to this point, Gracie had refused to spend more than a couple minutes on the top bunk.

His mother appeared behind Gracie. She was wiping her hands on a pale-yellow dish towel and wore an apron, slightly frayed around the edges, that he could remember seeing her wear when she'd fixed weekend pancakes for him and his friends during his teens.

"What's this, Lucas?" she asked. "You're bringing a woman home?"

"No, Mom." Good grief. "I asked Gracie how she'd feel if I invited a friend to come visit."

"I said yes," Gracie added for clarification. She nodded her head.

Lucas ignored his mother to focus on his daughter. "I'm not sure if she'll come, Gracie. But I think I'm going to ask her, if that's okay with you."

Gracie picked up on his more serious tone. Her exuberance calmed and she tilted her head. "Does she have any little girls?" she finally asked.

"No, baby. But she likes little girls." They'd talked about Gracie several times over the last few days and it had been apparent that Roni loved kids.

"Do you think she would like me?" Gracie asked.

His mother twisted her hands together.

"I'm positive she would like you." He wanted to say he couldn't imagine anyone not liking her, but Gracie had recently asked why she didn't have a mother. Someone at her dance class had told her that everyone had a mother. And Gracie was a bright kid. She'd come home that day and asked if she didn't have a mother because her mother didn't like her.

He glanced quickly at his mom and saw her worry as she stared at the back of Gracie's head. The last few years would have been far more difficult without his parents' love and support.

"But what if she doesn't?" Gracie continued. Her voice had grown nervously thin.

No words came to mind. What the hell did he say to that?

Yes, clearly there was at least one person who didn't care for Gracie. But he had no idea how to explain that some women were just selfish and immature, and didn't deserve the honor of being called a mother.

He didn't believe that about Roni.

Of course, there was much about Roni he didn't know. What if he was making another mistake and she *was* like Des?

He glanced at his mom again and she stepped forward this time and put her hand on Gracie's shoulder. "She's just a friend, Gracie," she spoke softly, and he was suddenly grateful she'd come into the room. "Like your friend Lisa who comes over to play with you. Your Daddy wants his friend to come for a playdate too." His mother shot Lucas a hard, wry look at the word "playdate" and he felt as if he'd been caught with his hand up a girl's shirt. "And if for some crazy reason his friend doesn't like you, then your Daddy would never invite her back."

That was the truth. Love his daughter, or don't let the door hit you on the way out.

Gracie tilted her head up and stared at her grandmother with such a serious expression that Lucas wanted to laugh. Only his insides had twisted until they'd become rigid. No laughter was coming up through that mess.

Then Gracie looked back at him. She nodded. "I think she'll like me," she declared. "She already talked to me. I hope she says yes when you ask her."

Her small, rose-colored mouth curved up and Lucas wanted to catch the next flight home just to pull his daughter close. He couldn't imagine a world without her in it. "I miss you, sweet Gracie."

"I miss you too, sweet Daddy."

~

The moon was a thin sliver that night, but it was bright. It hung low out over the ocean, shooting a narrow path through Roni's bedroom window and slicing over the two of them. Lucas lay there, his eyes open, staring blankly at the painting hanging on the wall opposite the bed while his brain worked overtime.

He'd done nothing but think about her all day. Her. And him. And Gracie.

Her and him.

Her and Gracie.

Her and him and Gracie.

He shifted his gaze from the painting, and it landed on the ceiling. He wanted Roni in his life. Yet he couldn't understand how his feelings could develop so quickly. Or so strongly.

It couldn't be love until he brought her fully into his world.

At least, that's what he kept telling himself.

She didn't know about all that Gracie had been through. Or what she might go through again. She didn't know that he worried every minute of every day that the cancer would come back.

But his heart kept saying something different. It taunted him that this was love.

They had a good time together. The sex was good—*the sex was great*—and they easily laughed and enjoyed each other's company. They'd even fallen into a comfortable routine. But it was more than sex and fun and comfort.

She was vulnerable behind her walls.

And every time he saw that vulnerability peek out, he found himself wanting to pull her close. He wanted to protect her and fix her world.

And he wanted her to fix his.

He turned his head to find her watching him. The clock on the bedside table behind her showed that it was just after one in the morning. He needed to tell her about Gracie.

But the words didn't come.

She was lying on her side, her curls sticking out in every direction, and one corner of her mouth slowly hitched up. The loneliness he'd gotten used to seeing in her eyes now showed up in her smile. He couldn't stop himself from reaching for her.

He pulled her to him, and neither of them spoke as their mouths met.

She opened her lips and welcomed him in, and he groaned deep in his throat as he thrust inside her mouth. She tasted sweet and hot. He gripped the back of her head to hold her as he feasted on her. He nibbled and tasted, and he swore he'd never get enough.

She gave as good as she got. He'd never seen her so greedy.

She sucked at his lips as her own hands clamped tightly around him. She reached deep inside. Her tongue slid along his and met him thrust for thrust. And the whole time, he would swear she was silently begging for more. Pleading for it. She was almost feral in her need.

When they broke apart, their hot breaths mingling and her cheeks flushed, she shoved the covers aside and threw a leg over his torso. The next instant she rose, proud and high above him, and he could do nothing but stare.

The moonlight hit her above her navel and cast a seductive glow over her entire body. The pink tips of her breasts pointed up, the silver barbell winked in the night. His hands balled up with desire. She was breathtaking.

His erection nudged against the cheeks of her butt, and he wanted to be deep inside her like he'd never wanted to be inside another woman in his life.

She must have been thinking along the same lines.

Before he could reach for a condom, she had one in her hand and was ripping it open with her teeth. She lifted above him and then she had him in her hand. His hips automatically pistoned with her touch. Her slim, soft fingers around his heavy weight got him every time.

In the next second she had the condom rolled over him and was easing herself down along its path. His balls squeezed tight with the feel of her.

She was slick and wet, and so damned hot that it almost hurt.

He didn't let himself pump, though he was near desperate to. He gritted his teeth and held back. She was in charge for the moment. He would follow her lead.

When she had him buried inside her, her eyelashes fluttered in the moonlight. She lifted her face and looked at him. Her dark eyes were almost emotionless, but it was as if everything she was feeling was transmitted wordlessly between them.

She hadn't expected this thing between them to be so real.

Neither had he.

She wasn't sure what to do about it.

He swallowed. Neither was he.

Then she began to move and he didn't want to think.

Her neck arched, her head tilted back, and her eyes closed. Her lips parted. She reached behind her until her hands splayed on the top of his thighs, and her breasts jutted high in the air. And all the while, her body moved up and down on his. Tight, pale curves were displayed in the glow from the moon, and he knew it to be the most erotic thing he'd ever seen.

He reached for her, settling his hand where they were joined. He spread his fingers wide. She had a narrow strip of hair there, trimmed short, and he took his time rubbing back and forth over the coarser texture. When his thumb dipped to touch her engorged flesh, she paused for a brief second, but then pressed herself more fully against him. He throbbed inside her.

With effort, he moved his hand up and slid over her stomach. The muscles beneath her skin quivered under his touch. His other hand gripped her thigh as she continued riding him. Finally, he reached her breast.

She arched her back farther, filling his hand with her.

She didn't make a sound. She merely rode him. He simply did his best to hang on.

He watched from half-closed eyes, unable to look at anything but her. And he just knew.

This wasn't a fling. It wasn't casual. It never had been.

It didn't matter how fast it had happened, or how much he really knew about her.

He loved her.

He wanted her in his life.

When she lifted up and pulled her hands from his thighs, he took over. It was either that or profess his love right then and there. And he feared that might scare her away.

He lifted from the mattress and put his mouth to her body. He sucked her breast deep between his lips. Finally, a sound came from her. It was soft and short. A high-pitched keening noise. He wanted to hear more.

Her hips rose and fell faster now, and he wrapped an arm around her waist. He worked one breast with his hand while the other got the attention of his teeth and tongue. He bit down right at the base of her beaded, oh-so-perfect nipple and he flicked the little barbell with his tongue. She made another noise. This time it was a groan.

She was holding on tight to her control and suddenly his purpose was to make her lose it. He wanted her screaming his name.

He pulled her down with him until his back was on the mattress and she was flush against his chest. He gripped her rear with both hands and pumped hard into her. They were sweating and sliding together and he couldn't get enough. He couldn't touch her enough. His mouth tasted and nipped at her neck as a hand scraped up her back. She was salty, but maintained the hint of berries that he always caught on her. He sucked a perfect circle of skin into his mouth.

She squeezed him tight from the inside, and his mouth popped free at her neck. The hand at her butt clenched as he almost called it done. Sweet Jesus, she drove him out of his mind.

She writhed, seeming almost out of control, yet he knew she wasn't. She twisted her hips in small circles, and it felt like she was pulling every last ounce of his energy out through his dick. She knew exactly what she was doing. And she was winning this round.

He went for her mouth, but she pulled away. She lifted up and braced her palms on his shoulders, watching him as she worked him with her hips. There was passion in her eyes now. And a hot, burning need. He could see that as plain as day.

But also determination.

He didn't know if she was determined to make this the best damned orgasm he'd ever had, or if she was determined to make sure he didn't mean as much to her as she feared.

He snagged her by the back of the head and burned a kiss to her mouth. He meant something to her, dammit. And he knew it.

Breathless, she pulled back and shoved him to the mattress.

This time, he let her have her way.

Her hips picked up speed, and she ground tight into him. Small little moves that had him making the most unmanly of noises. Her eyes lost focus and her lower jaw fell slightly open and he knew that she was about to dive over the edge.

He held on, refusing to go before she did.

And then she stiffened and arched. Her body began small, almost imperceptible twitches, and her breaths came out in short, staccato bursts. She immediately gasped them back in. Her fingers dug into his skin. Her thighs clenched him tight.

He gripped her hips and groaned from the torturous pleasure of it all. Her inner muscles squeezed him. Tight and fast. Over and over. And she continued to rock and grind against him. He hung on with the sheer determination to make sure she saw what she was to him before he finished. He refused to let her hide from it.

The instant her body began to relax, he said her name.

Her gaze locked with his and he let himself go. He emptied himself.

He pumped and throbbed, feeling like his orgasm would roar through him forever, and all the time, Roni didn't look away. He showed her everything he could. His love. His desire. And the fact that he was just as scared as she was.

This was big. They both knew that.

And it could so easily go wrong.

When he was spent, he eased his grip and she collapsed to his chest. They both breathed hard. He lifted his arms and draped them around her back and hugged her tight. His lips lazily curved upward when she didn't so much as move a muscle. She was as wrung out as he was.

Several minutes later, with neither of them having said a word, he felt her breaths deepen and grow steady. She would soon be asleep in his arms.

"Roni," he said softly.

Her breathing paused. Then she lifted her head.

She looked deep into his eyes.

"You want more," she stated, her voice calm and steady.

He knew she didn't mean more sex. She meant . . . *more*. More than these two weeks.

He nodded.

She dropped her head back to his chest and he felt her breath ruffle across his skin.

"So do you," he whispered into her hair.

She didn't respond.

He began drifting off to sleep with the idea of waking beside her in the morning, making love again, and then discussing where they went from there. He would tell her about Gracie. He was looking forward to it.

But when he awoke, he was alone in bed. He glanced at the clock. He'd overslept. For the first time in years, he hadn't woken automatically at the same time every morning.

Then he heard the piano from the other room, and he rose to go find Roni.

Chapter Twenty-Two

Roni had her neck bent over the keys and her eyes closed as she worked on the song that was in her head, but not yet on the page. She'd gotten out of bed that morning with something new running through her mind.

Actually, multiple things had been running through her mind. Lucas and what they'd done during the middle of the night, for one. That hadn't just been sex. It had been intense and honest and real. It had been a desperation for more.

And she'd been right there with him.

She'd also been thinking about Gracie. She didn't know what to think there. She hadn't talked to the girl again, but she wanted to. She wanted to get to know her. More than the details that Lucas had filled in. But mostly, she wanted to know what was going to happen when Lucas went home in a few days.

Then there had been the music in her head.

It had demanded to get out. It had been the easier thing to tackle at five in the morning, so she'd gotten up, put on some coffee, and left Lucas where he lay.

He'd mentioned before they'd gone to bed the night before that he had finished his work project, and she'd found herself wondering if he'd want to stick around this morning. It would interrupt her piano session, but she hadn't been able to make herself wake him and tell him he needed to go.

Her fingers finally hit on the notes she'd been after. She played it again and then quickly scribbled them down.

Lucas had made love to her last night like he was branding her. His every touch had scorched her from the inside out. She'd been unwilling to speak for the duration for fear that the wrong thing would come out of her mouth.

Love.

The idea of it had teased her all evening. Did she love him? Could she love him? Did she want to?

None of it made any sense. They'd barely just met.

But the mere idea of him heading back to Dallas and her not hearing from him again put an icy fear in her that she'd been trying not to explore too deeply for days.

He'd accused her of wanting more last night.

And yeah, she did. She just didn't know how much.

She replayed the piece from the beginning, and nodded when she finished. It was right. Then she realized that the music reflected her a bit.

The opening was fun and easy, yet she held slightly back with the tone. She imagined her life and how she often felt like she was standing just behind closed doors. She wanted to open them and step through. She wanted to see what was on the other side. But there was so much potential hurt that could be waiting for her.

So she hung out on the safe side and had a good time. She smiled and she laughed. And she pretended everything was okay.

But it wasn't. It hadn't been in a long time.

Telling Andie and Ginger about Zoe had shown her that. The conversation had released years of pent-up pain. She'd needed the time alone with her thoughts of Zoe, but she'd equally needed to share her love for the child with her friends. She could move on now. And she was ready to.

She closed her eyes and played the next part. She hadn't written the notes for this section yet, but they flowed from her fingers now as if she'd been practicing them for days. She built to a crescendo, the notes intense and exciting. The doors were opening and the sun was poking through. She'd taken off her running shoes, yet she was dying to sprint through to the other side anyway.

Only this time, she would run barefoot. She wanted to feel every grain of sand the world had to offer.

She wanted to feel and experience Lucas. And whatever feelings he brought out in her.

She lost the rhythm and stopped, then started that section over. This time, she wrote the notes as she went. When finished, she began to play from the beginning once more.

About halfway through, a noise pulled her attention and she glanced over to find Lucas standing in her darkened living room, his jeans pulled on, hugging his muscular thighs, and unbuttoned at the waist. It made her itch to dip her fingers behind the zipper and take him out.

His chest was bare and glowed in the lights of the Christmas tree, and her lungs swelled with the breath she took. He was gorgeous.

All strong and sexy and male. Testosterone oozed all over her house.

But it was the way he watched her that got to her.

He stood immobile, his eyes taking in everything about her at once. She didn't stop playing as he watched. And she didn't take her eyes off him. She also got the distinct impression that once the music stopped, he would want to talk about last night.

About his declaration that she wanted more too.

She didn't want to talk about that this morning. She needed to think things through first.

When she got to the end of what she'd written, she tucked her hands beneath her thighs and shot him a wry smile. "You woke up before I meant for you to," she said.

"Don't stop on my account." His voice was rough and sleepy and had a bit of an edge to it. It turned her on. "I won't interrupt," he added.

She chuckled and swiveled on her seat to face him, sliding one leg around to the other side of the bench. She had a robe tied loosely around her waist—and nothing more. It was a plain white cover-up that she often wore when she got out of the shower. A boring robe. Like one found on the back of the bathroom door in a hotel room.

Only, when she straddled the bench like she was doing now, the sides inched open and she suspected it suddenly looked a lot more interesting. The material clung to the inner swells of her breasts, leaving a tiny gap of skin right between them, and then opening wider the farther down it went. The sash remained knotted at her waist, with the ends draped down to the lacquered bench in front of her bare crotch.

Lucas's blue eyes crawled down her exposed flesh. His look made her nipples harden.

"You walked into my living room barely dressed, Lucas." Her voice was not good at hiding what he did to her. Not that she really tried to hide it anyway. She had a sudden vision of him laying her out on top of her piano. "I'm not sure how you expect that not to distract me."

"I didn't walk in here." His eyes burned on her body as he continued looking at her. "I was pulled in. I swear you're a siren. You reel me in every time I get near you." He slowly lifted his gaze to hers before letting it edge off to the side of her face. "Have I ever told you that I like your hair?" he asked.

She blinked. Her hair? He wanted to talk about her hair? While she sat there bare-assed and her crotch exposed? *Fine.* She could talk about her hair. She tugged the sides of the material over her body. "I look better when I straighten it," she said.

"No, you don't."

The words almost made her smile. She preferred it curly herself. As a kid, her tutor had been in charge of making her hair look "presentable" for performances. The poor woman had spent hours every week trying to turn the locks into something more than corkscrews. As a teen, Roni had taken this duty upon herself. She'd never managed straight at that age, but with its length, she'd found a happy medium with slight waves.

"Yes I do," she insisted. She touched a hand to her tousled hair. "I look more polished."

"But you don't look like you."

She eyed him. That was the very argument she'd always used when her dad had wanted her to straighten it. "You don't even know me," she said, but she didn't believe the words. This man somehow seemed to know everything about her.

He crossed the room until he stood directly in front of her. He was tall and hot and sculpted down to every detail of his body, and her fingers began to wiggle at the thought of pulling him down beside her. His gaze engulfed her.

"I know you," he said simply. The words were low and felt almost dangerous.

She caught herself leaning forward, as if hoping he would put his mouth to hers.

"What were you playing?" he asked instead. "Something you're writing?"

She rolled her eyes and pulled her leg back across the bench. Why all the talking? With a dirty look tossed his way, she retied her robe over herself. "Yes." She once again faced the piano. "I've been writing a few pieces lately."

She'd been thinking about calling her manager and discussing the possibility of a new CD. She'd been thinking about that a lot.

"Play something for me," he demanded.

"I just did." She glanced at him. Now that he was away from the Christmas tree, the pale gray light that was coming up beyond the ocean stroked lazily over his body. It didn't diminish his hotness one bit.

"You were playing it for *you*," he said. "Play something for me."

She put her fingers on the keys. "You did note that I didn't stop playing when I saw you, right?"

"True." He moved to the coffeepot and pulled down a cup. "But you were watching me like you wanted to eat me up," he said. "You weren't thinking about playing that piece for me."

She shook her head. No, she hadn't been thinking about playing that piece for him.

"Why are you way back there?" she grumbled. He seemed to be intentionally keeping his distance.

"I want coffee."

She began playing a soft medley of Christmas songs. "You could have *me* along with your coffee," she teased.

His big body suddenly stood directly behind hers and the heat from him burned through the robe at her back. He reached around and untied her sash with one quick move.

"Oh," she breathed out.

"Don't stop playing," he said.

She didn't stop playing.

The cotton parted in his hands. Slowly and with great precision he opened it wide and pushed it off her shoulders until it puddled around her hips.

While bent over her, he turned his face into her neck and deposited a very tiny kiss. She shivered. He'd probably kissed the red spot she'd discovered when she'd looked in the mirror that morning. He'd left a mark on her last night.

Then he stepped back and he was gone. She was left sitting there at the piano, playing buck naked except for the sleeves of her robe, which hadn't fallen off, since her hands were still on the keys.

"What are you doing?" she asked. She glanced over her shoulder to find him standing in front of the open refrigerator.

"Breakfast," he said. He took a sip of his coffee. He looked so perfect standing there in his jeans and rumpled hair, drinking from her coffee mug while searching out a bite to eat. She could get used to that.

She lifted her hands and turned to him, but he pointed a quick finger at her.

"Play," he said.

"Fine," she shot out. She turned back and played, but not before she slipped her arms free of the sleeves. The robe draped across the bench, threatening to slide to the floor, but hung on due to the fact that her rear was still sitting on it.

She picked a classical piece this time. One that she could pound out her frustrations to.

"You could get naked too," she pointed out.

"I could." Noises rustled behind her. The refrigerator closed and a cabinet door closed. Then what sounded like the microwave opening and closing.

Beeps sounded and a soft whirring hum began.

"I guess you're staying for breakfast then?" she asked, her voice heavy on sarcasm. It was Wednesday and she would be making breakfast for Mrs. Rylander in a couple hours, but she liked the idea of Lucas sticking around and fixing himself something in her kitchen.

"Yep." He didn't seem to be much of a talker this morning.

More rustling. This time it had the distinct sound of denim, and Roni couldn't help but peek over her shoulder again.

"Didn't I tell you to play?" Lucas asked when he caught her looking.

She'd been right. His jeans were now in his hand, no underwear, and he had about two-thirds of an erection going.

Her fingers never stopped. "I believe I am playing." She missed a couple notes, but didn't let that bother her. "What are you doing?"

"You wanted me naked."

She nodded. "Yes, I did."

Her breaths grew shallow and she had to turn back to the piano in order to concentrate. She'd never had a naked man in her kitchen before. And most certainly, not a hot, delicious-enough-to-serve-on-her-dining-room-table—if she'd had one—naked man.

"Um . . ." she began. It seemed like she should say something.

The microwave beeped and the door opened and closed.

"I can't eat," she managed to get out. "My neighbor is coming over for breakfast later."

Lucas stepped to her side and she looked over to find his penis in her line of sight. It was bobbing in the air as if greeting her with a hearty good morning. "Mrs. R?" he asked. "Cool. And I didn't fix you breakfast." He held up his plate, which had a piece of leftover quiche large enough for three people and two apples on it. "You're too busy playing to eat."

Without another word, he took his nakedness and walked to the far side of the piano. His butt cheeks were almost pressed up against the large glass pane of her window, while the two side panels were open, and she knew he had to be feeling the cool breeze waft across his body. It didn't seem to dampen his "spirit" any.

"When can I stop playing?" she asked. Her throat was dry and she'd grown wet between her legs.

"When I've heard enough."

He stooped to the floor, and she was surprised when he stood with a rather dead-looking plant in his hand.

"Forget to water something?" he asked.

She squinted at the light-pink planter he held. "I forgot that was there. I think one of the ladies at the senior center gave it to me back in the summer."

He lifted an eyebrow, then moved across the room and deposited the whole thing in her trash. He returned to his position at the other end of her piano, blocking her view of the ocean. He was most distracting, and she found herself wanting to forget the piano and drag him to the ground.

"When are you going to admit you miss playing?" he asked suddenly.

The music paused but then one hand began rolling through a series of scales. "I thought you weren't going to push about that?"

That had been the agreement. They would try this relationship thing, but he wouldn't push about the piano. His large shoulders shrugged. "I changed my mind," he said.

"Shouldn't we agree on that first?"

"Okay, then we'll talk about something else. Admit I was right last night. You want more from this too."

Damn. He had gotten out of bed prepared to push her buttons today.

"Because *I* do," he said. The words were spoken without a trace of uncertainty. "I want a lot more. I want to dig under your surface and learn what hurt you. And I want to help you through it. I want to share my hurts with you too." His voice slowed, softened, and Roni's heart raced as she watched him. She couldn't look away. "And I want you to come home with me and meet—"

"Fine," she raised her voice, interrupting him. She held a hand up in the air between them. She didn't want to hear him say that he wanted her to meet Gracie. Not yet. She wasn't there yet. "I miss playing," she admitted. "Are you happy? I miss it every day. Every single time I sit down and put my hands on the keyboard, I want to be in front of a crowd instead of here in my house."

She refused to admit out loud that she wanted more from them. Not until she had some idea of how much she wanted.

She lowered her head and went into a symphony she'd known since she'd been in elementary school, and she refused to look at him while she played. The notes rang out loud and hard. Her fingers throbbed from the pounding. Several minutes later, she pulled her hands back, out of breath, and looked up at him with a scowl. The ferocity of the music hadn't seemed to faze him. He merely watched her calmly.

He set his plate, now holding only two apple cores and a fork, on the windowsill with his coffee cup and crossed his arms over his wide chest. "Do the concert Saturday night," he urged. His voice was soft and coaxing. Not demanding. Yet it still hit her wrong.

He was pushing and she wasn't ready for it.

She stood from the piano and headed across the room. She reached for the coffee cup she'd left on the counter earlier but it was gone. When she found it clean and upside down on the side of her sink, she shot him a dirty look.

"Roni," he said calmly.

She shook her head. "I can't do it yet."

But she wanted to. She'd been playing with the idea of telling Kayla to set up the concert since she'd talked with her friends on Sunday. Nothing major. Maybe just the contestants and the business owners. She longed to sit in front of a packed auditorium, all of them waiting breathlessly. For her.

But then what?

She couldn't go back out on the road. She didn't want to be the person she'd been before Zoe. She didn't want to ache every time she played, remembering that she'd been chasing a career while Zoe had been alone and dying.

No. She couldn't be the person she'd been before. That person had existed with one goal. To be the best. And Roni had no clue how to combine the person she was now with the person she was then. Especially when she looked into Lucas's eyes and saw not only him and his feelings for her, but the knowledge of his little girl.

The knowledge that Roni had those feelings as well.

She could see herself in their lives. She wanted that.

She shook her head as Lucas came around the piano and reached for her.

"I'm scared, Lucas." She held up her hands as if to ward him off. "I'm not sure what I want. I agreed to play with the band Friday night, but that's all I can do right now."

"What happened?" he whispered. He ignored her feeble protests and pulled her to his chest until she rested her cheek against the strong beat of his heart. His skin was warm and comforting beneath hers. "Tell me," he pleaded. "Let me help." She nodded and snuggled closer. "I will," she said. "But not this morning. Mrs. Rylander is coming over and I don't want . . ." She let her words trail off and her shoulders sagged. She didn't want to be sad today. Not for her neighbor. But mostly, she just didn't have the energy right then to rip herself open. Again.

Lucas pulled back and looked down into her face. "Let's go out tonight," he urged. "After we finish at the convention center. Let me take you to a late dinner. Maybe a little dancing. I want to give you a fun night. Then we'll find a quiet corner, and we'll talk. I have things I need to tell you, as well."

Fear crept around the edges of Roni's vision. Could she really tell him how much she'd loved Zoe? That she'd wanted to die in her place when she'd come home to find her already gone? His warm eyes never left hers and she knew that she could. And she wanted to.

Like she'd told Andie and Ginger, it was time to move on. She needed to do what she'd never done before. Grieve. Say her good-byes to the child who had touched her world for such a short span of time. And then she needed to see if she could make a new world with Lucas. And his gorgeous Gracie.

She nodded. "Tomorrow night, though. I told Andie and Ginger we'd go out tonight. We have a pregnancy to celebrate."

His gaze zeroed in on her bare stomach.

"Not me, you big goof." She slapped him on the arm and he grabbed her by the wrist and pulled both her hands around behind his back. Suddenly all his nakedness was mashed up with all her nakedness, and all she could think about was him and her and how neither of them had to be anywhere for a while.

He put his mouth just below her ear and whispered, "I can picture you round with my child."

She sizzled in his arms. She could picture that too.

She sought out his mouth, and his touch scalded her. Before she could protest, he had her around the waist and was lifting her up to her countertop. She squealed at the chill of the granite under her bare rear.

"For someone who's such a clean freak, you'd think my bare ass on this countertop would bother you," she complained.

He chuckled. "I've already had breakfast." He put his hands down on either side of her and his mouth slanted hard across hers for five heart-stopping seconds. When he pulled back, she wasn't breathing steady. "But I will be sure to wipe it down before I eat anything else from your kitchen."

She reached for him, wanting his mouth back on hers. She didn't care about dirty kitchens or anything else at the moment.

He held back. "Were you finished playing?"

"No," she groaned. "But kiss me, will you?"

"I don't want to throw off your routine," he said, then leaned in and bit her on the shoulder. "Too much."

"Too bad. You've already screwed it all up. It's not bad enough you've been prancing around naked all morning. Now you're—"

"I never prance," he stated flatly. His hands remained flat on the counter on either side of her, but he pulled back. The look of disgust on his face had her laughing.

"I didn't mean 'prance,'" she said. "Just . . . you know . . . you've been in here, bothering me with all these yummy muscles and—" She slid her hands over his hard chest and groaned before lowering one hand to wrap her fingers around the very thick, large part of him that she liked so much. She stroked him from the base to his head. His jaw twitched with a clench. "—hardness," she finished in a whisper. "That kind of prancing."

He shook his head. "I don't prance," he repeated. "Of any kind."

She giggled. Men and their egos.

She still had him in her hand so she stroked again. Up and down. Up. And down. She lowered her eyes to watch her movements and teased him by poking her tongue out just a tiny little amount. She let out a throaty laugh when his chest rumbled with an anguished sound.

"Roni," he growled.

She rubbed her thumb over the drip of liquid spilling from him. "Yep?" she chirped.

"Say that I don't prance."

Her eyes slowly lifted from where she held him, literally trapped in her hand, to crawl up and over his heated flesh. Before she moved on from his chest, she pressed her mouth against him and swirled her touch around the dark nipple tucked in the middle of the slight patch of hair. He throbbed in her hand. She stroked him again.

His fingers gripped her hips and tugged her forward, spreading her legs wide around his hips. She shifted her gaze up past his strong neck, and over his hard-as-steel chin.

Blue eyes burned into hers.

"Say it," he demanded.

He tugged again and the head of his penis grazed against the most feminine part of her. Her hand squeezed him involuntarily before she forced herself to let go. She put both palms on his chest and thanked her lucky stars that he'd come into her life. Finally, she felt like she was beginning to live again. And she hadn't even known she wasn't.

"I have never," she began. She wiggled on the counter a little and he slipped a bit closer to where she wanted him to be. "*Ever*," she stressed. She pressed in to plant another kiss on his chest. As she did, his swollen head slid just past her waiting lips. He was now positioned right at her opening. She felt as if her entire body was vibrating, but wasn't sure if it was only hers, or Lucas's, as well. "Seen. You. Prance."

Lucas pushed forward with her last word and slid deep inside her in one smooth motion. He closed his mouth over hers and cut off the air she'd been trying to pull in.

He devoured her.

His hands on her rear held her where he wanted, and he plunged deep. He pulled back and drove in again. He was a machine.

"Oh God," she moaned. "It feels so . . . *Crap*—" Her words bit off as she stiffened. "You don't have on a condom," she breathed out.

He paused, still buried in her, and she saw the indecision pass across his face.

"*Shit*," he whispered.

Her legs crossed behind him and held him tight. "Don't stop yet," she pleaded. "In a minute."

They could try the pull-out method, she supposed. Though that was the last thing she wanted. She tightened her legs and he looked at her in disbelief.

"My mother would kill me if I brought home another pregnant girl."

Dry laughter escaped her. She dropped her forehead to his shoulder. "It wouldn't be my first choice either," she confessed.

Though the idea didn't scare her like she thought it should.

She lifted her head and looked at Lucas, suddenly wanting to tell him that she loved him. Because she did. But how in the hell she'd fallen in love with this man in less than two weeks, she had no idea.

Before she could figure out whether to blurt out the words, whether to ride him bareback until both of them were raw, or whether to run and hide and forget she'd ever met him, she noticed something on her deck.

Roni burst out laughing.

"Uh . . ." Lucas began. He turned her face to his. "Problem?" he asked.

"Our decision has been made for us," she said. She nodded her head to the window and Lucas followed her gaze. "We've been caught," she said.

Two pale hands were cupped around a scrunched-up wrinkled face. Pressed to the window on the other side of her piano.

CHAPTER TWENTY-THREE

Cheers rang out in one corner of the crowd as contestant number one, Gus Thompson, and his partner presented their soup to the judges' table.

They were at the senior center on Wednesday afternoon, and though the out-of-town turnout was down for the day, the numbers had been more than sustained by those who lived on the island. Hordes of women had come out to see these men cook. They were now crammed into the senior center, some spilling out onto the wrap-around deck. It was a gorgeous December day, and though a chill was in the air, no one seemed to mind.

Lucas and the other remaining five men were working diligently with their partners in the center's massive kitchen to get their French onion soup just right. Roni was just glad they hadn't been directed to make French *hen* soup since they were down to day three—Three French Hens—of the contest.

She looked across her table at Ginger and Andie sitting with her and smiled when Andie pressed a light touch to her stomach. Roni still couldn't believe one of them was going to have a baby.

They were keeping the secret for her, but given that Andie had spent hours every week with the seniors on the island before she'd moved away, some of the older generation were giving her a shrewd eye every time she turned a little green. Apparently her morning sickness was working well into the afternoon hours.

"You doing okay over there?" Roni asked her friend.

"I'm fine." Andie nodded. "Just . . . a little . . ." She put a hand to her mouth as if holding something back, and finally finished with, "*Ugh.*"

Ginny Whitmore, Andie's aunt, squeezed in beside Roni. Ginny's red curls were tied loosely at the back of her neck and she wore an armful of bright, jingly bracelets. They clinked together as she reached an arm across the table to Andie. "I brought you some herbal tea."

"Thanks, Aunt Ginny." Andie smiled wanly and took the cup. "Where's Mom?"

Andie had told her mother and Aunt Ginny about the pregnancy, and surprisingly, her mother had been a total mother hen the last few days. More so, even, than Ginny.

"She's handling something or another with the contest." Ginny waved a hand in the air as if she didn't have time for the details. Andie's mother had moved to the island earlier in the year and had essentially stepped in to cover Andie's absence from Seaglass Celebrations. It was a business decision that fit better than anyone would have ever guessed. Kayla ran the business now, but Andie's mother was the epitome of organized. She was turning out to be essential in growing the company.

From across the room, another round of cheers went up as contestant twelve finished his soup. It wasn't a race to the finish, merely to make the best soup. But these men didn't seem to know how to do anything but race. Every competition over the last week and a half had turned into either a show of brute force or a show of who was the fastest.

Lucas was working with a fifty-year-old today, and from the looks of things, the woman had never seen a kitchen, much less knew what an onion was. They were most definitely not in the lead for fastest today.

Earlier, when Lucas had been at the grocery store to get their supplies, he'd texted Roni since he knew she liked to cook. He'd asked about the best onions and cheese to use, and whether they should make their own croutons or go with the store-bought kind. Baguette slices were her favorite to use in the soup, but she'd held the information back.

Going outside his partner for help wasn't against the rules, but given Roni's position with the contest, she'd felt uncomfortable answering him. Instead, she'd texted him back a couple of links to recipes for making the soup. Anyone could Google the same results, so she hadn't felt like she was crossing any lines.

Roni watched him work, unable—as usual—to take her eyes off his über-hot body, and wondered if this would be the final day for him. She hoped not. Though granted, if she were selfish she'd want him kicked out. He had to stick around for the parade on Saturday no matter what, and if he wasn't in the competition for the next two days, then they would have more time to spend together.

But he was passionate about winning. She saw that every day as he worked with whatever partner he was given, and through whatever random contest the committee had thought up. He wanted to take that money home to his charity. Clearly it meant a lot.

Vanilla Bean and Chester Brownbomb, two regular attendees at the center, walked by, Vanilla's arm wrapped tightly through Chester's. Vanilla's blue-tinged hair caught the late-afternoon sun as she smiled broadly at the other gray-haired women in her midst. Chester was the catch to be had for that generation, and Vanilla had apparently had him for going on six months.

"I can't believe those two are still together," Andie murmured. She lifted her cup and took a sip. "He was such a horndog before I left."

Ginger leaned in and whispered, "I think he's seeing somebody else behind her back."

"Oh no," Andie said.

"From what I can tell," Aunt Ginny added, "it isn't behind her back. It's Judy Sevier, and Vanilla knows all about it. They play bridge together on Monday nights and Judy makes sure Vanilla knows when she's been with Chester. Vanilla merely pretends she doesn't know anything about it so she can go on acting like she has her a man. Chester even knows that she knows."

Roni laughed lightly at the gossip. The senior center was the place to learn things. "Then why does he put up with it?" she asked.

A pencil-thin red brow lifted on Aunt Ginny's face. "Because she makes the best pot roast on the island, my dear. And Chester is a red-meat man."

A third round of cheers slipped into the air for number fifteen, Scott Grainger. This one was given with far less animation than the others. The audience didn't like Scott as much. Yet day after day, he'd managed to bring in the votes. He'd even been in the top two a couple times.

Roni returned to Lucas. He still looked nowhere near close to being finished. He did look cute, though. His hair was standing on end in a couple places, and the elf apron he wore over the front of his jeans had all manner of smears. There was even a tiny white streak of flour just above his left eye.

Cooking wasn't his forte, apparently. But he did have other talents in the kitchen. Like taking her clothes off and setting her up on the counter.

She held in a groan as she remembered Lucas pushing into her that morning. He'd been bare and big, and so hot she'd about died when she'd remembered they weren't using a condom. She also thought about the fact that she hadn't wanted him to stop.

He had, though. Rather abruptly.

He'd pulled out of her and left her house in a fat hurry after Mrs. Rylander had interrupted them. Roni suspected his opinion of "her lovely neighbor" had changed a bit when he'd discovered she was also a Peeping Tom.

Roni's opinion had teetered as well. But she had invited the woman over, after all. As Mrs. Rylander had explained when Roni let her in, she was only looking through the window to see if Roni was fixing breakfast yet or not. Roni hadn't gone down the deck stairs to get her when she'd quit playing, and Mrs. Rylander didn't want to be late.

Like the woman hadn't been aware that Lucas was still at the house. She seemed to know everything that went on there. But Roni couldn't hold any hard feelings about someone wanting to arrive before Lucas left. He was a potent man. Anyone would want to spend time in his presence if they could. Even eighty-year-old women.

So she'd forgiven her neighbor, kissed Lucas before he'd run out the door—while he'd been carefully *not* looking Mrs. Rylander in the eye—and then made eggs Benedict and had a lovely time chatting with her neighbor. Roni hadn't gotten anything out of her concerning her family or why no one came to visit her, though. But that hadn't kept her from trying.

Instead, Mrs. Rylander had been more interested in seeing the house and what Roni had changed about it since she'd moved in. So they'd had their breakfast at the kitchen bar, had taken a slow sweep through the house—ending with the Christmas tree—and then Mrs. Rylander had offered a quick hug and headed home. Roni had helped her down the back steps, but Mrs. Rylander had refused any additional help beyond that.

Roni could understand the need for independence, so she'd backed off. But she had watched from her living room window, just to be sure she made it home okay. The woman had grown on Roni over the months, and she'd hate to see anything happen to her.

Kayla suddenly appeared at the table at Roni's side, jerking her back to the present. Andie and Ginger shifted their attention from watching the men cook to eyeing Kayla's tight expression.

She looked back and forth from Roni to Andie. "I need to talk to you two," she said.

Seeing that Andie still sported a nice green hue, Roni scooted over on the bench and patted the space beside her.

Kayla tucked a piece of dark hair behind her ear and her toe began to tap. "Can we—"

"Sit," Andie said. "Whatever has you worried, we can talk about it here."

Ginger and Aunt Ginny would eventually hear about it anyway, and Kayla had to know that. So she sat. She leaned over the table, putting her face toward Andie's, and Roni followed suit, her rear coming up off the bench as she leaned in. With all three of their heads together, Kayla whispered, "We have a problem."

Roni almost laughed. She'd already figured that out from Kayla's boardlike posture.

"I'm sure we can work it out," Andie soothed. "Just tell us what it is."

Kayla flicked her gaze toward Roni's and the line of her mouth went flat. "There's been an accusation." She swallowed and wet her lips before continuing. "There have been complaints that Roni's relationship with Lucas has kept him in the contest. She can afford a lot of votes." She shrugged. "So the theory is that she's buying his way through."

Not that that would be against the rules, either. But still . . .

Roni sat back with a thunk.

"I just knew this would cause problems," Kayla muttered to herself.

Roni trailed her gaze across the room to watch Lucas once again. She'd worried that her being with him would impact things, but until today she'd heard of no issues. In the end, she didn't care what was said about her. But she did worry about risking his chances.

She brought her gaze back to the women and reached for Kayla's hand, which was now clenched into a tight fist. "I haven't participated in the voting since I handed that man all my money during his table-top striptease," she admitted. She had donated a chunk of cash every day, though. Worry for Lucas wouldn't make her shortchange the local charities that were benefiting.

"But you've been seen at the voting booth every day," Kayla questioned. "With your checkbook." Large, panic-riddled hazel eyes surrounded by extra-long lashes blinked at her. Kayla really did have gorgeous features. She just needed to chill out.

"Not a single vote," Roni reiterated.

"But . . ." Kayla trailed off. She pursed her mouth and suddenly looked disoriented. "Why not?"

Because she loved him. But Roni wasn't about to blurt that.

Instead, she grabbed Andie's cup and took a sip. Bleck. Peppermint tea was not her favorite. She made a face and handed it back. "In case something like this happened," she said. "I've been making donations, but not casting a single vote."

Andie eyed them. Her coloring wasn't as green as it had been. "Can we prove it?"

"As long as Owen tells the truth." Owen worked in the kitchen at Gin's. He was barely legal and had a major crush on Kayla. Kayla had exploited the fact to talk him into manning the voting booth every afternoon.

"Whew." Kayla blew out a breath and the lines on her faced eased. "Of course Owen will tell the truth. Thank goodness." She chewed on her lip for a few seconds and a single line came back across her forehead. She looked at Roni. "It would help settle things down, though, if you'd just stop seeing him," she pleaded. "Surely you've had enough."

A huge grin splashed across Roni's face, as well as Andie's and Ginger's. No one at that table would walk away from sleeping with Lucas before they had to. Kayla blushed to the roots of her hair.

"Okay, fine," Kayla muttered. "If it was me, I wouldn't have had enough either."

"Not even close," Roni clarified. She watched the man in question as he slid the bowls for the tasting into the oven. "And if I have anything to say about it, I won't be done come Saturday, either."

Her friends' eyebrows rose. Ginger and Andie couldn't be too surprised by the fact after their Sunday-morning conversation, but no doubt the words shocked Kayla to her toes. No one had seen Roni serious about any of her island flings. And certainly not serious enough to keep seeing him after he returned home.

Aunt Ginny slid an arm through Roni's and squeezed with affection. Andie had spent the summers at Ginny's house when they were kids, and both Roni and Ginger had spent hours each day there, as well. She might as well be an aunt to all of them.

A series of tones began playing at Roni's side and she gasped as she made a quick grab for her Gucci purse. Embarrassment flooded her as she searched inside for the phone. Everyone was asked every day to keep their phones off or on Vibrate while the contest was playing out. Roni could swear that hers had been silenced.

She got hold of the thing and yanked it from her purse, only then remembering that she had Lucas's phone. They had the same models, and he'd grabbed hers in his hurry out of her house that morning.

The call was an incoming Skype. From Gracie.

Roni's throat tightened as she thought about Lucas almost asking her to go home with him to meet Gracie that morning. She didn't know if she was ready for that.

But she wanted to be.

She swiped the screen to end the incoming call, but accidentally swiped it the wrong way, and the next thing she knew, Gracie's face smiled back at her.

"Hi," she chirped, loud enough for all the tables around them to hear. "You're my daddy's friend."

Mortification filled Roni as all heads turned in her direction.

Heat drenched her cheeks and she shot up out of her seat and ran for the door. The chatter at the tables in her section had gone silent and she knew that every single one of them was watching her sprint out of the room.

Once she was in the hallway, she slumped back against the wall and squinted her eyes tightly closed. *Ohmygod*, she'd answered Lucas's daughter's call.

She had to talk to her. How could she not?

"Hello?" the young voice called out. "Are you there? All I see is green."

Roni had on a dark-green skirt and the phone's camera was pointed at it.

Slowly, and praying that she didn't say the wrong thing or do anything that Lucas wouldn't like, she lifted the phone to her face.

Big blue eyes and the cutest curls Roni had ever seen filled the screen. Gracie was perfect.

"You're his friend, right?" Gracie asked again. "His special one? The piano player."

Roni chuckled softly and nodded. *His special friend?* Had he talked about her to his daughter? "Hello," Roni managed to squeak out. "It's nice to see you again, Gracie."

An exuberant smile shone between two chubby cheeks. "It's nice to see you again too," Gracie politely chimed. "My Daddy said I might get to meet you. But not on the c'puter. I didn't know I would get to talk to you on the c'puter again. Are you coming home with him to see me? He said you might."

An invisible restraint held Roni against the wall as she listened to the girl chatter, and she caught herself smiling along with her. Oh yes, she wanted to go home with Lucas and meet this child. Every time Gracie asked another question, Roni found herself with the urge to know more about her.

"My Daddy isn't going to get me a dog anymore, did he tell you that?" She sighed dramatically. "We talked 'bout it and we're gonna wait for Santa to bring me one. He will, too. Cause Grandma took me to see him yesterday. I told him a dog was what I wanted more than anything in my whole life." Her blue eyes blinked back at Roni from the screen. "And a Barbie. The kind with a swimming pool. Did you have a Barbie with a swimming pool when you were little? Do you want to play wif' mine wif'me?"

Gracie finally took a breath, and Roni managed to get in a word. "Were you calling your dad for a specific reason, Gracie?"

From what she understood, he normally talked to Gracie in the mornings, and again at night before she went to bed. His daughter knew that he was busy in the afternoons.

"Oh." She nodded and one of her curls dropped down so that it hung in front of her eye. "I wanted to ask him if Gran'pa could take me to pick out a tree or if we should wait 'til he gets home. He's gonna be home in four days, but Gran'pa said he'd take me today if I wanted him to. He said Daddy wouldn't care, but I wanted to be sure. We use'ly pick it out together."

Oh my. Roni could so fall in love with this angelic child.

She had to go to Dallas and meet her. She would tell Lucas tomorrow night. They had a date planned for after they finished for the day. She intended to tell him about Zoe before the night was over. Seemed it might be the right time to ask if she could meet his daughter too.

"Are you my Daddy's girlfriend?" Gracie suddenly asked.

Roni looked at the heart-stopping face and bright-blue eyes and felt a little piece of her heart already finding its way to Dallas. She nodded. "I am."

"I thought so!" Gracie shouted. "I told Grandma you was. She said we'd see. But I knew." Gracie's head nodded excitedly. "Wait 'til I tell her."

"Maybe you should let your dad tell her." Worry began to churn inside Roni. She bit her lip. Should she not have said anything?

Gracie suddenly went quiet. It was an interesting sound coming from the child. Then she shook her head, and said, "No. I'm gonna tell her, 'I told you so.' I'll tell her it's a secret, though. I gotta go."

The call disconnected as quickly as it had started, and she was left standing alone in the hall. She pulled the phone to her chest with both hands and dropped her head back to the concrete wall. She wanted this so bad.

What had happened with Zoe was the past. She'd moved on, and she could handle whatever life threw at her now. She'd just needed the time to get there.

She heard cheers come from the other side of the wall and smiled, assuming Lucas had finally presented his soup to the judges. She wanted to move on in her life with Lucas. And Gracie.

CHAPTER TWENTY-FOUR

A Tim McGraw song blasted from the sound system of the Two-Step Bar and Grill as Lucas twirled Roni around the dance floor. It was their date night and he was trying his best to show her a good time. The day's competition, in honor of Two Turtle Doves, had been a two-step contest between the final four contestants. After finishing at the convention center, he'd had the brilliant idea to come over to the Two-Step. Dancing, dinner. Then a long, snuggling walk along the beach. Sounded romantic enough.

Only, the bar hadn't been a unique idea. A crowd had shown up with them.

He and Roni shuffled counterclockwise along with the rest of the dancers on the floor, and though he had their upcoming conversation on his mind, priority number one at the moment was the way she looked. And smelled. And had tasted when he'd managed to steal a quick kiss from her.

They hadn't seen each other the night before—Roni and Ginger had spent the night with Andie at her aunt's house. And who knew missing one night with a woman he'd only known for ten days could make a man crazy? But crazy he was. Her short dress and cowboy boots weren't helping matters any either. Her toned thighs had attracted the attention of every male who'd looked in her direction.

He wanted her so badly he was about ready to drag her to the middle of the crowded floor and get down to business. Only, the place was so crammed full that he doubted he could get her to the middle of the floor if he wanted to.

"You must be excited," she said. "About being down to the final two."

Her head tilted up to his, and as he peered down into her dark gaze in the low light of the room, he didn't care one iota that he was one of the two remaining men. With her dress gaping just enough that he could see the plump swells of her breasts, all he could think about was being buried deep inside her. Without a condom.

And how he hadn't wanted to pull out yesterday morning.

It had thrown him that the thought of continuing had even passed through his mind. He should have learned his lesson years ago.

Yet Roni was different from other women. She fit him.

And he wanted to get her pregnant.

Whoa. He looked away. He didn't need to go there. Not yet. There were still hurdles to cross. Specifically, a couple of important conversations to have, and then convincing her to meet his kid.

"Yeah." He nodded. He stared off across the crowded floor. "Absolutely. The money would go a long way for the kids and families who need it."

Roni grew quiet in his arms and he didn't try to fill the void. He had to get them out of there. "How about we—"

He cut off his words at the feel of someone poking him in the arm. He looked down, then jerked his gaze to Roni. Mrs. Rylander shuffled along beside them. He willed Roni to read his mind. *Get rid of her. She's seen me naked.*

She'd also seen him hilt-deep inside Roni.

That was not something he wanted to relive.

But instead of reading his mind—or maybe she did and she was just being evil—Roni turned loose of his hand and stepped back with a gracious smile. "I think Mrs. Rylander would like to dance with you, Lucas."

Was she kidding him? He burned a look into her, but it didn't stop her. She was gone, and left standing in her place was five feet of ornery.

And to think, he'd once thought this woman was sweet.

What was she even doing out late at night in a bar?

"You'd better give me your hand, young man; we're about to get run over," she informed him. She stood there with her right hand in the air, fingers up, and a black patent pocketbook dangling from her elbow.

Lucas put up his left hand. He didn't make eye contact. "Do you even know how to two-step, Mrs. Rylander?"

"*Humph,*" she mumbled. "Best call me Audra since I've seen your goods." Her fragile hand fit itself to his. "And don't shortchange me none, either. I want some of them twirls and do-si-dos."

He just shook his head and clasped his fingers around hers. Do-si-dos were not in the two-step. They were nowhere near the two-step. He positioned his other hand on her shoulder blade, and away they went. Surprisingly, her feet flowed instantly into the quick-quick-slow-slow rhythm of the dance.

"*Humph,*" she said again when he didn't comment on her apparent knowledge of what she was doing.

He kept his gaze trained over her head, and shot Roni an evil look anytime she came into his view. She was now dancing with Gus Thompson, contestant number one, and Lucas didn't think he liked that at all. Gus was the other man left standing in the competition, but that wasn't what bothered Lucas. It was seeing Roni smile into the younger man's eyes. She could be such a flirt when she wanted to. He also didn't like how the two of them looked a little too perfect together.

Jealousy and horniness were apparently the name of the game for him tonight.

He flicked a quick glance at his partner and added impatience to his list. The little old lady was wearing him thin.

She'd been in the house the morning before when he'd come back out of the bedroom—*dressed*—and though he hadn't looked at her, he'd felt her staring a hole through him. She'd been measuring him up. The woman was eighty, for crying out loud. What was he supposed to do with an eighty-year-old checking him out?

"Do you love her?"

The simple question was enough to finally pull his attention to her. "Excuse me?" he asked.

"Roni," she stated plainly. "Do you love her?"

It was a good time for one of those twirls she'd wanted. He sent Mrs. Rylander on a spin, but when she came back the same look was plastered on her face. It was a mix of determination and protectiveness. Wow. Who knew the little thing had it in her? She was going to protect Roni from him?

Like Roni would need it. His heart was the one that would get broken, if anybody's did.

"I saw that hickey you put on her neck," she tossed out. "As well as what else you were doing to her." She shook her head. "Your generation." Her tone was filled with disgust. "It's always about the sex."

"It's not about the sex," he said. It had been, yes. But then . . . Well, maybe it had never been, to be honest. He'd had a strong pull to Roni from day one.

He shook his head and didn't say anything else. Instead, he set his mouth and refocused his gaze on the crowd. He saw one of the twins he'd met at the party that first night. With her long, dark hair flowing down to the middle of her back and her body-hugging dress, she was a looker. He hoped she was the single one instead of the owner of the bar.

If not, the way she was wearing one of the other contestants almost as tight as she wore her dress would be highly inappropriate.

His mother had taught him manners in his early years, so guilt began gnawing at him for ignoring Mrs. Rylander the way he was. With a sigh, he grudgingly looked back down and responded to her question.

"Forgive me," he said as politely as he could muster, "but I don't see how my feelings for Roni are any of your concern."

She was still watching him. She was like a hawk. "Well," she began, "seeing as how someone has to watch after her, I've gone and made it my concern."

Another twirl. This time a double, and amazingly the woman kept up. He went for cordial when he brought her back around, and didn't point out that Roni had her own mother who could look after her. "Did you and your husband dance, Mrs. Rylander? You're very good at it."

A slip of a smile appeared between the wrinkles, and she nodded. "We used to push the furniture back against the walls and dance in the middle of the living room." They both grew quiet as she disappeared into her memories. When she came back, she looked up at him and said, "He never put me up on the counter, though."

Lucas's eye twitched. She could stop reminding him that she'd seen that particular show.

"But I can't say as I wouldn't have liked it if he had," she mumbled. Lucas ignored her.

The song ended and he thanked her and tried to excuse himself, but she kept a firm hold. "Not so fast, hot stuff. You didn't answer my question yet."

He ground his teeth together and started moving with the flow again, while on the other side of the floor Roni switched partners. She now danced with the twenty-one-year-old who had been kicked out of the contest within the first few days. Lucas didn't remember his name, but he did remember how he'd seen the kid looking at Roni.

The same way the boy was looking at her now. Every time his gaze dipped down the front of her dress.

Lucas's grip must have tightened because Mrs. Rylander let out a small "ouch."

He jerked his attention to her and loosened his hold. "I'm sorry," he apologized sincerely. Then he caught sight of another contestant standing on the sidelines with his eyes on Roni. This one had been kicked out of the contest earlier today and hadn't taken it well. He was eyeing Roni as if he blamed her for his loss.

"I certainly don't see what she sees in you if this is the kind of attention you pay your dance partners. And here I went and told her that she should keep you."

"You what?" He shifted his gaze between the jerk watching Roni and Mrs. Rylander.

The white head nodded up and down. "I said you were a good one. But I might just retract that. She listens to me, you know? She'll do what I tell her."

Her words pointed out that he most definitely was not being a gentleman to his partner. He shouldn't be ignoring her. His mother would have his hide. With the little amount of patience he had left, he forced himself to ignore the other side of the floor and focus on Mrs. Rylander instead. Had she just said that Roni listens to her? He chuckled lightly, shoved Roni from his mind, and took Mrs. Rylander for a couple more twirls, then tried a sweetheart move that left her facing the same direction as him.

She laughed with delight as she followed his lead, so he pushed a bit more. With every move, she was right there with him. A bit slower than some of the other women around them, but she most certainly knew what she was doing.

"I think I misjudged you, Mrs. Rylander." He leaned his head down to hers as he teased. "Too bad I didn't have you as my partner today doing the two-step. I suspect you would have wowed the crowd."

"I know I would have," she agreed without hesitation. "And I darn well should have been your partner. I bought ten tickets today. And I put all of them into your basket."

Entry into the daily lottery had changed a few days ago to allow participants to buy as many tickets as they wished, and to choose which contestant they wanted to try to win. It had tripled the amount of money being raised each day.

He stopped dancing with her declaration and stared at her. "You bought ten tickets and put them all in for me?"

"I did." She turned her nose up proudly.

They were bumped from behind and he scooted them over to the edge of the floor. Dancing continued beside them.

"Why?" he asked. He suspected it was to tease him about seeing his bare ass.

"Because I want to make sure you don't hurt her."

She was serious.

He shook his head and took her hands between his. He was serious too. "I won't hurt her," he promised. "I swear."

Mrs. Rylander nodded. "Be careful. I think she's been hurt before."

"I do too." He was certain of it. "But it won't happen again. Not on my watch."

"So you do love her?" she asked.

He looked at the older woman, then gave a nod. Yes, he did love her. And he intended to tell her.

Her hand clasped his. "Dote on her," she urged. "A woman needs a man to dote on her. Love her with your life. I want her to have someone like my Henry."

Lucas studied the woman, who suddenly looked frail, and made her a solemn promise. "I don't know your Henry, Mrs. Rylander, but I can guarantee that if Roni will allow me, I'll dote on her for the rest of my life. I'll be there for her. Always."

And he knew that he meant it.

He had no concerns about how she and Gracie would get along. They'd apparently talked on his phone the day before while he'd been busy making soup. Roni had explained the slipup when she'd shoved his phone back at him after he'd finished at the senior center. She hadn't gone into specifics about the conversation, but whatever had been said, Gracie had loved it. She couldn't wait to meet Roni. Now all he had to do was get Roni to Dallas.

"Be careful if you have kids, though." Mrs. Rylander's words grew almost too quiet to hear in the loudness of the bar, and Lucas leaned in close so she could talk directly into his ear. "Show them they're special too." She patted his hand as she talked. "And don't be too hard on them. Let them be kids."

He pulled back and looked into the pale eyes of the woman and recognized sadness in her depths, as well. Seems Roni wasn't the only one who had been hurt in her life. He nodded. "I will. And I'll tell you a secret that I don't share with many people." He put his mouth to her ear. "I already have a child. Her name is Gracie and she's the most beautiful person in the world."

Mrs. Rylander turned her head to look at him and her eyes suddenly watered. "She loves you?"

"She's four. She thinks I walk on water."

"Don't ever let her know that you don't." She patted his hand again, and then pulled his face to hers and pressed a cool kiss to his cheek, lingering for several seconds. "And you take care of my Roni."

Before he could say anything else, she turned, and with her head held high, marched to the front door of the bar and disappeared out the other side. Had she been there tonight only to talk to him?

Roni appeared at his elbow. "What did you say to make Mrs. Rylander leave?"

He shook his head. "I'm not sure." But he knew.

He'd let her see what she wanted to know. He wasn't playing with Roni. He was in it for the long haul.

Grabbing her hand, he nodded his head toward the door. "Let's get out of here."

She looked at him and he could just about swear it was love he saw shining back. "Exactly what I was going to suggest."

CHAPTER TWENTY-FIVE

The pop and hiss of the flames in Roni's backyard fire pit sounded in the quiet night as she and Lucas sat side by side. They each held a stick over the open flames. They'd left the Two-Step, stopped at the grocery store for hot dogs and the makings for s'mores, and had come back to her house for dinner.

Now they sat quietly, each working on their own food.

"Not much of a date, huh?" Lucas asked. He looked perturbed as he shoved yet another hot dog on one of the three-foot-long roasting forks she'd dug out of her pantry. The house had come with the pit and the forks, but until tonight, she'd never used the forks. "We should have just gone to the hotel restaurant," Lucas continued to grumble. He seemed to be in a foul mood. "It would have been quieter there than the bar. And I could have bought you a nice dinner."

"This is actually quite lovely," she said. She took in the quarter moon rising up out of the ocean, and the stars twinkling brightly above. The fire in front of them was not only sufficient to cook their dinner, but it was just enough to take the chill off the air. And the ocean could be heard rolling in the distance. "It's very romantic."

He grunted.

Roni rotated her stick to cook the other side of her hot dog, and peeked over at Lucas, who now had two sticks, each loaded with two dogs. She shook her head. The man—with all those muscles—ate more than anybody she'd ever seen.

"What's bothering you?" she asked.

He shot her a frustrated look. "We haven't gotten to do anything remotely resembling a date since we met. I wanted to show you a good time."

He was such a doll. She smiled and reached over to squeeze his forearm. "Being with you *is* a good time."

"You know what I mean." His mouth slashed down on one side. "You got all dressed up and everything."

She looked down at her paisley-print babydoll dress and the sweater she'd pulled on over it before they'd come outside. "Sweetheart," she said drolly, "this isn't dressed up." She held her legs out in front of her, her feet together, and twisted them back and forth, admiring the detail on her cowboy boots. This pair had been purchased in Nashville the last time she'd played at the Ryman. "This is fun and casual." She lowered her feet and half-turned in her foldout chair so she was facing him. "And I'm having the best time. Do you know how long it's been since I've had a hot dog? Much less, one cooked over an open flame."

He growled and she laughed. She went back to focusing on her dog. "You never did say what Mrs. Rylander said to you at the Two-Step."

He'd been suspiciously silent about his conversation with her neighbor. If his lack of words now was anything to go by, he intended to remain silent, as well. She sighed.

"Fine," she said. "Then tell me what you told Gracie about me."

"Huh?" He looked up from the fire. He seemed a million miles away.

"You talked about me to Gracie. She called me your 'special friend.'"

He laughed at her words and she felt her insides doing the gooey thing it did every time he made that sound. She lifted off her chair and scooted it closer to him until their arms brushed.

"I did tell her you're my special friend." He shot her a naughty grin and slid his hand along her bare thigh. His fingers slipped under the hem of her dress and inched to the inside of her leg. Her breathing grew shallow. "My mother told her you were the kind of friend I wanted to invite over for a playdate," he told her.

His face relaxed and his smile became as lethal as his ripped abs. It made her want to crawl into his lap and wiggle down real low.

"So you do want me to meet her?" she asked. Turned on or not, they had things to discuss. Sex would have to wait. "Because I'd like to," she finished softly.

His fingers stilled and his face turned somber. His eyes were black in the dark night. He nodded. "I would like that very much. She'll fall in love with you."

"I think I might fall in love with her too," she whispered.

A gleam flared in Lucas's eyes and he closed the distance and set his mouth to hers. He took his time as he kissed her, seeming to explore and taste every spot he encountered. As if he hadn't been there and done that before.

When he finished, she couldn't speak. He cared for her. A lot.

That had come through loud and clear.

"I told her I was your girlfriend," she confessed.

Surprise registered on his face, followed by an all-male kind of grin. The kind that made it hard to keep her clothes on. "That must be the secret she wouldn't tell me," he said.

"I suspect so." Roni laughed. "She caught me off guard when she asked me if I was." Roni shrugged. "I didn't know what to say so I just said yes. I hope that was okay."

He leaned into her again, but this time, before kissing her, he whispered hotly against her lips, "That was the perfect thing to say."

Then his mouth was on hers and his touch burned through her body. She wanted to get closer to him. She wanted his hands on her. She'd missed him last night.

Screw talking.

"Do you want to—"

Her words were cut off by a sizzle and a pop, and they both turned their faces to the fire to see that her hotdog had drooped too low into the fire. The end had burned black and had broken from the fork. It now lay in the flames. She groaned. "I never was any good at this."

"I've got you covered." Lucas pressed a kiss to her temple before he pulled away. He removed his forks from the pit and put his perfectly cooked dogs in buns. He then put three of them on his plate, and passed the forth one over to her.

"Thanks." She took the food, but she didn't take a bite of it. Suddenly, she wasn't in the mood to eat. It wasn't just Gracie she needed to talk to him about. She wanted to tell Lucas about Zoe. She wanted him to understand how much she'd loved the girl. And how she was a bit terrified at letting herself love Gracie the same way.

She picked at the bread of her bun while Lucas got busy adding relish and mustard to his. He held up the mustard bottle in her direction but she shook her head. She had no idea how to start, so she settled on starting years past.

"I loved my dad," she said.

The tone got Lucas's attention. With a hot dog at his mouth, he paused and cut his eyes over to hers. Then he set his food down without taking a bite and turned to her. He reached out a hand and she put hers in it.

"But he wasn't the easiest man to get close to," she finished. Then she glanced away from his probing gaze. She focused on the dark ocean off in the distance. "He was all about his career. And my career. He wanted me to be even better than he was."

"You are."

She made a face. "I'm not looking for platitudes. And no, I am not as good as he was. But I'm close." She grinned sheepishly. Her ego was still alive and kicking, apparently. "And if I hadn't quit . . ."

Lucas remained silent as she sat there and thought through her life. She appreciated his understanding that she didn't need him to fill every empty space with words. She just needed time to work through her feelings. And the facts were, if she hadn't quit, she would have surpassed her dad by now. He would have been proud.

And some days, not doing that really bugged her.

"What I told you before about traveling with him was accurate. It was the best time of my life." She rubbed her thumb back and forth against his palm. "But I was lonely," she added. "As far back as I can remember, I always felt like I was alone in the world. Mom and Danny would make it to a few shows, but not many. She didn't want to take Danny out of school. And Dad . . ."

She shook her head and then rested it on Lucas's shoulder and stared into the fire.

"He was always all about the piano. If we weren't practicing, we were talking about it. Strategizing where I needed to improve, and how to get me into the big halls. He loved me. He truly wanted the best for me." She paused and breathed in the warmth from the flames in front of them. It filled her lungs, comforting her on her inside, and made her want Lucas's arms wrapped around her on the outside. "But he never really fit me into his life," she added. "It was the piano, or nothing. And little girls need more than that."

She tilted her face up to Lucas's and waited until he looked at her.

"Girls need love," she continued. "They need hugs. And they need cheers, even when they have an off day. They need shoulders to cry on." She glanced back out at the dark night and her heart squeezed when he slipped his arm around her. That was one of the things she loved most about Lucas. She knew he was the kind of dad that a little girl needed. "Dad didn't have time for shoulders and tears," she said. "Or even special dinners on my birthday."

"Sounds like you needed your mom," Lucas whispered into her hair.

She nodded. "I did. I missed her all the time. But it was our life. She had to be home for Danny, and I had to be with Dad to be what I wanted to be. I got used to it." She paused again, then took another deep breath and pushed through. "And then Dad died when I was eighteen. Whether he was perfect or not, I was crushed. I'd idolized him. And then I *was* truly alone."

Lucas pressed his cheek against the top of her head and held her tight to his side. "Did your mom come for the funeral?"

She shook her head. "They'd been divorced for ten years. Danny came. But he was in the middle of finals and was working to get into med school. He had to finish out the week first. So I played a couple more shows by myself, the venues giving refunds if patrons weren't happy with getting only me, and by the time Danny got there, I had all the arrangements made. We buried Dad, and I was back out on the road the next day."

Lucas straightened and peered down at her. "You didn't take any time off?"

"I didn't need it. Plus, I had commitments. You don't veer from the schedule if you want to be the best."

He studied her until she began to fidget in her seat. She stood and walked to the other side of the fire so that she was at the ridge that rolled down to the beach. The moon was higher and bright enough now so that the sand glowed in the night.

"Roni." Lucas followed her. She crossed her arms over her chest and gripped her elbows on either side. "Did you ever get to take time off and deal with the loss of your dad?" he asked.

She glanced at him. "I told you. I was fine. That was the way we handled things."

It had been the way she'd watched her dad handle his divorce years before, and it had been the way she'd handled Zoe years after. She saw that now. And she recognized that maybe that hadn't been the healthiest of ways to deal with grief. But it was what she'd known. It had helped her survive.

"Years later I met Charles and for the first time, I didn't feel quite as alone." She laughed drily as she peeked up at Lucas. "And the funny thing is, for the two years that we dated, we were in different cities probably seventy-five percent of that time." She lifted a shoulder. "But it was comfortable. He played the violin and he was just as driven as me. He got me. I thought we had something."

"What happened?"

She stared at him and he went blurry through the tears welling up in her eyes.

"Oh, babe." He wrapped both arms around her and pulled her in close. "Do I need to go kick his ass?"

She shook her head against his chest and laughed lightly. "No. I didn't even really love him," she whispered. "But I fell in love. With a seven-year-old girl who had no one. She needed me. And I needed her."

Roni tilted her head back and stared up at Lucas. He wiped the tears from her face. "She was sick. I wanted to adopt her, but Charles said no. It was him or her." She hiccuped out a laugh. "Guess which one I chose?"

"I'm hoping it was the girl." His deep voice held a ton of emotion and Roni slipped her arms inside his jacket and around his waist. She rested her cheek against the steady beat of his heart. She nodded.

"Her name was Zoe. I knew she didn't have too many years to live, and she deserved to have someone love her until she died." Tears streamed down Roni's face now, soaking Lucas's shirt. "I didn't want to be like Dad. I wanted to believe I could put a child first. So I made the decision to cut back. I could teach in the city, or I could record CDs. I wouldn't have to leave her. I planned to finish out my tour and then I was going to be Zoe's mother for as long as I had her."

She swallowed against the pain, and a weight pressed down in the middle of her chest. She was so mad at herself for not being there for Zoe.

"I wasn't scheduled to be back in New York until a couple days before Christmas. But I didn't want to wait that long. So on my day off, I hopped a flight home. I went straight to the hospital to tell Zoe that she was going to be mine. She would have a home. And a mother. And someone to love her forever."

She stopped talking. Her voice had tightened and cracked. She couldn't go on.

Burying her face in Lucas's chest, she held him tight and great wracking sobs shook her entire body. She couldn't hold them off. Lucas stroked her back through it all. He kissed the top of her head. And he held her tight.

Several minutes later, the tears began to ebb and Roni got her voice back under control. "I failed her, Lucas." The words croaked out. "I got to the hospital and she had already died. I'd been out on the road. Just like my dad. My career was more important." Her breath hitched. "And the child that I loved died alone."

The sobs began again, and she finished with, "I should have done better."

~

Lucas held Roni close and fought his own tears. Seeing her so torn up ripped him in two. He whispered softly, trying to soothe her. He smoothed his hands from her shoulders to the base of her spine. He pressed kisses to her forehead. Nothing helped. She cried and cried. And she clung to him as if she would never let go.

He wondered if she'd had the chance to cry for Zoe before.

"What did you do the day after you found out?" he asked.

"What?" She sniffled.

He brought his hand to her cheek and tilted her face up. Her eyes were red and puffy, and tears continued to flow, but they'd slowed. He kissed each of her swollen eyelids and whispered, "What did you do the day after you went to the hospital?"

Her face scrunched up in thought. "I had a show in San Francisco the next day. I flew out that night."

"You didn't grieve."

Guilt crossed her features and she shook her head in a tight motion. "I didn't know how. And I didn't know I needed to."

"Poor Roni," he murmured. He stroked his palms over her cheeks and then pressed his mouth tenderly to hers. She was salty and wet, and her lips trembled beneath his. "Then it's time that you did. You take as long as you want. I'm here for you."

She tucked back against him and muttered, "And you thought the date was bad before. At least then you didn't need to wring your shirt out from where I cried all over it."

He cupped the back of her head and held her to him. "You cry on me every day if you need to," he whispered. He remembered all the days he'd wished he'd had someone to hold and cry with himself. He could be that person for Roni. He wanted to be that person for Roni.

As she'd told her story, he'd been unable to keep from thinking of Gracie as she'd been lying in her own hospital bed. While she'd been going through rounds of chemo.

She'd lost her hair. She'd lost weight. But she'd never lost her spirit.

And he knew the biggest reason for that was because she'd had support. She'd had him, and she'd had his parents. Maybe not a mother, but she had not been alone. Thank God.

"You did wonderfully for Zoe." He said the words, but he didn't expect her to believe them. Because he knew her. She cared for people. She took nosy, lonely neighbors under her wing when they had no one else. Of course she would have taken Zoe in too. "You were there for her as much as you could be. You were making arrangements to care for her. You thought she had more time."

She shook her head. "I should have cut back earlier. I should have been there." She pulled away and wiped her face, then walked to the edge of the yard. Her back was stiff and her arms were crossed tight over her body.

"How long had you known her?" he asked from behind.

"Six months."

"And how many times did you see her in those six months?"

She glanced over her shoulder, her eyebrows bunched. "I don't know."

"Well, when did you meet her?"

"In June."

"And were you on tour in June?"

She shook her head.

"So how many times in June did you go see her?"

Her eyelashes lowered before she turned back to face the ocean. "Every day," she murmured.

His heart swelled. No wonder he loved this woman. "And when you were on tour, how often did you see her?"

"Whenever I was in town."

"Did you call her while you were on the road?"

"No." She shook her head. "She had trouble talking. I sent her postcards instead."

Lucas took the three steps needed to be standing behind her and put his hands on her hips. She felt fragile beneath his fingertips, but he knew she wasn't. "Did she like the postcards?"

She tilted back until her shoulders rested against his chest. "She loved them," she murmured. "She liked to see the places that I traveled to. When I came to see her the next time, she'd let me know which of the places she wanted to visit when she got out of the hospital. She'd use her markers and put a purple check mark on the ones she wanted to go to, and a pink *X* on the ones she thought looked boring."

He crossed his arms in front of her and blew out a breath when she relaxed fully into him. "You were perfect, Roni. You did everything right. She knew you loved her."

A minute passed as the late-night air drifted around them, rustling through the grass at their feet while Roni seemed to be thinking through his words. Finally, she whispered, "But I wasn't there for her when she needed me the most."

He closed his eyes. He didn't know how to make that better. And then he thought of Des. She hadn't even wanted to be there when Gracie had needed her. There was a huge difference in the two women. He had to make Roni understand that she was special. That she had no reason not to forgive herself.

"Gracie's mother left the morning after Gracie was diagnosed with leukemia."

CHAPTER TWENTY-SIX

R oni froze in Lucas's arms. She could feel his heartbeat thumping steadily against her back. And his arms felt strong and secure around her. Unwavering. Almost as if he was unconcerned with anything. But did he just say . . . ?

She slowly tilted her head up where she lay against him and looked at the underside of his jaw. He stared out toward the sea, steady and firm. He was a rock. But he'd just told her that his daughter had cancer, and here he stood, miles away from his child.

What was wrong with him?

"Leukemia?" her voice came out strangled. She pushed out of his arms and turned on him. "Your daughter has leukemia?"

Oh, shit. Roni's chest rose and fell with a ragged breath. She was already in love with the man, and half in love with another child that . . . what? Would die? She put both hands to her mouth. She felt sick.

"Roni." Lucas moved toward her but she stepped back, out of his reach. "No," he said. He shook his head, the side-to-side motion fast and almost frantic. "She's not sick. Not now. She's fine. She's . . ."

Roni took another step back, holding up her hands to ward him off even though he hadn't made another move in her direction. She couldn't fathom going through it again. "You want me to fall in love with another child who's going to—"

"She is *not* going to die." He bellowed out. "Not on my watch." His words echoed back at them. "And don't even utter those words to me."

"But you said—"

"I started that all wrong," his words were clipped. "She's not sick. She was diagnosed three years ago. She *had* leukemia. She's had chemo. She's fine now. Really. She's just . . . well . . . she's my baby," he said. His voice broke on the last word. "I worry about her every day. How can I not? But she's fine. She's in remission. You've seen her. Did she look sick to you?"

Roni jerked her head back and forth. Her heart was still racing from the shock. "What are you even doing here? Shouldn't you be at home?"

"She's *not sick*," he repeated calmly. "Not now. She hasn't been for a long time. She's been in remission for eighteen months. They won't declare her cancer-free until it's been two years." He reached for her again but dropped his hand when she shook her head. "She's fine, Roni," he soothed. "She's perfect. And what I was trying to tell you before was that her own mother—the woman who was supposed to love her unconditionally—hasn't been there for her a day since she was diagnosed. She left *because* Gracie was sick. But you're different. You were there for Zoe. Zoe knew she was loved."

The panic started to subside, but the damage had been done. "I need some time," Roni whispered.

"No." He snapped out the word. And this time, he did take another step in her direction. She took a step back.

Then she was falling.

"Roni!" Lucas shouted.

Her feet couldn't find a hold as she hit the sloped ground beneath her. She rolled a couple times, down the sandy ridge, until she ended up sprawled on the beach with sand inside her panties and her dress twisted in a knot.

She lay face up, breathing hard and staring at the stars, and felt her tears begin anew. They didn't pour from her this time. Instead, a thin watery drip came from the corners of her eyes and spilled into her hair. She'd so wanted the idea of Lucas and Gracie to be real. She'd wanted to believe in them.

But she couldn't go through that again.

Especially when she was just realizing that she wanted her piano career too. In some fashion, at least.

She'd have to choose. Again. Be there for Gracie, or chase her career.

She lay there crying in the sand until Lucas finally stood over her, staring down into her face. He panted as if he'd been running.

"Are you okay?" he asked. "Did you hurt anything?" He bent over at the waist, hands on his knees, and stared at her.

"I'm fine," she mumbled. She just wanted to be left alone.

"Then let me help you up." He reached a hand out to her but she didn't take it.

"Go back to the hotel, Lucas." Her voice came out flat. She was out of energy. "I can't do this."

His jaw clenched and then he had his hands on her arms and was dragging her up off the sand. She pushed against him but he didn't budge.

"Let me go," she muttered. She slapped at his hands as he pulled her along behind him.

"I am not letting you go." Then he bent one shoulder to her waist and the next thing she knew she was hanging upside down over his back, her sand-infested rear flashing in the night.

"Are you crazy?" she shouted. Thankfully they were the only ones on the beach, but that didn't mean she would tolerate being manhandled. "Put me down."

He rounded the walkway leading from the beach to her property and stomped up the wooden steps, bouncing her with every motion.

"You're not walking away from us because you're scared," he announced.

"I'll do anything I want." She thumped her fists against his butt, then rolled her eyes at the ineffectual action. Damn the man and his tight ass. "You can't force me to go to Dallas, Lucas. And this behavior isn't winning you any points either."

She continued bouncing upside down with each of his long strides. He didn't stop until he reached the stairs to her back deck, and then he only brought her up and over his shoulder. He still didn't let her go.

"Put me down," she repeated. Her teeth clamped together, and she couldn't imagine being any more embarrassed.

He held her in front of him, her feet a foot from the ground, both of them practically steaming with anger.

"You're not walking away from this," he said.

"I just need some time." It was a lie. She was walking away. She would run if she could only get down.

"I promised Mrs. R."

She blinked, forgetting her anger. "What?"

He motioned with his head to the house across the yard. "That's what she wanted tonight. I promised her that I would take care of you."

"I don't need taking care of."

"Fine. I actually promised that I would dote on you," he ground out. "Happy? I said I'd dote on you, and that I would be there for you. So I'm not walking away just because you're freaking out."

She pulled in several deep breaths as she tried to calm herself, and shot a venomous look at Mrs. Rylander's house. The woman was butting into her love life, now? Roni needed to put a stop to her before things got worse.

"I'm fine, Lucas. But I want to be alone."

"Are you going to Dallas with me or not?" he asked. "I leave Sunday morning."

Threatening tears burned her eyes again and she lowered her head. "Just let me down."

Her whining voice must have done the trick. He loosened his grip and she slid along the length of his body. It was impossible to miss their differences as they moved over one another. He was hard to her softness. He was tough. She . . . not so much.

He wanted to take care of her.

She actually wanted to be taken care of. Sometimes.

But not right now.

"I don't know about Dallas, Lucas," she told him honestly when she had her feet on the ground. "Tonight was a lot. I need to sleep on it."

The planes of his face never wavered in front of her, though his eyes changed from hard-edged to tender.

"I love you, Roni."

Her throat closed and the tears she'd been holding off escaped. She dropped her forehead to his chest, but she said nothing.

He lifted her face. "It's real," he told her. "I love you. Your strength and your courage. The fact that you care about people. And I love that you're brave enough to take care of yourself when *you* need someone the most. But you don't have to anymore. I'm here for you. I always will be if you'll let me." His eyes roamed over her face and then he pressed a soft, closed-mouthed kiss to her lips. "Gracie and I will make sure you're never alone again," he whispered when he pulled away. "All you have to do is love us."

She didn't know what to say.

Her heart screamed yes, but . . .

She shook her head. "Go home," she pleaded. "Let me be alone tonight."

A muscle ticked in his jaw, but finally he nodded. He took a step back.

"We'll talk tomorrow," he said. "I'll put out the fire and wait until you're inside before I go."

The darned man was still trying to take care of her. *Fine.*

She turned to head up the stairs without another word. At the door, she shed her boots, her sweater, and even dropped her panties where she stood. They were all covered in sand. When she went inside, she left the lights out and watched through her back door as Lucas crossed her yard and worked at the fire pit. He doused the flames, then picked up the trash and carried it to the can beneath her deck. A few seconds later he returned to the pit and crammed the food they hadn't eaten into the grocery bags they'd carried it out in.

She saw him look at the house and then down at his hands. She slid the door open.

He crossed the yard, his long gait eating up the distance, and was at her back door in what seemed like seconds. Before she could tell him he could come in and go through the house to his car, he'd handed her the bags and was gone.

Neither of them said a word.

She slid the door closed and dropped the bags to the floor. Then she plugged in her Christmas tree and curled up beneath it.

There she cried for her dad's death. She still missed him.

She cried for her parents' divorce that had happened so long ago. She wasn't sure her dad had ever mourned the loss of his marriage, or if her mother had ever gotten over it, so she cried for the both of them.

And then she cried for Gracie and all that she knew Lucas and his daughter must have gone through.

She cried because Gracie's mother hadn't loved her enough to stay.

Quite a while later, she rose and pulled the innocuous-looking wooden box from her bookcase. She lay on her back under the tree with it, staring up at the lights, and she thought about all the holidays she'd spent with her mom. Her mom had made them special and filled them with love.

Then she thought about the Christmases before her mom and dad had split up. Those were the memories she cherished the most. A full, complete family. They would all sing around the piano together, or her mom and dad would dance while she played the piano. And she and

Danny would always awaken early to sneak down to the tree and see what Santa had brought them.

Never had they made it back to their beds. Their parents always appeared, as if by magic, as she and her brother stared wide-eyed at the gaily wrapped gifts. Then Christmas would begin. At whatever insane hour of the morning it had been.

She'd wanted to give Zoe at least one Christmas like that.

Roni had failed her.

When she'd been at the hospital on Thanksgiving Day that year, she'd noticed that Zoe had seemed weaker than usual. She hadn't looked healthy at all. Roni had even briefly considered canceling the remainder of her tour.

It was a thought that had never entered her mind before. But she didn't cancel shows. If her dad had been there, it would never have even crossed her mind.

So she'd packed her bags and headed back out. It was the last time she'd seen Zoe.

She opened the wooden box and pulled out the postcards the hospital staff had collected from Zoe's room, flipping them over to look at the backs. Purple check marks graced the top corner of most, but there was the occasional pink *X*. Roni turned one of the *X*ed cards over to see where it was from. Milwaukee. Zoe hadn't understood why anyone would want to go to Milwaukee. She thought the name sounded funny.

Roni smiled at the memory. She'd promised Zoe that no one would ever make her go to Milwaukee if she didn't want to.

Then Roni found the cards with no marks on the backs. There were three of them.

They were the postcards that Zoe had never seen.

More tears filled Roni's eyes as she curled on her side and pulled the cards to her chest. She should have done better.

She *could* have done better.

But she hadn't.

CHAPTER TWENTY-SEVEN

Roni eased her eyes open, unsure where she was or what day it was, and slowly looked around. Everything seemed off. As if the world had tilted on its axis. And her eyes hurt.

Then she remembered.

She was under her Christmas tree. She'd cried herself to sleep.

She closed her eyes again, and lay there in the early-morning quietness. The tree still glowed above her, and the sky outside her sliding doors showed enough light to let her know that she'd way overslept. She didn't move from where she was, tucked on her side, with one of her nephew's presents now smooshed under her head.

So much for her routine. She didn't even feel like playing the piano this morning.

Too many tears had fallen the night before.

But she did feel better somehow. More . . . calm. As if a weight had been lifted from her chest. Apparently she'd needed a meltdown.

Too bad it hadn't helped her come to any decision about Lucas.

No matter how many ways she'd twisted things during the night, she couldn't decide if they were worth the risk. She could be just fine right here the way she was. She might miss a few experiences in her life, but at least this way, her heart would stay intact. She wouldn't have to risk it being violently ripped from her body again.

And if that meant she was a coward, then she could be okay with that. She was good at it. Hadn't she hidden from her problems her whole life?

Like father, like daughter.

But then . . . staying here, staying stagnant, would mean she would never see Lucas again, either.

And he'd said he loved her.

She swallowed against a lump in her throat.

She loved him back.

But what if Gracie got sick?

She opened her eyes and this time she could focus better. She looked out the door and across the floor of the deck, right between two of the railing slats—which were running horizontal in her prone position—to where the sun was just beginning to come up out of the ocean. It was bright orange, and the sky and clouds around it were streaked in pink. She loved sunrises.

She sighed and rolled to her back. She needed to get up.

She pushed to a sitting position and then turned to look behind her. She studied the pile of postcards spread out under the tree. A few of them were still damp, others had been damp but now were stiffly dried, and the remainder looked to have been bent either in her hands or under her body at some point during the night. The packages hadn't fared much better. There was a nice head print in the one that had become her pillow.

Good to know that when she had a breakdown, she took everything in her path out with her.

She sighed and looked away from the mess. She really wanted to move on from her mistakes.

It felt like it was time. Lucas had done that for her.

He'd helped her to grieve. And in return, she'd . . . what? Pushed him away?

Was too damned scared to even try?

It hurt too much to think about.

She scooted around until she sat propped up against the end of the couch and stared out through the back door. She scratched at the side of her head. There was sand clumped in her hair from where she'd fallen on the beach the night before.

A noise caught her attention a second before Mrs. Rylander's head appeared at the deck stairs. Her tiny body followed. Roni watched as she took in the sand-filled clothes still strewn across the deck before turning her gaze to the back door.

Their eyes met through the glass.

"Are you okay?" Mrs. Rylander asked. Roni read her lips more than heard her. For once Mrs. Rylander seemed subdued. Concerned.

Roni shook her head. No. She was not okay.

She leaned forward until she could grasp the handle of the door then slid the door open and returned to her position against the couch. Her neighbor took in the scene on the floor.

"I saw the fight last night," Mrs. Rylander admitted. "Saw him hauling you up from the beach."

Roni wasn't surprised. She and Lucas hadn't exactly been quiet.

"Sorry if we woke you," she said.

A bony shoulder shrugged beneath a thick seaman's sweater. "I don't sleep much most nights anyway."

The heavy ribbed knit of the sweater was worn at the hem—which hung to the woman's knees—and looked to be years past its prime. And then Roni got it. It was Henry's sweater. All the times the older woman showed up in oversized sweaters and jackets . . . they must be Henry's.

Roni's heart broke for her.

To love someone that much. She didn't know if that was a good thing or bad.

Mrs. Rylander made her way past the mess on the floor and surprised Roni by plopping down next to her. "Want to talk about it?"

Two minutes ago, Roni would have said no. She didn't want to talk about it.

But she took a long, hard look at her neighbor now, and she saw years of experience written in the lines of the woman's face. There had definitely been some hard years and hurts thrown into the mix. And Roni knew that yes, she *did* want to talk about it. Because she didn't know what to do.

"I think I might have lost him," she said. "Pushed him away."

"Impossible."

She glanced at her neighbor again, this time with a sad smile. "Why do you say that? Because you butted in last night when you danced with him? Because you made him say he'd take care of me?"

Roni was still slightly annoyed by that move, but in the light of day, she began to see it as sweet. It was nice having someone who had her back.

"I didn't make him say anything," Mrs. Rylander corrected. Her lips pursed in her normal, obstinate way. "I simply asked if he loved you." She tilted her head to give Roni a shrewd stare. "He did tell you that, didn't he? That he loves you?"

Roni nodded. "He told me."

"And did you tell him back?"

Not, do you love him? But, did you tell him? She shook her head. "I couldn't."

"Well, why in hell's bells not?"

A light chuckle came from Roni. She really did care for her lovably eccentric neighbor. "Because I was too busy losing my mind."

"Why?" Incredulity sat heavy in the word. "Because he said he loves you?"

"No," Roni whispered. She returned to watching the sun move slowly up the sky. The pink streaks were fading now as blue took their place. Her chest was so heavy it almost hurt to breathe. "Because I'm scared. I lost a little girl once. One that was very special to me. Losing her shut a door in me that hasn't been opened until recently." She glanced at Mrs. Rylander and admitted, "Until Lucas. But I'm not sure I can step through it."

"Oh, sweetheart." A thin, bony arm settled around Roni's waist, and Roni found herself tilting her head to rest on Mrs. Rylander's shoulder. It was nice. A special moment the two of them had never shared.

"Tell me about this child," Mrs. Rylander urged.

So Roni did.

With this being the third time to share the story, she began to see things in a new light. She didn't just tell how she hadn't been there for Zoe, but she told of times she had. They talked about Roni's visits to the hospital, the special gifts she'd bring the little girl, and the time she'd gotten permission to take Zoe to the zoo. Zoe had loved animals. Roni had given her that.

When the words stopped, she felt lighter on the inside. As if Zoe was smiling down on her.

"I'm sorry that you lost Zoe."

The words were simple, but Roni felt the emotion behind them. She looked over at her neighbor. "What happened with you?" she asked. She wanted to be there for her neighbor too. "Why don't your kids visit?"

Pain laced Mrs. Rylander's pale blue eyes and turned down the corners of her mouth. "This isn't about me. And I won't bring my problems into your life."

And that was it. Roni knew she wouldn't get anything more out of her neighbor.

Whatever had happened, the woman was a fighter, but she had closed off her heart.

"Okay." Roni picked up her neighbor's hand and held it. "But I'm here if you ever need me. You know that, right?"

Mrs. Rylander stared out through the still-open back door for several long seconds. She didn't so much as blink. And then she nodded. "I know you are," she said in a frail voice. Her eyes closed. "And thank you."

Roni returned her head to her neighbor's shoulder, and the two of them sat that way while a slight wind occasionally drifted in to whisper across them. Finally, Mrs. Rylander put her free hand over Roni's. She patted it gently, the cooler skin of her gnarled fingers gentle against Roni's. "I had to make sure he wouldn't hurt you," she said. "That's why I talked to him last night. Why I butted in. I want you to have someone who loves you as much as my Henry did me."

The words meant a lot.

"I think he does." Roni smiled slightly. "But he has a daughter. And she has leukemia."

Mrs. Rylander gasped. "The poor baby."

"Yeah." Roni breathed in and out through her mouth as she worked to not let fear overwhelm her again. "He says she's been in remission for eighteen months. She's healthy now, I guess." But Roni didn't really believe it. "As healthy as she can be. Until it comes back."

"Are they expecting it to come back?" Mrs. Rylander pulled away and shock registered on her face. Roni just looked at her, noting the difference in the two of them. The very idea that it might come back shocked Mrs. Rylander to her core. Whereas, Roni simply assumed it would.

Could she be wrong?

"I don't know," Roni finally answered. "He didn't actually say he thought it would."

In fact, he'd said the opposite. She just hadn't believed him.

Mrs. Rylander gave a quick nod. "Then it won't. Lucas will see to it. He won't let anything happy to his girl."

Boy, didn't Lucas have a fan?

But the woman had a point. He was a good father. A good man.

He wouldn't be here if he thought anything might happen to Gracie. Not that he could stop it if it did.

But he would know his daughter's health best.

He wouldn't take off for weeks at a time if she wasn't truly on the road to recovery.

So Roni could trust in that. She could believe, in that way, Gracie was not like Zoe.

She picked up one of the postcards, and flipped it over to look at the back. There was no mark. She would miss Zoe forever, but that didn't mean she would ever forget.

"You need to keep him," Mrs. Rylander said. "I told you that already." She peered at Roni. "Don't be too scared to live."

And then she stood from her spot on the floor and headed out the door.

She'd said her piece and she was returning home.

Gathering the cards scattered around her, Roni smoothed them out the best she could and carefully put them back in their box. Then she returned the box to its spot on her shelf.

Once finished, she stepped through the back door to stand on the deck. She breathed in the fresh air. The wind gently touched her face, and the sun heated her skin. It was a gorgeous day.

And Roni knew Zoe was smiling down at her.

Zoe had been a good part of her life. And she would always be with her.

But it was time to move on.

~

Lucas hurried down the back hall of the convention center Friday morning, heading for Roni's dressing room. She'd texted him and asked him to meet her there. It had been a long, restless night after he'd left her place, and he hoped she'd calmed down. He didn't want to have to drag her all the way to Dallas just to convince her that what they had was real and worth fighting for.

As he neared the turn to take him to her room, several other voices caught his attention and he slowed. One of them was loud and overheated. When he heard the words "and I know you had something to do with it," Lucas picked up speed. Whoever it was, he didn't like the sound of it.

He landed at her open door and peered inside.

Roni sat in a chair in the middle of the floor, one leg crossed over her other knee and her features calm and polite, but he didn't miss how her fingers were clenched together in her lap. The tips were white. He also noted that her eyes were puffy right across the lids. She must have cried more after he left last night.

Kayla stood to Roni's side, along with two other men he'd seen throughout the contest.

Sprawled on the couch on the other side of the room was Scott Grainger, the contestant who'd been eyeing Roni on the dance floor the night before. He wore the same look of disgust as he had last night. Sitting beside him was a short, round man in a suit.

"What's going on?" Lucas asked.

The short man and Grainger jerked their heads in his direction. Both men wore looks filled with enough animosity that Lucas didn't wait for a reply. He stepped inside the room and filled up the space. He moved to Roni's other side so that she was now flanked on both sides.

He had no clue what was going on, but clearly the text Roni had sent had not been because she wanted to tell him that she'd be flying out to Dallas with him in two days.

"Mr. Grainger," Kayla began, motioning toward the contestant who hadn't quite made it to the final round, "is wishing to file a complaint."

Lucas looked at her. "About what?"

She swallowed and licked her lips nervously. "He claims that Miss Templeman has . . . *helped* you get to the final round."

"And I've no doubt she'll help him win too." Grainger came up off the couch. His chest puffed out and his cheeks turned ruddy, and Lucas was reminded of when they'd worked together once before. They'd both shown up for a shoot years ago, looking to score the same job. They'd each gotten a job, but Lucas had won the better placement.

Grainger had not taken the loss well then, either. He'd threatened a lawsuit, if Lucas remembered correctly. It stood to reason that he'd be blowing smoke here today too.

He couldn't stand Scott Grainger.

"Who's the suit?" Lucas asked, turning his head to look at the round man still seated on the couch.

The man rocked back and forth two times before managing to push himself to his feet. When he stood next to his buddy, he was a good six inches shorter than Grainger.

"I happen to be a close, personal friend of Mr. Grainger's. I'm his witness to this catastrophe."

"He also buys hundreds of votes every day." The younger of the two men standing alongside Kayla spoke up. He held out his hand to Lucas. "I'm Owen. I've been collecting the money for the daily votes."

"You're probably in on it too," Grainger sneered.

Owen ignored him. "Mr. Grainger is saying that Roni buys too many votes for you each day because you're sleeping together."

Lucas glanced at Roni.

"Not that that would be against the rules," the final man spoke up. "I'm Ken Tolley." He held out his hand to Lucas. "I'm head of the contest committee. And the rules state that anybody can buy any number of votes they wish."

"Then what's the problem?" Lucas asked.

The round man jumped in. "Mr. Grainger and I believe that you pursued Ms. Templeman with the specific purpose of winning."

Lucas raised a brow. "You think I'm sleeping with her because she has enough money to buy as many votes as she wants?"

Both men nodded, and Kayla shifted from one foot to the other.

Lucas peered down at Roni. "Do you have that kind of money?"

Honestly, he'd never thought about her money. He supposed she had plenty, though. She lived in a huge house, and best he could tell, she hadn't done a lot the last few years to make much. A pink hue touched the apples of her cheeks and he wanted to lean over right there in front of all of them and kiss her lips.

"I have enough," she murmured.

Lucas pursed his lips, impressed. "Hmmm. Guess I picked well then." He turned his gaze back to the two men by the couch and let his stare go cold. "I am not sleeping with Miss Templeman for her money. Not that it's any of your business. Nor have I once asked her to vote for me."

"Of course you didn't," Grainger said. "You wouldn't have to ask. Give her a little of the goods, and she'll pour the money your way."

Lucas took a threatening step toward the man, wanting to shove his head inside his body, but Roni stood from her chair, blocking his way. "Gentlemen," she said. She looked from Grainger to his sidekick, then to Lucas, Mr. Tolley, and finally to Owen. "It's my understanding that there's an accounting system for the votes. Yes, I've written a check. Every day. A big check." She glanced back at Lucas. "But since the night of the Nine Ladies Dancing competition, not a dollar of my money has gone toward a single contestant."

"She's telling the truth," Owen spoke up. He lifted a notebook. "She doesn't vote. She just donates."

"And you're probably a friend of hers," the round man said.

"As you pointed out earlier," Owen countered, "you're a friend of Mr. Grainger's. Should I tell the group how many votes you cast for your 'friend' each day?"

Everyone turned to look at the round man except Grainger. No one spoke.

Finally, Grainger stepped forward, slightly in front of his buddy. "What Ken puts in for me isn't the point. He's not sleeping with me." This brought out muffled chuckles around the room.

Lucas reached out a hand behind Roni and put a finger dead center in the small of her back. She jolted, but just as quickly stilled. He slipped his finger into the waistband of her black pencil skirt. She had on black platform heels to go with the skirt and a bright-blue blouse thin enough that he could make out the faint line of her bra strap running across her back. She smelled good enough to eat.

He took a small step forward.

She ignored him, but he caught Owen watching him. Then Owen's gaze shifted to Kayla, and Lucas almost laughed. The boy wore a sad puppy-dog look, as if he'd give everything he owned to be able to touch Kayla the same way.

"Gentlemen," Kayla spoke up now. "We have a contest to get to this morning. Mr. Tolley and I will discuss your views, and we'll get back to you with our decision."

"I'm not finished—"

"You can't—"

Both Ken and Grainger began to argue at the same time, but Mr. Tolley held up a hand, cutting them off. "Our decision will be final," he said.

And with that, people began trailing out of the room.

Roni didn't move, as Lucas still had his finger on the inside of her skirt.

Mr. Grainger and Ken both shot them a sneer, but let Kayla usher them out. Kayla then looked at him and Roni. Her gaze dropped to where his hand disappeared behind Roni's back, and then she turned and left the room, closing the door behind her.

Roni jerked away. "Did you have to touch me while they were in here?"

He nodded. "I had to. I missed you too much."

She rolled her eyes and put several feet between them. "You're impossible," she said.

"And you look like you cried more after I left last night."

Worry shaped her eyes before she jerked her gaze to the mirror. "Do I look that bad?"

He walked up behind her and stared at her reflection. He shook his head. "You just look a little sad."

Her eyes met his. "I am a little sad."

"I know." He slipped his arms around her, then relaxed the muscles in his shoulders when she didn't pull away. "And I'm sorry for my part in that," he added.

"It's not your fault." She tilted her head back and rested it against him.

"I meant what I said, though."

Brown eyes remained steady on his.

"I love you." In case she didn't know what he was talking about. "And I'm pretty sure you love me too."

She wouldn't admit it. She just watched him.

"Did you come to any decision last night?" he pushed.

Her jaw clenched, and then he watched her pull in a breath through her nose. Finally, she glanced away and answered with questions. "What if I did come down there, Lucas? What if I fall in love? With Gracie." She stroked him with her gaze. "With you. And what if she gets sick again? I'm not sure I'm strong enough for that."

"I'm sure you are." She was the strongest person he knew. Who else would plan to adopt a child who she knew would die?

"I need to pursue something with the piano again," she told him.

This lightened his heart. "Good," he said. "I've thought you needed that all along."

She sighed and pushed at his arms, but he just shook his head. He wasn't letting go of her. She slumped against his body instead. "What if I want it all again?" she whispered.

"Then we'll miss you while you're gone." He pressed a kiss to the side of her head. "And we'll come see you. Often."

"And what if Gracie gets sick?"

He stilled. He didn't let himself believe that Gracie would get sick. But Roni was worried about being on the road instead of being there for his daughter. Of course she would be. And he would never want to ask her to choose.

"Gracie isn't going to get sick," he said.

Hollow eyes met his. "It would destroy me," she told him. The emotion left her words. "And I just don't know if I can do it."

The words felt so final that he wasn't sure what else to say.

He wouldn't beg her to come to Dallas if she didn't want to. But he also couldn't imagine getting on the plane without her.

He lowered his hands and stepped away. Now *he* needed the distance she'd sought so desperately last night. Because for the first time, he worried that he just might lose her.

And that was another part of his life that he refused to think about.

Chapter Twenty-Eight

Male laughter rang out from the beach and every woman sitting on the aluminum stands paused in their conversations and turned their head to the sound. It was Lucas. His laughter was to women like dog whistles were to dogs. And Roni had to admit it made her a little jealous. Because she knew what those women were thinking every time they looked at him.

Same thing she was.

He and his day's partner were currently bent over about thirty feet out on the beach, laughing with each other as dozens of pears tumbled from their Christmas tree to their feet.

It was the last competition of the contest, and he and Gus had spent the day with their partners taking part in a scavenger hunt for enough pears to fill the wire-framed Christmas trees currently standing side by side on the beach. Today's game was to gather the many varieties of pears from their hiding spots on the island, make a *papier-mâché* partridge, and then assemble all the items on the tree.

Again, it wasn't about who was the fastest, but that was hard to tell from watching the two men work. They'd been rushing so much to finish that Lucas had inadvertently sent his pears rolling as he'd stretched high to place a round of a reddish-colored variety. His design had been based on rows of the different varieties of pears, whereas

Gus's was a mishmash with the more unique colors acting as ornaments, and the base being the typical green Anjou.

Roni had to admit that Gus's was prettiest. But maybe she was partial to it because Cookie Phillips had been chosen as his partner that day. Cookie owned the bookstore and was normally too shy to talk to someone as hot as Gus, so Roni had been thrilled when she'd pulled Cookie's name from Gus's basket. Roni was secretly hoping they finished their tree first, although she still wanted Lucas to win overall.

She knew what winning meant to him. A large donation to the Dallas Leukemia Foundation. The society had not only provided support when he'd needed it the most, but worked nonstop to ensure that kids like Gracie lived. That they could be cured for good. So yeah, it made sense to her now. Enough so that she was almost encouraged to put her own money toward Lucas that day instead of simply to the day's charity.

She was still irritated by that morning's attack. If she'd wanted to purchase a thousand votes a day for Lucas—or even ten thousand a day, for that matter—it would be none of Scott Grainger's business.

"Look at her go!" Andie exclaimed. She pointed out Cookie as she laughed with Gus. Roni, Andie, and Ginger were sitting together in the stands, cheering on the teams. And if Roni wasn't mistaken, as they watched, a hair flip got thrown in. Cookie had some flirting going on.

Apparently, put Cookie in the vicinity of a hot guy, and she became a wanton woman.

Roni watched a few more minutes, cringed when one side of Gus's tree came toppling down, then shifted her attention back to Lucas. She pulled in a deep breath and blew it out. She still hadn't quite decided what would happen next with them, but given the fact she'd about melted at his feet when he'd touched her that morning, she had a pretty good idea.

But first, she had to talk it out with her girls.

"We had a fight last night," she said, as if to no one, but she knew her friends would hear her and know who she was talking about.

They were sitting on the end of one set of bleachers, over by one of the portable heaters that had been set out for the day. It was chilly outside, so the city had done what it could to keep the crowd from getting too cold. Vendors were also selling hot chocolate and coffee as quickly as they could make it.

Ginger sat on the other side of Andie and scooted in close so that the three women were practically on top of each other. "What happened?" she asked.

"I told him about Zoe."

"And that caused an argument?" Andie looked appalled.

"No." Roni glanced around, then lowered her voice. "But when he told me that Gracie had been diagnosed with leukemia three years ago, I kind of lost it."

"Oh my God," Ginger breathed out. She shot her gaze to Lucas. "Poor thing. Is she okay?"

Roni nodded. "Remission for eighteen months."

The three of them fell silent while they all watched Lucas and his out-of-town partner work. His design still wasn't as good as Gus's. She needed to teach him a thing or two about Christmas trees.

"Did you break up?" Andie asked.

"Why would they break up?"

Andie cut her eyes at Ginger before turning back to Roni. "Because Roni is afraid to fall for Gracie now. What if something else happens to her? Is she going to risk losing another kid?"

Roni nodded while Ginger said, "Oh."

"So what happened?" Andie asked.

The pressure of tears pushed at the back of Roni's eyes again. She'd really thought she would be cried out from the night before. She looked toward the cool blue sky, hoping to keep the tears at bay.

"I told him I didn't think I could do it," she whispered. She breathed in and out a couple times and finished with, "And then he told me that he loved me."

"Oh!" Ginger shot another look at Lucas as if she was surprised he'd had it in him.

Andie hugged Roni.

Roni let a tear escape.

"What if it does happen again?" she asked. "It'll kill me."

Ginger got up and moved to Roni's other side. She put her arm around Roni too. "But you love him back, right?"

There was zero sense in trying to deny it. Even Lucas knew she loved him. "Yes."

Both girls hugged her tight. "We're so happy for you," Ginger whispered. She pressed her cheek against Roni's.

Roni chuckled. "I don't even know what I'm going to do."

"You're going to go to Dallas, of course," Ginger said. "And you're going to meet that little girl. And you're going to fall in love with her too."

Roni shook her head and felt two more tears track down her cheeks. "And what if she gets sick?"

"Then you'll be strong for her," Andie told her. "Just like you were strong for Zoe."

Roni didn't know if she could do that. However, the thought of *not* going home with Lucas was almost laughable.

"What if I decide to go back out on the road again?" she asked.

Ginger pulled back. "Are you thinking about it?"

Andie didn't say anything. She just continued holding Roni, while lowering her head to Roni's shoulder.

"I don't know," Roni said, "but I want to do something. I miss it too much."

"Then you figure out what you want," Andie instructed. "It doesn't have to be all or nothing."

Ginger nodded. "You can have piano and a life."

Roni stared at her friends. "And if Gracie gets sick while I'm away?"

"Then you'll know that Lucas will be there with her until you get back." This came from Ginger. Roni hadn't thought for one minute about the fact that if Gracie did fall sick again, she would still have her father there with her. As well as her grandparents. She would never be alone.

"Hmmm," Roni murmured.

Andie laughed softly. "She can make a good point when she wants to, huh?"

Ginger looked offended. "I make good points all the time."

Andie and Roni snorted with laughter, and Ginger finally joined in. Maybe she did, but mostly Ginger was just romantic. And Roni hoped she never changed.

Someone in the crowd gasped and the three of them forgot Roni's problems and watched the men on the beach. Gus was three pears and a partridge to being finished. Lucas was six pears. He'd already placed his partridge high up on the tree.

A surge went through the women as they all began to cheer on their favorite. Roni sat forward in her seat and watched. It was a good day. She had a good thing with Lucas. And Ginger had made an *excellent* point.

Did that mean she and Lucas *did* stand a chance? She certainly hoped so.

Because she wanted to see where this could go.

Gus placed the last pear and Cookie handed the partridge up to him and he attached it about two-thirds of the way up. Everyone held their breath, waiting to see if anything would fall. Lucas was one pear from being finished.

But he was too late.

Gus and Cookie's tree stood, and after Gus threw his hands in the air and the crowd cheered, he picked up Cookie and swung her around in a circle. Then he planted a huge kiss on her mouth, and the women cheered even more.

Andie and Roni grinned. Ginger sighed.

Out on the sand, Lucas hugged his partner. When they broke apart, he searched the clusters of women with his penetrating gaze, and he didn't stop until he landed on Roni. He didn't smile, just looked at her as if waiting for an answer.

She knew what he was asking. It was time to make a decision.

Suddenly everything felt right. Her and Lucas. The idea of calling her manager and telling him to put out feelers. She'd start with just a CD. She wanted to record her new music. Maybe she'd even consider more.

And her and Lucas and Gracie. They just might be able to work.

She nodded and watched Lucas go still. She wanted to go to Dallas. Then a wide grin broke across Lucas's face and she returned one of her own.

Kayla appeared at Roni's side and pulled her attention from the man she loved.

"They backed off," Kayla said. A look of relief swept across her face and the woman smiled a real smile for the first time in days.

Andie perked up. "Scott Grainger?" Andie hadn't been at the meeting that morning because she'd been hugging the toilet. "What happened?"

"Owen did some research on Mr. Grainger's friend. The man runs the charity that Scott planned to donate his winnings to."

Roni's jaw fell open. "You mean he was voting heavy for Scott so that Scott would win and his organization would get the money?"

"Exactly." Kayla shook her head. "Not exactly against the rules, but talk about unethical. When I presented the evidence, they decided it wasn't worth their time to push anymore. Those two have had me twisted up for days. I just want to kick their butts."

"How about I do something to make it better for you instead?" Roni asked.

Kayla looked at her. "You're going to kick their butts?" All four of the women laughed. Then Kayla sobered. "What are you going to do? Buy enough votes to ensure Lucas wins just so I can rub it in their faces?"

"That's an idea," Roni noted. "But I'll stick to my current strategy. It's been working so far."

"Then what?"

Roni smiled broadly. "I'm going to play for you tomorrow."

It took a couple seconds, but Kayla's eyes went wide. "The piano? We're having a concert?"

"How about a modified concert?" Roni suggested. "In the parade."

"You want to play in the parade?"

"You think you can make arrangements between now and then? If you can, I'll play a new piece I've been working on. No one has ever heard it." Except Lucas.

Kayla was a woman who loved a good challenge. She looked at Andie as if wanting to make sure her boss heard her loud and clear. "A piano on a float tomorrow. You got it. I'll make it happen."

CHAPTER TWENTY-NINE

And the first-ever Mr. Yummy Santa goes to . . ."

Roni smiled at the audience from the stage as she waved the white envelope in the air. According to Kayla, Lucas and Gus had brought in the most money for votes yet—not counting donations. Roni was nervous for Lucas. People liked Gus. Heck, she liked Gus. He could take this thing away from Lucas.

After all, his tree had been way better than Lucas's. And he'd had a local on his team.

She turned to the two men and looked at each one of them. Lucas watched her like an animal ready to strike. Since their silent communication earlier on the beach, they hadn't seen each other at all. She'd been rushed off to practice with Coyote Creek. She'd be playing some of their songs with them this evening. Lucas and Gus had been immediately surrounded by photographers. The island had drawn quite a crowd the last few days. Tourism was up, retailers were thrilled, and all in all, the whole thing had been a success.

Even Kayla was almost relaxed.

But Roni was nervous. For Lucas. And for the fact she would be going to Dallas with him.

For the fact that it felt like everything she'd ever wanted was within her grasp.

She slipped a nail under the flap of the envelope and pulled out the card.

"Good luck, Gentlemen," she said into the microphone. Lucas smiled at her. A slow, hot, naughty smile—filled with love. And she practically swooned.

She turned to the audience and lifted the card to read it. A smile bloomed across her face when she saw the name printed there.

"Lucas Alexander," she announced.

Shouts went up and confetti came down, and Kayla hustled a small step stool out to the middle of the stage. Someone else brought Roni a gold crown—reminiscent of the Burger King commercials—and a red-and-green sash with "MR. YUMMY SANTA" written across the front. She got the pleasure of putting it on the winner.

Unable to contain her joy, she headed over to Lucas where he now waited by the stool. Two steps up, and she was eye to eye with him. Thanks to her heels.

"Don't fall," he murmured in a low, sexy voice. The microphone picked up his words and the crowd chuckled. Many of them knew that the two of them were an item, and they were no doubt waiting to see if anything exciting would happen next.

Not likely. She was a professional. She wouldn't be laying a big one on him in front of the crowd, no matter how badly she might want to.

And she did want to. It had been over forty-eight hours since they'd been together, after all.

"Congratulations on becoming our first winner," she said as she slipped the sash over Lucas's once-again-naked chest. She didn't even let her fingers linger over his hot skin. How very grown-up of her.

The gleam in his eye suggested he was thinking he'd won something else, as well.

She went to place the crown on his head and as she leaned in to get it just right, his eyes met hers.

"I love you," he mouthed.

Her world went still. She was in front of him so no one could see his mouth, and she felt as if it were just the two of them in the middle of the whole place. She gave him a small, secretive smile, letting her own love shine through. She wanted this. She could do this.

"I love you too," she replied just as silently.

Then she realized her mistake. His gaze fired and then lowered to her lips.

"Don't," she said. The microphone was still in her hand and picked up her whispered word.

"Do," he replied salaciously.

The noise level behind her began to rise.

Before she could pull away, Lucas had his mouth on hers, and the crowd roared to life.

His big hands reached out to steady her as he took the kiss deeper, and all she could do was hang on. Literally. He pulled her from the stool and wrapped his arms around her and she was left dangling in the air.

Nothing like being a professional.

When the kiss finally ended, she couldn't even be mad about it. The man now wore her lipstick, so she reached out a thumb and wiped it off his lips. She just shook her head at his behavior. He put her down, and the two of them turned to the cheering crowd, arms around each other, and gave an unsteady bow.

Mr. Tolley was hustled onstage with the oversize check showing Lucas's award, and Roni took the moment to escape.

She slipped off the stage and stood on the sidelines watching. And catching her breath.

"Pretty hot out there," said Jason, contestant number nineteen, the cutie from Iowa with the dimples and the large hands. He was standing with several other men, all waiting for their cue to head back to the stage. One last chance for the crowd to see all twenty-four men in their shirtless glory.

"Thanks, Jason." She probably would have blushed, but she was still overheated from Lucas's kiss.

"Guess he had something I didn't, huh?" he teased.

She just smiled and nodded her head. He had her heart.

After the men were sent back to the center of the stage, Roni stepped to the podium and thanked everyone for attending. The place was so noisy, she doubted any of them could hear her speak.

"Please stick around," she yelled into the microphone, "as Coyote Creek is back tonight. They'll be here late, so enjoy yourselves. And be sure to come back next year!"

She waved and slipped offstage and headed to her dressing room.

The adrenaline was pumping. She would be at the piano in about thirty minutes, and play for the same amount of time. And then tomorrow would be her reintroduction to the world. Kayla had worked her magic and had lined up a piano on a float. Along with several nearby news crews.

This time there was no nerves, only excitement.

She was ready to do this.

She was also ready to see Lucas. She hoped he could manage to get away for a minute before she had to be back onstage.

She stepped inside her dressing room and reached into the mini-fridge for a bottle of water. The door behind her opened and she turned to find the man on her mind. He closed and locked the door.

"Oh," she breathed out the word. "It's going to be that kind of moment, is it?"

He nodded and moved toward her. "It's going to be that kind of moment." He reached for the hem of her dress. She'd changed earlier and now wore the best little black dress that she owned. "Did I mention that I like it when you wear tight dresses?" he asked. "All I can think about every time I see you is how I'm going to peel it from your body."

This time he peeled it from the bottom up. He stopped at her waist.

Then his wide hands covered her rear and she dropped the bottle of water to the floor.

"I've missed you," she whispered. It felt like it had been days since she'd seen him.

"And I love you," he replied.

She reached for him, wanting his lips on hers, but he pulled back. "Say it," he demanded.

A grin spread across her face. "I love you," she whispered. Goose bumps covered her flesh at the possessive look the words created.

"And you're going to Dallas with me?"

Her heart constricted. With both fear and excitement. "Yes," she rushed the word out. "I'm going to Dallas with you. I want to meet Gracie."

There was no more need for words.

Lucas lifted her to his erection, and then he backed her against a wall.

He pressed into her. The trunks he wore were flimsy and hid nothing about him. He was hot and hard and ready to go. And she was only a second or two behind. She pressed her chest into his, needing his skin on hers, but the top of her dress was in the way.

"Wait," she whispered. She reached behind her to undo the hook at her neck. She shoved the zipper down as far as she could reach, then yanked the sleeves over her shoulders and dragged each arm free. All the while, Lucas pushed against her sex. He rocked into her, his hard length taunting her with what was to come. He remained covered, and she had on a thong, but he burned so hot against her, it was almost as if they were already skin to skin.

When her dress bunched below her breasts, she opened the front clasp of her bra and Lucas swore.

"God, you're beautiful." He shook his head as if in wonder.

She gasped when he lifted her higher and brought his mouth to her bare nipple.

He pulled her between his lips. Her legs clamped around his waist and his thickness landed right where she wanted him. She pressed down, desperate to have him inside her.

"Hurry, Lucas," she urged. "I want you."

She didn't have to say anything more. He held her to the wall while he reached into his back pocket for a condom. "I love you," she whispered. She planted kisses along his corded neck and he paused. He slowed as he leaned back and took her in.

His gaze was hot and needy. Her breasts rose sharply with each breath.

Then he set her on the ground and an urgent whimper escaped her throat. She reached out for him. She needed him inside her.

But he had other needs. He peeled her bra from her shoulders and worked the zipper down until the top of her dress hung past her waist. Then he worshipped her body with his hands and mouth. He lavished attention on every square inch from her waist up. He drove her out of her mind.

When she barely had the strength to stand, he went to work on the lower half of her dress. He tugged the zipper over the curve of her rear, and the dress slid soundlessly to her ankles. She kicked it to the side and he took a step back and simply stared.

She wore a royal-blue thong and black platform heels, and had a thin silver chain around one slim ankle. She knew she looked good, but not as good as him. As he studied her, he shoved his shorts to the floor and her body wept at the sight of all that strength. He sprang loose of the material and she couldn't wait any longer. She reached for him.

He moaned when her fingers touched his heated skin. The sound made her crazy.

But it was his eyes that got her. When he looked at her this time, it was love that she saw, overriding the desire.

She had to trust that this was right. It had to be.

Without a word, she dropped to her knees and pulled him between her lips.

He stiffened and thrust forward on a groan. The power of it was intoxicating.

She sucked him hard into her mouth, then gentle with long, slow licks, tracing her tongue from his base to the spot just behind the head. She caressed him with one hand as she continued teasing his length with her tongue. Then she shifted just to the right, and closed her mouth around his swollen tip.

His fingers flexed in his hair.

"Roni," he groaned. "Baby, you've got to stop. I need to be in you." He panted as she rode his long length with her mouth, then finished with, "We only have a few minutes."

She'd forgotten about that. They were in her dressing room.

Hundreds of people were only a hallway away.

With more than a bit of regret, she released him. He lifted her and had her pinned to the wall before she could pull in her next breath, and his mouth crushed hers.

Hiking one of her legs around his hip, he rolled on the condom and shoved her panties to the side. He put himself against her. He felt too large for her body to hold, though she knew she could take him in. And he looked into her eyes.

It was a look she wouldn't mind seeing for the rest of her life.

And then he pushed.

He entered her and she lost her breath with the exquisite pleasure of it.

He pulled out and pushed in again and she felt her body already begin to tighten. She didn't need anything extra tonight. She just needed him.

"Fast," she whispered.

He grunted and pushed in again.

And then she wordlessly slid over the edge as stars exploded behind her eyes.

Her body sang in his hands. He hit his own release and he closed his mouth, once again, over hers.

"I love you," he mumbled against her lips.

She was out of words. All she could do was nod.

And pray that she could keep this.

~

Lucas stepped away from Roni, both of them shaken and wearing slightly bemused expressions, and just shook his head.

"I . . . uh . . . *didn't* mean to do *that*," he murmured.

One shapely brow rose in front of him as Roni adjusted her panties. "Right. So you always come into people's dressing rooms and lock their doors, do you?"

Busted.

He grinned sheepishly. "Well, I didn't mean to do"—he motioned with his hand, waving it in the air in front of her mostly naked body—"*all* of that. I just intended to get my hands on you for a minute. Kiss you a time or two."

Her smile widened. "You did that."

She slipped her arms into her bra and pulled the material around to the front. As the pink of her nipples peeked through the blue lace, he felt his body stirring again. He had to get himself under control.

"Damn," he muttered as he watched her. They were in a public place. Anyone could come to her door for any given reason.

Plus, she had to be back onstage soon.

"I want you again," he stated. "I can't get enough."

She looked up from fastening her bra, and matching desire glowed back at him.

"Sorry," he finally mumbled. He turned his back to take his eyes off her. They didn't have time for a second round.

She laughed. "You don't hear me complaining."

He looked around the room for a tissue and a trash can, trying to get his mind to focus on something other than burying himself back inside Roni. It hadn't occurred to him as he'd been plowing his way into her that there was no connected bathroom. She laughed again, and then an arm reached around him, several tissues clutched between her fingertips.

They worked silently, cleaning themselves up and straightening their clothes, and when he picked his shorts up, he realized his wallet and phone had somehow managed to slide across the floor. Probably when he'd kicked his shorts off like a crazed teenager.

But damn, he'd missed her. Two nights was too long to go.

He stepped into his shorts. "You really didn't vote for me?" he asked. He'd been surprised to hear her announce that morning that she hadn't put a dime in for him over the last eight days.

Wickedness lit her face. "Not a one."

"I could have lost."

"But you didn't."

And, he supposed, he could have walked away with the money unsure if he deserved it or not. If she'd paid his way through, he wouldn't have felt right about taking it. "I think I should be offended," he grumbled, teasing her. "You could have put in at least one vote."

"Nope," she said. "Just be impressed with yourself." She shimmied into her dress and his blood once again headed south. "I know I am," she murmured.

She stepped over to him and kissed him squarely on the mouth. Her tongue stroked leisurely against his and he couldn't help but think about her licking another part of him. Hell, he had to get out of this room before he stripped her naked again.

He set her away from him. "Behave or I'll make you late to get back out front."

"Late could be okay." She eyed him from beneath heavy lashes, and he had to concentrate hard not to pull her dress back off her body.

"Aren't you looking forward to playing tonight?" he asked, groping for something else to talk about. She'd admitted earlier today that she wanted her career back.

And just like that, the wanton look disappeared and excitement filled her face. She nodded. "And tomorrow. Kayla has a float for me with a piano on it. She even wrangled speakers to hang off each corner. I'm going to play a mini concert during the parade, Lucas."

Pride glowed from her and Lucas found himself just standing there, staring at her. She came alive at the piano, and she was doing the same at that very moment. Pure, unadulterated pleasure glowed from her face. The concert pianist was back.

"I'm proud of you," he said. He pressed a hard kiss to her mouth, then moved away before he could do more. He grabbed his wallet from the floor and shoved it in his back pocket. Then he picked up his phone. He'd missed a text from his mother.

We're at the hospital with Gracie. Will call after we see the doctor.

Fear spiked through him and he whirled around. Roni looked up from the mirror, where she was plucking at her hair. She froze.

"What's wrong?" she asked.

He jabbed the number for his mother's cell.

"Gracie." Impatience had him counting the number of times the phone rang on the other end. "A text. They're at the hospital."

Panic roared through him as no one answered. He tried the house phone, and then his mother's cell again. His father didn't have a mobile; he hated everything about them.

No one answered anywhere.

He typed in a reply: **What's wrong? Is she sick?**

And then he realized that Roni hadn't said anything. He looked at her and saw that she remained across the room. Her face had gone white and she was chewing on her bottom lip.

Someone knocked on the door and yelled, "Ten minutes."

Roni's eyes shot toward the sound before bouncing back to him. "I can't do this," she whispered. "I told you."

Anger fueled him. "She's not sick," he snapped out.

She couldn't be. It had almost killed her the first time.

It had almost killed him.

He called his mother's phone again. Nothing. So he looked up the number for the hospital closest to their house, but they couldn't get him any information either.

"Find someone who can!" he shouted as the phone went dead. "Dammit," he muttered. "I have to go." He shoved his phone in his pocket. "Is there any way off the island after the ferry stops running?"

"No." Roni shook her head. Her eyes were too wide. "You're leaving?"

She looked like she was in shock.

"My daughter is at the hospital," he pointed out. "Yes. I'm leaving." Then he forced himself to slow down and take a deep breath. Panic would do no good. "Come with me," he said.

She pointed to the door. "But I have to play."

He tried his mother's phone again as his teeth ground together. As it rang in his ear, he reached for Roni's hand and rubbed his thumb over her clenched fist. "I probably can't get off the island tonight anyway. Or get a flight out until tomorrow morning. Come with me in the morning." He kissed her fingers and felt better already knowing that whatever it was, he wouldn't have to go through it alone. They could do this. They could do whatever Gracie needed.

Roni had gone quiet again.

And then he noticed that her hand now lay limp in his.

He shoved the phone back in his pocket and looked at the woman he loved. "Roni?"

She didn't look him in the eye.

"Roni?" His voice hardened. He stepped directly in front of her and forced her to look at him.

She just shook her head. "I told you," she whispered.

"What? That Gracie would get sick? It could be anything." But he didn't believe that it was. He believed his worst fear was coming to life.

"I can't do it," she said again.

And then he got it. "You aren't coming with me?"

Her no was a tight shake of her head.

"Tomorrow?" he asked slowly. He assumed Kayla would have put the word out about Roni playing in the parade. Canceling wouldn't be good for anyone. "Or never?" he finished.

Roni pulled her hand out of his and tucked it under her arm. Her gaze lowered to the ground.

"Are you kidding me?" he barked.

She didn't reply.

"What a coward," he muttered. He couldn't believe this was happening. "I thought you were different, Roni. I thought you had a spine." He'd thought she was strong enough to be there for Gracie. For him. "When are you going to quit hiding from your life?"

He should have known better. Hadn't this already happened to him once?

"Good thing I didn't expose you to my daughter." He spat the words out. "She doesn't need someone like you in her life."

Without another word, he slammed out of the room and walked away.

He did not look back.

Fury churned with fear and guilt about being away when Gracie needed him.

He would go home and take care of his daughter all by himself.

Just like he always had.

CHAPTER THIRTY

A knock sounded at the hotel door as Lucas packed the last of his clothes into his open suitcase. The only things left were his laptop, and the clothes and shower essentials he'd need for tomorrow morning. Then he'd be good to go. And he wouldn't look back.

A wrenching pain twisted in the middle of his chest but he ignored it. He didn't have time to think about what he was walking away from. It had been her choice. Plus, he and Gracie were better off finding out who she was now instead of later.

If she was no better than that, he wouldn't spare her two more minutes of his time.

Grabbing his phone—in case his mother called with an update again—he headed to the door. It was probably Kelly. Lucas had texted him as he'd left the convention center to let him know he'd be leaving on the first ferry of the morning. Only . . .

He stopped in the middle of the room and eyed the locked door. It could be Roni.

It *should* be Roni.

He checked his watch. She'd be off the stage by now.

He still couldn't believe she'd frozen up on him. Chances were high it wasn't her. The way she'd acted, he didn't think she'd be changing her mind anytime soon. And if she ever did, it would be too late.

With a pathetic amount of lingering hope, he opened the door. A woman stood there. Average height, blonde hair, green eyes. Pretty. With guilt weighing heavy on her face. He thought he'd seen her around over the last couple of weeks, but he couldn't put a name to her.

She stuck out her hand. "I'm Ginger," she announced, before saying in an apologetic tone, "Roni's friend."

Ah, the guilt of association.

"What do you want?" he asked. His tone was rude, but he was beyond caring. Surely Roni hadn't sent her over to make excuses for her. There was no excuse.

"Ummm . . ." Ginger drew the word out, looking more than uncomfortable to be there. "I have a boat."

He was at a loss. "And?"

"I own the ferry business here on the island," she explained, "but I also have fishing boats. Roni asked me to ready one of my boats and take you over to the mainland tonight."

He stared. The woman he'd thought he loved, who'd balked on him when he and his kid had needed him, had sent her friend over. With a boat.

Well, he supposed that was something.

"She's not a bad person, you know," Ginger smiled a little too hopefully. "She just needs some time."

"Who? Your boat?"

A dry look came back his way. "Your girlfriend."

"She's not my girlfriend."

"Can't you just give her a chance?"

He turned his back to her and went to pack up his laptop. If he could get off the island tonight, then he'd take it. There had been an earlier flight for Dallas in the morning, but he hadn't booked it since he didn't think he'd be able to make it, given the ferry schedule.

"I gave her a chance," he stated flatly. He didn't look up as he worked. He shoved his laptop in the padded section of the carry bag, then went for his toiletries. "She made her choice."

When he turned back, he saw that Ginger had stepped across the threshold, but just barely. She looked at a loss for words, but as Roni's friend, she apparently felt she had to try. "She's had a rough time in the past."

Seriously? This was her reasoning?

He locked his hands on his hips and stared at the blonde. "My daughter almost died while I was holding her in my arms. She went through months of chemo. Twice. All her hair fell out. Her skin turned yellow. And her mother left her the day after she was diagnosed. I know Roni's been through a lot herself. I get that. And she's scared now. But I don't have time for it. Either she moves past it and is with me—through everything—or it's over."

He stopped speaking and looked around the now barren room as if to make a point. Then he refocused on Ginger.

"And since she's not here with me . . ."

He slung his carry bag over one shoulder, zipped his luggage, and headed out the door, leaving Ginger to follow.

But he stopped abruptly on the other side. She slammed into him.

"*Damn*," he muttered. He looked back. "I have a rental that I brought onto the island. I can't go tonight. I have to take the car back on the ferry."

Ginger shoved at his back, moving him out of the doorway. "She took care of that too," she informed him. "Our other friend, Andie, is going home tomorrow. She'll drive your car. I just need the keys."

He stared down at the woman, noticing how her face was pulled tight and her eyes were avoiding him.

"What?" she finally bit out as he kept standing there.

"Seems she's thought of everything," he said. A boat, his car. Hell, by the time he got to the airport, maybe she'd have his flight rebooked for him as well.

"Seems like." Ginger agreed. She stepped past him and headed down the hallway. But before she got too far, he heard her mumble, "Except for you and Gracie."

A crooked slash lifted his lips. At least her friend thought Roni was an idiot too.

Not that it helped.

~

The music wasn't flowing today. Not like it should.

Or maybe it was just her.

Maybe she had no music left in her.

It kind of felt that way.

Roni pulled her hands from the piano keys and stared out the window. No sun could be seen rising up out of the water this morning. Just gray. Rumbling thunder. And blah. She propped her chin in her hands and her elbows on the top of the piano and let out a long, weary sigh. She felt the same inside as the weather. Yucky and gross.

What a setup for the afternoon parade.

At least, if it kept raining, she wouldn't have to worry about sitting on the float and playing in front of everyone. But it wasn't nerves that were bothering her this morning; she knew that. She'd been fine when she'd played with the band the night before. Fine, but not happy. She'd actually been pretty darn miserable during every minute of it.

But she'd played beautifully. And no one had been able to tell that her heart was broken.

Nor could they tell that she was as ashamed of herself as she'd ever been in her life.

She'd played and smiled and entertained . . . while one of her best friends had been taking the man she loved off the island. Away from her. But most importantly, to his daughter.

Roni glanced at the phone on the bench beside her hip. No blinking lights.

She'd texted Lucas in the early hours of the morning, as she'd been unable to sleep. She was worried about Gracie. It wasn't that she'd really expected him to reply, but when he hadn't, it had crumbled even more of her heart.

Yet she'd done the right thing. She believed that.

She wasn't what Lucas and Gracie needed.

Hadn't she proven that by the way she'd frozen up when he'd gotten the news? She couldn't be a mother to that little girl.

But that didn't mean she didn't care.

Worry gnawed at her now, and she fought the urge to call the hospitals in Dallas. She had Lucas's address. Surely she could find the one nearest him. But she knew they wouldn't tell her anything.

Because she wasn't family.

By her choice.

She collapsed onto the piano top and rested the side of her face over her forearms. She closed her eyes. She missed him.

And her heart hurt.

Warm tears slid from her eyes. She didn't make a sound. No audible crying, not even a sniffle. Just tears racing from beneath her closed eyelids to land softly on her arms. Her cheek slid against the wetness on her skin.

She wanted to go back and do it over again. She wanted to get it right this time.

Only, when she replayed the moments from her dressing room through her mind, she feared she would make the same decision again. Gracie could very well be lying in that hospital for the last time. She could be dying.

Roni turned her head to bury her face in her arms. She was so tired of being alone.

So tired of letting people down.

She just wanted to quit feeling anything for a while.

A hand touched her back and she jerked her tear-dampened face up. Ginger stood beside her.

"How'd you get in?" Roni asked. She sat up and wiped the backs of her hands across her cheeks. It was time to quit feeling sorry for herself. She'd made her decision. She had to lie in the bed she'd made.

"You didn't answer my knock so I came around and tried the back door."

Roni glanced to the sliding door in the living room. Then she noticed that her tree was dark. She hadn't turned it on this morning.

"You messed up, you know." Ginger said. She picked up Roni's phone and sat her butt down on the bench in its stead. "He's a good man. You should have gone with him."

"I never said he wasn't a good man."

She'd called Ginger the night before, right after Lucas had stormed out of the room. Ginger had tried talking to her then, but Roni hadn't wanted to hear it. She didn't especially want to hear it now either, but she didn't have the energy to stop it.

Instead, she tried to play the piano again.

Her fingers struck a couple chords before they stopped. She sat there as if her mind and her hands were disconnected.

"You two belong together."

"I don't belong with anyone." That was the answer. She'd called her manager the day before and told him she wanted to start slow, but why go that route? She'd never done anything in her career slow. She'd call him back and tell him she wanted a full tour. A new CD, multicountry stops. Anything he could line up. She'd come back with a vengeance.

She'd be the same Veronica Templeman that she'd always been.

Then she wouldn't have to drown in the sorrow of her own life.

Ginger put her hands on top of Roni's where her fingers lay lifeless against the black and white keys. The simple action clutched at Roni's chest. She jerked her hands out from under her friend's.

"You," Ginger began softly, "belong with Lucas." She paused only for a second. "And with Gracie."

"I don't—"

"You're scared," Ginger interrupted. "You opened yourself up before. And you lost. But that doesn't mean you will this time."

Roni turned her head to her friend. "Gracie is already back in the hospital. I don't see how that's winning."

"And Lucas is by her side. Or heading that way. Where you should be."

"I don't want another kid to die on me."

"Who says she will? This might not even be about her cancer. Have you thought about that?"

Roni stared at her. Ginger just didn't get it. Roni wasn't strong enough to be that person.

"Go home, Ginger." She rose from the piano and went to pour herself a cup of coffee. "I appreciate you being here, you know that. I would do the same for you. But I want to be alone now."

Ginger stood. She didn't immediately leave.

Instead she said what Roni least needed to hear. "He's scared too."

Roni stared at her, her cup poised at her mouth, but unable to lift it any higher.

"And you left the man you love to deal with this alone."

CHAPTER THIRTY-ONE

The run was just what Roni needed. The rain had disappeared and the sun was beginning to peek out from behind the clouds. The cobwebs were clearing from her head.

Ginger's words before she'd left had upset her. Yes, Roni knew Lucas was scared. She knew he was alone. But this was his life. He'd already been through it. He was prepared to handle it.

And yeah, she supposed that made her a bad person. Because if she loved him, she should be there with him. But it wasn't that kind of love. That's the decision she'd come to. It was more like a healthy dose of lust.

It was an island fling. Just as the ones before him had been.

Her fling had gotten under her skin this time, but what she and Lucas felt wasn't real. Not the kind of thing that would last. Her defenses had been down because of the season and the anniversary of Zoe's death. It could have been anyone she'd hooked up with and she'd have "fallen in love."

Only, it had been Lucas.

She slowed as she made her way up the beach, trying to catch her breath.

And he was different.

She pictured him as he talked about his daughter. The pride that glowed on his face. The protectiveness that was always there. And she knew.

She was lying to herself.

It couldn't have just been anyone.

A bird swooped down in front of her and she watched it fly out over the water, heading for parts unknown.

But her lying didn't change things.

She wasn't going to Dallas, and she would never see Lucas again.

Unless he came to one of her concerts.

She stopped abruptly and lifted her face to the sky. There was no way in the world that Lucas would ever come to one of her concerts again.

She wouldn't if she were him.

She wouldn't so much as spare another thought in her direction.

Crushing pressure made it feel like her lungs were collapsing. What was she doing?

The very thought of one more day without Lucas destroyed her. She couldn't imagine the rest of her life without him.

And Gracie.

She was already half in love with the kid, sight unseen. How could something bad be allowed to happen to her? Where was the fairness in that?

Lowering her head back to a normal position, she stared at the ground ten feet in front of her and began trudging through the sand. She didn't have the energy left to run. Instead, she felt as if the very sky above her were leaning on her shoulders. She was worried about Lucas. She wanted to hold his hand while he waited for answers. Or possibly, he already had answers. But what were they?

She pulled her phone out of its hidden pocket and checked her texts again. Still nothing from him.

But she had missed one from her manager.

Call me. Got a spot for Christmas Day. Good money. Great way to come back.

It was happening. Her career would pick up right where it had left off.

She swallowed around a throat suddenly tight, her breaths growing short. Instead of calling her manager, she texted her brother. If she took the job, that meant her plans for the holidays would change. She'd never played on Christmas before. It had been a sticking point with her.

Looks like I might miss Christmas.

It took no more than fifteen seconds before her phone rang.

"What's wrong?" her brother's greeting was terse.

"Nothing," she lied. *Everything. I lost the love of my life because I'm too weak and scared to be the person he needs.* "I just found out that I can play on Christmas day."

She'd talked to her brother the afternoon before. Right after she'd called her manager and told him that she wanted to come back slow.

"I thought you were starting with a CD."

"That was the plan. And the parade later today. I agreed to play a new piece I've been working on."

"Then I don't understand."

"It's my career, Danny. It's a good opportunity. If I want to make a comeback—"

"What happened?" her brother asked. He had his big-brother, take-charge thing going.

Her words cut off. She hadn't told him about Lucas and Gracie. She and her brother were close. They always had been. And she told him a lot.

But for some reason, she'd held Lucas and Gracie back from him.

Maybe because deep down she hadn't expected it to last?

"I . . ." she began.

She bit her lip and turned toward the ocean. The waves were rough today due to the storm that had rolled in overnight, and her insides felt as if they were churning along with the water.

"What's going on, Roni? You aren't ready for a big concert. Two days ago, you weren't ready for any concert."

She nodded. He was right. She was doing it again. She was running from her problems.

She gritted her teeth to keep from crying any more. She was tired of crying.

"Roni?"

"I fell in love," she whispered. "He has a kid." She closed her eyes. "And she's sick."

The silence grew on the other end of the phone until it felt like a being all its own. Danny would understand like no one else. He was a pediatric surgeon, and though he hadn't experienced the loss of one of his own kids, he lived with it every day. Not every child made it home safe and sound.

Finally, Danny spoke. He was calm and he wore his doctor's voice. She could handle his doctor's voice. It wasn't personal.

"What kind of sickness?" he asked.

"Leukemia."

Two beats of silence before, "Is she in chemo?"

She shook her head. "She's been in remission for eighteen months."

A short burst of air sounded in her ear.

"But he got a text last night." She hurried before he could tell her that everything was okay. Everything wasn't okay. "His parents were at the hospital with her. Lucas went a little crazy when no one answered his call. He couldn't find out what was wrong. He . . ." She stopped to take a breath. "Ginger took him to the mainland so he could go home to Dallas this morning."

"And where are you?" Danny asked.

"On the beach. I just finished my run."

"But you said you love this man."

"I have to play in the parade today. I promised Kayla."

"So you're going to Dallas after?"

She didn't answer. He knew the answer anyway. She didn't face her problems head on; she buried her head in the sand and pretended they didn't exist.

"She might be dying, Danny." Her hand shook as she held the phone to her ear.

"What did he find out when he got someone on the phone?"

"I don't know. He just left. And then Ginger took him—"

"You said that. But didn't you talk to him after he got hold of someone at home?"

She shook her head again. "No," she whispered.

"Why not?"

Because she was a coward.

"I told him . . ." She let the words die out.

Her brother expelled a frustrated breath. "Do you love him, Roni? Really?"

"Yes," she said in a small voice. She did. It wasn't just lust. And it couldn't have been just anyone. Lucas saw who she was even when she didn't want to show him. He cared about people.

He cared about her.

"Then what are you doing?"

"I don't know if I can go through it again."

"You don't know if you'll *have* to go through it again. Or you could marry the perfect man, have the perfect child, and have both of them get taken away by a random car accident in the blink of an eye." She could almost see the you're-such-an-idiot look on his face. "Nothing is guaranteed, Roni."

"But she's—"

"A little girl," he finished. "And probably scared right now. As is her dad."

Oh, God.

"What are you doing there, Roni? You were once willing to put your life on hold for a child that you knew had limited time. It ripped you in two when she died, but you were the bravest person I knew. There's no way you would have walked away from Zoe."

But she had. That last time. And then when she'd come back . . . The back of her throat burned.

She'd been too scared to stay after Thanksgiving, and when she'd come back it had been too late. What if it was already too late with Gracie? She would never meet her. Never let her know that she cared. And Lucas.

A strangled whimper came from her throat. He would *never* have left her to deal with something like this on her own.

"I'm such an idiot," she murmured. What was wrong with her?

"You're not an idiot," he assured her. "You're just scared."

"And Lucas," she said. "I should be there with him."

Her brother went quiet and she just knew he'd changed to his smug, I-told-you-so look.

"Oh God, Danny. What if it's too late?"

"It isn't too late."

"But I should—"

"Go," he said. "Yes. You should be there. If this is the man you want forever, you should go to him."

She nodded. "I will."

Oh geez. She blinked and refocused her eyes. What was she doing standing out on the beach when Lucas was alone and worried sick about his daughter?

"I've got to go," she said.

"Hey, sis?" Danny stopped her before she hung up.

"Yes?"

"I'm proud of you," he said. The feeling coming through his words brought goose bumps to her skin. "You're still the bravest person I know."

She nodded and started jogging once again. She had to get home. "Thank you, Danny."

"You're welcome. And make sure I get to meet this guy—and his little girl—at Christmas, will you?"

Laughter rolled up and out of her. "You got it."

She reached her backyard and slowed to dial Ginger.

"Yeah?" Ginger answered.

"Can you take me on your boat?"

Roni felt Ginger's hug through the phone. "I'll be ready when you get here."

CHAPTER THIRTY-TWO

The noise coming from the other end of the hall sounded like a herd of horses as Gracie and her friend raced down the dark-stained stairs from the second floor. Dark curls and a startlingly white gauze patch appeared around the corner and Lucas held out his hands in front of him.

"Whoa," he said. "You were just in the emergency room last night. Slow down."

"I can't, Daddy. Lisa's the monster. She's gonna get me."

The dark curls were followed by long blonde hair as his daughter streaked out of the room with her best friend howling with laughter right behind her. Lisa had her hands up, her fingers pointed like claws, chasing Gracie in a straight-legged, awkward gait.

The two of them had been going at it all day. Gracie was fine. When he'd finally gotten in touch with his mother the night before, he'd found out that it had just been a fall. She'd busted open her head, right at the hairline, and had needed twenty-two stitches. But other than freaking out her father and grandparents, the kid was fine.

He'd arrived at his mom's earlier that morning, fresh from the first flight in and running on little sleep, and the relief he'd felt at seeing his daughter's smiling face had allowed his arm to be twisted. Since then, Gracie and Lisa had been running through his house as if the two girls hadn't seen each other in two weeks. Instead of Gracie not seeing her dad in that same amount of time.

His mother had come over about an hour ago with the ingredients for an afternoon snack, and was in his kitchen right now baking up a batch—or three—of Gracie's favorite Christmas cookies.

He peeked into the living room, where Gracie and Lisa had collapsed into a fit of giggles in front of the tree. They flipped over on their backs to stare up at the lights and ornaments as if in awe. And it was pretty awe-inspiring. His parents had put the tree up for him this year while he'd been gone. They'd used the ornaments that Gracie loved—the wild mix and assortment so there was no theme going—and thanks to his mom, the lights looked professionally hung. Not like when he did them.

Then he heard Gracie whisper to Lisa that Santa was going to bring her a dog. He shook his head. He had to go find a dog.

"I don't understand those girls," he said to his mom as he entered the kitchen. "They go from monsters to crazy laughter in five seconds?" He stepped over some sort of light-purple animal and bent down to pick it up.

His mother stood with her back to him, bowls, ingredients, and cookie sheets covering most of the counters, and he thought about all the space in Roni's much larger kitchen. His house wasn't huge, but it was cozy. It was perfect for him and Gracie.

Which was all that mattered.

Irritation threatened to piss him off again, but he tamped it back down. He couldn't change Roni, and he wouldn't take her as she was. It was over.

Not that she was beating down his door to come back.

"Before you know it," his mother began as she turned from the counter, mixing bowl in hand and eyeing him over the top of her glasses, "they'll have their Barbies spread out all over the floor, and will be planning a Barbie and Ken wedding and dragging you into the middle of it."

The back of his neck began to itch at the look she planted on him.

She hadn't asked about Roni since he'd been home, but he knew it was coming. Probably in about two seconds.

Gracie had asked about her, though. It had been question number one after, "Did you bring me a present?"

He'd gently explained that Roni had decided she needed to stay at her house, and then he'd brought out Gracie's present. He'd picked up a stuffed green sea turtle the first day he'd gotten there. Gracie loved stuffed animals. Which was evident by the purple thing in his hand.

"What happened?" his mom asked.

He ducked his gaze and opened the fridge, putting the stuffed animal on top of the appliance as he peered inside. "What do you mean? With the contest?" He rooted around in the fridge as if there were more inside than a twelve-pack of soft drinks and a carton of eggs that should have been tossed last week. He had to get to the store. "I won."

He knew that wasn't what she meant. But he didn't want to admit to his mom that yes, he'd fallen for yet another woman who hadn't stuck.

And he'd been so sure about this one.

He finally pulled himself back out of the fridge and turned to face her. She was watching him in the way that made him feel about six years old. He popped the top on his drink. He wasn't in the mood to talk about Roni, no matter how his mother scowled at him. Then his phone buzzed in his pocket and he stiffened. He wondered if it would be another text from Roni. She'd sent him one at three that morning. He'd been asleep, but the buzz had pulled him out of his troubled dreams.

And he'd almost replied.

He took a healthy swing of his soda and slipped the phone from his jeans.

"Why isn't she here, Lucas?" Her tone was serious, but she softened it just a bit in her motherly way. "You promised Gracie."

"I did *not* promise Gracie." And yeah, looking back, he probably shouldn't have said anything at all. But he'd been so sure. So certain that Roni felt the same way he did. "I told her I planned to ask Roni. That's all I promised. And I did ask her."

It was Kelly. Lucas's gut tightened. Just checking on Gracie.

He responded to the message and tossed his phone on a red-and-green dishcloth lying beside the sink. If it vibrated again, he didn't want to know. He didn't want to hope it was Roni, still worried about Gracie.

Because what the hell had that been about?

She didn't care enough to come to Dallas with him when he'd thought the worst, yet she felt she had a right to know?

Not on his watch.

"So she said no, then?" his mom asked.

"What?" He looked over at her and then remembered. They were talking about Roni. He was thinking about her, his mom was talking about her, and the fact was, she wasn't worth either of their time. Also, he didn't want to admit to his mom that it was worse than Roni just saying no. She hadn't had the guts. "Things changed," he answered.

"Umm-hmmm."

She returned to her task and focused on the rolled dough. She had cookie cutters in the shapes of stars, Christmas trees, and bells, and was lining the cookies up precisely, evenly spaced on the pan. It made him think about Roni saying his toiletries were lined up like little army men.

Lucas moved to stand beside her and helped out. He may not want to talk about Roni, but he knew his mother would. And in all honesty, he did want her opinion. He wanted to be married some day. He wanted a mother for Gracie.

But if all women were going to be like this . . . if they were going to run at the first hint of trouble . . . then it would be best to hear it now. Save himself the trouble of trusting again.

They worked in silence for a few minutes before he wiped off his hands and leaned back against the sink. His chest felt heavy. "She was planning to come back with me tomorrow," he admitted.

His mom glanced up, but she didn't slow in her task. "But that changed?"

"Yeah. That changed." He grabbed his drink and finished it. It felt like an invasion of privacy to talk about Roni's most painful hurts, but he needed to get out of his own head for a minute. "Something happened in her past. Something that . . . hurt her. Scared her. And when we got the text the other night . . ."

He quit speaking and hung his head. He couldn't get the horror on Roni's face out of his mind. He'd been furious at her for not being willing to go with him, for backing away and refusing to jump in with both feet. But she'd been terrified.

Once he'd gotten some distance, he'd known that. Fear had shrouded her.

If he hadn't been standing between her and the door, it wouldn't have surprised him to see her bolt through it as if the devil itself were chasing her down.

"You're talking about that text your father sent." His mother shook her head in disgust. Her lips twisted. "Before the idiot tossed the phone in the car and forgot about it. You know how inept he can be with modern technology." His parents had still been arguing over that mishap when he'd shown up that morning. His dad had done as she'd requested and sent the message. It had never occurred to him that Lucas would use the same phone to try to get back in touch with them.

"Yeah." He nodded. "We were together when it came in. I panicked."

"I'm sure," she grumbled. "Damn fool man. Just send a text like that with no explanation."

"It's okay, Mom. Really. It all worked out."

Her lines of cookies lost their perfectly aligned pattern as her motions got more rigid. "It is not okay. I didn't want to make you crazy. And I certainly didn't mean for you to come home early."

"It's fine," he promised. "I needed to come home."

She shot him a look. "To get away from Roni?"

He nodded.

"What did she say?" she asked. "When the text came in."

"That she couldn't do it. She *wouldn't* do it." He pressed his lips together and glanced toward the living room. It had gone silent in there, so he assumed the girls had returned to Gracie's room. "She's scared of Gracie getting sick again," he lowered his voice. "She refuses to even try."

His mother put the first batch of cookies in the oven. She set the timer and then faced him, hands on hips. Her look was no-nonsense. "Then that's best, right? Know it now? Before you bring Gracie into it."

"Yeah." That's what he'd wanted to hear. "Only . . ." Only, he missed her and he wanted her. And he wanted her to text him again. "Are they all going to be like that, Mom? No woman strong enough to ever stick with us?"

She looked at him over her glasses again. Her eyes, which so closely matched his, stared back at him, and then they softened. "What happened in her past?" she asked.

He pictured Roni in her backyard as she'd been telling him about Zoe. She'd seemed so sad. So alone. He wished he could have been there for her during that time.

"A kid died," he finally said. He glanced away and waited while his mother took that in, then added, "A sick kid. One she'd planned to adopt."

"Oh," she whispered. She pressed a hand to her chest. "Bless her heart."

"Yeah," he agreed. No one should have to go through something like that. "I'm sorry, Mom. I thought I'd chosen better this time. I didn't mean to bring another woman into our lives who would run at the first opportunity. I thought she was stronger than that. I thought she . . ." He shook his head. He'd thought she loved him enough. "I didn't mean to disappoint you and Dad again."

Confusion lifted her brows up toward her gray hair. "Disappoint us?"

He shrugged. "I know that Des was a mess. She bolted the instant Gracie got sick. I should have realized what I was getting."

"You think *we've* been disappointed in you? Over her?"

"Well, yeah." Lord knows he'd been disappointed in himself. His parents had always taught him to do the right thing. To be the best in whatever he did. And he'd messed up.

Twice, now.

"Lucas." She crossed to him and reached up to caress his cheek. Now he really felt like a six-year-old. "We were heartbroken for you and Gracie, but we've never been disappointed in you."

"But I screwed up."

"You took a chance. Des is the one who messed up. She's the one who doesn't have Gracie in her life."

That was true. It was most definitely her loss.

"I wanted her to be Gracie's mom," he admitted quietly. "I thought she was the one."

"I'm assuming we're talking about Roni now?"

He grimaced. "Yeah. Roni."

She patted his cheek and gave him a wink. Then she turned back to the next batch of cookies. "Maybe she still can be."

Nothing could have shocked him more.

"What?" he asked. "She deserted us."

"Because she was scared, right?"

"Yeah, but . . ." He glanced around the room, uncertain what to say. "She balked, Mom. She told me she loved me, and then in the next instant she freaked. She wouldn't even discuss coming here."

"Have you heard anything from her since then?"

Guilt gnawed at him. He glanced at his phone, still lying beside the sink.

"Did she call?" his mom asked, following his gaze.

He shook his head. He knew her text had come from honest worry. And he'd ignored her. "She texted early this morning."

"What did she say?"

Fear that he'd walked away too fast ate at him. But he hadn't had a choice. He'd needed to get home to Gracie. And Roni had . . .

He let out a harsh breath. "She asked about Gracie."

His mom nodded. "And you told her it was just a fall? That there is nothing whatsoever to worry about?"

He knew that she knew the answer to that. He *should* have told her that, but he hadn't. He shook his head.

"Lucas." Her tone was definitely disappointed now.

"You didn't see her, Mom. She practically shoved me out of the room. Wouldn't even discuss coming with me. I suggested she come today. After the parade she's playing in. But she refused that too."

"Yet you said she was scared."

"Why are you taking her side on this?" Frustration had him raising his voice. His mother stopped what she was doing and looked up at him, and he felt like he had when she'd caught him kissing their neighbor's kid behind the bushes when he'd been five.

"Do you love her?" she asked.

He didn't answer. This was not the way he'd expected this conversation to go.

"Doesn't matter," she said. "I already know you do. You wouldn't have considered bringing her home if you didn't. And that doesn't go away overnight. Not if it's real."

And dammit, it was real.

"So the way I see it is you have two choices." She opened a box that contained six small bottles of different-colored sprinkles and set them out on the counter. "You can either forgive her—"

"What's to forgive?" he cut in. Anger suddenly fueled him. "She's not here. She's sitting in a parade right now, starting her career all over again, and has probably already forgotten we exist."

It wasn't that he wanted her to choose Gracie over her career. He would never want that. They could find a balance. But a parade over his daughter's health? Over being there when he needed her?

That had hurt.

His mother eyed him shrewdly. "You said she loved you."

"She claimed she did."

"So you think she's already forgotten you?"

He stared at his mother. His jaw clenched. Did all women stick together whether they'd ever met or not?

"Never mind," he muttered. He stalked past her.

"Lucas Eugene."

He paused just for a second at the words, but then shook his head. She didn't understand.

The buzzer on the stove went off at the same time the doorbell rang. Perfect. An escape.

As he went down the hall, he glanced up the stairs to where he could hear the kids. That would be Lisa's mother at the door, but he didn't call Lisa down yet. He needed the distraction as long as he could get one. He suspected his mother was going to want to finish their talk when they were once again alone.

But when he pulled open the door, a five-foot, wild-haired, freaked-out woman stood before him. She looked like she'd taken a shower and thrown on the first thing she could find, whether clean or dirty, and had forgotten there was such a task as combing her hair.

"Is she okay?" Roni quickly asked.

His heart quit beating. She'd come.

CHAPTER THIRTY-THREE

Lucas nudged her back and stepped out on the porch, shutting the door tight behind him. "What are you doing here?"

She pleaded with her eyes. "Please, Lucas. I know you probably hate me now. And I deserve it. I should have been here. But I need to know—"

"Don't you have a parade to be in?"

He was so hard. Surely she hadn't lost him in one night.

But she'd deserted his kid. She probably had lost him.

She forced out a breath. "I went to the hospital first," she explained. "Three of them, actually. I couldn't find you. I couldn't find Gracie." She glanced over his shoulder at the solid door at his back, wishing he hadn't shut it. Surely there would be some sign in the house. Had she been too late?

"I'll go," she promised. She didn't want to, but she could see he didn't want her there. It would be best not to complicate things. "But I needed to make sure she's okay." She stared into his eyes and thought about the rest of the reason she'd come. "And I needed to tell you something."

Cold blue eyes peered back at her. She couldn't read a thing from the look, and the fear started in her again. Gracie had to be okay. *They* had to be okay.

She needed him.

"What did you want to tell me?" he finally asked.

Nerves tingled inside her and she thought about her friends, who had taken her over to the mainland that morning in Ginger's boat. Andie had come with them. The whole way over they'd coached her on what to say when she got to him. But not a single word of what they'd said then came to mind now. She didn't know what she was supposed to say. Other than . . .

"I love you," she whispered. A shimmery feeling swept over her from the neck down. "And I'm sorry. I let fear control me, but only for a while." She shook her head. "I won't let it happen again."

He had to believe her.

Yet the unchanging expression said he didn't.

She swallowed. "Please, Lucas. I know I don't deserve a second chance, but I want you to know that I would give you one. I would give you many. Though you'd probably never need as many as me," she finished lamely.

Geez, she sucked at this. She needed to remember what Andie and Ginger practiced with her. She was ruining everything.

"Why aren't you at the parade?" he asked. His face had not grown any softer, but she thought she detected a slight ease in his voice. It was enough to give her hope.

"Because you didn't answer my text and all I could think was that Gracie . . ." She bit her lip as the worst thing she'd thought ran through her mind. "I had to be here. I couldn't be too late again."

A muscle in his jaw twitched and she glanced frantically at the door.

"Lucas," she begged. Was she really too late?

"She's fine," he finally said.

All the air left her lungs in a rush and she thought she might fall down. Instead, she backed up to the railing and leaned against it. Her shoulders sagged and she covered her mouth with her hand. Gracie was okay. She was fine.

She looked at Lucas. There were several feet between them now, and she wanted to be next to him. In his arms. But knowing Gracie was alive was enough.

"You just left Kayla in the lurch?" he asked.

She nodded. One side of his mouth twitched up and she felt a tiny bit of the clench around her heart loosen.

"I'll bet she liked that," he said.

That wasn't quite the way it had gone over. But Kayla had understood. She'd even admitted that she would do the same thing.

"I had to promise her a full concert later, though," Roni admitted. "My first concert. She's a tough negotiator."

"When is it?"

She shook her head. "Not until . . ." She stopped talking and just stared at the man she loved. He might reject her, but she had to tell him what she wanted. She had to go for it. "Not until Gracie is okay," she told him solemnly. "I won't go back to the piano until Gracie is one hundred percent. She comes first."

"I never asked you to choose."

"I know. And I'm not. I'm just putting her first. I'm putting *us* first. I always will. If you'll let me." She gripped her hands into fists at her sides as he continued giving her nothing in return. "The piano is just my job," she stressed. "I want you and Gracie to be my life."

She glanced at the door again, still needing to see for herself. "Is she here? Can I meet her?" She turned back to Lucas, worry still tormenting her, and asked in a small voice, "Will she need chemo again?"

His eyes changed then. The hard edge left them and the blue turned warm. And then she moved toward him, and whimpered when he took a step toward her. He didn't pull her into his arms, but he took her hands.

"Can I meet her?" she asked again.

He nodded. He squeezed her fingers in his. "But there's something important I have to tell you first."

"Oh God." The words came out breathless. "What? She's bad, isn't she? I knew it. She—"

"Fell and cut her head."

Roni's words froze as she tried to comprehend what Lucas had said.

Falling had triggered the cancer to return? That made no sense.

"She got twenty-two stitches," he added. He turned loose of one of her hands and pointed to his hairline, just above his eye. "Right here. And she's pretty darn proud that she didn't even cry when they gave her the shot to numb it."

Roni stared at him dumbly, nothing making sense. And then a lightbulb went off inside her and she got it. Her eyes grew wide and finally, Lucas began to smile.

"You're telling me she fell last night?" she asked. "And that's all?"

He nodded.

Relief poured through her, but at the same time, she wanted to pummel his chest with her fists.

"You let me worry about her all night long?"

His smile was fully in place now. "I want to say you deserved it."

"I did," she admitted with a groan. "I know I did. I should have left with you last night."

He cupped her cheek in his hand and she swayed toward him. The rougher skin on her cheek was the best thing she'd felt all day.

"You didn't deserve it," he said gruffly. "You have plenty of reasons to be scared. I get that. I just forgot last night. I was worried about Gracie."

"I was too."

He pulled her into his embrace and she slid her arms around his waist with a moan.

"I'm sorry," he said. He kissed the top of her head. "I should have let you know she was okay. I'll be more supportive of you too. I promise."

She tilted her head back and looked up at him. "I think I'm going to be okay," she said. "I really do. I've grown a lot these last few days. I've overcome some things."

"You've overcome a lot." He smiled gently and caressed the backs of his fingers over her cheeks. "You're the bravest person I know."

That was the second time someone had said that to her today. And she loved both the men.

"Kiss me," she begged. "I've missed you too much."

∾

Nine days later . . . Christmas morning.

Roni cracked open her eyes at the touch of something scratchy against her cheek. It was still dark in the room, but she could make out shadows from the night-light she'd left on in the hall. She was back at her house on Turtle Island. Lucas was with her—though not in the bed with her—and Gracie was there as well.

Lucas's parents were at the hotel. They'd be over later in the morning. Roni's family would be arriving on the ferry midmorning. And Ginger had promised to stop by as well. Even Mrs. Rylander had agreed to come over. It would be a house full of people, and Roni couldn't be happier. It was the kind of Christmas she'd wanted to give Zoe. Roni knew the little girl was smiling down on them now, and that was good enough.

Their first Christmas on the island.

She only hoped for many more.

"Daddy said I could bring this to you," Gracie whispered right next to her ear.

Roni let out a shriek and jumped upright in bed.

She flipped on the lamp next to her. Gracie stood there in the red-and-white-striped nightgown she'd picked out for Christmas morning, holding a bright-red poinsettia with a green foil wrapper around the bottom.

"I wanted to get you a flower," the little girl explained. She held it up higher. It was almost too big for her to hold. "Daddy said this would be the bestest kind."

A deep chuckle sounded at her door and Roni looked over to find Lucas leaning against the doorframe. He wore green plaid pajama bottoms hanging low on his hips and a Santa hat on his head. Nothing in between.

"Ho ho ho," he murmured in a low sexy voice.

Roni's pulse raced.

She gripped her fingers into the soft material she wore as she eyed him. She had on his matching top. She'd stolen it from him when he'd snuck into her room overnight.

Giggling brought her back around to the little girl, who was now climbing onto Roni's bed, the plant tilting precariously on its side.

"Thank you, Gracie." Roni ignored the hunk at her bedroom door and reached out to take the flower. Once she had both child and flower nestled in beside her, she motioned with her head for Lucas to join them. He studied them briefly as if he was afraid that if he did he wouldn't be able to control himself, but then pushed off from the door.

After he settled beside her, she smiled at them both. This was what she wanted. Now her life truly was good.

"This is the most beautiful flower I've ever gotten," Roni informed the girl. Gracie smiled brightly.

The two of them had spent countless hours over the past nine days getting to know each other. They'd gone shopping together, eaten ice cream together, made hot chocolate together, and had even worked on a present for Lucas together.

It had been everything she'd ever dreamed of.

She loved Lucas's house, and she thought his parents were perfect.

They'd all stayed in Dallas until a couple days ago, but Gracie had begged to come to the beach for Christmas, and Lucas had suggested it might be a good tradition to start.

She hoped that meant he would eventually trust her enough to ask her to marry him, but she wasn't pushing it. She'd tested things hard the night she hadn't gone back to Dallas with him. Plus, they'd only known each other a few weeks. She had to give him time; he needed to trust that if anything were to happen to Gracie, Roni would be there.

She knew she would be there. She would never be anywhere else when the child needed her. Not ever again.

Cancel shows, cancel tours. Whatever was called for, she would do it. Because like she'd told Lucas, they were her world. Nothing else was more important.

But she got that Lucas needed time to make sure. So she'd give him that.

Yet the second he proposed, wedding plans would be in the works. In fact, she already had Kayla on standby. She was that positive about them.

She looked down at Gracie snuggled close to her side. "Should we give your Daddy his Christmas present?"

Gracie nodded, her curls bouncing around her head. "Now?" she asked. "Can we?"

"Absolutely." Roni glanced at the clock, seeing that it was barely five. "And then we'll see if Santa brought us any gifts."

"I already peeked," Gracie said in a hushed voice. "He did."

Roni and Lucas laughed, and then Lucas leaned over before she could climb off the bed and kissed her full on the lips. "Good morning, gorgeous," he murmured against her. "I missed you."

"Daa-ad," Gracie moaned. "No more kissing. We have a present for you."

Roni shrugged as if to say they had to do what the kid wanted, and then trailed off after her. She'd racked her brain for the perfect gift for him, and nothing had come to mind. And then she'd thought of what might be a very special moment. Not simply for Lucas, but for all of them. And she'd set out to make it happen.

When they reached the living room, she saw that Lucas had already turned on the tree and started the fire. The room glowed in the dark of the morning, with reflections shimmering off the many packages below the tree. Santa had definitely come during the night.

But instead of heading to the presents, she and Gracie took each other's hand and marched to the piano. As they sat side by side, she caught Lucas's eye. So much love poured back at her that she almost felt undeserving. He was such a good man. And she'd almost lost him.

"I love you," she mouthed the words.

He nodded. "I love you too."

Then she and Gracie put their hands on the keys, and they began to play "The Twelve Days of Christmas." Gracie was a little rough. They'd only had nine days to practice, after all, and the kid was only four. But her determination made up for all the missed notes.

As they played, Lucas came to stand behind them. He put a hand on each of their shoulders, and she met his gaze in the reflection in the window on the other side of the piano. They looked like a family. One tall, gorgeous man, and two girls with out-of-control curls.

When they finished the song, Roni smiled widely and Gracie clapped.

"Yay!" Gracie cheered. But Lucas didn't say anything.

Roni tilted her head back to look up at him and gasped when he held a ring in front of her face.

"Marry me," he said.

Gracie giggled beside her, and Roni glanced at the girl. "Did you know about this?"

She laughed harder. "You and me snuck a present for him, and we snuck a present for you."

"It looks like you did," Roni agreed. And then she turned her attention to the man.

He was everything she'd ever wanted. Good. Kind. Caring.

And he loved her more than the world.

It was a no-brainer.

"Forever." She nodded.

"For always."

As he scooped her up, Gracie—and everything else—disappeared. All Roni knew existed was the man who held her in his arms, whose mouth was on hers. This was where she wanted to be for the rest of her life.

When he broke the kiss, she smiled and nuzzled into his neck.

"I'm going to want more babies, you know?" She'd been doing a lot of thinking about that the last few days. "Gracie needs a sibling."

Lucas's grip tightened on her. "Then I'm going to work extra hard to give them to you."

They kissed again until they heard Gracie gasp from the living room. Then they smiled secretly at each other and broke apart.

"What is it, sweet Gracie?" Lucas asked.

A tiny finger pointed with great excitement toward the back door of Roni's house. "Is that my dog out there? Did Santa bring me a dog?"

Lucas opened the door, and a small cocker spaniel with floppy ears and a precious face stuck his nose in. He wore a red bow tied around his neck, and a large tag that said, To Gracie.

"Is he mine?" the little girl asked.

Roni moved to Lucas's side and wrapped her arm around his waist.

"He has your name on him," Lucas said. "He must be yours."

Wide blue eyes looked up at her daddy as if he'd just roped her the moon. Then Gracie dropped to her knees and the dog poured kisses over her face.

"This is the bestest Christmas ever," the child whispered.

And Roni had to agree. She met Lucas's gaze and showed him her love through her smile.

The bestest. Christmas. Ever.

ABOUT THE AUTHOR

As a child, Kim Law cultivated a love for chocolate, anything purple, baton twirling, and creative writing. She penned her debut work, "The Giant Talking Raisin," in the sixth grade and got hooked on the delights of creating stories. Before settling into the writing life, however, she earned a college degree in mathematics and then worked as a computer programmer while also raising her son. Now she's pursuing her lifelong dream of writing romance novels; she has won the Romance Writers of America's Golden Heart Award, has been a finalist for the prestigious RWA RITA Award, and currently serves as president for her local RWA chapter. Kim is the author of *Caught on Camera, Sugar Springs,* and the Turtle Island novels, *Ex on the Beach* and *Hot Buttered Yum.* A native of Kentucky, she lives with her husband in Middle Tennessee.

Kindle Serials

This book was originally released in Episodes as a Kindle Serial. Kindle Serials launched in 2012 as a new way to experience serialized books. Kindle Serials allow readers to enjoy the story as the author creates it, purchasing once and receiving all existing Episodes immediately, followed by future Episodes as they are published. To find out more about Kindle Serials and to see the current selection of Serials titles, visit www.amazon.com/kindleserials.